CREATURE COMFORTS

By the same author:

Sowing Secrets
A Winter's Tale
Wedding Tiers
Chocolate Wishes
Twelve Days of Christmas
The Magic of Christmas
Chocolate Shoes and Wedding Blues
Good Husband Material
Wish Upon a Star
Finding Mr Rochester
Every Woman for Herself

TRISHA ASHLEY

Creature Comforts

AVON

AVON
A division of HarperCollins*Publishers*
1 London Bridge Street,
London SE1 9GF

www.harpercollins.co.uk

First published in Great Britain by HarperCollins*Publishers* in 2015
1

A catalogue record for this book is
available from the British Library

ISBN-13: 978-0-00-810225-8

Set in Minion by Palimpsest Book Production Limited,
Falkirk, Stirlingshire

Printed and bound in Great Britain by
Clays Ltd, St Ives plc

MIX
Paper from
responsible sources
FSC C007454

Find out more about HarperCollins and the environment at
www.harpercollins.co.uk/green

For my dear friends and fellow authors, Mary de Laszlo and Norma Curtis, with love.

Acknowledgements

I would like to thank my son, Robin Ashley, for his sterling research and editorial assistance over the summer, without which this book would never have been finished. Also, my grateful thanks to my many internet friends, who sent me their brilliant dog treat recipes – I could choose only one for the book, but I intend to make them all.

Prologue: Halfhidden, West Lancashire, 1993

That evening, Baz Salcombe's old Range Rover, which was mainly used by his teenage son, Harry, and his friends, passed through the stone gateposts of the Sweetwell estate and paused briefly in the blackest of shadows by the turn to the Lodge, before pursuing an unsteady course up the dark, tree-lined tunnel of the drive.

The road beyond the first sharp bend first hunched itself up and then dipped deeply into a hollow, but either the driver had forgotten that or was recklessly convinced that the car would fly over it, for it suddenly leaped forward with a roar – then the brake lights flashed and it swerved, flipping sideways into the trees with an almighty crash.

The ominous sound, together with the incessant blaring of the jammed horn, carried as far as the Lodge and set off a cacophony of barking from Debo Dane's Desperate Dogs Refuge. Judy Almond, her friend and housekeeper, who was starting out for the local pub to collect Debo's niece, Izzy, stopped dead with the car keys in her hand, heart racing.

Tom Tamblyn was halfway down the woodland path that led to his cottage by the Lady Spring when he heard the crash, but Dan Clew, Baz Salcombe's gardener, was first on the scene, for he'd been so close by that he actually felt the resonance of the impact through the soles of his feet. Arriving at a run, he found the crumpled car lying on its side in a thick tangle of old trees, wheels still spinning and the head-lights blazing out at a crazy angle.

The uppermost doors had burst open and, to his great relief, he saw his son Simon climb out and then stagger up the bank, where he slumped with his head in his hands. A girl was screaming hysterically and even before Dan had fished out a torch from his pocket and investigated, he guessed it would be Cara Ferris, the local vet's daughter.

Cara, her face masked with blood from a deep cut, was already frantically scrambling out of the back seat and it looked as though she'd had a lucky escape, for a branch had impaled the car from front to back, as if preparing to spit-roast it.

Dan moved the torch beam to the front and could see at a glance that his boss's son, Harry, had taken the brunt of the collision and there was nothing to be done – and the girl slumped next to him had a bad head injury and didn't look in much better shape. He paused for a moment, looking over his shoulder as if to check for any sign of other rescuers, before reaching in and gathering up her small, slight form.

Tom Tamblyn was just in time to see Dan lift the uncon-scious figure out of the front of the car, before laying it down on a bit of flat turf next to the drive.

'Is that young Izzy Dane?' Tom gasped, still panting for breath, for he was somewhat beyond the age of sprinting up steep paths. 'Eeh, she looks bad – and you shouldn't have moved her with that head injury, Dan.'

'Thought I'd better in case the car goes up – there's an

almighty stink of petrol,' Dan said shortly, looking up. 'She was in the front with Harry and they had the worst of it – my lad and the Ferris girl were in the back and got themselves out.'

He nodded at Izzy. 'If you think *she* looks bad, you should see Harry.'

'Like that, is it?' Tom got out his own torch, took a look inside the car, and came back, shaking his head.

'Poor lad,' he said. 'But he's in the passenger seat so . . . are you saying young Izzy was driving? She's not old enough to have her licence yet.' He took off his old tweed jacket and laid it over the still figure on the grass, after checking her airways were clear and she still had a pulse.

'She was in the front next to Harry – it's clear enough what happened.'

'Your Simon always drives them back from the pub, though, doesn't he?' Tom said. 'On account of being teetotal.'

'Not this time.'

'This is all Izzy's fault!' Cara exclaimed hysterically, the wadded hem of her T-shirt held to her bloody face. She'd scrambled up the bank and was sitting next to Simon, who was still slumped with his head in his hands. 'I'm going to be scarred for life – and Harry?' Her voice rose shrilly. 'What's happened to Harry?'

'It was Howling Hetty's ghost that did it!' Simon slurred, looking up with a face as milk-pale as any wraith, and then he threw up copiously into the grass next to him, narrowly avoiding Cara.

Tom blanched and said uneasily, 'Nay, never say you've seen her!'

'Of course he hasn't! Simon, pull yourself together and

3

ring for help, if you haven't already,' Dan snapped. 'What's the matter with you?'

'Teetotaller or not, he's drunk,' Tom said, fishing a mobile phone the size of a brick out of his trouser pocket and dialling 999.

'I'd better go down to the Lodge and tell them . . .' Dan stopped, glancing at Izzy, still lying unconscious on the grass.

'No need, they'll have heard that damned horn and be here any second,' Tom said. 'The whole of Halfhidden will have heard it.'

And he was right, for the sound echoing urgently up and down the valley was a siren for a disaster that had ended one young life and would forever change those of the other occupants of the car that night, but most especially Izzy Dane's.

Chapter 1: All Fools' Day, 2012

'Izzy – just the girl I need,' Harry said as I came level with the Range Rover, heading towards the steep path up through the Sweetwell woods to the Lady Spring and beyond it the Lodge, where I lived with my guardian, Aunt Debo, and her friend and housekeeper, Judy.

He was leaning his tall, skinny frame against the open door of the car, as if he might fall down if he didn't – and going by the sparkle in his green eyes, he'd drunk more than enough for that.

'Who, me?' I asked, pausing uncertainly.

My recurring dream reran its usual course, a brief video clip of a golden evening and four young lives full of hopes and aspirations.

Harry and his friends had seemed so grown up and sophisticated to my sixteen-year-old eyes. They were all about to go their separate ways: Harry to medical school, and quiet, unassuming Simon to study horticulture at a nearby college, while Cara, who'd grown as tall and thin as a beanpole, had only days before been spotted by a top modelling agency and, much to her parents' dismay, was poised to turn down her place at Oxford.

I always wished I could hang on to the dream long enough to see exactly what madness made me get behind the wheel of that car, but instead I usually woke suddenly, jerked right out of the past, just as I'd been summarily ejected from Heaven when I was in a coma in hospital after the accident . . .

For once, however, the picture dissolved as slowly as morning mist in the sun and I swam back up into wakefulness and the rattle of the ceiling fan in my Mumbai hotel room . . . *and* the unwelcome memory of the previous night's phone argument with my fiancé, Kieran.

Well, I *assumed* he was still my fiancé, though that might change once we met up at his parents' house in Oxford on Monday and I laid on the line exactly what I intended to do next and, more importantly, where I wanted to do it.

It was ironic that our relationship had gone pear-shaped only once we'd finally decided the time was right to stop working abroad and settle down together in the UK. And last night, when I'd told him I'd already invested some of the small legacy left to me by my father into commissioning stock for the online retro clothes shop I was going to set up, he'd been furious, even though I'd never made any secret of my plans.

He was even angrier when I added firmly, 'And don't count on the rest, because I'll probably need all of it to bail Aunt Debo out. The kennels are having a *huge* financial crisis.'

'Your aunt's affairs are always in financial crisis,' he'd said dismissively. 'She overreaches herself taking in all those dogs that are too vicious to be rehomed, so there's no point in throwing good money after bad.'

Then he'd claimed that we'd agreed to use my legacy as

part of a deposit on a house, even though we'd never so much as discussed it. And at that point I started to wonder if he'd ever taken in a single thing I'd said to him.

Until we'd visited his parents in Oxford the previous year, he'd certainly never mentioned to me that he had any intention of going back there to live and work. He seemed like an entirely different person once we'd set foot on UK soil . . .

'Look, I've got to go and pack. We'll discuss it all on Monday, when I'm back,' he'd snapped finally, then put the phone down on me.

I felt angry, confused and very upset. Why, over the course of our three-year engagement, had I never realised that the laid-back, good-natured, popular and cheerful Kieran I'd tumbled headlong in love with existed only as long as everyone else was falling in with his plans? But then, we'd spent most of our engagement on separate continents and even when we had managed to make our vacations coincide, we'd spent them on romantic breaks in exotic locations, watching the sun coming up over the Serengeti, or setting over the Taj Mahal, so I suppose it wasn't really surprising that we appeared to have entirely misread each other's character.

It was unfortunate that I could never sleep on planes, since the long flight back gave me way too much time to think. Appropriately, it was due to arrive in the UK on 1 April, All Fools' Day.

I was jammed between two large, sweaty, heavy-drinking businessmen in suits, who sprawled thoughtlessly, legs wide apart and arms akimbo, as if the seat between them was empty. I might have spent the whole journey bolt upright, with my feet together and arms clamped by my sides, except

that although small and skinny I have *extremely* sharp elbows
. . . and also an unfortunate habit of kicking intruding ankles
very sharply.

After a few mutterings and dirty looks, to which I
responded with sweetly smiling apologies for my nervous
tics, they gave in and subsided in opposite directions away
from me and I was left to my unwelcome reflections.

The previous night's argument with Kieran, unsatisfactor-
ily conducted over a patchy phone line, only added to the
feeling of acute cold feet I'd recently been developing about
our relationship. Now I suspected there was more than a
hint of frostbite setting in around my toes.

It wasn't that I didn't still have feelings for Kieran – a
vision of his blunt-featured face with its slightly wonky,
rugby-bashed nose, under a mop of sun-bleached fair hair
popped into my mind and slightly weakened my knees, if
not my resolve – but did he love me enough to change his
plans, rather than assume it would be the other way round?

I suspected not.

When we first met, it felt so right that I thought falling
in love with him must be part of my preordained destiny.
Even though my best friends, Lulu and Cameron, teased me
about my conviction that I had a near-death experience and
went to Heaven while I was in a coma after the accident,
and was sent back only because I had some important
purpose to perform in life, I *knew* it was real. Since then I
just had to tune inwards to the voice of my guardian angel
from time to time to check I'd taken the right turning . . .
only with Kieran, I think I must have fallen for him so hard
that I misread the message.

My path through life had appeared clearly marked till

then, for after studying Textiles and Design, I'd accepted a job with the Women's World Workshops Foundation, which sent me on assignments all over the world, though the majority were in India. The pay was minimal, but the job satisfaction immense: discovering the skills and artistic heritage of each area and finding ways of utilising them in the making of beautiful garments, the sale of which could transform the lives of the local women involved in the scheme and, through them, those of their families and even their whole communities.

And all the time I was amassing a huge portfolio of colours, designs, patterns, ideas and contacts, ready for the day when I would finally go home for good to Halfhidden, the small village in west Lancashire where I grew up, and set up my own business selling retro-inspired clothes.

Yes, the way forward had unrolled in front of me like an inviting magic carpet . . . until I literally bumped into Kieran in Pakistan, where he was working as a doctor for a medical charity and I was helping some enterprising local women to set up a co-operative making woven jackets.

It seemed like sheer serendipity that we should have been in the same place at the same time . . . though not so seren-dipitous afterwards, since we rarely managed more than snatched days together whenever we could make our leaves coincide.

Perhaps if we'd spent more time in each other's company, we wouldn't still have been engaged.

I'd always believed that Kieran was a wonderful doctor who loved his work as much as I loved mine – it was just that until a few months before, he hadn't mentioned that he'd always intended joining his family's GP practice in

Oxford. When I discovered this, he'd suggested that I could just as easily set up my business there as anywhere else.

But although Oxford was a lovely city, it wasn't *my* city. I'm a country girl, used to living on the edge of moorland, a short drive from endless expanses of beaches, not a hemmed-in-by-dreaming-spires one.

And then, Kieran's parents were a bit of a shock, too. Miranda, his overbearing mother, and Douglas, his sarcastic, know-it-all father, not only assumed I'd fall in with Kieran's plans, but had already started to look for a house for us. Miranda was even trying to take charge of my wedding, checking out reception venues at stately homes within easy reach of Oxford. That was the last straw.

'I think you're being very ungrateful, when my mother's taking all this trouble,' Kieran had said, when I'd rung him, furious. Then he'd added that since I was always banging on about *my* destiny, I should realise that joining his parents' GP practice was *his*.

We'd had so many arguments recently and that last one had reached a sort of crisis point, so that although I intended going straight from the airport to Oxford, as we'd arranged, I resolved that when Kieran arrived the following day the discussion was not going to go the way he so clearly expected it to.

Suddenly my inner voice was telling me, loud and clear, to go home to Halfhidden and that I was needed there – not only by Aunt Debo, but also by my friend Lulu.

Lulu had been living in France for years, in an increasingly abusive relationship with an older man called Guy, who'd turned out to be an alcoholic – and since he had his own vineyard, that gave him rather a lot of scope. He hadn't been physically abusive to her, but instead sapped her spirit and self-confidence over the years with the drip, drip, drip of criticism. Cameron and I had both worried about her, but there wasn't a lot we could do.

She efficiently ran the self-catering holiday *gîtes* and B&B rooms in the small manor and outbuildings of the estate, while Guy occupied himself with the making and consumption of wine. I'd visited only once and, on the surface, he'd been jovial, charming and welcoming . . . though since Lulu, Cam and I emailed each other most days, I knew that he was jealous of any other men who might show an interest in her.

Cameron went out there every summer to teach watercolours at their annual artists' week, and Guy tolerated his presence because he was under the misguided impression he was gay!

Then, at the end of the last summer school, Guy had been off on a bender and Lulu had finally snapped, packed a bag, grabbed her passport and left with Cam.

Now she was living in a static caravan in the small paddock that had once been occupied by her pony, Conker, behind the Screaming Skull Hotel in Halfhidden, and trying to expand the Haunted Weekend breaks set up by her parents into week-long Haunted Holidays.

'I need you,' she'd told me during our last brief phone call. 'My brother, Bruce, and his wife, Kate, have taken over the pub and restaurant, leaving Mum and Dad to concentrate on the hotel side, and I'm sure they only handed over the management of the Haunted Weekends to give me a role. So my Haunted Holidays simply *have* to be a success. I need way more ghostly goings-on and you have a better imagination than I do.'

11

'Why don't you ask Cam's grandfather, Jonas?' I'd suggested. 'He told me all kinds of old legends and stories when I was little, so I'm sure he could come up with some ideas – especially if it brings more visitors to the Lady Spring, too. In fact,' I'd added, 'why not call a meeting and get other people from the village on board? This could bring visitors to the whole valley, not just the pub.'

'Great idea,' she'd enthused. 'See, I said you have lots of imagination!'

Now she was going to do just that, holding the first meeting on Tuesday evening – so if Kieran and I had the almighty falling-out tomorrow that I suspected was on the cards, I'd be back in time for it.

'I'm so looking forward to seeing you again,' Lulu had said. 'Do you know, it's been nearly four years? And Cam hasn't seen you for even longer. It's lovely that Cam has moved back here too, but it's not the same when it isn't the three of us.'

'No, you're right,' I'd agreed, and then suddenly I'd longed even more to be at Halfhidden again, that Shangri-La of my childhood. It was pulling me back and, despite what had happened in the past, it would always be the place where I felt I truly belonged.

I got off the plane in much the same sticky and dishevelled state I'd got onto it, though at least I'd sent most of my heavy luggage on to Halfhidden and only had one suitcase with me.

Kieran's father was meeting me, which made me feel a little awkward, anticipating the next day's full and frank discussion. I wasn't sure what would happen after that, except I'd be going straight home, leaving the ball in Kieran's court.

There had been no getting out of it, though: Douglas had to be in London for some meeting or seminar the day before, and had stayed up to have lunch with friends before heading home, and he'd insisted on collecting me from Heathrow on his way back to Oxford.

'Rough journey?' he said, after failing to recognise me until I went right up to him. This lack of tact only hardened my resolve as we set off towards Oxford, and since I was thinking ahead to what I was going to say to him and Miranda when we arrived, it was a while before I noticed he was driving very fast . . . and also, unless he'd taken to using whisky as an aftershave, he'd been drinking.

And on that very thought, even though we were just approaching a sharp bend, Douglas recklessly swung out to overtake a lorry – straight into the path of a small blue car coming the other way.

There wasn't enough room to get past and Douglas jammed on the brakes, jerking me sharply forward . . . Then the weirdest thing happened. It was as if, for just a second, the fabric of time ripped open and I fell through, right into the Range Rover on the night Harry Salcombe died.

Then, equally suddenly, I was catapulted out again, into a gentle, familiar bright light, filled by a soft susurration of wings and a hint of celestial music . . .

I found I was now hovering above the car, which had spun right round and was facing back the way we'd come, while the small blue one was in a ditch. I could see myself sitting like a statue in the passenger seat, eyes wide with shock, and hear the thin thread of Douglas's voice, as if through water.

'Come on, Izzy, be quick – change places with me!' he demanded, pulling at my arm urgently, as if he could drag me across into the driver's seat. 'Izzy, come on, I'll lose my licence,' he snapped. 'Pull yourself together, you're not hurt.'

Then he sharply slapped my face and instantly I was back in my body and gasping with shock, partly at the blow and partly from once again being wrenched back from Heaven.

Chapter 2: Fault Lines

'By then other drivers had stopped and the police were there in minutes,' I said, trying to describe the scene to Daisy Silver, one of Aunt Debo's oldest friends. 'An ambulance came soon after, and then it all got a bit confusing.'

'I expect it did, after such a shock,' Daisy said in her calm, warm voice, pouring me a mug of coffee and pushing it across the wide, battered pine table in the cosy basement kitchen of her Hampstead house.

Her ample curves were enveloped in a familiar old rubbed purple velvet kaftan and she had loosened the thick plait of hair that usually circled her head like a silver crown so that it hung down her back to her waist . . . or where her waist would have been, had she had one.

'Douglas is an awful man! I mean, he's a doctor, yet instead of getting out to see if the people in the other car needed any help, he just kept on and on at me to say I was driving. Luckily no one was seriously injured, but the mother and two small children in the other car were really shaken up.'

'He does seem to have entirely disregarded his Hippocratic oath,' she agreed drily.

'Yes and even when the police were questioning him, he

insisted the driver of the other car was at fault and wanted me to back him up.'

'Which I'm assuming you didn't?'

'No, of course not. I told them it was entirely his fault for overtaking on a bend and then, of course, he was even more furious with me. When they breathalysed him, he was *way* over the limit, so they charged him with drink-driving as well as dangerous driving and goodness knows what else . . . though, come to think of it, I didn't tell them about him asking me to pretend to have been the driver.'

'It sounds like he'll be in enough trouble without that, so I wouldn't worry about it.'

'It would be just my word against his anyway, wouldn't it?'

She nodded. 'What happened next?'

'We had to go to the police station, but eventually they said I could go, so I got into a taxi and came here. I never gave a thought to how much the fare would cost until we arrived, but I'll pay you back tomorrow.' I clamped my hands around the mug of hot coffee.

'That's not important, and you know I'm always glad to see you, whatever the reason.'

'I do, and it seemed natural to head here,' I said gratefully, for as well as knowing Daisy from her frequent visits to stay with us in Halfhidden, I'd spent several weeks convalescing with her after the original accident when I was sixteen. She was a child psychiatrist by profession, but I hadn't been her patient; it was just that Debo had thought a total change of scene would do me good.

'Very sensible,' she approved. 'In fact, you behaved extremely well, given the shock you'd had.'

'It could easily have been a fatal crash.' I shivered. 'All because he drank too much and drove like an idiot.'

'Health professionals have all the human failings, just like anyone else,' Daisy said. 'But I'm horrified he should have asked you to change places in the car with him.'

'I don't suppose Kieran ever told him about the accident I was involved in – in fact, Douglas probably doesn't even know I can't drive.'

'He should never have *thought* of asking you, whether he did or not. It's wonderful that the family in the other car weren't hurt.'

She smiled at me and pushed over the open tin of coffee-iced biscuits. 'Have some soothing sugar.'

'Thank you,' I said, taking one and crunching into the crisp coating.

For a few moments we munched in amicable silence.

Then Daisy said with her usual acuity, which I suppose was a vital component of her success as a psychiatrist, 'Did something else happen, Izzy?'

'Yes – or rather, two things happened just as we hit the other car. One of them was that I briefly went back to Heaven, like I did after the first accident . . . and then I was right out of my body, looking down.'

'So you went through the bright tunnel again?' she asked, interested.

'There wasn't any tunnel this time, I was just momentarily enveloped by light and colour and a strange kind of music . . . it was lovely. But right before that, just as we struck the other car . . .'

I tailed off, trying to frame the words for what I had experienced, and Daisy didn't push me. Any more than she had when I'd arrived by taxi half an hour before in a distressed condition, and she'd merely greeted me with her usual, 'Oh, there you are, Izzy! Come in,' as if I was the most welcome and expected visitor in the world.

She'd always made me feel that way, especially when I was convalescing with her after that first dreadful accident. It was during that stay, after a trip to the V&A Museum, that I'd developed the consuming interest in textiles that eventually enabled me to help other women escape from grinding poverty. If you looked, there seemed to be a reason for everything that happened in life, good or bad . . . and that thought brought me back full circle to what I needed to say.

I looked up at her familiar apple-cheeked, wise face with its clever dark eyes. 'It was the weirdest thing, Daisy, just as if time was a curtain that ripped open to let me slip through – because suddenly, I was there in the Range Rover on the night of the accident when Harry . . . when I . . .'

'That's interesting,' Daisy said, 'because you had no recollection of even getting into the car, let alone subsequent events.'

'So you think it *was* a memory?'

'Possibly, because a sudden shock can bring back things the subconscious has hidden – though it can also create new "memories",' she gently suggested.

'You mean, I might have imagined the scene I saw? But it seemed so real! We were going along the lane up towards the Green and the others, Harry, Cara and Simon, were all singing. They'd been celebrating their exam results and Harry wanted me to go back to Sweetwell Hall with them to a party, but I'd already told him I couldn't. If I wasn't home by ten, Judy would go down to the pub to look for me . . . and that's the last real memory of that evening I have.'

Aunt Debo, who had become my guardian after my mother's early demise, had tended to lose track of my movements and the passing of time, while Judy, her best friend, who'd originally moved in to help with the childcare but never left, was more practical and firmly set the boundaries a teenager needed.

'Judy was surprised you'd disobeyed her, but we knew Harry must have persuaded you. But to return to the flashback you had, if everyone was singing and happy, that was a good memory?'

'I suppose so,' I said, and though I think she guessed I was still holding something back, she didn't press me. I changed tack.

'I had another argument with Kieran on the phone last night and I'd decided things weren't going to work out – or not the way he wanted them to – so I was going to have it out with him tomorrow, when he got back.'

'You did seem unhappy about the way his parents were taking over your plans, last time we spoke.'

'That was certainly part of it. Do you know, his mother had even started planning a huge wedding in Oxford, when I'd told her I'd always dreamed of a small one in the Halfhidden church.'

'Well, Izzy, you certainly couldn't have a big one in St Mary's, because it can't hold more than about thirty people at once, can it? And it's *your* wedding, so you must have it where you want it.'

'Or not at all. And there's more. They've found us a house round the corner from theirs, which they think I'm going to put that legacy from my father into. Kieran can't see any problem with any of that. In fact, he's entirely failed to see my viewpoint at all, and last night after we argued he put the phone down on me!'

'I'm very sorry to hear it isn't working out, but it's better to find out whether you're entirely compatible before you get married, rather than afterwards,' Daisy said. 'If Kieran's set on joining the family GP practice in Oxford, you'd definitely have to see a lot of his parents.'

I shuddered. 'I don't even want to live in Oxford.'

'It's a very lovely place.'

'I know, only it's not *my* place.' I tried to explain. 'I know I wasn't born in Lancashire, but despite what happened there, Halfhidden still feels like home and the one place where I truly belong. It . . . pulls me back.'

'You were only about five when Debo and Baz Salcombe became an item and you all moved into Sweetwell Hall with him, so you probably don't recall much before that.'

'No, nothing at all. I think I remember Judy and I had our own suite in the Victorian wing of Sweetwell, where the housekeeper and her family live now, but mostly my memories are of after the affair finished, when we all moved to the Lodge.'

'Debo does have the knack of staying best friends with her former lovers,' Daisy said with a smile. 'And it made sense to stay in the country, because by then she and Judy had got about eight or nine rescued dogs between them, way too many for town.'

'Baz liked dogs, too,' I said. 'He never minded when Debo's escaped and ran around the estate, or that she extended the kennels beyond the garden into the grounds.'

'He was a very likeable, easy-going man,' Daisy agreed, for she had got to know him on her frequent visits to the Lodge.

I sighed sadly. 'He was, and the nearest to a father figure I've ever had. I missed him so much after he went to live abroad . . .'

Baz had been so broken by the loss of his only child that he'd shut up Sweetwell and gone to live permanently in his beachfront house in the Bahamas, leaving the housekeeper as caretaker and Dan Clew to look after the garden and keep an eye on the wooded grounds.

Baz had rarely visited after that and never at times that coincided with my visits, though he and Debo had always remained friends – and occasionally, I suspected, more than friends.

'Kieran absolutely idolises his father,' I said, following this train of thought. 'So he's going to be a bit upset about the accident, though I don't know if Douglas will tell him I refused to take the blame for it.'

'If he does, since Kieran knows about your history, he'll hardly be surprised about that. And if he truly loves you, he'll be more concerned with how it's affected you.'

'I'm not at all sure he really does love me, and in any case, when push came to shove, he seemed quite prepared to override what I wanted to please his parents.'

'It certainly sounds to me as if you two at least need some breathing space apart,' Daisy said. 'Things will seem clearer then and you may even find that you do have a future together.'

'Perhaps,' I said doubtfully. 'But if so, it definitely wouldn't be in Oxford. And not only have I already used some of this

21

legacy they seemed to have been counting on, I'll probably have to bail Debo out with the rest.'

'Oh, I don't think it will come to that. Debo does stagger from financial crisis to crisis, but she always manages to raise the money she needs from somewhere,' she said, surprised. 'I mean, for a start she can get as much modelling work as she wants and she often pops down to stay with me for various assignments.'

Debo had been a famous model in the sixties and seventies, and even though she was now the wrong side of sixty, she was still much in demand. Tall, thin and elegant, with huge grey doe-eyes and cropped ash-blonde hair, she hadn't changed much since her heyday. Judy always told me I looked like a miniature version of Debo, but with my father's dark colouring and lack of height, though I think she was just being kind . . .

'Debo hates leaving the dogs though, so if she's been down a lot recently it shows how bad things have got – and this time there's no Baz to come to the rescue,' I pointed out. 'She was devastated when he died so suddenly – not to mention the shock of finding out the whole estate had been left to some illegitimate son she'd never heard of!'

'Actually, when she rang to tell me, the main shock seemed to be more that Baz must have had a fling with Fliss Gambol, an old enemy of hers from her early modelling days, even though it was before Debo took up with him,' Daisy said. 'Even worse, she's always blamed Fliss for your mother's death.'

'Oh? In what way?' I asked, puzzled. I knew from Debo that my mother had been sweet, but a bit of a wild child and died young from an accidental drug overdose. I was the result of a brief fling with a married American artist twice her age. Although he'd known about me, we'd had minimal contact until, to my surprise, he'd left me a little bit of money a few years ago. 'Fliss Gambol was some sixties singer, wasn't she?'

'Yes, until drink and drugs got the better of her. Lisa, your mother, was very young when she came to live with Debo after your grandmother died and, unfortunately, she fell in with Fliss's crowd and under her influence.'

'That makes it a bit clearer,' I said. 'I can see now why Debo would be upset . . . and Fliss's circle must have seemed very glamorous and irresistible to an impressionable young girl, so I understand better how she came to such a tragic end. Poor Lisa!'

I sighed. 'This must have raked up some unhappy memories for Debo. Baz always promised he'd leave her the Lodge and the land round it where she's extended the kennels, and instead this son of Fliss Gambol has scooped the lot!'

'She does have the Lodge for life, though, and Baz may have thought if he left her any money she'd spend it on even more dogs,' Daisy said astutely. 'Or if he gave her the Lodge outright, she'd mortgage it.'

'Perhaps,' I admitted, because Debo did tend to pour every penny that came her way (except for what Judy could snatch away for housekeeping) on her Debo's Desperate Dogs Refuge. 'Anyway, I'll have to see when I get home. With Baz's son having all the land, she won't be able to keep as many dogs.'

'I can't see her being happy about that,' Daisy said. 'And I don't think she'll want to take any of the money your father left you, either, however desperate things are.'

'We'll see,' I said, sitting up straighter. 'You know, I believe

23

meeting Kieran was a wrong turn. I confused what *I* wanted with what I was supposed to be doing.'

Daisy smiled. 'I think it all comes down to following your heart. But sometimes you also need to use your head.'

'Both seem to be telling me to go back to Halfhidden and set up my mail-order company there. I want to go home at last, and not go away ever again,' I finished.

Daisy regarded me thoughtfully. 'Hmm . . . that might still be the shock talking and the cold feet about the wedding. But time will tell.'

'It will – and there's something else I'm going to do when I get home, that I should have done years ago: I'm going to meet the past head-on,' I said with new resolution.

'You mean, the accident?'

'Yes, I want to fill in the blank bits and try to understand why I was driving that night. I mean, I remember clearly that I was working in the pub with Lulu and Cam and that I left to walk home early, because my old dog, Patch, was ill. And then in the car park I passed the red Range Rover and Harry invited me to the party at Sweetwell. I told him I couldn't, though that bit's fuzzy . . . and then I remember absolutely nothing until I came out of the induced coma in hospital weeks later.'

'But you've been told what happened?'

'Yes, mainly by Lulu and Cameron, because by the time I'd convalesced with you and got home again, no one ever mentioned it to me – it was like the elephant in the room. Even Judy and Debo didn't want to talk about it.'

'Well, they did think at one point they'd lost you, so it isn't surprising that they wanted to put the whole tragedy behind them.'

'Perhaps, but because I can't remember what happened, it's always made it very hard for me to accept what I did and move on. So now I'm going to talk to those most involved, especially Cara and Simon. I haven't seen Simon since then and Cara's always avoided me, or cut me dead. Lulu says it's because she blamed me for the scar on her face that ended her hope of being a model,' I added. 'Lulu and I were amazed when she married Sir Lionel Cripchet after she left Oxford University, because he is more than twice her age and horrible! But his estate, Grimside, is only the other side of the hill from Halfhidden, so at least it means she lives nearby.'

'I can see where you're coming from and the need for closure,' Daisy said, 'but sometimes it really is better to let things lie. Cara's anger is probably based on guilt because she was sober enough to realise that you shouldn't be driving, yet she let Harry persuade you.'

'If I really *was* driving,' I said, looking up at her. 'Because the thing is, Daisy, in that flashback I had, I *wasn't*. I was in the back seat, with Cara.'

'Darling,' she said, leaning across and squeezing my hand, 'that might not have been a genuine flashback, because don't forget that the first two people on the scene after the crash said you were in the driver's seat, didn't they?'

'Yes, though I don't trust Simon's father, Dan Clew, in the least . . . but Tom Tamblyn said so too, so I suppose you're right,' I sighed. 'Tom has always been my friend.'

A message popped into my phone and I looked at it for a long moment. 'Kieran. His mother must have got hold of him and – well, he's not pleased with me, let's put it like that. She's on her way to spring Douglas from the clink, but

Kieran says his father will lose his driving licence and probably be prosecuted, so it will make his life very difficult.'

'That's not your fault, is it? I expect Kieran will see sense once he's had time to think of it from your viewpoint.'

'He'll have to, because I'm not shouldering the blame for things I didn't do, when I still have to come to terms with the things I *did*,' I said.

Before I went to bed I rang Lulu.

'I'm sorry it's all gone horribly wrong,' she said when I'd told her my news, 'but I'm really glad you're coming home because we all need you! And if you're back tomorrow, you can be at my Halfhidden Regeneration Scheme meeting on Tuesday, can't you? It's in the Village Hut.'

'*Regeneration?*' I echoed and she said mysteriously that she'd taken some of my ideas about involving the whole village and run with them.

'Cam has to teach an evening watercolour class in Ormskirk, so he'll probably get there only for the very end of the meeting, though he knows all about it. He's been helping me draw up maps and stuff. So I'll really need your support,' she added, refusing to be drawn on the details.

'Are you upset about Kieran?' she asked.

'Yes – no, I don't know,' I confessed. 'I did fall in love with him and . . . somehow, I seem to have just as suddenly fallen out of love again. Or perhaps I fell in love with a Kieran who didn't really exist.'

'I know the feeling,' she said sadly. 'I never want to fall in love again. My friend Solange says that that woman Guy's living with keeps coming into the café and crying into her coffee, and it's rumoured they're having huge rows.'

Lulu's ex, Guy, was still occupying the house in the Dordogne from which she'd finally fled. He'd assumed she'd left because she'd found out about his affair, but she'd had no idea till afterwards, when her friend in the village told her the woman had moved in. Still, at least it meant that he left her alone.

'I can't say I'm surprised,' I said.

'No, Guy was always a mistake – a controlling, bullying mistake, and I'm glad I got away.'

'With Cam,' I said slightly pointedly, for I knew their old friendship had taken a slightly different turn on their journey home from France.

'Cam has been a huge comfort to me, but we don't want to rush into anything and spoil the friendship we have . . . I mean, it's always been the three of us, hasn't it? And we all need space to get our lives back on track.'

'True,' I agreed. 'Time will tell – about many things!'

Chapter 3: Moving Pictures

'No we don't *need* her,' snapped Cara from the back seat of the Range Rover. She was tall, ice-princess-fair, beautiful, nineteen, and hated Harry showing interest in any other girl. She hadn't deigned even to acknowledge my callow, adolescent presence when I'd been out in the beer garden earlier collecting empty glasses, though Harry and Simon had said hello . . .

I woke with a start and sat bolt upright, heart thumping, for my hazy dream, as familiar as an old friend, seemed to have come more sharply into focus, revealing words and details I'd previously forgotten . . . if they *were* memories and not, as Daisy had implied about the previous day's flashback, something conjured up by my subconscious.

Cara Ferris was the only witness with clear recollections of all that had happened and I was going to do my best to get them out of her, one way or another . . .

I lay back for a few minutes, listening to the faint sounds of Daisy, who was a very early riser, clashing about in the basement kitchen. It was strangely soothing. My inner body clock was totally messed up after the long flight back and I wasn't sure quite what time it thought it was now, except that all at once I was ravenously hungry.

There were no further messages from Kieran on my phone, but he would by now be well on his way home. I'd sent him a brief reply last night, saying that once he'd thought about things calmly, he must see that I couldn't have acted any differently and that the crash had not only come as a great shock, but brought back memories of my previous one.

Then I'd added that I was heading home to Halfhidden, and left it at that. His move next – and I think he owed me a major apology for his last text.

Before our arguments reached their recent crescendo, he'd had the habit of leaving a loving 'Good morning, darling!' message on my phone for me to wake up to every day. He had one of those fancy watches that told you the time wherever you were, though he was quite lazy, so I suspected he'd found some kind of app that worked the time difference out and sent the message for him . . . only now he appeared to have turned it off, along with the charm.

After all these years, it left a Kieran-sized hole in my morning.

I rang home after breakfast and got Judy, as I'd expected. Debo would be out in the kennels with Sandy, the kennel-maid, but on weekday mornings Judy could usually be found in the kitchen, baking bread and cakes that never seemed to have any effect on either Debo's figure or mine, only on her own expanding girth. Judy didn't care, though: she'd given up her struggle against weight gain, along with her career on the stage, when she'd moved in to help her best friend with my childcare, the housekeeping and their shared passion for rescuing dogs.

When I told her I'd be home some time that afternoon, she expressed mild surprise.

'I thought you were going to go and stay with Kieran's parents in Oxford first?'

'There's been a slight change of plan . . . or even a *big* change of plan. I'll tell you both about it when I get back. Did my boxes arrive? There should be three of them. One's got fabrics and some sample dresses I had made up in it.'

'Yes, all safe and sound and in your studio,' she told me.

Debo and Judy had created the studio-den out of the old conservatory at the side of the house as a welcome-home surprise for me when I'd returned from Daisy's after my convalescence. She'd told them how interested I'd become in textiles, so they'd installed an old sofa, a small handloom, an easel and a scrubbed pine table, on which sat an antique black Singer sewing machine inlaid with mother-of-pearl. I'd cried when I saw it, but in a good way . . .

'Debo will be pleased to hear you're coming home today and now I know, I'll bake your favourite coffee walnut cake.'

'All your cakes are my favourite,' I said, for while Judy's loaves tended to be dark, dense affairs that took a fair bit of chewing, her cakes and scones were so light they practically floated off the plate.

'If you tell me what time your train gets in I'll come and meet it,' she offered.

'I'll ring you just before I get there,' I promised.

As the train ate up the miles between London and Lancashire, my heart lightened. My decisions, too, seemed just as valid now they were exposed to the daylight, especially since there had been no further word from Kieran.

By now he should be back in the UK, although unless his mother picked him up from the airport, he'd have to go to Oxford on the train, because presumably his father was grounded.

I sighed, looking out of the dirty window at a watercolour-grey sky. I sort of missed Kieran, though perhaps I just missed the familiarity of having him in my life. But if he really loved me, I supposed he would follow me north – by which time I hoped to have laid Harry's ghost to rest and made a new beginning.

I really wasn't looking forward to the first of those interviews with the others involved in the accident, but my inner voice, now I had tuned in again, assured me that it was the right thing to do. So I took out the spiral-bound notebook I'd bought at the station and began to jot down a list of the people involved in the accident that I needed to talk to.

At the head, of course, were Cara and Simon, the two most important witnesses, though Cara definitely wouldn't want to speak to me and I had no idea where Simon was working. The last I'd heard, he was under-gardener at some big National Trust property in the south.

The next two witnesses in order of importance were Dan Clew, Simon's father, the Sweetwell gardener who had pulled me out of the wreckage of the car, and Tom Tamblyn, who'd arrived just in time to see him do it. I dreaded trying to talk to the horrible Dan. He'd accosted me soon after I'd come home from my convalescence with Daisy and almost shattered my fragile and hard-won equilibrium by telling me no one wanted me back in Halfhidden and to leave Simon, alone. However, now I was no longer a fragile sixteen-year-old but a confident woman of the world in her mid-thirties, so I would give it a go even though he probably wouldn't tell me anything anyway, or if he did, it would be unreliable. But I'd believe Tom, if only I could get him to open up about what he saw. He was my friend Cam's uncle and, along with his father, Jonas, keeper of the Lady Spring in the Sweetwell woods.

Apart from them, there were just Lulu, Cam, Debo and Judy, who might add a bit of peripheral detail. I decided I'd get those interviews done first and out of the way, before I got to the trickier and more important ones.

Judy was waiting patiently at Ormskirk station for me in her battered estate car, sitting on the open tailgate along with two old friends: a one-eyed, white bull terrier called Vic, and Ginger, a drooling rotty-boxer cross, who were the current house dogs. Also, staring mournfully out was a large, shaggy mountain of black fur.

'What on earth is *that*?' I said, holding back the two dogs from jumping out, and already slightly covered in dog drool and hair from their enthusiastic welcome. Judy, smallish and plumply pear-shaped, was clad in tartan trousers of a shrieking orange shade that was unlikely ever to have been worn by any Scottish clan, and which echoed the hennaed colour of her madly curling hair. When I kissed her, she smelled of roses as usual, though since she lived in the permanent doggy fug of the cottage, I could never work out how she managed it.

'That's Babybelle,' she said. 'There's a Newfoundland in there somewhere, under the hair and blubber. She lay on her last owner's small child and nearly suffocated it, so they were all for having her put down, till someone contacted Debo.'

'She's so vast I don't suppose she even noticed the child was there and she seems friendly enough,' I said, stroking her. She heaved herself up into a sitting slump and licked my hand.

'Oh, she's daft as a brush and wouldn't hurt a fly on purpose. But I think she must have been fed a diet of junk food, because she was even fatter and in really poor condition. She's already lost a stone.'

'She looks very sad,' I said, stroking her head. Her eyes were like lumps of dark, moist amber.

'They're supposed to be faithful, one-person dogs, so she's probably missing her owners, even if they were useless – but she certainly seems to like *you*.'

She pushed the dogs back and closed the hatch door. Then she added, as she turned the car out of the short-stay car park and headed towards home, 'Perhaps you could be in charge of Babybelle once you've settled in? She needs encouraging to take exercise.'

'I could take her out a bit,' I agreed cautiously, because since my dog Patch died I'd avoided getting too attached to any of the dogs, mostly because I was away so much.

I looked round, and saw a flat, black, furry face and two sad amber-brown eyes staring through the mesh of the dog guard at me. She whined. At least, I hoped it was Babybelle and she wasn't lying on the other two dogs.

We drove through the sizeable village of Middlemoss and turned into the high-hedged lane that would lead eventually to the Screaming Skull Hotel and the turn up the valley to Halfhidden.

'How is everything?' I asked. 'Debo sounded very upset about Baz's will and this new heir suddenly appearing on the scene.'

'She certainly is, but I'll tell you all about it when we get home, because Debo said we needed a council of war.'

'Has this man actually arrived?'

'Well, he's been up a couple of times, but he hasn't moved in yet, since he has to relocate his business from Devon first. Garden antiques, apparently.'

'So, you've met him?'

'*I* have, but Debo was away working when he was around. A magazine flew her to the Maldives for a shoot – it's all right for some! – and then she had a cameo role in a film. Anyway, we'll save that for later, or I'll be repeating myself. And then you can tell us both what's brought you home early, because I can see something's up.'

'Fair enough,' I agreed, and she began to update me on the local gossip, though of course I'd heard some of it as Lulu and Cam had been emailing me all the time now they were back living in the village.

'I was going to give a talk in the Village Hut tomorrow, on knitting with dog hair,' Judy said, dawdling behind a slow tractor, 'but Lulu's plans seemed more urgent so she's talking tomorrow and I'll give mine later. You know about Lulu's meeting?'

'Yes, but she was very mysterious and wouldn't go into details. The Halfhidden Regeneration Scheme sounds very grand.'

'We're all agog to know what she's up to.'

'I gather it's part of her plans for expanding the Haunted Weekend breaks into week-long Haunted Holidays.'

'Then it'll be interesting to find out how that will regenerate the whole of Halfhidden, won't it?' Judy said. 'Did you know that old Jonas has moved to live with his daughter,

Lottie, behind the shop and Cameron has gone to take his place at the cottage by the Spring?'

'No, but I thought Cam had been quiet these last few days! He must have been busy moving, though I do know about the art gallery he's trying to set up.'

Cam, after teaching art in a London inner-city school, had returned to Halfhidden to live with his widowed mother a few months ago, intending to create a studio and art gallery in the old garage next to her shop.

'Jonas is into his nineties now and his rheumatism was playing him up, so he's better living with his daughter. And Cam will take over the Lady Spring from his uncle one of these days anyway . . . or he should do, though of course it's tied to the Sweetwell estate, like Dan Clew's cottage, so until the new owner makes his presence felt, we don't know *what* he intends.'

'He can't change how things are at the Lady Spring, because that's how it's always been,' I said quickly. 'They pay a pepper-corn rent for the cottage, I remember Tom telling me once.'

'Yes, they're the guardians of the Spring, so long as there's a male Tamblyn to carry on, as I understand it,' Judy said.

'Well, he *is* a Tamblyn, it's even his middle name – Cameron Tamblyn Ross,' I said.

'*There have always been Starkadders at Cold Comfort Farm,*' Judy said deeply, and then we both giggled, for a love of reading was something we shared.

The tractor finally rumbled off up a farm track just before the pub and Judy paused the car briefly so I could admire the huge, freshly painted sign outside, which boldly proclaimed: 'WELCOME TO ONE OF THE MOST HAUNTED HOTELS IN BRITAIN!'

'Is it?' I said dubiously. 'I thought really it only had Howling Hetty's skull behind the bar, the footsteps on the backstairs at night and one haunted bedchamber.'

'It is now,' Judy said drily.

'The car park's empty,' I commented, as she drove off again.

'Monday's always quiet, with the weekend visitors gone home and the restaurant closed, and I don't suppose Tuesday is ever much busier, so it's a good night for Lulu to talk to everyone.'

'Yes, that's true, though it sounds as if she'd like to fill the hotel every night. She just sent me a text to ask me to go to the Hut early tomorrow to help her set things up for the meeting.'

'What things?'

'She didn't say. I think she wants to surprise me.'

'There are rumours that she's been going up and down the valley talking to all kinds of people, but if she did, she must have sworn them to silence till the big reveal tomorrow night.'

The road took a sharp turn between dark hawthorn hedges starred with silvery constellations of blossom, and then began to climb. The dark and densely planted conifers of Sir Lionel Cripchet's estate, Grimside, crowded up to the backs of the cottages on our left, while the tangled ancient woodland of Sweetwell lay to the right. Oddly, although Cripchet's estate was well known to be overrun with grey squirrels, they never crossed the road into Sweetwell. Tom Tamblyn always reckoned that this was to do with the taste of the water there, which despite the name is anything but sweet.

I put my window down and inhaled the familiar scents of home appreciatively. Already spring seemed to have arrived in the valley and all the buds and blooms were bursting forth at once, with bluebells, saffron-yellow gorse and daffodils along the grass verge, and creamy magnolia and bright yellow forsythia in the gardens.

The cottages edging the lane grew in number for, although Halfhidden straggled all the way up the steep lane to the Summit Alpine Nursery, most of the important buildings, including the tiny church, formed a defensive huddle around the circular Green.

Here stood the large house from which Cara Ferris's parents ran their veterinary practice, Lottie Ross's general shop, and the Hut, a half-brick, half-wooden hall, renovated more than twenty years before by Baz Salcombe in a fit of philanthropy.

Judy steered the car past the deserted bus shelter where, twice a day at an inconvenient hour, the Middlemoss bus stopped before returning whence it came, and turned between the lichen-scabbed stone gateposts of Sweetwell – and I saw at once that a large sign reading 'Rufus Carlyle Garden Antiques' had replaced the 'Debo's Desperate Dogs' one.

I spotted that a moment later, half-concealed in the shrubbery by the turn-off to the Lodge. Unfortunately, the sign was the only thing that was concealed, for ramshackle kennels and rusty wire pens ran right up to the edge of the drive, and the sound of barking, which had been increasingly audible as we approached the Green, now became deafening.

'Good heavens!' I exclaimed. 'Things have expanded a bit since I was last home. How many dogs have you got now?'

'Nearly forty at the last count,' Judy admitted. 'Debo can't seem to say no.'

The cottage, a low honey-coloured building with windows set under the eaves, looked just the same. The deep scarlet door was flung open as we got out and the tall, slender and elegant figure of Debo, clad in jeans and wellies, was swept out on a wave of Desperate Dogs.

'Darling!' she cried, tripping over a rat-tailed little white mongrel and practically falling into my arms. 'Welcome home!'

Chapter 4: Desperate Dogs

Sandy, the kennelmaid, loomed silently up and waded into the scrum, chasing all the dogs back towards the kennels in a yapping, noisy pack, and I finally managed to get through the door.

Debo didn't let me have time to do more than dump my bags in my old bedroom up in the eaves, before calling me back down to the small sitting room for the council of war.

Vic and Ginger, the two house dogs, had vanished with the rest, but Babybelle lay like a furry Mont Blanc in front of the empty fireplace.

'Belle refused to go out with the others and she's too big to drag, unless one pushes and one pulls,' Judy said, seeing my glance.

I sat down on one end of a rather hairy sofa and Belle heaved herself up and wearily plodded over, then subsided heavily onto my feet with a sigh. My toes instantly went numb.

Judy exchanged glances with Debo. 'There, I told you she'd taken to Izzy.'

'I suppose we'd better try and get her into her kennel before we start, because Sandy will feed them all when she comes back and then Belle will be desperate to get at her dinner. She'll howl for hours afterwards, too, wanting more food,' Debo said.

'That must go down well with the neighbours,' I commented.

'Oh, well, most of them don't mind and it's not as if we're right next to anyone. Dan Clew's cottage is the nearest and he did report the barking to the council last year, but luckily we didn't have quite as many dogs in at the time and when they measured the noise, it wasn't so bad. Anyway, they don't bark *all* the time.'

'*I'll* get Belle out,' Judy said, and fetched in a sort of plastic ball with holes in it, filled with doggy treats that Chris, Debo's canine behavioural specialist, had recommended. I think she could produce an adoring male specialist to provide free advice in *any* department.

Babybelle looked up when she heard the food rattle; then, as Judy backed out of the room, she slowly hauled herself to her feet, her eyes fixed longingly on the toy.

'She has to chase it round her run to get the treats out and they're low calorie, because Judy bakes them herself. Exercise and food – such a good idea,' Debo said.

'She is huge!' I commentated as the bear-like creature ambled out.

'Quite a lot of that is fur, because the Newfoundland breed has a special double layer to keep them warm when they're swimming in the icy sea. And she's got webbed feet too.'

'Really?' I said, fascinated. 'Weird!'

Debo poured coffee and pushed the milk carton my way. The china was a mismatched collection of thick, white, cheap pottery, one or two remnants of Victorian chintz-patterned loveliness and a couple of eighties Portmeirion plates.

'We can get the biscuits and cake out now without Babybelle bothering us,' she said happily, opening a tin to reveal Judy's home-baked pecan biscuits and another containing the coffee and walnut cake that Judy is convinced is my favourite.

Debo cut hefty slices from it and took one for herself.

'It's a miracle you aren't twenty stone, with the amount of sugary things you eat,' I said.

'Good metabolism, darling, like you. It's so lucky you took after my side of the family that way, even if you ended up titchy, like your father.'

Judy returned, dogless. 'That should hold her for a while,' she said, sinking back into her usual wing-back chair. 'If we can get some more weight off, we should be able to rehome her eventually. She's good-natured enough with people and other dogs. I'll miss all that lovely hair for my knitting, though.'

Since Debo's Desperate Dogs was a kind of Last Chance Saloon, rescuing dogs that, for one reason or another, were facing being put down, there was a core group of permanent residents who were unlikely to leave, as well as a fluctuating population of arrivals and departures. But recently there appeared to have been a population explosion.

I said so. 'I see you've had to get Tom to make you some more runs out of old wooden pallets and wire mesh, Debo – they're right up to the edge of the drive, now!'

'We were bursting at the seams and it's flat just there. Besides, I had to put them *somewhere*,' she said reasonably.

'But you're only licensed for a certain number, and there wouldn't be quite so many if you didn't take in dogs that could be easily found new homes by other charities,' Judy pointed out.

'But the poor things have had such hard lives that they need a little time and love so they can recover first,' Debo protested. 'And anyway, when Baz came back last year – his first flying visit for yonks and he'd put on so much weight that that heart attack was on the cards, Izzy – he didn't say anything about there being too many dogs, or the kennels spreading round the front just a *tiny* bit, so I'm sure he wouldn't mind about the extra runs.'

'The new owner of Sweetwell might not be quite so sanguine about having what looks like a shanty town up the side of his drive,' Judy said.

This reminded Debo of her grievances and she said indignantly, 'That will! I'm sure someone must have persuaded Baz not to leave me the Lodge, because he always promised he would. If I had any money, I'd challenge the will on the grounds of undue influence, but he didn't leave me any of that, either!'

'If you'd had any money, you'd have instantly spent it all on the dogs,' Judy said. 'We've got so many unpaid bills, we could wallpaper the entire office with them.'

'You have got the Lodge for life, haven't you?' I asked. 'That's what Daisy said.'

'Yes, but that's not the same as owning it outright. I mean, apparently I can't even make small changes to it without permission from this Carlyle man! And he's already had my sign taken down from the front gate without asking me first, though I got Tom to put it by the turning to the Lodge instead.'

'I suspect people could find the kennels *without* a sign,' I said drily. 'But I did notice the new one for Rufus Carlyle Garden Antiques – it would be a bit hard to miss, since it's so big. That's his name, Carlyle?'

'Yes, Rufus Carlyle. I do vaguely remember Fliss getting pregnant by some man of that name, back in the mid-seventies, because there was a bit of a scandal in the papers. So since he took his name, this Rufus is probably his child and not Baz's illegitimate son at all. They should check his DNA against Baz's, before he moves himself and his business in, lock, stock and barrel.'

'I'm not even sure you can do that at this stage, but even if you could I think you're way too late, because a big removal van passed earlier, while you were out,' Judy said. 'Myra says she expects him to arrive any day and she's spring-cleaned the house ready.'

Sweetwell Hall was an ancient, long, low, black and white building with a small brick-built Victorian wing blobbed onto one end like an afterthought, in which the younger of Tom Tamblyn's two sisters, Myra, her husband and their son, Olly, occupied the upper storey. Myra, Sweetwell's house-keeper, was such a fanatical cleaner that she practically caught the dust before it hit any surface, so the place was probably already buffed and polished to within an inch of its life.

'The outbuildings are full of garden antiques now, lorry-loads of them . . . whatever they are,' Debo said. 'When did you talk to Myra, Judy?'

'I didn't. Lottie told me when I popped over to the shop for a packet of walnut halves, and she said that Myra was going to make some proper Lancashire hotpots ready for his first dinner in the house, so he could start the way she intended him to go on.'

'I didn't think she cooked for Baz,' I said.

'Not often, but she did stock the freezer and fridge, so she had a lot of control over what he ate. He always said he

43

didn't know why he bothered leaving out a list of things he fancied, because she always ignored it.'

'Presumably they've already completely proved this Rufus Carlyle person *is* Baz's son, or Baz wouldn't have acknowledged him in the will,' I said, returning to the original subject.

'That's true, Izzy. Baz was easy-going but he wasn't stupid, and he must have known Fliss Gambol would have said *anything* if she thought there was money in it,' Judy said.

'She certainly would,' Debo agreed, her face darkening. 'She was always trying to take my boyfriends away . . . and if she hadn't drawn your mother back into her crowd after you were born, Izzy, I'm sure she'd still be here with us.'

'Daisy told me all about that,' I said.

'Lisa was very young for her age and impressionable,' Debo explained. 'I always felt I should have taken better care of her.'

'You had a career too, don't forget, and you did your best,' Judy told her. 'I haven't heard much about Fliss for years – what's she been doing?'

'I think she's been on an endless cycle of rehab stays and career relaunches that never quite took off. Now up she pops as the mother of the heir and, reading between the lines of that story she sold to a Sunday rag, she'd let the Carlyle bloke think he was the child's father until she decided she could get more out of Baz, only a couple of months before he died. I think Baz met Rufus only once – then he goes and leaves Sweetwell to him!'

'Rufus Carlyle is certainly no child,' Judy said. 'He must be a year or two older than Izzy, in his late thirties.'

'Well, you've seen him and I haven't,' Debo said. 'I was away earning an honest crust both times he came to inspect his windfall, so you'd think he was trying to avoid me. Probably a guilty conscience,' she added darkly.

'Guilty conscience?' I asked. 'If he was really Baz's son, then I suppose he couldn't help that.'

'No, but then he must have got round Baz and talked him into leaving him everything, even the things he'd promised to *me*,' Debo said bitterly. 'It's so unfair!'

'But Baz did make sure you could live in the Lodge for the rest of your life, so that's not so bad. I mean, I know you can't do anything radical with it, or leave it to anyone else, but he can't get you out.'

'But he *could* object to the kennels encroaching onto his land, or us building any more,' Judy said. 'And though I didn't tell you at the time, Debo, because I knew it would upset you even more, Fliss came for a snoop round one day, with Dan Clew in tow.'

Debo stared at her. 'When was this?'

'When you were away the first time. I opened the door and there she was, looking like one of the Living Dead. I told her she had a nerve, showing her face anywhere near you – and it was just as well you weren't there, Debo, or you'd have set the dogs onto her.'

'Too true: I would.'

'She said the kennels were a total eyesore and her son wanted them cleared away as soon as possible. Then Dan Clew put in his two pennyworth and told her Baz had been trying to get us to remove them from his land for years, not to mention complaining about vicious dogs constantly escaping and the noise problem, but we hadn't taken any notice.'

'Dan Clew is a lying toad who would do anything to get

45

us out of the Lodge! And the brazen cheek of the woman, coming to my home after what she did!' Debo said furiously. 'I hope you didn't let her set foot over the threshold.'

'No, and I told her Dan was lying and Baz had been a dog-lover who completely supported what we were doing with the Refuge. Then she said even if that was true, Rufus certainly didn't feel the same way and then I slammed the door on her. She seemed to be getting on *very* well with Dan,' she added.

'Well, she would – she'd sleep with anything male and *he's* never been that fussy, either.'

'She's a fast worker though, because Myra said afterwards that she'd been staying with friends not far away and only called in out of curiosity to have a quick look at the place.'

'She hasn't got any friends,' Debo said. 'It was probably another rehab clinic.'

'We've only got her word for it that her son wants the kennels removed,' I said. 'He might be another dog-lover.'

'I don't think so,' Judy said, 'because actually he did say something about the kennels near the drive not giving a good impression to customers when he opened the garden antiques centre for business. And then Goldie – he's a big mastiff cross, Izzy – got out that very night and went up to Sweetwell. Myra was too terrified to hang the washing out next morning until I'd been and collected him.'

'He only hates men,' Debo said. 'And he didn't actually bite, he just threatened to.'

'Perhaps, but you can understand that he wouldn't want big, vicious-looking dogs bouncing up to customers,' I said.

'Well, Goldie's gone to live with a woman in an isolated Scottish croft now, and she loves him to bits,' Debo told me.

A lorry covered in a flapping tarpaulin went past and on up the drive, rattling the diamond-paned windows. 'That's probably another load of garden antiquities,' Judy said. 'When we took some of the dogs up there first thing this morning, the courtyard was full of old wrought-iron gates, fountains, wheelbarrows and even bits of ancient farm machinery.'

'What's this Rufus Carlyle like?' I asked her.

'I don't really know. He's always called at dusk, like a vampire. A bit brusque, deepish voice, quite tall, late thirties.'

'Fliss must have had her fling with Baz a couple of years before he and I became an item, if Rufus is his,' Debo said. 'I wouldn't have looked at him if I'd known she'd got there first.'

'According to that newspaper article, it was only a brief encounter in a storage cupboard at a well-known restaurant,' Judy said.

'She certainly put it about a bit,' Debo said disparagingly.

'So did you,' pointed out her friend with brutal honesty.

'I had *relationships* – one at a time – and I was fond of them all,' Debo said indignantly. 'I still am and they're all still good friends. That's what makes Baz's betrayal over the will so much worse – and I don't think I could bear it if Fliss moved in to Sweetwell, too.'

'Oh, I shouldn't think she will. I'm sure she has her own place in London and that must be much more her scene. In fact, she said Halfhidden was Hicksville and she couldn't imagine how we could stand living here,' Judy said.

'Good, because I'd have to kill her if she did move in. Where could we hide the body?'

'We'd think of somewhere,' Judy said.

Debo sighed and said gloomily, 'I don't think any son of

Fliss Gambol can possibly be nice. And moving my sign without asking, then complaining about the kennels just shows you what he's going to be like.'

'I expect Dan Clew has been poisoning his mind against us,' Judy said, turning to me. 'That man's been all bitterness and bile since he made that heavy pass at Debo and she turned him down in no uncertain terms.'

'As if!' Debo said scathingly.

'After the accident, he took against me, too,' I said. 'Remember how he told me when I got back from Daisy's not to try to contact Simon, when the thought hadn't even entered my head?'

'He got the wrong end of the stick,' Debo said. 'It was Simon who tried to contact you when you were still in hospital, but you weren't well enough at the time. And then afterwards, Dan sent him to stay with his sister in Durham till his college term started.'

'You never mentioned that before,' I said, staring at her. 'I wonder what he wanted to see me about.'

'I think he blamed himself for not realising his drink had been spiked that night, but of course it wasn't his fault,' Judy said. 'He was distraught after the accident, so I suppose you can't really blame Dan for trying to protect his son, in his own misguided way.'

'Simon was always a nice boy, so his mother must have been lovely, because he can't have got his good nature from Dan,' Debo said.

'Is Dan still going round with a shotgun under his arm, pretending he's the estate manager?' I asked.

'Yes, darling,' Debo said, 'but don't worry because it's unloaded. He knew Baz would have sacked him instantly if he attempted to shoot even a rabbit on his land, because he was only easy-going up to a point.'

'Dan's a horrible man,' I said, taking another slice of cake. There is something perfect about the union of coffee icing and walnut halves . . .

Debo suddenly sat up straighter. 'What if this Rufus isn't like Baz and thinks Dan ought to shoot any loose dogs running round on his property?'

Judy thought about it. 'Oh, I don't think so. He seemed all right really.'

'Maybe it would be an idea to invite him to tea and try to win him over to our side?' suggested Debo cunningly.

'Good idea! I can stuff him full of fairy cakes to sweeten him up, and you can exert your charms on him,' agreed Judy. 'He must have some of Baz's genes, so it might just work.'

'True, and I expect once we've had a chance to explain what we're doing, he'll understand how vital it is to rescue these poor dogs,' agreed Debo, brightening up in her usual mercurial way. 'Maybe he'll even help support our work.'

'I think we'd better get to know him a little before suggesting anything like that,' Judy cautioned her. 'And there are bound to be some changes. Tom's worried that he'll want to alter the way things have always been at the Lady Spring.'

'We'll just have to wait and see,' I said. 'Meanwhile, you said you had a huge financial crisis, Debo.'

'We certainly do,' Judy said grimly. 'I've only just found out the half of it.'

'The thing is, that when Baz promised to leave me the Lodge, I sort of borrowed some money against it,' Debo confessed. 'It was when I had that enormous vet's bill for Benjy, though we had to try the operation, and then afterwards the pills cost hundreds a month . . . And in the end the poor old boy died, though we had a lovely few extra months with him.'

'I don't think borrowing against a house that wasn't actually yours was a good idea,' I said with restraint.

'I know, but I'd got behind with Sandy's wages and then the suppliers said they wouldn't send me any more dog food until I'd paid the bill in full for the last lot . . .'

'And now we keep getting final demands from the electricity company, plus we ran out of oil for the central heating in February,' put in Judy.

'I *thought* you'd turned if off a bit early this year!'

'Luckily it's been quite warm, except in the evenings,' Judy said.

'I managed to get a couple of donations from friends to tide us over, but I suppose I am in a bit of a hole,' Debo admitted.

'You can say that again,' I said. 'How much do you need?'

I whistled when she told me. 'It's just as well I'm going to be around from now on and I'll bail you out with what remains of the money my father left me. It should clear the major outstanding debts, at least. That's a start.'

'You'll do no such thing,' Judy said firmly. 'Debo's made sure your money was safe all these years, to give you something to start you off when you settled down.'

'That's right. I'll just have to squeeze my friends a bit harder and maybe take more work when it's offered, even if I do hate going away so much,' Debo said. 'That legacy was for you, to start your own business, or buy a place of your own. Didn't you tell me that Kieran wanted you to use it as a deposit on your first home together?'

'That was never going to happen and I've told him so. We've had a few arguments lately and . . . well, I've made up my mind that I'm staying here, in Halfhidden,' I told them. 'I've already bought the first stock and I can start my business in a small way in the studio and then, when it takes off, buy a place of my own. So you see, I don't need the rest of that money.'

'But . . . what about Kieran? I mean, you were going to get married and although I know you didn't take to his parents—' Judy began.

'Understatement of the year,' I said, and then told them what had brought me home earlier than expected, and my resolution to face the past and forge a new future here in Halfhidden.

'That Douglas man sounds like a complete tosser,' Debo said critically. 'And as to Kieran's mother – well, Judy and I were planning the sweetest little economy wedding in the Halfhidden church, with a tent on the Green for the reception. I know a sheep farmer with a big marquee who would lend it to us for the day. He uses it to put his in-lamb ewes in when the weather's cold and wet.'

'That was exactly what I wanted and I've already made my own wedding dress,' I agreed.

'It could still happen because you might feel differently when Kieran turns up on the doorstep,' Judy said thoughtfully. 'Once he's seen sense, that is.'

'*If* he sees sense, and I'm not convinced he ever will. But one thing I am certain of is that I'm home for good, so even if we did have a future together, he'd be the one making the concessions and moving up here.'

'Attagirl,' Debo said. 'All those years of negotiating with

stubborn village elders and minor officials has given you a bit of attitude!'

'And I *want* you to have the money, Debo – think of it as a loan.'

'A loan I'd probably never be able to pay back,' she said honestly.

'Oh, I don't know. Just think how much they paid you for that cameo part in a blockbuster film a couple of years ago! That would have practically been enough on its own. But I do have one or two conditions for lending you the money . . .'

'Conditions?' Debo echoed, her large grey eyes widening.

'Yes. I know that Judy runs the household affairs and pays those bills, and I don't want to mess with that – though I'd like to know where she gets the money from,' I added, the thought only just occurring to me.

'Oh, Debo puts a bit into the joint household account whenever she earns anything,' Judy said. 'We've got to try and keep a roof over our heads and eat, after all. But I've got a small income and my pension too, though it never seems to go far enough.'

'You shouldn't have to put all your own money in! Wasn't Debo paying you a wage at one time?' I asked.

Judy shrugged. 'At first, when you were a baby and I looked after you full time, but later . . . well, I live here too, so it was share and share alike.'

'But if anything happens to Debo, you won't even have a roof over your head now, have you thought of that?'

'*I* hadn't!' Debo exclaimed. 'How awful of me! Judy darling, we should be paying into a pension for you, or something, just in case!'

'Too late, and in any case, you're the thin, rangy sort who'll live for ever, while by now my heart is probably totally encased in fat,' Judy said. 'Anyway, leaving aside the household expenses, what are your conditions, Izzy?'

'That I take over the kennels paperwork,' I said. 'The office looks as if someone removed the ceiling and tipped in a lorry-load of scrap paper. I know the only thing Debo's kept in order are the dogs' records, and those are out in the shed, so that's probably partly Sandy's doing.'

'She does keep them updated and runs a tidy shed,' Judy agreed.

Sandy Lane, a local farmer's daughter, was by nature taciturn and solitary, apart from the dogs, and liked to eat her lunch, drink her tea and do her paperwork in a converted shed, where she had a comfy chair, radio, table and smelly paraffin stove.

It was there, when they did manage to rehome a dog, that she made the new owner pay a small fee and buy a suitable collar and lead before letting them leave.

'I don't mind in the least if you want to take the office side over, because it's a nightmare – I mean, I'm a *charity*,' Debo said, as if that excused her from any form of paperwork. 'I shove all the receipts into a box and once a year the accountant comes here and sifts through them, but he says he despairs of me.'

'I'm not surprised. If ever the taxman decides to do a complete inspection of the books, they'll wipe the floor with you.'

'Is that it – you just want to help me with the paperwork?' asked Debo.

'Pretty much. I think we need to find better ways of

ordering things and making ends meet, but I'll work on it. And you have to admit you have way too many dogs!'

'I don't like to turn them down,' she said sheepishly.

'I know, but some of them are not desperate dogs at all, they just need rehoming, so you could pass those on to larger rescue places where they can find new owners more easily.'

'Sandy and I have both told her that,' Judy said. 'We have contacts who could help, and they could always return the dogs if they can't rehome them.'

'I suppose you're right,' Debo conceded reluctantly.

'If we do end up having to remove all the kennels outside the garden boundary, it's going to be the only way we can carry on,' Judy pointed out.

'Well, think about it while I deal with the financial crisis and get things back on an even keel,' I suggested.

'I still don't think you should rush into giving us your money, Izzy. You've had a shock and you've been working so hard,' Judy said. 'You need to rest and recover before you make a big decision like that.'

'No, go with your heart,' Debo urged me. 'Not about the money, but about where you want to live and work.'

'I've already made my mind up about all of those,' I said, 'and what's more, now I'm back for good, I also intend facing up to my past head-on.'

'What *do* you mean?' asked Judy.

'That I'm on a mission to talk to everyone closely involved in the accident that killed Harry, so I can get as true a picture as possible of what happened that night. I should have done it years ago, because I'm sure when I have I'll really be able to put it behind me at last.'

They exchanged worried glances.

'I'm not sure that's the best idea. It was so long ago, everyone has forgotten about it,' Judy said.

'But I don't think they have, they just don't *talk* about it. Even you two have never really discussed what happened with me, but now you're going to have to.'

'Well . . . we will if you really want us to,' Judy said, and Debo reluctantly agreed.

'I don't think you should rake it all up again, but if you're determined to do it, then we'll help you, of course.'

'We don't even like to think of it,' Judy said. 'At one point we really thought we'd lost you, when the line on the monitor went flat . . .'

'I expect that was while I was in Heaven, before I had to come back,' I said. 'I know neither of you really believe that I went there, but it was totally real – and anyway, if it wasn't, then how did I know that Harry and Patch were both dead?'

'That *was* odd,' Debo admitted. 'But the nurses might have talked about the accident and we may have mentioned Patch, so your subconscious probably absorbed the information.'

I gave up on that tack. 'Apart from the visit to Heaven, the last thing I remember before waking in hospital was being in the car park on my way home from the pub and telling Harry I couldn't go to the party with him and the others. There's a huge blank to fill in, so I'd really appreciate any help you can give me.'

And they did answer my questions about that night, though of course by the time they'd arrived on the scene of the accident, everyone except Harry was out of the car and the ambulance was on its way.

It obviously upset them to remember it, but I also had the oddest impression that Judy was holding something back . . .

After that, I went upstairs to unpack my things, and then into my studio for a while. Whenever I'd returned I'd always been grateful that it hadn't been turned into emergency kennelling but was always just as I'd left it, with my old sketchbooks, rolls of fabric and drawers of odds and ends awaiting me.

It felt comforting, even with the niggling worry about whether this unknown son of Baz's would change things – or, worse still, that his mother would turn up again and start interfering, though from the sound of it she hadn't found the quiet backwater of Halfhidden to her liking.

But I certainly did, and as the car had headed up the hill on my way home, I'd felt sure I was following my true destiny once again.

Now, that certainty folded softly round me with the downy warmth of angel's wings.

Chapter 5: Hounded

'Shut up, Cara – I want Izzy,' Harry snapped, before turning back to me with the smile that always made my heart beat faster.

'Dad's away, so all our college friends are coming over to Sweetwell for a party. Come with us?'

After dinner everything suddenly caught up with me – the whistle-stop visit to the two workshops in India that were making the clothes for my new business, the increasingly acrimonious arguments with Kieran, the long flight home, and then Douglas's accident. It wasn't surprising that exhaustion hit me like an express train. When Judy ordered me off to bed, I slept right through until almost lunchtime next day.

I had so much to do, what with the Desperate Dogs paperwork, a business to set up and, sandwiched somewhere between the two, interviews with the remaining people on my list – but I also longed to go down for a dip in the healing pool below the Lady Spring, which was something I usually did most mornings when I was home and the weather wasn't totally freezing.

The source of the Spring lay in a little cave set back in the rocky outcrop above it and then the water fell into what was once a natural pool. According to old Jonas Tamblyn, who wrote the pamphlet about the local legends that they sold in the entrance hut, it was for centuries a pagan site, and various objects have been found nearby, or washed into the lower pool, including a very pregnant clay figurine. I expect that's where the local belief that the water is good for fertility came from.

It had always been called the Lady Spring, though the identity of the Lady in question has changed with the centuries, as the old pagan goddess was first absorbed into a Roman deity, and then later became identified with the Virgin Mary and Christianity. It was no wonder the clearing around it always felt heavy with history.

I jumped out of bed, put on jeans and one of the vintage Indian cotton tops from my extensive collection, on which I'd modelled some of my new range, and went down to find Judy already laying the kitchen table for lunch. There was a heavy, sullen-looking loaf of bread cooling on a wire rack. It was odd how brilliant she was at baking almost anything but bread . . .

'There you are,' she said. 'We thought we'd let you have your sleep out and then you'd feel all caught up and yourself again.'

'It worked, because I do, *and* I'm ravenous. Has anyone rung me?'

I'd already checked my mobile and there were no messages from Kieran, though of course he might still have been asleep.

'Lulu rang earlier to say she'd be out all day, but she'd see you at the Hut a little before the meeting and catch up with you then.'

'Right, and I'm sure she said Cam was off teaching a watercolour group today, so he may not be around either, but I think I'd just like a quiet afternoon anyway.'

Debo came in then, with Vic and Ginger frolicking round her feet, and Judy dished up bowls of delicious thick mulligatawny soup, then broke the heel of the old loaf (not without some difficulty) and tossed it to the dogs under the table, before cutting into the new one.

After lunch we toured the kennels so I could visit permanent residents and meet some of the latest arrivals.

Most of them were the big breeds of dogs and over half were some kind of bull terrier, several permanently scarred from being used for fighting. Debo told me their sad histories, where she knew them, but really, you could read a lot of it in their eyes. The ones who timidly crept up and begged for love were the most heartbreaking.

The more recent kennels and runs had been roughly knocked together for free by Tom Tamblyn, out of materials he'd found in skips, and I could see why the new owner of Sweetwell might not like his customers seeing them as they drove up to his garden antiques centre.

Judy had been quite right about some of the inmates not being Desperate Dogs at all, but eminently rehomable, including the cute little white mongrel I'd seen when I'd arrived. I said as much to Debo and suggested that her friend Lucy, who was in charge of a large dog rescue centre in Cheshire, had a much better chance of quickly finding them a forever home.

When I also added persuasively that then she would have a little more room for the *really* desperate cases, Sandy, who'd been following us round, supported me and said she'd draw up a list of all the ones that could be moved right away, like Babybelle.

'Yes, she's perfectly friendly, just too fat and lazy and costs us a fortune in dog food,' Judy agreed.

'Oh, but I think she's already quite attached to Izzy,' Debo protested. 'Look at her little face pressed up against the wire!'

'*Big* face,' I amended. Babybelle had indeed plodded up to the front of the pen when she spotted us and was now staring intently, though I suspected that was probably from the hope of food, rather than from any new-found affection. I pushed a hand through the mesh and stroked her and her tail thumped heavily a couple of times.

'I think she ought to be rehomed too,' I said, hardening my heart, and Babybelle looked at me reproachfully.

'We'll see,' Debo said. 'Meanwhile I'll have to have a look at Sandy's list. What are you going to do now, darling?'

'I think I'll go down to the Lady Spring and take a little dip in the pool before any visitors turn up.'

At that time of year the Lady Spring and the healing pool below it were only open to the public from two till four, and it wasn't much after half-past one now. Often, Tom didn't even see a visitor at all on weekdays in early spring, so he might be pottering about in his garden, or round his beehives. There's a big brass bell visitors can ring by the turnstile if they do turn up and he's not in his hut.

'It's a bit chilly for swimming,' Judy objected, shivering at the thought.

'I know, but the water's always OK once I'm in – not warm, but not unbearably cold, either.'

I went in to fetch my things and Babybelle set up a howling the minute I turned my back that continued until

60

my return. Then she instantly stopped and instead barked at me imperatively.

'She wants to go with you,' Debo said, elegantly resting her arms on top of her yard brush and looking as if she was posing for a magazine picture, rather than cleaning an empty dog run. If anyone could make dungarees and wellies fashionable, it would be Debo.

'No way,' I said. 'Tom won't allow a dog into the enclosure, and anyway, she'd probably take a year to plod down there.'

'Pity, because she does need the exercise and she's definitely taken to you.'

'But we don't *want* her to get attached to me, because I'm sure she could find a good home with someone else,' I said. 'If she's costing a fortune in dog food, the sooner, the better.'

'Perhaps Tom might like her,' Judy suggested. 'He rang to say he might pop in sometime later today to see if any of the dogs took his fancy. He lost Duke recently, you know.'

Tom and his father, Jonas, had now rehomed two of Debo's Desperate Dogs and they'd both reached a good age. They always seemed to give them regal names, too.

'If they took Babybelle, she could find herself a Princess or a Queenie,' I said, with a grin.

'I don't think she's his kind of dog,' Debo said doubtfully. 'Jonas, now he's living with Lottie behind the shop, says he wouldn't mind a little dog to keep him company, only we mostly get the big ones, as you know.'

I did indeed: it was the bull terriers, Rottweilers, Alsatians, Dobermans and large mixed breeds of the canine world that generally got dumped first, and some of them had been treated so badly they never could be rehomed. Others, however, when

Debo's dog therapist friend, Chris, had worked his magic on them, were placed with new owners.

'I'm off to fetch a greyhound in a minute,' Debo said, looking at her watch. 'Judy's coming with me, for a change of scene.'

'A greyhound? You haven't had one of those before, have you?'

'No, because there are specialist greyhound rescue places. But this is urgent – if I don't fetch her by three this afternoon, she's going to the vet's to be put down. She's retired from racing, but her new owners put her out in the back garden when the pet rabbit was loose, and you can imagine the result.'

'Yes. Bit silly of them.'

'It was the neighbour who suggested me and rang up. She said it was a nice dog, but they were going on like it was a blood-crazed monster and had locked it in the garden and left it there. But they've given permission for me to take it if I pick it up before they get back, and the neighbour will let me in.'

'That might be one to send straight to your friend Lucy, to rehome,' I suggested.

'Maybe, but I've just had a thought: greyhounds don't need a lot of exercise and they make good pets, so I might be able to persuade Jonas that he'd like her instead of a little dog.'

'So long as he hasn't taken to breeding rabbits. Or what about that little white mongrel, Snowy?'

'Unfortunately he barks his head off whenever the TV's on, so until we can break him of doing that, he's going to be a bit difficult. Chris is thinking up a plan.'

'Let's hope it works,' I said, then set off for the Spring, with Babybelle's imperative barks turning into long, blood-curdling howls behind me.

I slowed down once I was out of earshot – or perhaps Babybelle had just given up. I had so much on my mind that I really needed a little peaceful time to be alone and let the birdsong and the buzz of busy insects soothe me . . . but unfortunately, I didn't get it, because Dan Clew, the Sweetwell gardener, stepped out of a side path right in front of me, blocking my way.

He was a big, bullishly handsome man, in a heavy-jawed kind of way, with a high complexion and small, dark eyes. He seemed to hold a certain charm for some women, though now that he was getting on a bit, his black hair was liberally streaked with grey and his strong frame starting to run to fat, the latter probably due to the pies and pasties he consumed most evenings in the public bar of the Screaming Skull. He had a handful of cronies there, but he wasn't popular, due to his bad temper.

As usual, now that he fancied himself as gamekeeper-cum-estate manager, he had a shotgun under his arm, though even if Baz had allowed him to load and use it, there wasn't anything to shoot in the overgrown woodland that circled Sweetwell Hall. I mean, the red squirrels weren't vicious, and anyway, they were a protected species.

Still, it wasn't exactly helping to dispel the faint air of menace that always hung around him.

Dan eyed me in the way he did all women, as though examining dubious heifers at a cattle show.

'You're back visiting, then?' he asked.

'Hi, Dan,' I said levelly, though my heart was still thumping from the suddenness of his unwelcome appearance. 'I'm back indeed – but for good this time.'

His eyes narrowed. 'You're staying here in Halfhidden? I wouldn't have thought you'd want to do that. No one wants you here after what you did to Harry. You're not welcome.'

'So you say, but you seem to be the only person who thinks so, or who holds me to blame for letting Harry talk me into driving that night,' I said evenly, standing my ground, for as Judy had pointed out, I'd had years of battles with obstinate village elders and petty officials while working abroad and I was no longer a traumatised young girl able to be scared off by bully-boy tactics.

'Cara Ferris told me straight that you insisted on driving and wouldn't even stop at the Lodge to let Harry take over. And my boy, who they'd made drunk, was out of it in the back seat.'

'Well, you can't blame *that* on me,' I said. 'Spiking his drink was another of Harry's bright ideas. And I still don't remember a thing about what happened, not even getting into the car, let alone driving, so she could say anything, couldn't she?'

'You're calling her a liar?' he demanded.

'I'm saying that I know I would have been so terrified at the idea of driving the car on the main road, that I'm certain I wouldn't have insisted. So yes, that has to be a lie, at least.'

'Sez you!' he sneered.

I looked at him and suddenly decided to take the bull by the horns and get one interview I was dreading over with. 'Actually, Dan, I want to ask you some questions about the night of the accident, and what you really *saw*.'

'I saw you behind the wheel, that's what I saw,' he said. 'And Harry next to you, with a dirty great branch sticking through him, dead as a doornail.'

I felt slightly sick. 'Judy said I mustn't have been wearing a seat belt and was thrown forward, that's why I had such bad head injuries. But you got me out of the car, didn't you? Why did you do that?'

'It was on its side in the ditch and there was an almighty smell of petrol,' he said shortly. 'Simon and Cara got themselves out of the back, but I thought the whole thing might go up any minute and better to move you than you be burned to a crisp.'

'Well . . . that was kind of you, then,' I said, disconcerted.

'Tom turned up as I was getting you out; he'd have done it if I hadn't.' He shrugged.

'Was there anything on the drive that might have made me swerve?'

He shook his head. 'Nothing. You probably just came too fast at the dip and then slammed the brakes on. You could have killed my boy, like you killed the boss's son.'

'Not on purpose,' I reiterated, thinking that he himself had actually done all right out of the tragedy, because he'd lived an easy life since Baz moved abroad. And Simon seemed to have got on well too, working his way up the career ladder as a gardener with the National Trust.

'How's Simon doing?' I asked on that thought.

He gave me a darkly glowering, suspicious look. 'I suppose they've already told you he's head gardener over the other side of the hill, at Grimside, now,' he said tersely. 'In charge of that herbarium, or whatever fancy name they've called the walled herb garden.'

'Herbivarium?' I suggested, and he shrugged.

'Old Cripchet charges people through the nose to see it, then sells them half-dead plants for stupid prices.'

'Actually, I didn't know Simon was there, but I'm glad he is, because I want to talk to him as well. In fact, I'm going to talk to *everyone* who was there on the night of the accident,' I said. 'I should have done it years ago.'

Dan's face darkened alarmingly and he took a hasty step forward, gripping the shotgun tightly, though more as if he'd like to beat me to death with it than shoot me. That was not a comfort.

'You leave him alone – you'll leave us *all* alone, if you know what's good for you,' he threatened. 'And you'd better tell that aunt of yours to look for another place to take her mutts, because Rufus, the new owner, doesn't want her on his land.'

Then he turned on his heel and went off up the private path towards Sweetwell, slamming the small wicket gate behind him. I hoped Howling Hetty would get him.

Angry and unsettled, I stared after him until he disappeared among the trees, before carrying on towards the Spring. Goodness knows, I needed soothing even more now than I did before! But on the plus side, at least I'd got the most dreaded interview over with and I now knew that Simon was working within easy reach. I could just walk through the gates like any other visitor to the herb garden and then look for him.

Come to think of it, since Cara had married Sir Lionel Cripchet, I should be able to kill two birds with one stone . . . or I would, if Cara deigned to acknowledge my existence.

I wasn't holding my breath on that one.

Chapter 6: Water Cure

I hurried down the path as fast as the overgrown bushes and brambles along it would allow, for I now had an almost overwhelming urge to immerse myself in the strangely opaque greeny-blue waters – and not only in my usual 'wash away my sins' manner, but now, after the encounter with Dan, a 'wash that man right out of my hair' one, too.

The clearing lay dreaming in the crisp April sunshine, the usual hint of magic tingeing the air. Tom's small stone cottage looked as if it belonged in a fairy tale, tucked behind a white picket fence, with a neat row of beehives at one end and a dovecote at the other, where there was a slight flurry of wings as an occupant exited.

The wild wood pigeons called and somewhere a blackbird whistled sweetly. Then a red squirrel bounded gracefully and airily across the grass, pausing briefly to turn its tufty ears and bright, inquisitive eyes in my direction. I thought there couldn't be a spot that had more spirit of place – somewhere where the passing of centuries seemed tangible, soft and enfolding. You could feel a connection with the earth, or the life force – or even, if you'd been bashed around the head enough, an inner angelic voice telling you what to do.

Mine was telling me to go and get into the pool.

The stone wall surrounding it was silvered with circles of lichen and I had a plastic token for the old turnstile at the entrance, which had once graced Southport pier. It let me pass through with a well-oiled clanking noise, and once inside, everything was just as it had been on my last visit.

When the Romans rediscovered the pool, they deepened and extended it into a rectangular bath big enough to swim two or three strokes each way in. They'd roofed it, too, and built other rooms off it, heated by an ingenious hypocaust system, but all the stones were taken to make Spring Cottage, and now the only evidence that there had once been a super-structure lay in the hummocky shapes under the short turf.

I climbed up to the cave, took a pointed paper cup from a stack on a shelf inside and had a drink of the water, which tastes weird, though not unpleasant.

Then I changed in one of the wooden sentry huts by the pool, before sliding into the water, which, because I'm so short, came to about shoulder height. I ducked under and it closed over me as softly and silkily as cold milk. Then I turned and floated starfish-wise on the surface and the spring sun fell golden on my closed eyelids.

Debo once told me that the young Roman soldiers would have swum naked, and ever since then I had often thought I could hear echoes of them laughing and chatting . . . but then other times I'm convinced I can hear faint pagan chanting.

That day I wasn't aware of any past swimmers sharing the space with me, just the softness of the water on my skin, the sun warming my eyelids and the sweet warbling of birds in the trees.

I always brought my worries and fears to the pool and

now I felt them drain away, leaving a sense of peace and lightness behind in their place.

I was prepared to let go of Kieran, too, though not without some regret for the love I'd once felt for him and the hopes I'd had for our future.

He'd seemed such a kind, generous man, easy-going and popular with everyone . . . except, now I came to think of it, with Debo. She'd flown out to India for a visit just after we'd got engaged and immediately befriended one of the local stray dogs that attached itself to her. She'd decided to take it back home to Halfhidden with her, though of course, she couldn't do that straight away, and I was left in charge of organising all the vet's checks and inoculations and the rest of it, until I finally managed to get the dog onto a plane and off to her new life. (She was a sweet golden brown creature we called Rani, who was eventually adopted by the family who own the alpine plant nursery at the top of the village.)

Kieran hadn't understood why Debo should make such a fuss about a dog, when there were children suffering so much poverty and hardship. In fact, he made no secret of it that he thought Debo's Desperate Dog Refuge was a stupid idea altogether and a total waste of money.

'Why take in dogs that aren't suitable for rehoming?' he'd asked, puzzled. 'I mean, they must bite, or have some other antisocial behaviour, so putting them down would really be the only sensible option.'

So no, he and Debo were never going to see eye to eye. And though I could see his point about the children, animals deserve better treatment, too, and they were where Debo's heart lay.

Apart from that one glitch over Debo's Dogs, everything about our relationship had seemed entirely serendipitous, from our first meeting right up to the moment he introduced me to his parents for the first time . . .

I flipped over, took a deep breath and then swam underwater to the other end of the pool, where I let myself slowly float back to the surface, looking down into the opaque depths. I always think coming up is a bit like being born again. One minute it's dark turquoise murk and the next – out you pop into bright light and a birdsong 'Hallelujah' chorus.

But this time, just as I was about to turn over, there was the sudden shock of an almighty splash right next to me and next minute I was wrenched out of the water, taking an involuntary gulp of it in the process, then upended inelegantly over someone's arm. A hard hand thumped me between the shoulder blades and I choked and spluttered, then began to struggle.

'You're alive!' said a deep voice, thankfully.

Turning me the right way up, the man waded to the side and laid me down on the stone edging, before climbing out.

I sat up, still coughing up water, and exclaimed indignantly, 'Of course I'm alive, you idiot! I was *swimming*!'

'My God,' he said blankly, looking down at me from a great height, 'I've rescued a pixie!'

His hair was darkly plastered to his head and his clothes dripping, but there was something strangely familiar about him. Then, when he reached down and hauled me to my feet, I found myself staring up, stunned, into a distinctive and unforgettable pair of eyes the soft green of sea-washed bottle glass, edged with smudgy black around the iris.

'Harry?' I whispered, my heart suddenly stopping, then restarting, but faster and more erratically.

It was he who broke the long eye contact, frowning and letting go of his grip on my arms so suddenly that I nearly sank down again.

'I'm Rufus – Rufus Carlyle,' he said, looking at me strangely.

And of course, after that first brief shock I could see he was a total stranger. He might be much the same age as Harry, his half-brother, would have been by now, but other than the eyes, his face was entirely different, all planes and angles, with a cleft chin and a Roman nose that wouldn't have looked out of place under a plumed helmet on the obverse of an ancient coin.

In fact, it occurred to me that if he hadn't been wearing clothes, he would have been a dead ringer for the fantasy Roman soldiers I'd often imagined sharing the pool with me.

I felt a slightly hysterical bubble of laughter trying to escape my lips and clamped them together, but I must have looked weird, because he asked tersely, 'Are you all right?'

I nodded and then swallowed. 'Yes. Or at least I was, until you started half-drowning me and bashing me around.'

'Only because you were floating face down and looked drowned. What on earth were you doing in there, anyway? The place is closed to visitors until two. Did you climb over the fence?'

He looked me up and down and then added, before I'd had a chance to get a word in among all the questions, 'Presumably *not* dressed like that. You looked so small in the pool I thought you were a child – but now, obviously not.'

I'd forgotten what I was wearing – or *not* wearing. My old and modest one-piece swimsuit appeared to have vanished in my absence, so I'd grabbed the first alternative that came to hand, the white bikini I'd bought years before when going on holiday to Corfu with Lulu and her parents. It hadn't looked particularly skimpy when I was a skinny teenager, but I'd acquired a few curves since then and I have to admit it had been a struggle to fasten the top . . .

I crossed my arms over my chest defensively. 'I'm local, so I've got a token to get through the turnstile and Tom doesn't mind my having a swim whenever I want one.'

'So, who are you?'

'I'm Izzy,' I said reluctantly. 'Isabella Dane.'

He took a sudden step back, as if I'd offered him a poisoned chalice and suggested he take a tiny sip for his health's sake.

'*You're* Izzy Dane? Dan Clew told me all about you, but he said you lived abroad.'

'I *bet* he's told you all about me,' I said bitterly. 'And I *was* living and working abroad, but now I'm back. For good. And *we* didn't even know *you* existed till a few weeks ago. Debo thinks you're probably an impostor,' I added, even though I'd known straight away that he wasn't.

'Then she's wrong,' he snapped. 'You think I *wanted* to discover the man I'd thought was my father all my life, wasn't?'

We stared at each other, and then I shivered violently.

'Presumably even pixies can get pneumonia,' he said. 'Hadn't you better get changed? Or do you walk around the woods like that?'

I gave him a look and stalked off across the grass to the changing hut, slamming the door after me. The sun was well down now, one stray beam shining through the heart-shaped cut-out high in the door, like a celestial message. I only wished I knew what it was saying.

When I came out, towelling my urchin crop into an even more pixie state, he was still there, dripping gently onto the short turf.

He'd taken his fleecy blue sweatshirt off and was wringing it out, revealing a broad-shouldered frame tapering to a narrow waist. He wasn't heavily muscled, but either he worked out, or wrestling heavy bits of garden antiquities about was more strenuous than I'd imagined.

With some difficulty, he put the garment back on again. 'I'm not sure that's an improvement,' he said.

'I thought you'd have gone home: you're going to catch your death, hanging about in wet clothes,' I said, and this actually seemed a good idea to me; so I didn't offer him my towel to dry his hair with.

'We're presumably going the same way, since I expect you walked through the estate from the Lodge?'

'It's actually an ancient right of way,' I said defensively, wondering how it was that he constantly made me feel in the wrong. 'It goes all the way from Middlemoss, across the main road at the bottom of the hill, and then up behind the pub to here. Then it cuts through the corner of your estate and comes out by the Sweetwell gates. That's why there's that wooden door in the wall just there.'

He frowned. 'Which door?'

'You probably didn't notice it because it's painted the same green as the ivy. But most people just walk up to your drive and then go through the gates, because they're always open.'

'Dan said the path *wasn't* a right of way above the Spring; it ends here.'

'Dan says a lot of stupid things,' I remarked, pushing through the turnstile and setting off home. He followed suit and then fell into step beside me, squelching.

'So, it wasn't true when he said you'd killed my half-brother, Harry, drink-driving?'

I stopped and glared at him. 'I may have been driving, but I certainly wasn't drunk – and it was an *accident*!'

'Oh, well, that's all right then,' he said sarcastically.

'Look, I don't even remember what happened, because I had a head injury,' I said angrily.

'That's lucky,' he remarked. He seemed to be a very bitter and nasty person and I strongly felt I could do without his company.

'Well, that's good, coming from the son of the woman responsible for the death of my mother!' I snapped furiously, without thinking what I was saying. 'I bet she didn't tell you *that* when she found out Debo was living at the Lodge.'

'What on earth are you talking about?' He gazed at me in astonishment. 'My mother's done a lot of crazy things, but at least, unlike you, she's never killed anyone.'

My fists clenched and goodness knew what I would have said to him next if my attention hadn't been distracted by a sudden loud crashing noise in the bushes. A vast, black hairy creature bounded out and threw itself at me and I fell flat on my back.

The monster landed on top of me with all four giant feet, and then started licking my face with a tongue like a sheet of wet sandpaper.

'Get off, Babybelle!' I ordered crossly, when I'd managed to gasp some air into my lungs, and tried to push her away, to no avail.

'And you –' I said to the man – 'don't just stand there, but this time do something useful, before she suffocates me. Haul her off!'

Obediently, he took hold of Belle's collar and pulled. She resisted, but eventually gave in, so he must be pretty strong. I got up gingerly, picking leaves out of my hair. 'I'm bruised all over, you stupid creature!'

'Which one of us?' he asked, though through lips so tight he could have started a new career as a ventriloquist.

'Both,' I said shortly, then threading the belt of my jeans through her collar, I hauled Belle off towards home. She followed me like a lamb . . . as did Rufus Carlyle – or so I thought, until I reached the drive and turned to find he'd vanished silently, presumably up the side path.

I tried not to wish pneumonia on him . . . just a *teeny*, but very snotty, running cold.

Judy was standing on the drive and looked relieved when she spotted us.

'Oh, you've got her! Debo headed up towards the house, because Sandy saw her go that way.'

'The daft creature suddenly jumped on me while I was walking back and knocked me flat.'

Babybelle took the opportunity to sit down, mostly on my feet, and pant in a pleased sort of way, as if she'd rescued me from mortal peril.

'I'm bruised all over, though actually some of that was from being manhandled by Rufus Carlyle.'

'What on earth do you mean?'

'He thought I was drowning in the pool and rescued

me. He's a horrible man, because when he found out who I was, he said Dan had told him I'd killed his half-brother, by driving while drunk.'

'That Dan Clew is poison,' Judy said. 'I'll give him a piece of my mind next time I see him.'

Debo appeared round the bend and we waved before heading for the Lodge, Babybelle plodding after us.

'I told him that was rich, considering his mother had killed mine,' I confessed to Judy. 'I didn't mean to, he just made me angry.'

'Well . . . possibly that was slightly rash, considering he has the power to make our lives difficult if he wants to,' she said, 'but it was probably irresistible, given the provocation. And Debo's just as likely to speak her mind when she finally meets him – you know what she's like.'

And it was true: Debo was prone to saying exactly what was in her head, sometimes with disastrous consequences.

'Let's not tell Debo I've had a run-in with him just yet,' I suggested. 'She looks much more cheerful now.'

'She is, because she's decided that, having carefully not touched your money for years, it's now perfectly OK to accept it as a loan. She's convinced she'll be able to pay you back, though you do realise that that's unlikely, don't you?'

'Oh, yes, and I don't want it back. I've put aside enough to get the business going.'

'Don't you think you should wait till you can see Kieran again before making a final decision? I mean, if he's worth his salt and loves you, he'll move north, and then you might want some of the money for a house deposit after all.'

'No I won't. I never agreed to use it to buy one in Oxford

in the first place, and anyway, at the moment I'm not sure I even want to see him again, let alone marry him.'

'He still hasn't rung, or anything?'

'No, not even a text message to say he's back,' I said shortly, and she let it lie.

Debo caught us up and after a tussle we got Belle back in her kennel, though I had a feeling she could get out again any time she liked, just by leaning on the fence till it gave way and then walking over it, much as she'd walked over me.

I hoped I hadn't let Rufus Carlyle walk all over me too . . . but on the whole, I thought that honours were so far about even.

Chapter 7: Regeneration

I walked down to the Hut early for Lulu's Halfhidden Regeneration Scheme meeting, but Rita and Freddie Tompion, who ran a clock repair shop in the village, were already there, carrying out stacks of tubular metal and canvas chairs from the curtained-off storage area and arranging them in neat rows.

It looked like they were expecting a full house.

From the tiny church of St Mary's next door, the strains of a small organ playing 'Nearer, my God, to Thee' wafted across. Jonas was giving the pedals some welly. Now he'd moved in with his daughter, Lottie, he was practically next door, so I expected he often popped in to practise. He played for the monthly service when the new young Middlemoss vicar came over, too.

It was lovely to see Lulu again and give her a big hug – and even better that already she looked subtly different from the last time we'd met, when she was still firmly under the thumb of the increasingly jealous and controlling Guy. Cam and I had been so worried about her.

She hadn't yet entirely lost the slight look of apprehension, but she was no longer quite so worryingly skinny and the blue shadows had gone from under her eyes. She'd always been the confident, gregarious, lively one of the three of us, till Guy got his hands on her, so now we'd just have to help her get some zippity back into her doo-dah.

She returned the hug, looking both pleased and relieved to see me. 'Thank goodness you're here!'

'You said to come early, but it doesn't look like you need me except for support, because you're very well organised.'

She had a flip chart, a blown-up wall map of the whole valley, with numbered stickers all over it, and a stack of printed leaflets. She also carried a fat notebook and had a pencil stuck in the thick dark curls behind one ear.

'Outwardly, perhaps, but inside I'm petrified!' she confessed.

'It'll be fine,' I assured her. 'Come on, I've got some pecan biscuits here from Judy, for refreshment time, so let's add them to the supplies.'

There wasn't a kitchen as such because the Hut was too small, but tea, coffee, milk and a kettle were arranged by the small sink in the curtained-off storage alcove, along with a stack of paper cups and plates. There was a biscuit tin there already.

'Myra's bringing one of her famous marmalade cakes and Bruce's latest batch of madeleines are in that tin,' she said, following me over. 'He says he's perfected them now, but he's had so many attempts lately, we're all completely sick of them.'

Her brother was an excellent chef and since he and his wife, Kate, took over the restaurant side of the Screaming Skull, I'd heard it had gained quite a reputation for good food. When I said so, Lulu sighed.

'He and Kate have really made a success of it and Mum and Dad could manage the hotel and pub side of things in their sleep, so I know they only gave me the Haunted Weekend breaks to give me something to do. I really feel I've got to make my own mark by expanding the holiday bookings.'

'Well, that's what tonight's all about, isn't it?'

'Yes, and that's what's making me nervous, because maybe I'm being too ambitious in trying to involve everyone else. And you do look lovely, by the way,' she added enviously. 'Is that dress made of sari material?'

'Yes, do you like it?' I gave a twirl. 'My own design, and it's going to feature in my first collection, with a matching quilted patchwork jacket.'

'It wouldn't suit me, now I'm so skinny.'

She'd always had more curves than I, so it was odd that now I was the one with a modest figure, though if Bruce kept feeding her up with madeleines, she could soon overtake me again.

'I'm sure it would look good on you because I've draped it sari-style and saris suit every size and shape. But I'll design something especially for you one of these days, and then you can model the prototype for the online catalogue. Meanwhile, here's a little something I brought you back.'

I gave her an amber silk scarf, which was a colour that really suited her, and a pair of silver and citrine earrings. She put them on straight away and draped the scarf around her neck so the two ends drifted behind her as she walked. It looked a little incongruous with her plain white T-shirt and jeans, but then, I liked incongruity. The clothes I was designing might be inspired by my collection of vintage

Indian cotton garments from the seventies, but there was also more than a hint of classical Greek drapery and other influences thrown into the mix.

'I've had an eventful afternoon,' I told her, after the Tompions, having decided we might need yet more chairs, had gone to raid the stack kept in the church vestry. By then, Jonas had switched seamlessly to 'Jerusalem', by way of 'Lead, kindly Light'.

'I went down to the Spring for a dip just after lunch and had a run-in with Dan Clew on the way, which I'll tell you all about later. But then I had another – with Rufus Carlyle!'

'Who?' she said absently. She was now riffling through her notebook, her mind obviously elsewhere.

'The new owner of Sweetwell! You know, the missing heir who popped up just in time to scoop the jackpot when Baz had the heart attack?'

'Oh, right.' She looked up and focused. 'Is he living in Sweetwell now, then? I knew he was moving his business here from Devon because there's a garden antiques sign over the gateway, but if I'd known he'd be around, I'd have invited him to the meeting.'

'Judy said Myra wasn't expecting him till tomorrow, so running into him earlier was a bit of a shock . . . especially when I wasn't wearing any clothes.'

'What?' she said, giving me her full attention at last.

'Remember when we both bought white bikinis, for that holiday in Greece with your parents?'

She nodded. 'I still have mine somewhere, but I don't know why, because I haven't been that plump for a good ten years and it would just drop off me.'

'I have the opposite problem, because I've definitely got much more hip and boob than I used to. Anyway, I couldn't find my old cossie and I haven't unpacked my bags yet, so I grabbed the bikini instead. I wasn't expecting anyone to be around at that time of day, not even Tom, but once I realised how tight the bikini was I double-checked that the clearing was deserted before I left the changing hut.'

I gave her a graphic description of my 'rescue'.

'There wasn't a soul about when I got into the water and I was floating there feeling soothed and quite happy, considering I'd not only just broken up with the love of my life but also had an encounter with the ghastly Dan . . . Then suddenly, a total stranger had me draped over one arm and was thumping me on the back, before tossing me out onto the side of the pool like a drowned rabbit.'

Lulu giggled and I gave her a look, before reluctantly grinning myself.

'OK, I suppose it was quite funny, in retrospect. But at the time it wasn't, and when I'd finished coughing up all the water I'd inhaled when he grabbed me and got my first real look at him . . . well, it was a bit of a shock, because for a second I thought he was Harry.'

'Why, is he so like him?'

'Not really, it was just a momentary impression, though he does have the exact same green eyes as Harry and Baz did, and his hair is that really dark chestnut shade when it started to dry out a bit.'

'It's hardly surprising that Baz passed his colouring down to both sons, is it? Is he nice?'

'No. I think if he'd known who I was before he rescued me, he'd have let me sink instead,' I said morosely. 'Dan told him I'd killed his half-brother while drink-driving and of course he lapped it up.'

'I don't know what Dan's problem is,' Lulu said indignantly. 'He seems to have a down not just on Debo, but you and Judy too.'

'Hell hath no fury like a gardener scorned,' I said.

She went back to staring at her notes. 'I'd have invited this Rufus man to the meeting anyway, if I'd known he'd moved in. What does he look like, apart from the green eyes, in case I see him about?'

'Big, broad shoulders, angular sort of face with a cleft chin and a proper Roman nose. He seemed naturally sarcastic and bad-tempered – and he said *I* looked like a damp pixie, which didn't exactly help to endear him to me.'

'But everyone *did* call you Pixie Ears at school,' she reminded me, grinning.

'That was quite a long time ago, *Bendy* Benbow,' I said pointedly, and she winced. 'Those days are long behind us, and anyway, I can't help it if my ears are a bit pointy and I'm small, can I?'

'I expect he thought you looked cute.'

'I hope not,' I said, revolted, because being small and looking years younger than my age meant I'd spent all my adult working life striving to be taken seriously. 'And he didn't seem to like me even *before* he found out who I was. What's more, he's got Debo worried that he'll want her to move all the new kennels off his land.'

'Do you think he will?'

'I wouldn't be surprised. At the moment she's managed to convince herself he won't, but you know what Debo's like, she can swing from unfounded optimism to the depths of despair in minutes . . . and I've got so much to tell you, but the rest will have to wait till we can have a good catch-up when we won't be interrupted.

Perhaps Cameron could join us, too,' she said.

'Ah, yes – you and Cam,' I said meaningfully. 'Just what happened between you two on the way back from France?'

'Nothing – it was only that I needed comfort and—' she broke off, going slightly pink. 'Really, it was nothing, Izzy, and I don't want anything to change the friendship between the three of us. Cam understands that. He'll be here tonight, but he's got an art class first, so he'll be very late.'

'All right, I won't mention it again,' I said, 'though I'm sure the three of us would always be best friends, whatever happened.'

'Any word from Kieran yet?' she asked, changing the subject firmly.

'Nothing, just that one nasty message after his father was arrested, then silence.'

'By now I thought he'd have seen your point of view and be texting you apologies every five minutes.'

'Yes, so did I, really,' I admitted.

'He'll come round,' she said. 'Only if he does, I really don't want you to leave Halfhidden, just when the three of us are back together again.'

'That's OK, because I'm not going anywhere,' I assured her. 'I must be mega-fickle, because I seem to have fallen right out of love with him again – and I'm sure now he was a wrong turn up a dead end, and actually I was *supposed* to come back and live here on my own.'

'An angel voice told you so?' she said, half joking.

'Something like that, though I never actually hear a *voice*, you know – I just get a sort of inner feeling that something is right or wrong.'

'I wish I'd had any kind of message, angel or otherwise, warning me not to go and live in France with Guy,' Lulu said with some bitterness.

'You probably did, you just weren't listening to it. Or like me with Kieran, you only heard what you wanted to.'

'Or the ding on the head made you mad as a box of frogs, so there aren't really any angel voices at all.'

'There is that,' I conceded.

'Maybe Kieran will follow you up here, you'll go weak at the knees again and the voice will tell you to marry him and live happily ever after in Halfhidden.'

'I don't know how I would feel if I actually saw him again,' I confessed honestly. 'I have wondered if I'd feel differently. But that whole scenario is probably not going to happen anyway, especially once he knows I'm definitely using what's left of my legacy to bail Debo out of her current financial crisis, because oddly enough, both he and his dreadful parents were banking on it for a house deposit.'

'Then they shouldn't have counted their chickens before they were hatched, should they? And here are Rita and Freddie with more chairs. Come on, we'll help put them out.'

We managed to squeeze them all in, though I hoped everyone was feeling friendly tonight, because the rows were tight. On each seat we laid a copy of a leaflet grandly entitled 'The Halfhidden Regeneration Scheme: A Plan to Bring Prosperity to the Whole Valley, by Increased Visitor Numbers'.

People began to arrive, first clustering curiously around the wall map, before finding a seat, though some came over to say hello and how glad they were to see me back again.

More and more shuffled in until the room was so full that the heat was getting a bit Black Hole of Calcutta and the doors had to be opened.

Everyone seemed to be there – or everyone in Halfhidden who *mattered*, for the local families were out in force, including Tom Tamblyn, his sisters, Lottie Ross from the shop, and Myra, the Sweetwell housekeeper, along with her husband, Laurie, and their son, Olly. Then there were the Ferrises – Cara's parents, the local vets – and of course, the Tompions. It's always a surprise to me that though there has been much intermarriage between the local clans over the centuries, the tall, flaxen-fair, blue-eyed Tamblyn genes and the stockier, dark, brown-eyed Benbow ones continually reappear.

'It's a pity your parents couldn't make it,' I said to Lulu. 'I know the restaurant is open tonight, so Bruce and Kate can't.'

'I think I'd rather they weren't here, actually, because they know all about my plans and they think I'm mad.'

'The jury's still out on that till the rest of us have heard what they are,' I told her. 'Go on and do you stuff – it looks like everyone's here that's coming and it's time.'

'I suppose you're right,' she said, hands clenched so tightly on her notebook that her knuckles were white.

'You'll be fine,' I assured her, then went and sat in the front row next to Judy and Debo, who'd been saving me a seat. Judy pointed out some newcomers nearby, who were actors in the *Cotton Common* period soap drama they shot locally.

'Only minor characters, though, because all the big names seem to have bought places around Middlemoss,' she whispered. 'They've stayed longer than we thought they would, too, since they made it through the winter without putting the "For Sale" notices up.'

There was a bit of a stir as one or two latecomers arrived and slipped into the back row, and when I turned round for a quick peek, I spotted a familiar dark chestnut head that could only belong to Rufus Carlyle. Dan Clew was sitting next to him.

Lulu walked to the front of the hall, looking horribly nervous. Her ex really had dented her self-confidence and I wasn't sure the old Lulu would ever totally bounce back, but I hoped she would. If someone tells you for years that you're useless and ugly and no other man would look at you, it must be like water dripping onto a stone and wearing it away.

Everyone was still chatting, but Tom Tamblyn, who was sitting at the end of the front row, rose to his feet, his shock of once-flaxen hair framing his face like a silvery halo, and held up his hands for silence.

'Quieten down, you lot,' he shouted without ceremony. 'Let's give the lass a chance to speak her piece.'

'Thanks, Tom,' she said gratefully.

'Yay! Go, Lulu!' I called and she gave me an uncertain half-smile, then stepped forward in front of the flip chart.

Chapter 8: Haunting

'First of all, a warm welcome, everyone, and especially to our newcomers,' Lulu said, looking round the Hut, and then I think she must have caught Rufus's eye, because she blinked and seemed to lose the thread for a moment.

Then she turned and flipped back the top sheet of the chart on the stand to reveal, in large print, 'POINT ONE: INCREASED VISITOR ATTRACTIONS'.

'Right, I'll begin by outlining my plan, which I've already discussed individually with those it would most directly affect. Basically, it's a scheme to bring greatly increased visitor numbers to the whole valley and, with them, more money and employment. Once I've finished, I'll be very interested to hear any suggestions, or answer questions, and there'll be refreshments.'

'Our Myra's marmalade cake,' I heard Jonas pipe up with satisfaction, and someone shouted, 'Hurray!'

'As most of you know,' Lulu carried on, ignoring these asides, 'the village was once much more prosperous, especially during the Victorian era, when there was a great enthusiasm for spas and that kind of thing. Day trippers travelled for miles to Halfhidden, to drink the waters. That's why the pub was called the Spa Hotel until recently, and I've discovered there was once a tea garden further up from the Green, at the Old Mill.'

'That's right,' called Hannah Blackwell, who lived there. 'The old open-fronted glass veranda is still as it was then, but they had tables all over the lawn, too, when it was fine.'

'Yes, there's a picture of people taking tea on the Mill lawn among the copies of early photographs I've pinned to the board near the door, and others showing crowds of visitors walking up the path to the Spring from what was then the Spa Hotel, or picnicking by the waterfall near the alpine nursery.'

'My father put a gate across the path to the falls after the Saxon Hoard was discovered, to keep away people trying to dig for more, so it's much more overgrown than in the photos,' said Brandon Benbow, who with his family ran the Summit Alpine Nursery. 'The gorse and brambles soon take over.'

'There are still plenty of visitors to the Lady Spring in the summer, including some of the people staying at the pub on Haunted Weekend breaks,' Lulu said. 'I think they're mostly looking for Howling Hetty, after seeing the skull behind the bar and hearing the story. And it was while I was trying to think of a way of extending those Haunted Weekends into complete week-long Haunted Holidays that I suddenly saw how that could potentially benefit the whole community.'

'I don't really see how,' said Tom Tamblyn, 'though I'm all for it if you can.'

Lulu flipped another page on the chart to reveal, 'POINT TWO: MORE GHOSTS'.

'We already have enough spectral goings-on at the pub to keep our visitors happy for a weekend,' Lulu said. 'Howling Hetty's skull behind the bar, three haunted bedchambers and the ghostly footsteps on the backstairs.'

'I don't remember there being that many ghosts in the pub,' Lottie Ross exclaimed, surprised.

Lulu grinned. 'There are now!'

I knew from Lulu's emails that most of her bookings were from people wanting to spend the night in a haunted chamber, so that figured.

'So, my plan is to entice visitors to stay at the pub for a week, with the promise of a complete ghost trail to follow round the whole valley.'

'Is there a ghost trail?' Will Ferris, Cara's father, one half of the local husband-and-wife vet team, asked.

'No, but there will be, if everyone supports the idea. My plan is that we start by scaring visitors witless at the pub, then after that they can take the path up through the woods haunted by Howling Hetty to the Lady Spring, where Tom will curdle their blood with tales about the ghostly Roman soldiers and the pagan chanting you can hear on nights when the moon is full.'

'Oh, yes, I remember Father telling us about the chanting, but I've never heard it myself,' Myra said.

'Nor anyone else, except Jonas,' a farmer said drily.

'It's the truth, so help me,' declared Jonas, half hidden in the corner. 'I wrote about it in those pamphlets we have for sale up at the Spring.'

'Of course it's true,' agreed Lulu.

'You go on, lass – never you mind them,' Jonas urged.

'Yes, do go on, Lulu, this is fascinating,' I said. 'We've got the visitors up to the Lady Spring, where they'll pay their money to drink the waters or even have a dip in the pool if they want to, and then as usual they'll exit through the back of Tom's hut, giving them a chance to buy pamphlets, postcards and souvenirs on the way. But where do they go after that?'

'Up the footpath through the woods, with more possibilities to meet Howling Hetty, and on to the Green,' she said.

'That's not a public footpath above the Spring, that's private,' called Dan Clew in a loud and aggressive voice, and the audience turned as one to stare at him.

'Nay, you daft bugger,' said Jonas forthrightly, 'it's been used by the whole village as a shortcut to Middlemoss since time immemorial, as you'd know if you were local and not an oft-comed-un.'

Dan might have lived in the valley his entire adult life, but he was still a newcomer as far as Jonas was concerned.

'Why, the Morris Men still dance the whole way up the footpath from Middlemoss to the Green on the first Sunday after May Day – always have, and always will. Aye, it's public, right enough,' Jonas continued, and there was a general murmur of agreement.

'Not above the Spring, it isn't,' Dan insisted belligerently, with a sideways look at his new boss, Rufus.

'You've been fancying yourself estate manager ever since Sweetwell was shut up, Dan Clew, and got too big for your boots,' Tom Tamblyn told him, for there was no love lost between the men. 'But that time you tried putting a gate across the path above Spring Cottage, someone took the lock off with bolt cutters the same day. And then next night, the gate vanished too. People won't stand for it.'

'I think we can guess who did that,' Dan said, with an ugly look at him.

'*Is* the path from the Spring to the Green actually marked as a public right of way on the Ordnance Survey maps?' said the now-familiar deep voice of Rufus Carlyle, and Lulu said it was.

'Though people do exit through the Sweetwell gates, instead of using the original small door in the wall further down.'

'And the Ramblers Association together with local volunteers go up it every year, cutting back the brambles and weeds,' Tom told him.

'That would seem to be clear enough, then,' Rufus said, surprisingly reasonably.

'But you won't want your property overrun with crowds of visitors if this scheme goes ahead,' Dan objected.

'Going by the overgrown state of the woods, they'd have trouble getting off the public footpath, except where it joins one of the private ones, and those are all gated, with signs on them,' Rufus said.

'Yes, and you could put another gate where the path branches off to the drive, so they come out onto the Green where they should,' Tom Tamblyn suggested.

'That's a very good idea,' Lulu agreed. She turned back towards her flip chart. 'Now, where was I? Oh, yes, the visitors walk up path and emerge onto the Green, where they'll have an opportunity to buy drinks, sweets, more postcards and all kinds of other things at Lottie's shop.'

'Hear, hear,' called Lottie. Then she asked, as an afterthought, 'Postcards of what?'

'Well . . . the local beauty spots, perhaps, maybe complete

with a hint of a ghostly presence? Cam and I could probably fudge those; we're both good with a camera.'

'I expect you could,' she agreed. 'And then after my shop, they can go into Cam's Hidden Hoards gallery next door. That's where our Cam's just opening his studio and gallery, in the old garage,' she added, mainly for those newcomers not expected to know these things through the grapevine.

'Great . . .' Lulu said, making a note. 'I don't suppose the old garage was haunted, by any chance, was it?'

'It was the blacksmith's before it was ever a garage, so I dare say it might have been,' Lottie said thoughtfully. 'And maybe I've heard ghostly hoofs passing in the night, when there are no horses to be seen . . .'

'My sister-in-law keeps a white horse in the paddock behind the pub where my caravan is, and it's spooked me more than once at night, even though I knew it was there,' Lulu said. 'The White Horse of Halfhidden!' She made another note. 'OK, after they come out of Hidden Hoards, they cross the stream and go on up the hill past Stopped Clocks.'

She looked at Rita and Freddie Tompion. 'I don't know if it would affect your business at all, because I know your customers come to you specially, or you go to them if it's a museum or a big clock you have to repair *in situ.*'

'I've always got a few watches and antique clocks for sale in the window,' Rita said. 'I could get a little more stock in.'

'And I know a story about a clock that was supposed to be haunted,' said Freddie, literally getting into the spirit of things. 'They brought it to my grandfather to be mended, because it chimed every night at the exact time the last owner died and they couldn't stop it. It turned out he'd been murdered, and when they hanged the man who did it, the clock stopped chiming.'

'Great story,' Lulu enthused, scribbling that down too.

'It was the heir that did the foul deed, so he never came back to collect it,' Freddie said. 'It's the grandfather clock with the ship face that's in the corner by the door.'

'Wow! We'll put it in the guidebook – I mean, we will if everyone agrees to my plan and there *is* a guidebook.'

'If there's going to be enough business, then I'd reopen the Victorian tea garden at the Old Mill and I'm sure our Shirley would love to move back and help me,' Hannah Blackwell said. 'Will the trail go up that far?'

'It certainly will, because the next stop will be the Haunted Falls, up by Uncle Brandon's alpine nursery,' Lulu assured her.

'That's right,' agreed Brandon Benbow.

'Which haunted falls?' Debo asked, puzzled.

'The little waterfall. Apparently, as well as being inundated with some kind of nasty imp things called boggarts, there's the ghost of the Saxon warrior looking for the hoard he buried there just before he was killed,' Lulu told her.

'I've never heard about any Saxon hoard before today – or about the boggarts,' said our kennelmaid, Sandy Lane, who was sitting next to her younger sister and her equally taciturn father, who was a farmer up the hill.

'It was found way back in the nineteenth century,' said Cameron's voice, so he must have slipped in unnoticed at some point.

'That's so,' confirmed Jonas. 'I heard tell of that.'

'It's the reason why I called my gallery Hidden Hoards,' Cam said. 'You can see photos of what they found in the

Middlemoss Folk Museum, but the gold is in the British Museum now. There wasn't a lot, just a crumpled brooch and the inlaid handle of a dagger.'

'We could have a display and souvenirs about the hoard in the nursery,' Brandon suggested. 'We're already getting more visitors, ever since we turned one of the greenhouses into a bit of a garden shop and started selling stuff like wellies and gardening tools painted with flowers, the sort of tat that people seem to want these days.'

'I quite like that kind of thing,' Judy confessed. 'Hedgehog boot scrapers and pink watering cans.'

'I'll do you a good discount if you want to come up, Judy,' Brandon offered.

'I'll hold you to that,' Judy said. 'And if visitors are going to be walking near the Lodge, maybe we could have a collecting box and information board about Debo's Desperate Dogs, too?'

'Good thinking, Judy,' said Debo. 'We might even manage to rehome some of the dogs with visitors, you never know.'

'Lulu, this really could revitalise the whole valley,' I said admiringly.

A thin, middle-aged woman with pale golden hair and no discernible chin stood up. 'I'm Floriana Winthrop. You may have seen me in *Cotton Common*.'

There was a small chorus of agreement, since the period soap was very popular locally. I'd watched it myself, because Judy was addicted, but I couldn't remember seeing this woman in it.

'Now I've heard your plans, I'm quite horrified!' she continued. 'We really don't want the village to be overrun with *tourists*. I mean, I only moved here because my friends in the next cottage assured me it was totally quiet and other-worldly.'

'It wasn't always this quiet, as Lulu said,' I remarked. 'You only have to look at the photos to see that.'

'That's right, it was still a busy, bustling place when I was a small lad,' said Jonas. 'The blacksmith got all the carriage trade from the hotel and they used to turn their hand to anything – they even made those wrought-iron gates to Sweetwell, that would look a whole lot better if Dan stopped poncing about with a shotgun and painted them.'

'Why should I? I'm not the handyman,' Dan said angrily.

'You're not anything, so far as I can see, except a great streak of nowt,' Jonas said scathingly.

'I think we've strayed away from the point about not everyone welcoming lots of visitors,' Lulu interrupted quickly.

'But most of us *would* welcome more visitors spending their money locally, and it's not exactly going to be like Blackpool on a bank holiday, is it?' Brandon Benbow said.

'It's what most of us want,' Tom agreed.

Lulu flipped her chart again and revealed, 'POINT THREE: PLANNING, MAPPING, SIGNPOSTS, LEAFLETS, INFORMATION BOARDS AND INTERNET PUBLICITY OPPORTUNITIES'.

'These are some points to think about if we do go ahead with the scheme,' she said. 'We can do most of it ourselves, keeping costs to a minimum.'

That appeared to be the end of the presentation, and we had a more general discussion, after which Tom called for a show of hands for those in favour of the scheme, which was almost everyone except the handful of newcomers, who voted against.

'That seems almost unanimous,' Lulu said. 'So now I think we should have some tea and coffee – and Myra Graham's famous marmalade cake.'

It was no surprise to anyone that Jonas, despite his rheumatism, got to the marmalade cake first.

'Everyone's all for your plan,' I said to Lulu, when we'd secured cups of coffee and paper plates of cake and biscuits. 'There are some great new ideas, too.'

'It's just as well, because we'll need the whole village to come together to sort out the route and clear paths, put up signs, get pamphlets and maps printed . . . all of that. There's so much to do. *And* we need to find enough ghosts to keep the visitors happy!'

'I think from the sound of it, there'll be one for every square foot of Halfhidden,' I said, grinning.

'Except up at Sweetwell?' suggested a familiar deep voice in my ear, making me jump. 'Apart from having hordes of people traipsing across my land and visiting the Lady Spring, what's in it for *me*?'

'Oh, hi,' Lulu said, looking up at him with big, innocent brown eyes, just as if she didn't know he'd wrestled my half-naked self out of the Lady Spring pool earlier in the day. 'You're Rufus Carlyle, aren't you?'

'That's right.' He glanced at me with those unnerving light green eyes. 'I see my fame has gone before me.'

'If I'd known you'd already moved in, I'd have sent you an invite to the meeting. I'm glad you came, though, because if you're running a garden antiques business from Sweetwell, then you must be interested in more customers?'

'I'm not sure your ghost-hunting tourists will be in the market for garden antiques.'

'Of course they will, and I could put you on the map and in the brochure. In fact, Howling Hetty was said to have been a servant at Sweetwell in the seventeenth century and it was rumoured she'd been killed by a son of the house after he got her pregnant, so you really *ought* to be on the ghost trail anyway.'

'Why is Hetty howling?' he asked. I don't think that's what he meant to say, he just couldn't help himself.

'I expect she's looking for her head, but they found it years later and it's behind the bar in the pub, displayed in a special alcove,' Lulu explained.

'Nice,' he commented drily.

'Well, they can't move it, because it would bring terribly bad luck,' she said reasonably. 'So poor Hetty has to keep looking for it.'

'Where's the rest of her?'

'No one knows. The skull was washed into the lower pool near the road below the Lady Spring.'

'If there's a pool below the Lady Spring, why does anyone pay to go to the other?' Rufus asked.

Jonas, who was passing by with an empty plate, presumably heading for more of his daughter's cake, paused long enough to say with some surprise, 'Eh, lad, you wouldn't want to bathe in the same water what had run out of a pool a lot of diseased people had swum about in, would you?'

There was a small silence, broken only by the sound of Lulu's pencil writing something down in the bulging notebook.

'Right,' she said, 'I've made a few changes, so that now after the waterfall, the visitors will go back down to the Green and visit the ancient church of St Mary's, one of the smallest in the country; then up the drive to Rufus Carlyle Garden

98

Antiques and the stable block, where it was rumoured that Howling Hetty was a kitchen maid in the seventeenth century.'

'She wouldn't have been a kitchen maid in the stable block,' Rufus objected.

'It incorporates an even older building that was once a separate kitchen,' I told him. 'They used to do that centuries ago, because so many burned down, so that way, the rest of the house wouldn't burn with it.'

'Isn't it going to take them more than one day to do all this trail of yours?' he asked Lulu.

'Of course: I'm *designing* it as a complete circular trail, but I expect them to do it in bits. The garden antiques centre alone could probably happily occupy half a day.'

'But I didn't say I wanted . . .' Rufus began, but Lulu had seen Hannah Blackwell trying to get her attention from the other side of the room and was off like a whirlwind.

'I don't see why you should object to a bit more business,' I told Rufus, and he scowled down at me.

'Holidaymakers aren't going to do more than look around the place and take photographs. They won't buy anything.'

Then his attention shifted and focused elsewhere and I turned to see he was staring at Debo, who was in animated conversation with Will Ferris and his wife, Agnes, probably about the treatment of one of the dogs. She hadn't bothered changing out of a ratty jumper and jeans, but she still looked as if she was posing for a glossy magazine.

'Is that your aunt, Debo Dane? I've tried to talk to her a couple of times when I've been around, but she was always away. Or so the woman who opened the door said,' he added darkly.

'That was Judy Almond, my aunt's friend who lives with

us, and she was telling the truth: Debo still gets lots of modelling assignments, commercials and even some small film parts, so you just chose the wrong time. She has to take everything she's offered, to keep the kennels going.'

'Ah, yes, the kennels . . . and all those dogs,' he said. 'That's mostly what I wanted to discuss with her.'

'Shall I introduce you to Debo now? She'd really like to talk to you – especially since she found out that while she was away, your mother, Fliss Gambol, visited the Lodge with Dan Clew and told Judy you wanted all the kennels gone from your land as soon as possible – and if she didn't do it quickly enough, they'd be bulldozed off,' I said tartly.

'She did?' He frowned. 'I knew my mother had called in to have a look at Sweetwell one day when she was visiting friends nearby, but – anyway, I need a serious talk with Debo, so tell her I'll be round tomorrow afternoon.'

'That sounds ominous,' I said, staring at him. 'Baz was a great dog-lover and he never objected to the kennels, so—' I broke off as I caught sight of Cam's familiar, sensitive, thin face through the crowd and cried out, 'Cam!'

He headed over, grinning, lifted me off my feet and swung me round. He might *look* weedy, but he's surprisingly strong.

'Izzy!' he said, giving me a hug and kiss, before putting me down again, and I'd just remembered Rufus and started to introduce them, when I realised that he was no longer there. I could see his dark head and broad shoulders above most of the crowd as he made his way out of the hall, not stopping to talk to anyone else.

'That was Rufus Carlyle, Cam – and he didn't even try Myra's marmalade cake!'

'Aunt Myra usually makes two at a time, so perhaps he'll

get some at home,' he said. 'Meeting go OK? I missed most of it.'

'Yes, it seemed to go down a storm with practically everyone, and it looks like Lulu's just going to call it to order again and round things off.'

Lulu, flushed and looking excited and rather pretty, tapped her spoon on the side of her cup and called, 'Attention! Could anyone who'd like to be on the Halfhidden Regeneration Committee stay behind? We'll need a group to keep things moving, though we'll post information up on the village noticeboard as we go. And we'd better start up a fund to pay for things like trail leaflets, new signs and information boards.'

Those who stayed behind because they had volunteered for the committee – or were volunteered without being asked – consisted of me, Cam, Lulu, the Tompions and Jonas, who said he had nothing much better to do these days and could get across the Green, whether his rheumatism was playing him up or not.

'Good,' said Lulu, 'because you have all the best stories about Halfhidden.'

'Yes, Granddad, and on the drive back from Ormskirk tonight I remembered one you told me when I was a little boy,' Cameron said. 'I don't think Lulu's heard it – the one about the Sweetwell Worm?'

'*Worm*?' I echoed.

'Ah, yes, the Worm,' Jonas exclaimed. 'Damned if I hadn't gone and forgotten that one, till you reminded me!'

'I'm not sure a story about a worm—' Lulu began doubtfully.

'You mean as in a serpent or dragon?' put in Rita Tompion,

101

interested. 'I've heard an old legend about the Lambton Worm.'

He nodded. 'That's right. When I was a tiny lad, my great-grandfather told me about the dangerous Worm that lived in that rocky outcrop up in the woods above Sweetwell, where the moorland starts.'

'Oh, a dragon!' enthused Lulu. 'That's more like it!'

'It's not a nice story, really,' Jonas said, frowning as he tried to remember it. 'The local people – this would be a long, long time ago, when they were all heathens – used to choose one young lass every year as a sacrifice to the Worm and leave her tied to a tree near the rocks.'

'I suppose it was a sacrifice to good harvests and fertility, really,' Cam suggested.

'The serpent would come out and eat the poor girl, and then leave them alone till the next spring,' Jonas said. 'But eventually St George came riding by and found the maiden tied to the tree, rescued her and took her home. The Worm came rampaging down the hill, breathing flames and stinking of sulphur. But it was all right in the end, because St George killed it.'

'Well, that's very exciting . . . and something like that happens up at the Little Mumming Revels every year, doesn't it? They act out a St George and the Dragon scene,' Rita said. 'Perhaps the serpent went over that side and wanted an annual maiden from them, too?'

'You're right. One wouldn't keep a serpent going for a year,' agreed Cameron.

'Where's that Rufus bloke got to?' asked Lulu. 'He should know he's got a Worm as well as Howling Hetty on his land.'

'He left suddenly and I don't think he was that enthusiastic

102

about your plans,' I said. 'Maybe we should start the annual sacrifice up again and make him the first?'

'Or Dan,' Lulu said. 'It's got to be someone we can spare easily.'

'Ho, ho,' said Dan, who had lingered behind unnoticed, probably, since he was a greedy man, to snaffle the last leftover biscuits, for he was shoving something wrapped in a paper napkin into his trouser pocket as he left.

'Did you ever see that film *The Wicker Man*?' I asked Lulu, and she giggled.

'Oh, don't tempt me!'

Then we helped the Tompions put the chairs away and clear up, before we went outside onto the twilit Green.

'I'll be spending all tomorrow working on my gallery,' Cameron said to me and Lulu. 'Why don't you both come round for a good catch-up – and lunch? You two bring it,' he added, cunningly.

Chapter 9: Disconnected

'I really can't, Harry,' I said regretfully, because this was the first time he'd asked me to join him and his friends. Perhaps he'd finally noticed I'd grown up?

He'd always been carelessly kind to me, in an older-brother sort of way, and only the week before he'd let me get behind the wheel of the Range Rover a couple of times and take it up and down the long, bumpy Sweetwell drive, his hand warmly over mine on the gearstick . . .

It had been another long and eventful day, ending with Judy belatedly remembering to tell me that Kieran had rung just after I'd left for the Hut.

'He couldn't get an answer from your mobile.'

'I'd left it recharging in my room, but he hadn't left any messages on it. So . . . what did he say?'

'He seemed surprised you hadn't rung him, but I said he could hardly expect you to, in the circumstances! Then the connection suddenly went dead.'

'Judy's sure he put the phone down on purpose,' said Debo, and I thought she was probably quite right. It seemed to be getting a habit with him, whenever he was hearing something he didn't like.

By then I was too tired to ring or text him back even if I'd wanted to, which I can't say I did, because by now it felt as if he was on another continent and it was slowly drifting away. There might still be the narrowest isthmus of land bridging the ocean between us, much as a silver filament had once connected me to my body when I was in Heaven, but if so, I didn't think there was a lot of twang left in it.

I didn't wake up next morning until I heard Judy come back from walking the dogs and make a start on cooking breakfast . . . or maybe it was the smell of bacon frying that woke me.

Knowing Daisy Silver to be an early riser, I rang her before going downstairs and told her about the dreams I'd been having since I got home.

'It's basically the recurring dream I've always had, only it's as if it's suddenly been brought into sharp focus and there are all kinds of details and bits of conversation I hadn't recalled before.'

'And you remember it all when you wake up?'

'Yes, clear as crystal, and they feel like new memories coming to the surface.'

'Does it move forward beyond the point of your last memory of that evening?' she asked.

'No . . .' I admitted reluctantly. 'And I haven't dreamed of being in the back of the car again . . . So maybe that *was* a figment of my imagination.'

'I expect you'd been in the back of the car before that night?' she suggested.

'Yes, several times,' I agreed. Then something occurred to me. 'In fact, Harry had given me and Cam a lift back up to the village from the pub only a few days before and everyone was singing then, too. So . . . that might simply be a memory from that night.'

'It's a possibility, but it still may be that some of the latest dream sequences are actual memories coming to the surface.'

I digested that for a moment. 'So I might not have *entirely* lost my memory of the accident, just buried the painful bits away somewhere?'

'That's right, and now, due to the shock of the second accident, it's starting to surface. It will be interesting to see if the dream progresses beyond the cut-off point it's previously reached, won't it?'

'Yes, fascinating,' I said wryly. 'I'll let you know if it does.' And then after a bit more conversation she had to go, though as always, I felt better for talking to Daisy, even if I was no wiser about what was reality and what wasn't.

Judy called me and I'd just sat down at the table with a mug of coffee and a loaded plate when the back door slammed and Debo came in, with Babybelle determinedly plodding after her. At the sight of me, her flag of a tail waved, sending the nearest seat cushions flying like chintz Frisbees.

'Flattened her pen again,' Debo said in explanation. 'I think she was looking for you, Izzy.'

'Can't you put her in one of the stronger runs?' I asked.

'No, we need those. At the moment we have two dogs that really might bite someone if they got out and panicked.'

Babybelle plumped herself down heavily against my leg with a long sigh, as if she'd trekked across a desert to be with me again.

'Oh, sweet – she loves you,' Debo said fondly.

'Actually, I think she just loves the idea of breakfast. She's drooling over my feet.'

'Don't give her any,' Judy said firmly. 'If she's going to be your dog, she'll have to learn that we don't give scraps at the table, just like Ginger and Vic have.'

I was about to refute any intention of adopting Babybelle, when she looked up at me with those big, sad, amber eyes and laid an ingratiating webbed paw the size of a soup plate on my knee.

I said to Judy, '*You* tell her about the house rules, then.'

Debo asked me what I was going to do with myself that morning.

'I thought I'd make a start on sorting the paperwork in the office and then I'm going to have lunch at Cam's new gallery with him and Lulu.'

'I'm baking some curry puffs in a bit,' Judy said. 'I'll make extra, so you can take some with you.'

'Great!' I loved Judy's hot and spicy curry puffs.

Debo, lavishly spreading about half a pound of butter onto her toast, said, 'I expect you'll think of all kinds of clever ways to economise! Judy's been suggesting we make cutbacks for ages, so I really should have listened to her.'

'Better late than never,' Judy said, firmly removing the depleted butter dish to the other side of the table, out of reach.

'I've been thinking, Izzy darling, that we'll need more money to get us back on an even keel than just what's left of your legacy, so I'm going to phone a friend or two after breakfast to help make up the rest,' Debo said brightly.

'If any of your friends and former lovers will actually

answer the phone when they see it's you after their cash again,' Judy said.

'Of course they will,' said Debo, opening her already huge grey eyes even wider in surprise. 'Because they know if they don't, then I'll just go and stand on their doorstep and ring the bell till they let me in!'

She would, too, and later, when I'd shut myself in the office (determinedly accompanied by Babybelle) and was staring slightly desperately at a mountain of paper, under which might possibly be a roll-top desk, I heard her talking on her mobile in Judy's cherished little rose garden outside the window.

'Oh, *no*, Elton, darling,' she was saying sweetly. 'Of course I'm not after you for your money again! What on earth made you think that?'

You have to give her full marks for trying and, usually, succeeding. It's just a pity she spends it faster than she gets it.

By twelve I had all the papers roughly sorted into stacks on a folding card table and, having found the keys to the filing cabinet in the desk drawer, discovered that it was completely empty, apart from several cellophane-wrapped packets of sage-green cardboard hanging files.

There was no method in Debo's madness. Old bills that had been paid were tossed back onto the heap with the new, while a whole bundle of ominously red-printed final demands appeared to have been purposely hidden away in the cubbyholes of the desk. Out of sight, out of mind.

The only positive thing was that, since her accountant had sorted and removed the paperwork for the previous tax year, there was a lot less of it than there might have been.

By late morning I was ready for a break, and once I'd washed off the dust, Judy coaxed Belle out to the kennels while I set off for Hidden Hoards, laden with still-warm curry puffs swaddled in tinfoil and a thick tea towel.

I felt oddly furtive as I walked out of the Sweetwell gates, because it had suddenly occurred to me that perhaps Rufus Carlyle would expect us to come and go by the little gate in the wall now, like everyone else. But then, I'd still have to cross the drive and cut through a private path to get to it, so it wouldn't really make sense.

The Green lay quiet and still under a cloud-soft sky, apart from the library van, which was parked in front of the church. I could see Lottie Ross just climbing into it, so unless old Jonas was minding the shop then she must have closed for five minutes.

The garage, which had fallen into disuse long before I was even born, was next to the village store. Once the black-smith's, it showed signs of its later evolution by the single ancient faded blue petrol pump that stood outside. Cameron had cleaned it up and left it there, like a piece of found art. The front of the building, where there had once just been huge wooden doors, was now glazed to let lots of light into the gallery and there was a Hidden Hoards sign over the door.

Cameron opened it as I arrived and said, 'Hi, Izzy! Come on in – Lulu's already here.'

I walked past him, pausing to take in the interior: it went back much further than I'd expected and was surprisingly light, what with the new glazed front and a couple of windows at the sides. A floor of reclaimed wooden timber had been laid and the walls freshly painted a plain, soft white. At the far end, under a large skylight, Lulu was laying out a motley collection of foodstuffs on a small, square table, so I went over and added Judy's contribution.

'Isn't this a great space for a gallery?' I enthused. 'It's a Tardis of a place!'

'It's huge, isn't it?' agreed Lulu. 'There's a *vast* storage area at the back and a little room with a sink and kettle and stuff.'

'And a convenient convenience,' Cam said. 'The plumbing and wiring were all ancient, so replacing those, putting in the windows and laying the new floor cost a fortune. It was lucky I could live with Mum and sink all the money I made from selling my London flat into the renovation.'

'How are you going to arrange the interior – leave it as one big space?' I asked.

'No, my studio will be up at this end and I might hold art classes here, too, eventually. I've got a folding glass-and-wood room divider coming next week, so I can keep the studio separate, or throw the whole space into one for an exhibition, if I want to.'

'He's really figured it all out,' Lulu said, exchanging warm smiles with him and then munching into a spicy curry puff. 'Mmm, these are good!' she added appreciatively.

I clocked the warmth of those exchanged smiles with interest, for, as I'd suspected, their feelings for each other had moved on from friendship to something deeper, even if Lulu was currently in denial. I'd thought I might feel excluded by such a change in our triangle of togetherness, but in fact I just felt sort of benevolently pleased.

'Judy made the curry puffs this morning. Do you want the recipe?'

'Yes, please,' Lulu said. She loved to cook, though she'd

never had any desire to become a chef, like her brother, Bruce.

'Here, have a ham and mustard sandwich,' Cam offered, pushing a paper plate in my direction. 'Mum made them, and there's a chunk of pudding cake in that plastic box.'

We munched companionably. The thing about having best friends is that no matter how long it is since you've seen them, the moment you're back together, it's as if no time at all has passed.

'When are you aiming to open?' I asked Cameron.

'I was hoping this weekend, just in time for Easter, but it's all taking longer than I expected. As well as my own work, I'm going to stock locally made arts and crafts – not cheap manufactured tat, but really good stuff.'

'You'll need a counter with a till on it, then, won't you?' Lulu suggested.

'I know, and luckily I've just managed to source an old wooden one on eBay, so I've hired a van and I'm going to collect it tomorrow from Birmingham.'

'You really are organised!' I said admiringly.

'I have to be, because if the gallery fails, I'll be back to teaching art in an inner-city school, and I feel I've served my time doing that.'

'But it won't fail, and once we get the Haunted Holidays trail up and running, you'll have loads of visitors eager to part with their cash for something unique and original, you'll see,' Lulu assured him.

But she said it with less bounce and enthusiasm than she'd shown at the meeting, and for the first time since I'd arrived, it occurred to me that she might have something on her mind.

Cam seemed to have noticed too, for he said, 'What's up, Lu? You've got dark circles under your eyes and you keep sighing.'

'It's nothing really,' she said. 'Just that I had an email last night from Solange, my friend in the village, telling me that Guy's mistress has left him and gone back to her husband and children.'

'Well, that didn't last long,' I commented.

'No, but at least it meant he was too preoccupied with her to follow me after I ran off with Cam. I'd been afraid he would, because he was always so jealous – and then it turned out he'd been seeing this other woman for ages.'

'He was never jealous of Cam, though,' I said, and she grinned wryly.

'True, but only because he thought he was gay.'

'I can't think how he got that idea,' Cam said indignantly.

'No, nor anyone else,' I agreed. 'Did Solange say anything more, Lulu?'

'Only that his mistress came into the café just before she left, moaning about Guy again. She said he'd turned cold and strange as soon as she'd moved in and also seemed to think she was some kind of servant, who would cook and clean the house and service the *gîtes*, between visitors, while he went out drinking himself senseless with his friends. He's a slave driver.'

'Well, we already knew that,' I said. 'You were run ragged doing all the practical stuff while he played the jovial host and pottered round his vineyard.'

'That's how it turned out, though it seemed more of an exciting joint venture when I first went to live in France with him,' she said. 'He helped more then and didn't drink quite so much.'

'What do you think Guy will do now?' Cam asked. 'He surely won't follow you over here, after all this time.'

'I hope not. Perhaps he'll just get another slave? I didn't quite realise how much I was doing, or how exhausted I was, till I left – and that was thanks to you, Cameron.'

They exchanged warmly affectionate smiles again. I was sure they didn't realise they were doing it.

'I feel guilty that you've lost your annual painting holiday week in the Dordogne, Cam,' she added.

'It was nice while it lasted, but I only really did it so I could see you,' he said. 'But maybe I could offer painting classes to some of the Haunted Holidaymakers?'

'Oh, great idea!' Lulu pulled out the bulging notebook that seemed to be a permanent feature in her handbag now and made a note. 'If the weather's nice, you could hold the classes at the Spring, or up at the waterfall . . . though then I suppose you'd have to shut the gallery while you were out.'

'I expect Granddad would mind the shop. He likes to keep occupied.'

'I've had three Haunted bookings for this weekend,' Lulu said. 'That makes things easy from the haunting point of view, because there are two ancient rooms that naturally creak a lot in the night and another right by the backstairs, which do the same. Old houses make a lot of noise; I suppose it's all the timbers expanding and contracting, or something.'

'Or maybe it really *is* haunted?' suggested Cameron. 'I'm sure Uncle Tom believes in Howling Hetty, because he won't have her name mentioned in the house.'

'He seemed OK about all the other haunted stuff at the meeting,' I pointed out.

'Yes, it's just her. I don't know why.'

'I've drawn up a list of all the extra signposts and information boards we'll need, and where they should be sited around the village,' Lulu said, thumbing through the notebook to find the right page. 'I thought we might discuss—'

'Just stop right there,' I told her, getting out my own notebook. 'Because first of all, I'm on a mission and I need your help . . .'

Chapter 10: Sparks

I told them both about the flashback to the accident when Harry died, where I'd been in the back seat of the car, not the front, and how ever since then my recurring dream seemed to have expanded, showing me scenes and details I hadn't previously remembered.

'So – do you think perhaps you *weren't* driving?' Cameron asked.

'No, not really. Daisy Silver said I might have seen what I wanted to have happened, rather than what really did. And of course, you and I *had* been in the back of that car only the previous week, Cam, when they gave us a lift home and we were all singing.'

'Yes, that's true.'

'But it has made me feel determined to find out exactly how the whole sorry mess unfolded. I'm tired of feeling guilty for something I can't even remember doing, and sometimes I even feel angry with Harry.'

'I can understand that,' Lulu sympathised. 'It was his own stupid fault, after all! If he hadn't thought spiking Simon's tomato juice with vodka was a funny thing to do, he'd have been able to drive them safely home, like he always did. So no one blamed you except Cara, and she was all bitter and twisted because she had to turn that modelling agency down and take up her place at Oxford University instead.'

'No one who was directly involved has ever really talked to me about it,' I said, 'though Judy and Debo have only just told me that Simon tried to see me in hospital, so he might have wanted to.'

'He blamed himself, even though it wasn't really his fault, either,' Cam said. 'So, this mission you're on is to talk to everyone involved and get as much of a true picture of what happened as you can?'

'That's it in a nutshell,' I agreed, opening my notebook. 'I've drawn up a list, and of course Cara is the most important witness, followed by Simon, Dan and Tom. But I also added Debo and Judy, because they were there within minutes, and you two, who were the last to see me at the pub.'

Cam, Lulu and I had helped out at the Screaming Skull for pocket money. Lulu and I had cleared tables in the restaurant and collected empty glasses, while Cam had been general kitchen dogsbody.

Cam said, 'I don't think some of them will be that keen on talking to you.'

'No, especially Cara, the one who should know all the answers, if anyone does,' Lulu agreed. 'I think she'd drunk quite a bit, but not nearly as much as Harry.'

'I know she told at least one lie at the inquest, because I'd *never* have insisted on driving, so that's made me wonder what else she might have lied about,' I said.

'At the time of the inquest, you weren't expected to recover, so it probably seemed safe to put all the blame onto you,'

Cameron said. 'She wouldn't expect you to be around to contradict her.'

'I suppose not, and it certainly won't make her any keener to talk to me now. Still, at least she's at Grimside, within easy reach.'

'I don't think she and Cripchet are getting on,' Lulu said. 'He's away quite a bit at his place up in Scotland, or his London club, and there's a lot of talk. Did you know he'd taken on Simon Clew as head gardener at Grimside?'

'Yes, but only because Dan thought I already knew and let it slip yesterday when I ran into him on my way to the Spring. I've ticked Dan off my list already, since I asked him about the accident then, and it's plain I won't get any more from him than he's already said.'

I sighed. 'I don't know if he's telling the whole truth or not, though he certainly did pull me out of the car in case it went up in flames, which I suppose was kind.'

'*Kind* doesn't really fit in with the Dan we know and don't love,' Lulu commented drily.

'But Tom saw him lifting me out, so I know that bit has to be true,' I said. 'Only *Tom's* never wanted to talk about it, either.'

'I'll explain to Uncle Tom how you feel,' Cam promised.

'If you could persuade him, that would be wonderful,' I said gratefully.

'Auntie Pauline died from pneumonia around that time,' Cam said. 'That's probably why he doesn't want to look back. She'd been very difficult for a few years with the early-onset dementia, but he must have still loved her, because he was really cut up at her funeral.'

'Yes, Jonas said much the same to me the first time I went

to the pool for a swim after I'd got back from my convalescence with Daisy,' I admitted. 'Remember how Jonas always used to call us over to the cottage and make us drink that revolting nettle tea to warm us up afterwards?'

'He still drinks it – he calls it his secret rocket fuel,' Cameron said. 'He's well past ninety now, so there must be something in it!'

'After Jonas told me that Tom never mentioned that night because of Pauline dying soon after, he said that since Lady Cripchet had been killed in a point-to-point a couple of weeks later, that that made three sudden deaths and so there wouldn't be any more.'

And then it suddenly occurred to me that perhaps guilt had been partly responsible for Tom's grief. In the weeks before the accident, I'd spotted him and Judy having secret assignations in the woods – Judy's flame-red hair had been a bit of a giveaway . . . Maybe that was what had made Judy seem a bit shifty while I was asking her questions, too?

'I'm not sure *we* can add much more to what happened than you already know,' Cameron said. 'But fire away with the questions if you want to.'

'OK.' I turned to a fresh page. 'Cam first. You were in the kitchen most of that evening, weren't you?'

'Yes, I didn't go out at all, since you were collecting empty glasses and Lulu was clearing in the restaurant. I prepped some vegetables, then after that I was scraping plates, washing pans and stacking the dishwasher.'

'So you never saw Harry and the others at all that night?'

'No, though I do remember you coming in from the beer garden with some glasses and saying that Harry, Cara and

Simon were there, and though the other two were friendly, Cara had snubbed you.'

'She usually did. I expect a sixteen-year-old was below her notice.'

'Then you said you were leaving early and you'd walk up by yourself, because you were worried about Patch,' Cam continued. 'That was it.'

'And you said goodbye to me on the way out,' Lulu said. 'Then not long after, there were sirens going past and eventually someone told us what had happened.'

'Later that night, when I knew you'd been taken to hospital and weren't expected to survive, I phoned Lu up . . .' Cam said. Then he smiled at me. 'We're so glad you did, though!'

'To backtrack a bit, Lulu,' I said, 'that night, you'd taken the food out to Harry, Simon and Cara, hadn't you?'

'Yes, but they'd come into the bar to get their drinks – or rather, Harry had. He was the one with the cash and, as you know, he liked to drink. Mum said he'd had quite a lot, but she wasn't worried about him driving, because she knew Simon was teetotal and always drove. She thought the vodka and tomato juice was for Cara.'

'I suppose she was too busy in the bar to really give it much thought anyway,' I suggested. 'You weren't out in the beer garden while I was leaving, were you?'

'No, unfortunately, or I'd have been able to see the car park. You just said you were going early and you'd see me next day. And I said I hoped Patch was OK . . . though, actually, we all knew he was really old and on his way out.'

'True, but I just wanted to be there, really,' I agreed. 'Harry and the others must have gone to the car just before I set out for home, since Cara was already in the back seat when I got there. Harry was standing by it and Simon sitting in the front . . . presumably feeling drunk, or sick, or both at that point.'

'The police tried to find any witnesses to what happened next, but there weren't any,' Cameron said. 'The midges were out in force and everyone who'd been in the beer garden had gone into the pub.'

I closed the notebook. 'I don't think that gives me anything new, just makes it a bit clearer. Apart from telling me about Simon trying to see me in hospital, Judy and Debo didn't really add much either. Perhaps none of the other people on the list will, but I have to try. So I'm going to be pretty busy, what with starting up my mail-order clothes business and trying to sort out the kennel finances, too. Did I tell you I'd taken that over? They're in a big mess.'

'No, but I can imagine, and it's probably going to take you ages,' Cam said.

'Oh, I don't know, I think I'll be able to get on top of it quite quickly. And once I've filed everything, sorted out all the bills and persuaded Debo to let other rescue charities rehome any dogs without major problems, it'll be a much tighter and easier-to-run operation.'

'Good, because I'll need you and Cameron to help me with the Regeneration Scheme,' Lulu said.

'I'll do my best, but I'll have to go home in a minute. Judy's invited Rufus Carlyle for tea this afternoon, in the hope we can soften him up a bit about the kennels.'

'His manners seemed abrupt, but he was reasonable about the right of way, once he knew all the facts,' she said.

'Yes, but he was totally horrible to me when we first met.

120

Did Lulu tell you about that, Cam? He seems to think I killed his half-brother while drink-driving.'

'Yes, and I thought it was pretty mean. But he obviously doesn't know what really happened.'

'I'm not sure I entirely do, either,' I said wryly. 'Anyway, we'll see what Mr Rufus Carlyle is like this afternoon and then, after that, I might have time to start sorting out the studio into my business hub. The first batches of clothes I ordered will arrive from India any minute and I'll have to figure out where I'll keep all my stock.'

'If you need more space, you can use the storeroom at the back of the gallery,' Cameron offered. 'I'll need only about half of it and it's dry and warm.'

'That would be wonderful! Thank you, Cam.'

'What about Kieran?' Lulu asked. 'You haven't mentioned him again, but surely he's rung up to apologise by now, or at least sent you a text? One minute you're about to get married, the next you're not even talking to one another!'

'He did ring yesterday while I was out, but I don't know if it was to apologise or not, because apparently Judy tore him off a strip before he got the chance.'

'He's probably on his way up to abase himself in person by now,' Cam suggested.

I felt a pang at the thought of seeing him, but it was more a remembrance of how I'd have once felt, rather than how I really wanted to feel now.

'I don't think so. And he couldn't persuade me to live anywhere else but here in Halfhidden now, because I'm here to stay.'

When I left, they were working out how to get the ghostly photographic effects for the brochure and postcards. Cameron had suggested, with his attractive crooked smile, that it might give the right effect if Lulu posed in various locations wearing a diaphanous white Victorian nightgown.

He appeared to have been totally immune to our charms for all these years, but he had a definite teasing gleam in his blue eyes now when he looked at Lulu.

Despite Cam's flaxen fairness, willowy frame, eloquent thin hands, sensitive face and a predilection for arty velvet or white linen suits, I couldn't imagine how Guy could ever, even for a single moment, think he was gay. Certainly no woman ever made that mistake, for he had his own, very definite appeal.

Chapter 11: Charming

Rufus must have arrived by way of the kennels, for the first we knew about it was when Sandy threw open the kitchen door with a crash and shoved him in, using a firm hand between the shoulder blades and the words, 'The bloke from the house.'

'Oh, thanks, Sandy,' said Debo. 'Would you like some scones or cake to take back with you?'

'Nah, got HobNobs and fig rolls in the shed,' she said tersely, then left and, with surprising stealth, Babybelle appeared in her place.

'She can't keep away from you, Izzy darling,' said Debo. Then she turned her huge grey eyes on Rufus and gave him her famous and irresistibly puckish grin. 'I'm very happy to meet you at last, Rufus! I've heard so much about you.'

He didn't look noticeably softened by the grin and replied slightly ominously, 'I've heard quite a bit about *you*, too.'

'Debo, you and Izzy take Rufus through to the sitting room and I'll make the coffee – or tea, if you'd rather?' Judy asked Rufus.

'Coffee is fine.'

Debo and I picked up the cake stand and tray and led the

way through. I tried to shut Babybelle into the kitchen, but short of squashing her face in the door, it wasn't possible. She and Rufus, both large solid creatures, padded with disconcerting quietness after us.

Debo exerted her charm, which just naturally oozed to the surface in the presence of an attractive man . . . and there was no denying that he *was* attractive, in a taciturn, sombre sort of way. Anyway, I'd seen his muscular torso clad only in a wet T-shirt, so I knew some of his hidden charms.

When Judy had brought in the coffee, they plied him with finger sandwiches, miniature scones and chocolate butter-cream fairy cakes. Babybelle, firmly rebuffed while attempting to help herself to these delicacies, retired behind my chair to sulk and drool, but I was just glad she wasn't doing it over my feet, like at breakfast.

Rufus ate and drank whatever he was offered (so Judy's speculation about his being a vampire was evidently wrong), but said little, until suddenly he turned his sea-washed green eyes on me and remarked sardonically, 'You're very quiet in your corner, Miss Eyre!'

I jumped, startled at how closely attuned he seemed to have been to my thoughts, not to mention his familiarity with the novel, but replied primly, 'I'm always quiet, for I know my place, Mr Rochester,' and he grinned, which all at once made him look younger and less formidable. It was just a fleeting thing, though, gone so fast I wasn't sure if I'd imagined it or not.

'Izzy tells us that you two had already met before last night . . . but didn't perhaps get off on the right foot?' Debo said pointedly, recklessly tossing a slight spanner into the charm offensive, which in any case hadn't seemed to be softening him up in the least. Judy must have changed her mind and told her what happened at the Spring.

'You can hardly be surprised that I wasn't delighted to discover who she was, given the circumstances.'

'You mean, the circumstances of her having killed your half-brother while drink-driving?' she suggested, with deceptive sweetness.

'Well, from what I understand from Dan Clew—' he began.

'I'm afraid Dan is *not* a reliable source of information,' Judy interrupted. 'In fact, he'd tell any lies to try to turn you against us. He attempted it with Baz, but got nowhere, and now he's at it with you.'

Rufus wrinkled his brow over that wonderfully Roman nose. 'You're saying it was a lie and that Izzy *wasn't* driving?'

'Izzy *was* driving, but she was only sixteen and certainly not drunk,' Judy said.

'*Sixteen*?' he repeated blankly.

'Yes, and of course, she shouldn't have been driving at all, but Harry must somehow have persuaded her into it. She had serious head injuries after the crash and can't remember anything about it.'

He looked at me. 'Dan said Harry and his friends got drunk celebrating their exam results at the pub and you were the one who insisted on driving them back to Sweetwell.'

'But I was two years younger and never part of Harry's crowd,' I told him indignantly. 'In fact, I was only at the pub that night because I had a part-time job clearing glasses and plates. I left to walk home a bit earlier than usual . . . and I don't remember anything after I saw Harry and two of his friends in the car park, so I've no idea what on earth possessed me to get behind the wheel.'

'We know you wouldn't have done it if Harry hadn't talked you into it,' Debo said. 'It really wasn't your fault.'

'That's right, Harry really brought it on himself,' Judy said, and then explained to Rufus about Harry thinking it would be funny to spike teetotal Simon's drink.

'It had more of an effect on Simon than Harry expected, and he was afraid to drive back himself because his father had said if he got any more points on his licence, he wouldn't get a sports car for his birthday,' I said.

'Yes, it all came out at the inquest,' Judy agreed. 'But the poor boy certainly paid for his silly prank.'

'I suppose that changes things a bit,' Rufus admitted slowly. 'Sorry,' he added grudgingly to me.

'That's all right. You weren't to know Dan was twisting everything.'

'No, I wasn't – but then, there's what *you* said about Fliss – my mother – too.'

'Don't mention that vile woman's name in my home,' Debo snapped, ceasing to loll elegantly against the sofa cushions and sitting bolt upright. 'You tell her that if she ever comes anywhere near the Lodge again, I'll set the dogs on her.'

Rufus looked taken aback by this sudden fierceness. 'I don't suppose she will. She only dropped in the once because she was staying not far away with friends. She never mentioned that she'd been anywhere near the Lodge.'

'She certainly had! She showed up with Dan Clew while Debo was away,' Judy told him. 'I didn't let her in the house, of course, but she said if all the kennels and runs that were outside the garden boundary weren't removed immediately, they'd be bulldozed and taken to the tip.'

'I never even mentioned the kennels to her!' Rufus protested.

'Dan got her on side pretty quickly, then,' I said. 'He certainly never misses a chance to get back at us.'

Debo belatedly recalled her charm offensive and gave Rufus a warm smile. 'Well, I'm sure you've taken after Baz in character, rather than your mother. You even have his colouring, too, though you're much taller.'

'Izzy thought I was Harry, when we first met.'

'Only for a second! You're not really like him . . . though I suppose it's hard to say how he would have turned out by now.'

'Yes, and it's hard to discover you had a brother you'll never get the chance to meet,' he said.

'But at least you met Baz, and he must have really taken to you because he left you everything,' Debo said brightly. 'Lucky you!'

'Actually, I only spent one week with him and not a lot of bonding went on. I was still in shock after finding out the man I'd always thought was my father wasn't. And now Hugo Carlyle is thinking of suing Fliss for all the maintenance and school fees he paid out for me, not to mention the deposit to start up my own business.'

'I suppose finding out you'd been an impostor all your life must have been quite traumatic,' Judy said thoughtfully.

'More of an unwitting cuckoo in the nest. Hugo Carlyle married after I was born and has three children, so he'd have spent the money on them instead, if he'd known. He hasn't spoken to me since it all came out . . . and I thought he was quite fond of me, in his own way, even though his wife wasn't,' he added bitterly.

'Baz must have liked you,' Debo pointed out. 'He didn't have to leave you everything.'

Rufus shrugged. 'He *didn't* leave me everything. He told me that since I looked like a Salcombe and blood was thicker than water, I'd inherit the estate. But the house in the Bahamas and any other assets went to the family who'd looked after him there.'

'Yes, but as well as Sweetwell you got the Lodge, Spring Cottage and the tied cottage in the village that Dan occupies,' Judy said.

'Dan doesn't pay rent, it goes with the job. Same for Spring Cottage – so long as there's a male Tamblyn to occupy it, apparently.'

'You can toss Dan out on his ear any time you like and no one will mind, but there have always been Tamblyns looking after the Spring and there always will be,' Judy said firmly.

'But Dan told me there's only Tom left in the male line, because his sisters, Myra and Lottie, and their children don't count.'

'It's totally outdated, all this male inheritance stuff,' Debo said. 'Lottie married a Ross, but she insisted on Tamblyn being Cam's middle name, and of course he'll take over the cottage and look after the Lady Spring eventually.'

'He's just moved in anyway, since his grandfather's gone to live with Lottie. They've sort of swapped places,' I told him.

'But technically, he's not a Tamblyn, he's a Ross,' Rufus insisted.

'He's Tamblyn enough,' said Judy, with an air of finality. 'There have been Salcombes at Sweetwell since some buccaneering ancestor was given the estate by Elizabeth the First, and Tamblyns were already looking after the Lady Spring even then.'

'Dan says . . .' Rufus began and then stopped, perhaps at last perceiving that all his local information was coming from the same, possibly untrustworthy, source.

'I can imagine *everything* that Dan says,' Debo said. 'Did he tell you that Baz had always promised he would leave me the Lodge?'

'But he did – you've got it for life.'

'No, he meant he'd leave it to me outright, to give me security. And he loved dogs and often gave me a donation to keep things going, so I thought he might have left me some money in his will too . . . But then, I expect he thought you would keep up the good work,' she added hopefully.

'I suppose Dan had something to say about *that*, too?' I guessed, reading Rufus's expression without difficulty.

'He did indeed. He said that Debo and her dog rescue charity bled Baz dry for years and he was too soft-hearted to ask her to clear the overflow of kennels off his land, or stop loose packs of savage dogs roaming round the house, terrifying Myra.'

'That was only once – and Myra *likes* dogs,' Debo said indignantly. 'She called to tell us where it was and Judy collected it within minutes. That one was all bark and no bite anyway, and it's been rehomed now.'

'But you do have to admit that the kennels have got out of hand. It looks like a shanty town, and being right next to the drive it'll hardly give the right impression to my customers when they arrive,' Rufus said quite reasonably. 'Nor would incessant barking, or loose dogs with uncertain temperaments roaming around the estate.'

'It's usually only one or two dogs who escape at a time, and actually, they haven't done it so much lately,' Judy said, then she frowned. 'Now I come to think of it, it's usually around the weekends, too. That's odd, isn't it?'

'How *do* they get out?' I asked. 'I can see that Babybelle just has to lean against the netting till it's flat and then walk over it, but what about the others?'

'The bigger ones often do the same, but I think sometimes a fox must get them overexcited and they fling themselves at the gates,' she said. 'They're only secured with cheap hook-and-eye latches that Tom bought in a job lot, so they probably just bounce out.'

'"Secured" would seem to be a bit of an overstatement, then,' Rufus said.

'We've accepted more dogs than we should lately,' Judy admitted. 'So we had to house them quickly. But from now on, we're going to send any rehomable strays straight to other charities and return to accepting only the absolutely desperate, last-chance ones that no one else will.'

'You mean all the huge, vicious, uncontrollable ones? Great,' he said gloomily.

'Though we could still do with a *little* more space than the Lodge garden,' Debo coaxed.

'Not if it looks like a scrapyard.'

'A nice trellis fence along that bit of the drive would hide everything, and with climbing roses planted along it, it would actually make a nice feature,' I suggested.

'Oh, yes, with a bit of funding from you, we could certainly do that,' Debo said eagerly.

'Using what for money? I live off what I earn,' he protested.

'But – Baz's literary estate? He was a major bestseller,' she said, for until Harry's death, Baz had produced a big, block-buster thriller every three years with clockwork regularity.

'"Was" is the operative word. He hadn't written for a long time,' Rufus said. 'And apparently, the royalties on the books have been slowly decreasing. I've got his agent to help me, but Baz left strict instructions in his will that he didn't want anyone else using his name to write his novels. And of course, there are expenses like death duties to pay.'

'So you haven't got pots of lovely money?' Debo said.

'No. I need lots of lovely customers for that. If I can get them past flimsy pens full of huge rabid, slavering dogs, that is.'

'Don't exaggerate,' Debo said mildly. 'We'll sort it. Izzy's going to help us get straightened out and she's very practical.'

'Is she?' He gave me another of those unfathomable looks, half-human, half-merman.

'She certainly is. And meanwhile, you can tell Dan to stop harassing us and threatening to shoot my dogs, because if he did I'd prosecute him . . . if there was anything left of him after Sandy got her hands on him.'

'She's a very tall girl,' Rufus commented. 'She practically frogmarched me right in here with no trouble.'

'Six foot. The Lanes are a tall, well-built family. You should see her little sister.'

Rufus rubbed his forehead, as if we had somehow given him a severe headache. 'I won't have any guns or shooting on my property, so I'll speak to Dan about that. And perhaps he's been overstepping his mark, but as estate manager, I suppose he had my best interests at heart.'

'Baz employed him as a gardener, that's all. Dan just started fancying himself as some kind of estate manager-cum-game-keeper after Baz went abroad,' Judy said bluntly. 'There isn't that much estate left. Most of it was sold off to local farms a couple of centuries ago. I mean, it's not like there's game to protect, or acres and acres of managed woodland, like Grimside.'

'Grimside?'

'Sir Lionel Cripchet's estate on the other side of the village, though most of the house and most of the land is over the hill nearer to Mossedge, so we don't see much of him in Halfhidden,' Judy said.

'Which is fine, because he's a horrible little man. He made a pass at me once, while his first wife was still alive,' said Debo. 'I told him even if I'd been interested, which I wasn't, he'd have needed a stepladder.'

And as to Dan gardening, Myra's son, Olly, does what he can, otherwise the whole place would be a wilderness by now,' Judy said. 'Myra says Dan's never touched a garden tool since Baz left.'

'I do seem to be paying Olly Graham for two days a week gardening,' Rufus admitted. 'But I thought, with his mother being housekeeper . . .'

'It's not any kind of favour to Myra, if that's what you're thinking,' I said indignantly. 'Olly's a hard-working, wonderful gardener and already has a weekend job up at the alpine nursery. Just because he has Down's syndrome, it doesn't mean he isn't great at what he does.'

'No, of course not. I wasn't implying that at all! It's just I haven't really seen anyone I'm employing in action yet. Even Myra pops in and out of the door from the Victorian wing like one of those wooden figures on a weather house.

132

She told me she only cleans, she doesn't cook or anything, but then leaves pies and cakes in the kitchen and stuffs the freezer full of food. I'm going to be the size of a house at this rate.'

'Did she give you a marmalade cake?' asked Judy, interested. 'It's her speciality.'

'Yes, a whole one with lemon icing.'

'Then she must like you,' Debo said encouragingly.

He gave me an unfathomable sideways look from those sea-glass eyes. 'I'm glad someone does.'

'Myra likes to cook and clean, so she's probably enjoying herself,' Judy said. 'Her husband, Laurie, has his own job. He's a university librarian, though I think he retires soon.'

'I'm used to looking after myself,' Rufus said. 'It's odd to have staff – Dan and Olly and Myra – and I'll need someone to help me renovate the garden antiques who can also hold the fort when I'm away on buying trips. The man I had in Devon didn't want to relocate.'

'Oh?' Debo said, perking up. Then she exchanged looks with Judy.

'Are you thinking what I'm thinking?' Judy asked.

'Foxy Lane?'

'That's it,' Judy agreed.

'Where's Foxy Lane?' Rufus asked, baffled.

'It's not a place, it's a person,' I told him. 'Foxy is the younger sister of our kennelmaid, Sandy, and she's the village "handyman", so to speak.'

'All the Lanes have got reddish hair and nicknames to match,' Debo said. 'Sandy and Foxy were christened something everyday, like Jane and Susan. Everyone still calls their father Ginger, though he's bald as a coot.'

'Right . . .' Rufus said slowly. 'Is she like Sandy? Only when I asked her if she worked for you, she behaved as if she suspected I was going to steal something.'

'Sandy's not really a people person. Foxy's more sociable because of having to deal with customers, but she's not finding enough of those locally and she won't travel.'

'Let me guess,' he said morosely. 'The valley is really Shangri-La and she'd crumble to dust if she left?'

Debo was not a great reader, so this allusion puzzled her. 'No, it's all called Halfhidden,' she assured him.

'Fox has epilepsy so she never learned to drive,' Judy explained. 'But she's totally stable on medication and never has fits.'

'She'd be perfect!' Debo said enthusiastically. 'She'd enjoy all the renovation and cleaning stuff, run the place while you were away, plus she's completely honest.'

'Yes, and anyone trying to nick an antique would be sorry, because she's done a bit of karate, so she'd probably pin them down and stamp on them, or whatever it is they do,' Judy agreed.

They beamed at him. 'There, problem solved,' Debo said. 'I'll get Sandy to tell her to come and see you to sort out the details.'

Rufus looked slightly stunned. 'Thank you . . . I think.'

'Have another cake or a cheese scone. There are plenty left on the bottom tier of the stand,' Judy offered hospitably.

'I would, but that huge dog has just eaten the last one,' he said.

And he was right, because with a stealth I would never have believed, the greedy creature had snaffled the lot.

Chapter 12: Reverse Alchemy

After Rufus had gone, Judy and Debo decided that he might prove to be quite malleable on the subject of the kennels after all and I didn't say that I thought they were deluding themselves, because only time would tell.

We walked those of the dogs safe enough to be taken out in a group, though even divided between four of us, this meant stopping every five minutes to untangle leads. Vic and Ginger ran free, as did Belle, though in her case she didn't run but instead followed me so closely that her wet black nose constantly bumped into the back of my legs.

We took a circuitous route from the Lodge that avoided the vicinity of the big house, since we didn't want to rub Rufus up the wrong way – or not any more than we already had.

After that, we had dinner, before Judy and Debo went out to settle the dogs down for the night. Being early risers, they generally went to bed at around eight or nine, unless some exciting entertainment was on offer, and there were not many of those in Halfhidden.

I decided to have another go at the paperwork. I'd bought

a couple of big lever-arch ring binders from Lottie's shop on the way back from the gallery earlier, in which to file the bank statements and invoices in date order. I thought that would be a good start.

But before I could begin, Cameron rang to say he was back at Spring Cottage and Tom had agreed to talk to me.

'If I were you I'd come now,' he said, lowering his voice. 'He's really reluctant, but I explained about the confusing dreams and how you'd like to understand what happened so you could finally put it behind you, and in the end he said yes.'

'Oh, thanks, Cam,' I said gratefully. 'I'll grab my notebook and be there in ten minutes.'

It was still light and I could hear Debo and Judy clanking buckets and rattling bedtime treats into bowls as I tiptoed past the kennels: Babybelle really hadn't wanted to go back in after the walk but had been lured into one of the stronger pens by the prospect of dinner.

It was darker in the woods, but I was never afraid of meeting Howling Hetty for, despite what Lulu told her visitors, she only ever appeared on the drive to Sweetwell, nowhere else. You wouldn't catch me or any of the locals walking along it in the dark . . . which, now I came to think of it, made it even stranger that I'd driven the Range Rover up there that night, since I must have realised I'd have to walk back down it on my own to get home.

I did have a strange feeling of being watched, though . . . but probably the way Dan suddenly appeared last time had made me edgy.

In the hushed twilit clearing, Spring Cottage looked even more like something from a Grimm's fairy tale than usual.

I tapped gently at the door and Cameron let me in. I'd miss old Jonas calling me into the cottage to drink foul nettle tea out of thin Japanese porcelain cups painted with dragons, but on the whole, it was a tradition I was prepared to do without.

Tom was in the armchair by the fire and though he looked up and smiled at me, it seemed rather strained.

'Here we are, Uncle Tom! Izzy only has a few quick questions, so it'll take no time at all. I'll just make us a cup of tea first, shall I?'

'You do that, lad, and then let's get it over,' he agreed, as if he was at the dentist facing his worst fears.

I handed Cameron some of Judy's gingerbread, which I'd purloined from the kitchen on the way out, and by the time he came back with it on a tray, along with three mugs, Tom and I were talking about Prince and Duke, the dogs he'd had from Judy and Debo, and how well they'd turned out.

'We're ready to get another, though one hasn't taken my fancy yet,' he said. 'But if it's a young dog, our Cam may have to take it on if I get past it.'

'You're only seventy, Uncle Tom,' Cameron said affectionately. 'And look at Granddad – he's bright as a button and pretty spry most days, despite the rheumatism.'

'The Tamblyns do tend to live to a ripe old age,' Tom admitted. Then he sighed deeply and looked at me.

'Well, let's get it over with. I never wanted to talk about what happened that night because it was such a terrible accident . . . not to mention my Pauline taking ill and dying right afterwards.'

His face twisted at some remembered pain. 'But anyway,

Debo and Judy asked me never to speak of the accident to you.'

'I think they asked everyone and I suppose they meant it for the best, but because of the head injury, I've got no recollections of my own about the accident. The last thing I remember is seeing Harry, Simon and Cara in the car park when I was on my way home.'

'None of us thought you'd survive,' Tom said. 'Debo and Judy were beside themselves when the hospital started talking about turning the life support off.'

'I expect that was when I was in Heaven with my mother, before she sent me back.'

He nodded, for like his father, Jonas, accepting I'd been to Heaven and the existence of guardian angels had never been a problem to him.

'It's hard to shoulder the responsibility for something so awful when you don't remember a thing about *why* you did it.'

'I suppose that's true enough. What do you want to know?'

I opened the notebook. 'That night, you were in the woods when you heard the crash, weren't you?'

He gazed away into the heart of the fire, as if he could see it pictured there. 'That's right. I'd been to our Lottie's for supper and a game of Scrabble and I was on my way back here when I heard an almighty bang and then the horn blaring, so I headed back up the path.'

'So you got to the scene of the accident quite quickly?'

'Well, the path's all uphill, as you know, so it took a few minutes, but Dan Clew was practically on the spot when it happened.'

'And what did you see?'

He closed his eyes as if the picture in the flames hurt them, and then opened them again: they were the same clear, periwinkle blue as Cam's.

'I came out onto the drive and when I turned the sharp bend, I saw the Range Rover lying on its side in among the trees and bushes. The headlights were still on . . . and there was a great big branch sticking through the car, front to back.'

I shivered. 'Who could you see, at that point?'

'Simon. He must have got himself out, because he was sitting on the bank, looking pretty ill. Dan was lifting you out and then he laid you down on the grass near Simon.'

'Did you actually *see* him getting me out of the front of the car?'

Tom frowned. 'It's all such a long time ago now . . . but yes, I'm sure he was just lifting you out when I turned the corner. Then that Cara climbed out of the back with her face all bloody and screaming like a banshee.'

'And then?' I prompted.

'I told Dan he shouldn't have moved you with a bad head injury, but he said there was a strong smell of petrol so it seemed the best idea. And I think I asked him if you were driving and he said you were, then told me to take a look at Harry, which I did, poor boy.' His hand holding the mug trembled.

'I'm sorry to bring it all back to you, Tom,' I said.

'It haunts me anyway. Maybe it will be good for *me* to talk it through – you never know.'

'Did anyone else say anything?'

'Cara said everything was your fault, but she'd had a shock

and she was hysterical. And I could see that Simon was drunk straight away, even if his father didn't believe me.'

'Did Simon say anything?'

I thought Tom wasn't going to reply for a minute and he seemed now to be studying the pattern on his mug more intently than it merited. 'Only something about having seen a ghost,' he finally grudgingly admitted. 'I took no notice and his father told him not to be daft.'

A shiver went down my spine. 'Was it Howling Hetty? Because that's the spot she haunts, isn't it?'

'So he said, but I've never seen her, nor has anyone else that I know. It's an old wives' tale, that one.'

'But surely something must have made me swerve off the road?'

'You'd barely been behind the wheel before, so I reckon you just forgot about the dip after the sharp bend or maybe mixed up the brake with the accelerator. But whatever caused it, take it from me that it wasn't a ghost,' he insisted stubbornly.

'I really can't imagine driving up from the pub at all and I must have been petrified! So if Harry had talked me into it, surely I'd have stopped by the Lodge so that he could have taken over the wheel? He would have been safe from the police once he was on private land.'

'We don't know, except that Cara told the coroner you'd insisted on driving them from the pub all the way up to the house, which neither he nor anyone else with any sense believed. But then, you weren't expected to live, so I suppose she thought she could safely lay all the blame on you.'

'Yes – you and Lulu said much the same earlier, didn't

you, Cam?' I said. 'But what about Simon, Tom? Couldn't he remember anything?'

'He said it was all a blur after they got to the pub that night. He wasn't just drunk, he had some kind of reaction to the alcohol, which I suppose accounts for why it never had any attraction for him.'

'I think Simon probably felt guilty about the accident too, though with less cause, because when it comes down to it, I had a choice about whether to get behind that wheel or not, while Harry spiked Simon's drink without his knowledge.'

'But if he hadn't done that, then none of it would have happened at all, would it?' Cameron pointed out reasonably. 'Go on, Uncle Tom – what happened next?'

'I rang 999, seeing no one else had had the sense to think of it, and then Debo and Judy arrived . . . It seemed a long time till the police and ambulance came, but it wasn't really.'

'And they took me off to the hospital – and presumably Cara and Simon, too?'

He nodded. 'Judy insisted to the police that you couldn't possibly have been driving, but the evidence was against her.'

'Cara hasn't spoken to me since that day,' I said, 'but Debo and Judy said Simon wanted to talk to me while I was in hospital, only I was too ill.'

'Simon was in a state, poor lad. Harry was his best friend as well as his father's employer, so he was lost.'

'I suppose he must have been. How awful of me that I've never really thought of how Simon felt about it until recently,' I said contritely.

141

'That's natural enough,' Cameron said. 'It was a big shock when you found out you'd been driving.'

'I think I've told you everything I can remember,' Tom said, looking relieved, but also unusually shifty, much like Judy had when I'd finished asking her questions, so maybe it *was* just that they'd been having one of their secret trysts in the woods that night. And if so, then it really wasn't any of my business.

My mobile rang just after I got back to the Lodge, where only the two house dogs were awake to greet me.

'Izzy?' Kieran's voice demanded aggrievedly. 'Got you at last! Why haven't you been answering my calls? I've even tried the landline a couple of times and had Debo and Judy tearing me off a strip.'

'Well, I noticed you seemed to have lost the power to text, though I kept checking for messages, but Debo and Judy said you'd rung only once, yesterday evening,' I said, surprised. 'They must have forgotten the other call. But I've been really busy since then anyway, and I had to go out again this evening. In fact, I've only just got back in.'

'I don't see what could be more important than talking to your fiancé,' he said. 'I've been waiting for you to give me some kind of explanation for your behaviour – even an apology.'

I stared at the phone as if I'd discovered a gremlin hiding inside it. 'Explain about which behaviour? What are you talking about?'

'The way you disappeared back up north after the accident, leaving my father at the police station. You didn't even ring my mother and let her know what had happened.'

'But you of all people should have understood what a shock being in another car accident was. All I wanted to do was get away. Anyway, on TV the police always allow people they've arrested to phone someone, don't they?'

'This wasn't some trashy crime series, but real life. I'd have expected my fiancée to stand by my family.'

'Look, Kieran,' I said, with more patience than I felt, 'the last I heard from you was a text blaming me for refusing to take the rap for your father's drink-driving! Is it any wonder I haven't rung you?'

'He was not drunk,' Kieran said coldly. 'Perhaps he was slightly over the limit, but the crash was all the fault of the other driver.'

'Oh, don't be silly,' I snapped. 'He overtook just before a blind bend – and he'd been driving recklessly before that. The car coming the other way tried to avoid him, that's how the poor woman ended in the ditch. And thank God she and the children were all right,' I added devoutly.

'That's not how my father described what happened, and if you'd only backed up his story, things wouldn't now be looking so grim.'

'Well, I'm very sorry if he's in deep doggy doo-doo, but he dug himself into it and there was no way I was lying to get him off. I don't know how you could even suggest I should have taken the blame, knowing as you do what happened when I was sixteen.'

'But that was entirely different,' he said. 'Anyway, this hasn't exactly endeared you to my parents, I can tell you, though for my sake they're prepared to forgive and forget.'

'That's very big of them. But actually, Kieran, the way they were trying to take over our lives and *my* wedding didn't exactly endear them to *me*, either! And what's more, even before the accident I'd had some doubts about our future, once it became clear you'd been making big assumptions about things.'

Kieran made the sort of gobbling noises that could get you into big trouble around Christmas, but I carried on regardless.

'I'd made up my mind that I didn't want to live in Oxford, but instead needed to come home and put some space between us.'

'And you were going to tell me this *when*, exactly?'

'When you arrived in Oxford. It seemed fairer to do it face to face, and then I could travel back to Halfhidden right afterwards.'

'How kind of you to want to tell me in person,' he said sarcastically. 'I don't know what's got into you, when you always knew I intended going into practice with my parents.'

'But I didn't. You only told me that last year, when we visited them for the first time. And *I* always talked of coming back here, to Halfhidden.'

'I thought you just meant to visit, not to live, because after we got engaged you must have known you'd have to change your plans. I thought you'd be grateful there was a family practice for me to go into and that my parents were willing to put in some money for a house deposit.'

'Yes, to add to the legacy I got from my father! I was surprised to find you were all counting on that since I always intended to use most of it to set up my clothing business. I mean, I even delayed returning to the UK till I'd visited the workshops where my designs were going to be made and seen how the first orders were coming along, so what did you think I was using for money?'

'I presumed you had some savings and weren't touching your capital.'

'No: I was never paid enough to save anything and I knew I didn't have to because the money would be there when I needed it. And now I'm using what's left to bail Debo and the kennels out of a financial hole and get them back on an even keel.'

There was a pause, during which I could hear him breathing deeply and, possibly, grinding his teeth. Laid-back, good-natured, affectionate Kieran would appear to have permanently left the building.

'Your aunt will just squander it, like all the other money that's run through her fingers. But it's yours, so I suppose you can do what you like with it,' he conceded, with gritted-teeth magnanimity.

'Thank you,' I said drily. 'Just as I can do what I like with my own life.'

'Look, Izzy,' he said in a softer voice, though with an irritating overtone of one talking to a halfwit, 'I don't know how we came to fall out like this in the first place, but I'm sure we can work things out. Why don't you come down here for Easter weekend? I miss you,' he added, coaxingly.

That tone had once weakened my knees and blinded me to his true nature . . . but now the effect was only momentary.

'I haven't got time to come down, even if I wanted to. As well as starting the ball rolling with my own company and sorting out the kennels' affairs, I've decided to interview everyone involved in the accident I had as a teenager.'

'Why on earth would you want to rake all that up again?

145

It would be much better to let it drop and live somewhere else far away from it all, and I'm sure once you've seen a bit more of Oxford you'll love it.'

'Oxford is a beautiful place, only I don't want to live there. So I think we've reached an impasse, haven't we?'

'If you really loved me, you wouldn't say that!'

'If you'd really loved me, you wouldn't have expected me to cover up for your father's actions – or taken it for granted that I'd let your parents run my life.'

I didn't see how there could be any going back now, for the foundations of our love had taken so many knocks that they were crumbling, and the whole airy edifice was now as shaky as a stage backdrop.

'They were only being kind,' he said stuffily.

'Perhaps they were, in their way – but it isn't my way. I love Debo and Judy and Halfhidden, and I believe in what they're doing with the dog refuge. They need me.'

'I need you more,' he said flatly.

'I don't think you do, or you'd have considered working up here. I mean, you're a doctor with years of experience; it can't be that hard to find another practice, can it?'

'I grew up in Oxford and my family and friends are all there,' he said. 'Besides, my parents are counting on me to go in with them.'

'Well, you can see why I thought our engagement had run its course, can't you?' I said. 'Impasse!'

'Oh, come on, Izzy,' he said more persuasively. 'I'm sure if we could get together you'd see sense.'

'I am seeing sense,' I said firmly and then quickly switched the phone off before we could go round in any more unproductive circles.

I did shed a few tears once I was in my narrow bed up under the eaves, but they were more for the love I'd thought we'd had than the kind it had really proved to be, for by a process of reverse alchemy, my solid gold had turned to lead.

Chapter 13: Disengaged

'No, I really mean it, I can't come – you know what Judy's like. If I'm not home by ten, she'll be really mad and start looking for me.'

I didn't tell him I also wanted to rush back to be with my little dog, in case I sounded soppy.

'But it's like I said, we need you, Izzy . . . and we can give Judy the slip,' he said persuasively, catching me in the traction beam of his smile, like a rabbit in the headlights.

'Need me? You said that before, but why on earth would you need me, Harry?' I asked, puzzled.

I sat bolt upright, my heart racing, for that snatch of conversation had taken me onwards, into uncharted territory. Was it a memory surfacing? Or just my vivid imagination embroidering what I had since learned?

It was impossible to know.

The back door slammed as Judy and Debo went out to the kennels and I lay back on the pillows, calmer now and listening to the birds sweetly singing in the trees.

I thought about the conversation with Kieran last night and how, although the sound of his voice had stirred up echoes of the love I'd once had for him, the substance appeared to have entirely vanished.

Would I feel the same if I came face to face with him again? I thought I probably would, since I seemed to have fallen as headlong out of love as I'd fallen into it. But then, I'd thought I'd known what kind of man he was, only to discover that he was scheduled to morph into a clone of his father at the drop of a stethoscope.

I sent him a text message, saying that I didn't think we had any future together as a couple, but hoped we would stay friends and I wished him all the best.

After that I felt in need of a purge, so, despite it being overcast and with a distinct crack-of-dawn chill still in the air, I decided on a quick dip in the pool *and* a good long drink from the spring in the cave. I didn't know what was in the water, but something tasting that peculiar had to be good for me.

So off I trotted down the path, keeping a wary eye open for Dan, though due to his late boozy nights at the Screaming Skull he wasn't generally noted for early rising. At one point something did go crashing away in the undergrowth, but it was more likely to be a teenage badger heading back to the sett after a night on the tiles than a hung-over pseudo-gamekeeper.

There was no sign of anyone at the Lady Spring either, but a hazy, translucent blue plume of smoke rose from the cottage chimney, so Tom was probably cooking up a hearty breakfast.

Cameron had said he was going to leave really early to fetch the shop counter he'd bought on eBay, so he was probably already halfway down the M6 by now, stoking up with trans fats at a motorway services.

I let myself through the metal turnstile, which gave its usual well-oiled clunk, and drank two whole pointy paper cups of water from the spring in the little cavern, after which I started to feel revitalised, if slightly nauseated. There's nothing like a good purge, of one kind or another.

It was still so chilly that I was reluctant to take my clothes off and it was certainly no day for floating about dreaming – of naked Roman soldiers or anything else. I had the quickest dip ever, and though as usual the water felt a little warmer than the air, it was not enough to make me linger. Before I worked abroad I used to do this from early spring to very late autumn, so I have clearly turned into a lily-livered wuss.

As I came out of the enclosure, half-woman, half-Popsicle, I spotted Tom walking away from me towards the back garden, but either he hadn't noticed I was there, or he didn't want to talk to me this morning. The latter was quite possible, given that my questions last night must have stirred up many sad memories . . . and maybe a touch of guilt.

He and Judy seemed to have reverted to being just good friends after his wife died, though, so it had probably been one of those brief affairs that fizzle out.

I returned to the Lodge for breakfast with a *huge* appetite . . . where I discovered Babybelle in the kitchen, feeling much the same after her walk. After we'd both eaten, she insisted on staying and keeping me company in the office, while I carried on with the paperwork. She occupied the whole of the middle of the floor, spread out like a huge black bear rug, so I was constantly falling over her.

It was amazing how a large filing cabinet could so easily and hungrily eat up a ton of paper *and* make it possible to lay your hands on whatever you wanted without a five-hour search.

I'd just about finished popping things into freshly labelled hanging files when Judy called to tell me lunch was ready. It didn't seem five minutes since breakfast, but that certainly got Belle up on her huge, hairy feet – or maybe it was the enticing smell of food that wafted through the door when Judy opened it.

Over delicious chicken soup, accompanied by slices from a leaden and sulky sourdough loaf, Debo said that Tom and Jonas had been round to look at the dogs, and Tom had not only fallen for the greyhound, but he'd already taken her away with him!

'And Jonas is going to have Snowy when he's cured of barking at the TV,' she added. 'Chris is picking him up later and taking him back to his place for some intensive therapy. He reckons he can cure him of the barking in about a week.'

'So that will be two dogs rehomed. When several of the others have gone to Debo's friend Lucy's kennels, there'll be much more space,' Judy said. 'Four are going this afternoon and the next batch tomorrow.'

'I'll miss the poor darlings,' Debo said sadly.

'As long as we get down to a more manageable number soon, that'll be fine,' I said encouragingly. 'You're doing really well.'

'Until the next phone call about a dog on death row,' agreed Judy. 'And the one after that, and the one after that . . .'

'We can't turn the desperate cases down; that's what we're about,' Debo said. 'But I do promise to send the others straight off to Lucy.'

'Great – and the paperwork's almost sorted, too. I've paid

the most outstanding bills online and ordered some oil for the heating.'

'And I was promised some good donations when I rang around a few friends,' Debo said. 'Once they come in, we should be fine, shouldn't we?'

'For the moment,' I agreed. 'As soon as the dogs have gone to Lucy's, we can clear away the kennels and runs nearest to the drive and replace them with a small purpose-made block and runs further away, where the old greenhouse used to back onto the garden wall. I've been looking at them online.'

'Can we order that nice fence to hide them from the drive, to keep Rufus happy?' Judy asked.

'Yes, and you're in charge of planting the roses along it.'

'Of course, I've already been looking at the catalogues. I'd like to make a long rose bed in front of the fence, as well as planting the climbers,' Judy said enthusiastically.

'Nothing too pricey,' I warned.

'Perhaps Rufus will pay for the roses?' Debo suggested brightly, with her brilliant, gamine smile. I could see she'd soared off into one of her moods of unfounded optimism again.

When he'd come to tea, he hadn't been as awful as I'd expected after our first encounter at the Spring; but on the other hand, he hadn't been *that* nice, either.

After lunch I looked up the phone number for Grimside and tried calling Cara Ferris – or Lady Cripchet, as she was now, I supposed. But it rang for ages and then switched to an answering service, so I just left a message saying I needed to speak to her and asking her to call me. I didn't really think she would, though.

After that, Judy drove me to Ormskirk so I could buy four extending clothes rails on castors, and a shelf unit, ready for when my first consignment of stock arrived. I thought I'd keep one rail in my studio and the others and the shelf unit in the end of Cam's large storage room. I also, in an inspired moment, bought a folding pasting table with a carrying handle, because I thought I could set it up whenever I had orders to pack.

Back home I assembled one of the rails and then pressed and hung all my clothes samples on it – floaty scarves, dresses and quilted jackets in Indian printed cotton, several based on vintage originals from my by-now extensive collection. Some were embellished with bits of mirror and embroidery, tassels or little bells.

I'd had two sari-inspired dresses and one Grecian tunic made up in silk, and they looked quite beautiful, if I said so myself . . . as did my wedding dress, which was ivory with lace overlays and a lot of tiny silver mirror work and embroidery on the bodice and hem. I zipped it firmly away in a plastic cover and hung it in the back of my bedroom wardrobe.

Shades of Miss Havisham.

Debo, popping into the studio to admire my creations, said they took her right back to her early modelling days and she only needed a good dab of patchouli oil on her wrists to be completely transported.

Now I could see all the samples together, I was pleased with my basic stock. I would add extra styles over time. Currently I was working on a design for a maxi skirt that would have fullness in the hem and an elasticated waist, but wouldn't be so bunchy it made the wearer look like Widow

Twankey. And it would be lined in thin cotton too, so you didn't get the see-through Lady Diana experience. I had the drawing pinned on a board on the easel and it was now veering from Indian Classic towards Flamenco, but in a good way.

Later, I rang Cameron to see if he was back and asked him if I could take the other rails and the shelving over.

'Of course, and you should come and see my counter anyway because it's amazing: antique and made of mahogany.'

'Will that fit in with all the white walls and oak floor?'

'Yes, because it's beautiful in its own right, and anyway, the floor's stained quite dark. The van I hired is still out the front, so I'll come over and pick you up, if you like.'

He'd hired the rental van from Deals on Wheels, a garage near Middlemoss, so transporting my stuff across took us only minutes. Unfortunately, we had to transport Belle, too, since she heaved herself into the back of the van while we weren't looking and then lay there immovably.

'Do you mind if she comes too? I can lure her out with food if not,' I offered.

'No, I'm not bothered, so long as she doesn't pee in my gallery.'

'She seems totally house-trained, so she should be all right, though she leaves a trail of shedded hair wherever she goes, despite Sandy brushing her every day. At least Judy's happy about it because it gives her lots of hair to knit with.'

'She's a lovely dog. Is she yours now?'

'Looks like it,' I said ruefully as she padded into the gallery after us.

The counter truly was a thing of brass-handled beauty.

Cam had already started polishing the mahogany surface and the gallery smelled deliciously of beeswax and lavender.

Since my previous visit he'd arranged a series of white-painted open wooden cubes in the front window, ready to display local crafts, and hung a few of his rather amazing watercolours on the walls. In one that I particularly coveted, a cloud of bees were leaving a hive in an explosion of black and deepest saffron yellow.

'It's all really taking shape,' I said admiringly.

'It has to, because I now intend opening on the 14th,' he said. 'Luckily the folding room dividers are coming tomorrow, way earlier than I expected.'

'There won't be a huge amount more to do, then?'

'I still have more display cubes to paint white and then the craftspeople whose work I'm showing will bring their items in and I'll list them and mark up the prices and commission.'

'I suppose there are all kinds of things to think about before you open. Thank goodness for the internet, because I'd already sourced things like clothes labels and packaging long before I came home *and* blocked out a basic website.'

'As fast as I think of one thing, another pops up,' he admitted. 'I'll have to get a credit card machine and learn to use an electric till.'

'The devil's in the detail,' I said.

We set up my rails and shelves, and then, since there was loads of space, the pasting table. Even then, I only took up one end of the room. Cam unfolded an old wicker screen partway across as a divider.

'His and hers storage,' he said, with a grin. 'I'll only really need my bit for canvases, packing materials and framing. I'll get some artist's donkeys and easels for classes later – I'm scouring eBay for those, too. You can find anything on there, if you look hard enough.'

'It's going to be a great success,' I assured him. 'Are you getting some celebrity to officially open the gallery?'

'I hadn't thought of it. Like who?'

'There's that *Cotton Common* star living in Middlemoss – Judy told me because she's a big fan. I think he's called Ritchie something.'

'I suppose I could. Anyone except Sir Lionel Cripchet, because he's a little creep and, anyway, he's not liked in the village.'

'We never *see* him in the village.'

'How about keeping it local and asking Debo to do it?' Cam suggested. 'I could have a ribbon for her to cut, and fizz and nibbles in the gallery.'

'Sounds perfect. And she can wear one of my designs, so *I* get a plug in the local paper, too!'

'Good thinking. Here's to success for both of us,' he said, and we toasted each other in coffee from the little machine he'd installed in the corner.

I dropped a few hints about him and Lulu, in case he wanted to confide anything interesting to me, but to no avail. I'd just have to watch and await developments.

That afternoon I took Babybelle down a really overgrown path to the deep natural rock pool that lay in the woods below the Lady Spring.

It was certainly true that Newfoundlands loved water, for she leaped in with delighted abandon and swam about for ages. When she finally deigned to emerge, she shook herself vigorously, soaking me from head to foot in the process.

She did dry off surprisingly quickly, so I gave her another brushing when we got back. She seemed to enjoy it and I added the hair to the bag in the shed with the rest that Sandy had been saving for Judy's knitting.

If anyone wanted to commission a Newfoundland jumper, I could put them in touch with just the right person . . .

It was quite quiet at the kennels, since Sandy and Debo had taken the first four of the dogs over to Lucy's in the estate car. I could hear Judy briskly brushing out a dog run and singing excerpts from *The Sound of Music* in a wavering soprano. She was sixteen, going on seventeen.

It had become abundantly clear that Belle would not be leaving for Lucy's and I'd finally accepted my fate: I was stuck with the ridiculous creature for ever. But she'd still have to spend her nights and part of the days in the kennels, because she was a bit too huge to be a house dog in a tiny cottage.

I tried explaining that to her, but she accompanied me back into the house anyway.

I walked down to the pub after dinner, collecting Cam from Spring Cottage on the way.

Dan was already in the public bar when we arrived, so we went through into the snug. Lulu popped in from the hotel side for a chat and to impart a bit of gossip.

'You'll never believe this,' she said, 'but Mandy, one of the barmaids, just told me that she overheard Dan Clew telling his cronies that he'd not been in the pub so often at weekends lately because he'd been down in London staying with a pop star called Fliss Gambol!'

'Really?' I exclaimed. I'd already updated Lulu and Cam

on what I'd learned about Fliss's tragic influence on my mother, so they both knew who she was. We'd looked her up on Google, too, and her biography to date didn't make pretty reading. 'That seems fast, after a brief meeting – if it's true.'

'I don't think he'd have the imagination to make it up,' she said. 'And we did notice he wasn't around so much, because he's such a fixture in the public bar.'

'I bet Rufus doesn't know his mother's having an affair with his gardener,' I said. 'Or the man who *should* be his gardener, if he was actually doing any work.'

'It's probably just a brief fling,' Cameron suggested. 'I mean, she's been about a bit, so I'd have thought his novelty value would wear off fast.'

'I expect you're right,' Lulu said. 'She'll probably drop him just as quickly.'

'Granddad says you've asked him to come and tell ghost stories to the visitors on Saturday night,' Cameron said, changing the subject. 'He seems very taken with the idea.'

'I've told him the spookier and more blood-curdling the better, because after all, the Haunted Weekends are advertised for adults. If it's a success, it could be a regular Saturday event, whenever we've got enough interested visitors.'

'You're bound to get a lot of people following the haunted trail with families, when that's up and running, though,' I pointed out.

'Yes, but I'll make it clear that Jonas's ghost story sessions aren't suitable for young children. Of course, we never put families in the haunted chambers anyway, only in the newer part of the hotel.'

The newer part was added during the early nineteenth

century and then substantially extended during the Victorian era, but I suppose that *is* new compared to the rest of it.

'Nowadays most children seem to be brought up on a diet of *Hunger Games*, horror and vampires, so they wouldn't be that scared,' Cameron said. 'Anyway, I'll drive Granddad down here on Saturday night and take him home again afterwards. I'd like to stay for the story session too, if that's OK?'

'Yes, of course, you're both welcome to come,' she said. 'There are only three bookings for the Haunted Weekends, all couples, so it'll make more of an audience. Mum says we've quite a few other visitors arriving tomorrow for the long weekend, though – and once the Haunted Holidays start, I hope the whole hotel will be booked solid! Wouldn't that be wonderful?'

'It certainly would,' I agreed. 'When do you think you might start them?'

'Early May, but it depends how much we can get sorted out at the Halfhidden Regeneration meeting on Tuesday. Cam and I have made a start on designing leaflets and things already.'

'That reminds me, I roughed out that leaflet header you wanted,' Cam said, handing her a folder. 'See what you think.'

'Come for a Haunted Holiday in Halfhidden!' it proclaimed, over an eerily backlit photograph of Howling Hetty's head. Underneath, it invited visitors to 'Stay at the Screaming Skull Hotel, explore the most haunted hidden valley in Lancashire, drink the curative mineral water of the Lady Spring and bathe in the magical healing woodland pool.'

'Sounds wonderful,' I said. '*I'd* go there!'

'It's going to be a glossy threefold brochure with a map

of the trail inside. All the attractions will be numbered, with the details in little boxes round the edge, and I thought every business featured could pay a small fee towards the cost of printing it.'

'That seems fair enough: I'm up for that,' Cameron said.

'And me, too! I could advertise my website, even though I'm not actually selling direct to visitors, couldn't I? Cam's going to help me put the finishing touches to my website, so it can go live soon.'

I told her we'd thought that getting Debo, as a local celebrity, to officially open Cam's gallery, would generate some good publicity. 'And if she's wearing one of my designs, for me, too.'

'Good idea,' Lulu said. 'And we can tell any reporters who turn up about the Ghost Trail: publicity all round!'

She had a slight Baileys habit and was nurturing a glass of it, clinking with ice cubes. Now she took a sip. 'I'm going to be busy here all weekend. What are you two doing over Easter?'

'My folding doors are coming tomorrow, so I'll be at the gallery all day,' Cameron said. 'I've got a lot still to do there anyway.'

'And I'm going to finish all the kennel paperwork off. I transferred most of what's left of my money into the Desperate Dogs account when I was in Ormskirk, and Debo managed to wangle a couple of big donations from old friends, so I should be able to pay off all the outstanding debts and they can start again, on a smaller scale, with a clean slate.'

'If it *stays* on a smaller scale,' Lulu said doubtfully.

'I'll be keeping an eye on things from now on, don't worry.

And after tomorrow, I'll have all the time I need to concentrate on launching my own business.'

'We'll drink to that!' Lulu said, raising her glass. 'Here's to Izzy Dane Designs!'

Then she had to go and help lay the tables for breakfast, so Cam and I walked back home through the quiet woods, and no Howling Hetty crossed our path.

I tiptoed the last bit to the Lodge, in case Babybelle woke up and decided to break out, but she must have been fast asleep, for all was silent under the stars.

Chapter 14: Sweetwell

Simon Clew, who was sitting in the driving seat with his legs dangling out onto the grass and his head hanging down, looked up just then and gave a strange smile. He was deathly pale and sweating so much he had to keep pushing his heavy-framed glasses back up his nose.

'What's the matter with Simon?' I asked, distracted.

It was a much brighter morning and I again grabbed my things and set off for a swim while Judy and Debo were still out with the dogs, hoping they'd managed to drag Babybelle with them.

I'd decided that since living in India so long had turned me into a wimp, I'd just have to toughen up again, and the sooner the better.

The air was still chill under the trees, but the hawthorn blossom glistened and rabbits hopped away at the sound of my footsteps. That morning there were no stop-out teenage badgers on their way home, or whatever it was that was crashing about in the bushes the previous day, but as I neared the clearing, I spotted Rufus talking to Tom by the beehives.

Instinctively I ducked below the fence and ran quickly

past, hoping they hadn't seen me. I was not keen on another meeting, for I felt distinctly ambivalent about Rufus . . . though definitely not about his mother now I knew what part she'd played in the death of mine.

The sun was warm and golden in the clearing. I had a good drink from the spring in the cavern, after arranging a few bluebells in a nearby water-filled crevice as a tribute to whichever Lady happened to be in charge at the moment.

I splashed about a bit in the pool and then floated lazily, with the sun growing stronger and beginning to warm my face. But when I shut my eyes it wasn't the familiar young naked Roman soldiers I imagined sharing the water with me, but a damp and dishevelled Rufus Carlyle . . .

So when I opened them a few moments later to find him sitting on a block of stone watching me, it was a bit of a shock.

'How long have you been there?' I demanded.

'About thirty seconds. But don't worry, because this time I decided to let you drown, if you wanted to.'

'I saw you talking to Tom when I came down the path, but I hoped you hadn't seen me and would go away,' I said rudely.

'Do you want to be alone? I could go,' he offered.

'It's a bit late now,' I replied ungraciously, especially considering that the pool I was in and everything around it actually belonged to him. 'But I like being alone here in the mornings. It sort of recharges my batteries.'

'I was exploring some of the paths, though the smaller ones are very overgrown,' he said. 'Then I spotted Tom and since I meant to have a chat with him today anyway, I thought I might as well do it there and then.'

I stood upright, the water lapping at my pointed chin, and pushed wet elf locks of hair out of my eyes. 'Was it about Spring Cottage and how the Tamblyns have always lived there, guarding the Lady Spring?'

'Yes, though when I searched, I didn't find any family documents about it, so it must be an unwritten tradition.'

'Oh,' I said, digesting this. 'You mean, you could make them leave the cottage, so you could rent it out, or something, if you wanted to? Though, actually, there's no vehicle access to it, so I don't think you'd find many takers.'

'No, it wouldn't be worth it even if I wanted to do that, which I don't,' he said. 'Though I think they're getting a good deal: a cottage for free and an income from visitors to the Spring.'

'There haven't been many visitors for *years,* so Tom's always had to do handyman stuff in his spare time to make ends meet. He knocked together all those extra kennels for Debo.'

'That's not exactly an advertisement for his skills, is it?'

'Only because Debo was so hard up that he had to make them out of free stuff from skips and the tip,' I said indignantly. 'But if Lulu's Regeneration Scheme gets underway and the Spring is busier, he probably won't have to do anything else.'

'Ah, yes, the lively Lulu,' he said. 'Tom was telling me how you, his nephew Cameron and Lulu had been best friends all your lives . . . and I presume Cameron was the thin, fair-haired man you were so enthusiastically embracing at the end of the meeting?'

'Well, I hadn't seen him for ages and ages because he'd been working in London and was never home when I was.

But now all three of us have come back to live in the valley at the same time, which is so wonderful that it was obviously *meant* to be.'

'Actually, I assumed he'd come back to take over Spring Cottage from his uncle.'

'Oh, no, he'd just had enough of teaching and wanted to come home and start up his own gallery. He only moved in with Tom because his grandfather had such bad rheumatism that he needed to live with his daughter, who has the village shop. They swapped places.'

'If you say so. It just seemed a bit timely, moving in as soon as I came on the scene.'

'Does it matter, since he'll be looking after the Spring eventually anyway? That is, if you're going to let things carry on as they always have?' I added.

'I suppose so,' Rufus said. 'I can see I'll be portrayed as a monster to the whole of Halfhidden if I don't.'

'I think if you want to be accepted as part of the community, you'll have to respect the local traditions,' I agreed. 'Though that doesn't extend to employing Dan Clew if he doesn't pull his weight. No one likes him and he isn't local anyway. He only moved here when he got the job with Baz.'

'It may come to it, because now I've talked more to Myra and Tom about him, I can see that what he's been telling me hasn't always been entirely truthful.'

'That's the understatement of the year! He's already tried to spread all kinds of horrible rumours about Debo round the village, though luckily no one believed him.'

'But I suspect some of the things he said *did* have more than a grain of truth in them, like Debo taking advantage of Baz's good nature to extend her kennels into the grounds, not to mention using the estate as a giant dog run.'

'Baz loved dogs, so I really don't think he minded, and anyway, he was rarely here for more than one night a year after Harry . . . after the accident.'

'Be that as it may, I still don't like having bits of old wooden pallets and rusty wire netting up the side of my drive.'

'I did tell you it would look much better very soon,' I assured him, 'and it will, because I'm on the case. Things only got out of hand because Debo finds it hard to turn any dog in need away, but her main aim was always to give a last chance to dogs that would be put down if she didn't take them. From now on, the others will go straight to a rescue centre. In fact, they took four dogs there yesterday and four more will go today.'

'Great! So all that stuff at the side of the drive can be cleared away immediately?'

'Well . . . yes, but we'll still need a few extra kennels, only proper ones, set further back from the drive and hidden behind lovely fencing with a trellis top and climbing roses. In fact, Judy's offered to make a rose bed in front of it, too, if you pay for the plants.'

'I knew there'd be a catch in it somewhere,' he said gloomily.

'It would make the entrance look much nicer when your customers drive in,' I said persuasively. 'And it would look even better if Dan cut back the trees and bushes along the drive because at the moment it's one long, gloomy tunnel.'

'I asked Myra whether Baz expected Dan to do anything other than the gardening and keeping the paths and drive clear, like you told me,' Rufus said. 'She said no and he was so lazy that he did as little work as possible after Baz moved permanently to the Bahamas.'

'Aunt Debo told Baz when Dan started calling himself the estate manager and harassing her and anyone else that set foot on the estate.'

'Yes, Myra said that, too,' he admitted.

'Baz rang him and told him to get a grip and get on with the gardening, or find another job, but he didn't take any notice and Baz didn't follow it up. He did start paying Olly for part-time gardening, though, when Debo told him he was the only one doing any.'

'Olly does seem to put in a lot of hours. He was out there in the vegetable garden at first light this morning,' Rufus said. 'He's transparently honest, too, so I know anything he says is the plain truth.'

'Yes, there's no subterfuge with Olly; he says exactly what's in his mind.'

'When I asked him about Dan, he told me he'd overheard him telling Baz last time he came over that *he* was doing all the gardening and Olly just mowed the lawns. But Baz told him he knew Olly did more than that, because he'd just seen him pruning the roses.'

'I'm sure Baz *did* know that Dan still wasn't pulling his weight, but he just didn't have the heart to make any changes.'

'He kept the house in good repair, though.'

'Well, Myra is a demon cleaner, it's a compulsion with her, so the place is always spick and span, and anything that needs attention gets sorted out.'

'I've noticed. I even caught her steam cleaning the down-stairs cloakroom the other day and when I said there was no need to go that far, she asked me not to spoil her fun.'

'Oh, she loves it, and there are only so many hours she can spend cleaning her own flat in the kitchen wing because it's not that big. Did she say anything more about Dan?'

'Only that Olly is still doing most of the gardening, despite working at the alpine nursery at weekends. And she seems to be right, though Dan has made one or two token gestures when I've been about.'

His jaw hardened and I thought if Dan expected the new owner to be as easy-going as Baz, he'd mistaken his man.

'Tom's also confirmed how little Dan has been doing, so since I don't need any kind of estate manager, either he puts the full-time work into his real job, or he's out on his ear. And the gun, loaded or not, goes now.'

'He's not going to like that, after having such an easy life for years.'

'I'm paying his wages and he's getting his cottage rent free, so he'd better buckle down if he wants to keep it. He can make a start on cutting back the drive tomorrow and then, after that, clear all the paths. That should keep him occupied for a while, and by then I'll have a whole list of other stuff for him to get on with.'

'What about Olly?'

'He says he's happy to carry on being in charge of the walled garden and the vegetable patch. In fact, he seems to consider those his personal domain.'

I shivered suddenly and realised the sun had gone behind a cloud. 'I'm getting out, I'm freezing.'

'I'll wait and walk partway back with you . . . or maybe you'd like to come up to the house?' he suggested, to my surprise. 'You can see how the garden antiques centre is taking shape and I'll give you a cup of coffee to thaw you out. Come on,' he added as I hesitated, 'I've got that alarming woman Debo made me hire starting today, so it's the least you owe me!'

I wavered, but curiosity got the better of me. 'OK,' I said.

We emerged onto the drive by the higher path, after walking silently through the woods.

As we headed up to the house, Rufus said, out of the blue, 'Fliss rang last night. I call her Fliss, by the way, because she always hated being called Mum. She warned me not to let Debo take advantage of me, and then said I should take Dan Clew's advice, because he knew what was what. This, after meeting the man once!'

Remembering what Lulu had told me about Dan's boast of spending weekends with Fliss in London, I said cautiously, 'Judy said when they turned up at the Lodge they were as thick as thieves, so they seem to have hit it off straight away, don't they? What did you say?'

'I told her to butt out and mind her own business,' he said bluntly, his jaw setting. 'She's done enough damage already, making some other man pay for my upkeep all these years when she must have been sure I was Baz Salcombe's son all along. I mean, I always wondered where I got my colouring from, because I wasn't a bit like Hugo Carlyle.'

He sighed, rather wearily. 'I suppose I'd better get on to changing my name to Salcombe.'

'Oh, well, one thing at a time. And I can understand how hard it must have been, discovering the man you thought was your father, actually wasn't.'

'After he found out, he didn't even want to see me, especially when Fliss sold the conception-in-a-cupboard story to a Sunday rag. You can imagine how I felt about that.'

'Horrible,' I agreed, thinking that at least I knew who my father *was*, even if I'd never met him. By the time I was born, the result of a brief fling, he'd gone back to his wife in New Mexico.

'Hugo wanted to sue Fliss for the money he'd spent on my maintenance, school fees and all the rest of it, but apparently he's been advised it would be difficult. I wrote and offered to repay the money he'd put into helping me start up my first antiques yard, but he didn't answer. He's cut off all contact.'

I could see he was deeply hurt by all this and, despite my loathing of the woman who'd been instrumental in my mother's death, I was touched that he'd chosen to confide in me.

'Were he and Fliss together for long?'

'No, a brief affair, but she battened onto him like a leech once she knew I was on the way.'

'Perhaps she wasn't sure herself who your father was?'

'Maybe not, but once I'd seen pictures of Baz *and* my half-brother, I could see the resemblance in colouring myself.'

'Those light green eyes especially are unmistakable, although you don't really look like either of them in features. You don't seem very like Baz in *nature*, either,' I added.

'I didn't get much chance to know him. To be honest, by the time I met him I was too full of anger, some of it directed at him, to give him a chance. And when I found out I'd had a half-brother but he'd been killed in a car accident, I'm afraid some of that anger was directed at you, too, because I'd never get the chance to meet him. But . . . there's clearly more to that story than I realised.'

'There is, though the accident was ultimately still my fault. I was the one behind the wheel.'

'But there were mitigating circumstances – it's not like it sounded when I first heard about it.'

By now we'd turned a bend and there lay Sweetwell, sprawled in its usual rather ungainly fashion behind a stretch of ragged lawn.

'I'm surprised Olly hasn't kept the grass down with the sit-on mower that Baz bought him after Myra told him how long it took to cut.'

'Which sit-on mower?' Rufus demanded, puzzled. 'I asked Olly about the lawn and he said he cut it when he had time with an ancient petrol mower.'

I frowned. 'I wonder if it broke down? Olly was definitely riding round on it the last time I was home, though that's quite a while ago.'

'Strange. I'll look into it,' he said.

The drive divided into two and I saw that the way to the front of the house was now barred by a new five-barred gate, marked 'Private'. A large sign pointed customers the other way, towards the car parking area behind the separate court-yard, with its surrounding stables, coach houses and barns.

'It's a pretty perfect set-up for your line of work really, isn't it?' I said, thinking about it for the first time. 'You can keep the business and the house separate.' A thought struck me. 'If you change your name, aren't you going to have to change all your signs, too?'

'Yes, but I'll have to, because Baz stipulated in the will that I become a Salcombe within a year of inheriting.'

'In that case, you'd better stop being stubborn and get on with it. When are you opening for business?'

'Monday, if I can get everything straight. I usually shut Mondays, but this one's a bank holiday,' he said. 'Come on.'

He led the way across the courtyard to the office he'd made in the building at one end, which had started life as accommodation for grooms and then later the chauffeur, before finally falling into dusty disuse.

'This has taken shape already,' I said, perched on a nice old leather office chair.

'It was just a matter of bringing everything up from Devon and installing it here instead. There was already electricity, but next week I've got someone coming to update it and put new light fittings into all the outbuildings. Some of the sockets are so old, they're two-pin Bakelite ones.'

He looked around the room. 'I've got more room here than I had in Devon, and I could do with another filing cabinet.'

'I need one for my business and I saw just the thing in Ormskirk yesterday, only I'd gone there to buy a storage unit and lots of clothes racks, so there wasn't enough room left in Judy's car.'

'I have to go into Ormskirk tomorrow morning, so you could come with me,' he offered, to my surprise. 'I'll take the van, then there'll be no problem getting everything back.'

'Ormskirk will be very busy tomorrow, since it's market day *and* Easter weekend, so we'd have to leave very early,' I warned him.

'I was going to go in early anyway. I don't like crowds.'

'OK – and it's very kind of you.'

'Actually, it's just that I don't know my way around very well yet and need a free guide,' he said, with a brief glimpse of that rare, devastating smile.

Unleash your secret weapons! a robot voice droned in my

head, but I told it to shut up, because there was no way I'd ever get ideas about any son of Fliss Gambol!

After our coffee, he gave me a tour of the premises.

'It's good to see the place taking on a new life. I used to come up here with Cam and Lulu to play sometimes,' I told him. 'But not Harry and his friends, because they were two or three years older. Harry was at boarding school until he went to the local sixth-form college and he was like a slightly annoying older brother really . . . right up to that spring when I turned sixteen and suddenly got a crush on him.'

I don't know what made me blurt that out.

He gazed at me with those strangely opaque green eyes, so like Harry's. 'Did you? I can see that that would explain a lot about the accident.'

'Yes, though looking back I've no idea why I suddenly felt that way about him.'

'Well, we all have unsuitable crushes at that age,' he said. 'I was in love with my art teacher and she was not only old enough to be my mother, but married with two young children.'

The outbuildings were stacked with bits of old wrought-iron furniture, barrows, signs, pots, statues, railings, watering cans . . . you name it, if it was remotely connected with gardening, it was in there. There were racks of old gardening tools and ancient mowing machines, garden paving and Victorian twisted-top terracotta flower border edging.

Against one wall stood several old agricultural implements and the sort of scythe the Grim Reaper might pop in to purchase.

'I get a lot of things from France, especially garden furniture, and I go over there on a buying trip about every three months or so. But if I hear of anything interesting for sale anywhere in the UK, I go and have a look.'

'That sounds like fun,' I said enviously.

The biggest pieces were all in the centre of the courtyard and included a splendid fountain of a nymph with dolphins, which was probably white marble under the muck and green algae, and some curved stone seats.

'The small, valuable stuff is in the room next to the office,' Rufus said. 'Easier to keep an eye on what people are trying to walk out with.'

He stood and looked around his domain with some satisfaction, the breeze enthusiastically whipping his glossy dark chestnut hair about. 'I didn't have as much room in the last place and the yard was just rented, so this is so much better . . . *if* the customers will come all the way to Halfhidden, that is.'

'It's exciting starting something new, isn't it?' I said. 'The first consignments of clothes for my online business should arrive any minute.'

'What sort of business?' he asked.

'I've designed a range of clothes in Indian silk and cotton, retro-styled, based on ethnic clothes of the late sixties and seventies – you know, floaty fabrics, little bells, embroidery, quilted jackets?'

'No, not really,' he admitted.

'Well, anyway, it's retro with a twist. I've spent the last few years working for a charity that sets up small-scale women's co-operative textile workshops, so I had all the contacts in place. I brought back the first samples and I hope my website will go live soon.'

'Sounds like you've got it all clear in your head.'

'Yes, though I've got something to get out of the way first. I'm on a mission. There *were* two things, but I've already almost finished sorting out Debo and the kennels.'

'What kind of a—' he was beginning to ask, when he suddenly broke off and a faint look of horror crossed his face. The tall and sturdy figure of Foxy Lane slowly cycled into view on a too-small pink bicycle, her bright copper hair standing up like the crest on a helmet. Seeing us, she took one hand off the handlebars to wave, wobbled a bit, and then came on.

'I'll just set her onto cleaning up that marble fountain and then I'm going to hide in the office,' he said. 'She's scary.'

'Wuss,' I said, then called, 'Hi Foxy! I'm just off back to the Lodge – have fun!'

I totally finished the kennel paperwork when I got home, so that everything could tick over quite nicely from now on with minimal effort, provided we kept Debo on a tight rein. Or at any rate, a tight lead.

I showed her and Judy the two in-trays, one for kennel stuff and the other for any domestic bills, and they promised to use them.

Then I told them that Rufus had agreed to a new smaller kennel block, the fence and the roses, though I couldn't remember if he'd actually come out and said so. On the other hand, he hadn't said he *disagreed* . . .

'There, I told you he'd turn out to be a nice man, just like Baz. It's unfortunate his mother is Fliss, but I suppose he can't help that and we'll have to try not to hold it against him,' Debo said.

'It was just a brief encounter in a broom cupboard, and Baz was probably drunk,' Judy suggested. 'Not Rufus's fault.'

'No, and his father, or the man he *thought* was his father, has totally rejected him since he found out he wasn't his son. He even wanted to sue Fliss to get the maintenance back.'

This cheered Debo up no end, though she was disappointed that he'd changed his mind.

Chapter 15: Mission Statement

'S'Izzy,' Simon slurred, with a lopsided grin.

I stared at him in amazement. 'Are you . . . drunk, Simon?'

'Harry thought it would be funny to spike his juice with a bit of vodka – big mistake,' Cara said tartly from the back seat.

'Well, I wasn't to know it would affect him like this, was I?' Harry protested indignantly.

I woke in the middle of the night, Harry's voice echoing in my head, and it was quite a while before I fell asleep again. But this time I dreamed I was swimming up and down the pool at the Lady Spring with a naked Roman soldier bearing a striking resemblance to Rufus Carlyle, and when I woke the second time I was feeling strangely refreshed.

Babybelle now expected to come into the Lodge for break-fast every day after her walk, after which she clearly felt that her place was by my side . . . or under my feet. But today Judy distracted her with a bit of bacon while I made my escape to meet Rufus at the gates. I felt slightly shy, given the way last night's dream had panned out . . .

His Transit van had seen better days, most of them quite

a long time ago. It was also emblazoned up the side with 'Rufus Carlyle Garden Antiques', so that would be another thing he'd have to change.

I said so when I got in.

'I know and it's going to be really weird getting used to being Rufus Salcombe, though at least I have some right to the name. I'm seeing the solicitor about changing it by deed poll next week and then I'll work my way through altering the website, the cards, the van, the signs . . .'

'That's going to cost quite a bit,' I commented, 'and everything connected with running one's own business seems time-consuming, though at least before I came home I'd already sourced most of the labels, packaging and business cards for Izzy Dane Designs and started creating a website.'

'Izzy Dane Designs? Is that what it's called?'

'Yes, though at first I kept coming up with brilliant ideas for names that reflected what it's all about, like Eastern Fusion or East Meets West, only of course when I checked online, all the good ones were already being used.'

'There wasn't another Rufus Carlyle Garden Antiques online and I don't suppose there's a Rufus Salcombe running one, either.'

'I could have used my father's name,' I said, 'but although it sounds foreign, it's the wrong *kind* of foreign for what I'm making, and anyway, I don't see myself as a Rodriguez.'

'That sounds Spanish? You've never mentioned your father, except that he left you some money.'

'That's because I never met him, so there's not a lot to say. He was a sculptor, lived in New Mexico and was married, but he had a brief fling with my mother when he was over here. He knew about me, but he didn't send any maintenance or anything, so it was a surprise when he left me some money.'

'At least you're sure he *was* your father,' Rufus observed, trundling the van sedately through the sleepy village of Sticklepond, where the only sign of life was an elderly lady holystoning the doorstep of the Falling Star pub, opposite the Witchcraft Museum.

'He didn't leave me as much as Baz left you, only a small nest egg. I've blown some of it on my first clothes collection, with a little kept back for unseen contingencies, and the rest has gone to settle Debo's outstanding bills.'

'Then I think you've just thrown good money away.'

'No I haven't!' I said indignantly. 'It's only Debo's soft heart where animals are concerned that got her into debt, but with Sandy and Judy primed to keep her on the straight and narrow, and me to keep a tight rein on the bookkeeping, she'll be fine now. She's great at getting donations from her celeb friends, too.'

'I can imagine,' he said slightly drily. 'So . . . are the clothes you're going to sell the kind of thing you usually wear?'

Today I had on a jade-green and silver floaty tunic top and a matching quilted jacket, worn over jeans.

'Yes. I think they're going to appeal to all ages, because they'll be new to the younger buyers and familiar to older ones. And I'm going to stock big sizes too, because they look great on curvy women.'

'I think it sounds like a winner and I do like the clothes you wear,' he said unexpectedly. 'That green top and jacket make you look more like an exotic leprechaun than a pixie, today.'

'I think you're very rude,' I told him severely, but smiling.

*   *   *

179

After we'd bought our filing cabinets and other odds and ends and loaded everything into the van, we walked into the centre of Ormskirk and had coffee at the Blue Dog café, which Judy had recommended.

The entrance was next to a new shop called The Happy Macaroon and we stopped to admire the mouth-watering display in the window.

As well as the trays of multi-hued macaroons, there were realistic models of a traditional tiered wedding cake and a French croquembouche one, an airy pyramid of choux buns covered in sugar strands. At one side was a more prosaic tray of gingerbread pigs with iced curly tails and raisin eyes, which reminded me of the gingerbread dogs that Judy baked for me when I was little.

In the café, I insisted on buying the coffee and toasted teacakes, since Rufus had driven me in and then hefted the filing cabinets about, and we found a quiet corner.

'What did you mean yesterday when you said you were on a mission and would have to complete it before you could really get on with your new business?' he asked, looking up from the task of spreading copious amounts of strawberry jam onto half his teacake.

'Oh, that . . .' I said. 'It's just that I intend discovering as much as I can about the accident when Harry was killed. I've no recollection of that night beyond setting off for home from the pub, and after I got out of hospital Debo sent me to London to convalesce with Daisy Silver, one of her oldest friends. By the time I got back, everyone had clammed up about it. Now I'm going to talk to all those involved.'

'Is it a good idea to stir it all up again, after all this time?'

'It is for me, because I feel I need some kind of closure, and I've already made a start, though of course some people are more reluctant to talk about it than others.'

'I can imagine.'

'The only person I've ever really discussed it with in depth is Daisy Silver – she's a child psychiatrist by profession so very easy to talk to – and I still do ring her when something is bothering me . . . like the way my dreams have been turning very strange lately.'

'Dreams about the accident?' he asked gently.

'Yes. I mean, I've always had a recurring one about meeting Harry and his friends in the car park that night, but lately it's been more frequent and . . . well, *detailed*. More like a clear memory than a dream.'

Then I found myself pouring out to him how I'd recently been a passenger during another car accident, which seemed to have sparked off a flashback, as well as turning my dreams from grainy black-and-white to vivid Technicolor.

'The trouble is, I don't know if it's actual memories of that night surfacing, or just my subconscious adding details.'

'That would be unsettling,' he agreed. 'And you just can't tell with dreams. They can seem real and then suddenly go off at a tangent.'

'That's more or less what Daisy Silver said. But the thing that really threw me was the brief flashback I had during the second accident – because in that one, I wasn't in the driver's seat of the Range Rover, I was in the back.'

'So then you wondered if you really had been driving that night?' he said astutely.

'Exactly! But then Daisy said it might just be a flashback to another occasion when I *had* been in the back of that car with Harry and his friends, or even just my subconscious showing me what I *wanted* to have happened.'

'I understand now why you're feeling confused and want to get it all clear in your head,' Rufus said. 'But are you likely to find out any more than you already know?'

'I don't know, but I'm going to give it my best shot. I'm working my way towards the central witnesses, and I've already talked to Lulu and Cam, who were working in the pub with me that evening, and to Debo and Judy about what they saw when they arrived at the scene of the accident. Dan Clew got there first, of course, but he wouldn't tell me any more than had come out at the inquest, which was that he'd found me in the front of the car. When Tom Tamblyn confirmed that he'd seen Dan lifting me out, I knew it must be true, no matter how much I'd love to believe otherwise.'

'It's better to be certain, though, isn't it? And now I know you a bit better, I'm sure Harry must have talked you into driving, so everyone is right and it wasn't your fault.'

'I still can't image how I agreed to do it, but Cara Ferris is really the only person who can tell me – if she will. I've left a couple of messages on her answering service and she hasn't got back to me. I need to see if Simon Clew remembers anything too, though Dan warned me off speaking to him. But anyway, they're the two final and most important witnesses.'

'You're clearly a woman of great determination,' he said, a slight smile in his green eyes. 'Myra told me yesterday that you were engaged to a doctor you'd met abroad?'

He glanced at my left hand, which was entirely bare of an engagement ring. I hadn't taken it off; Kieran had simply never got round to buying me one.

'I was, but now I'm not, because things didn't work out. I feel that I'm meant to live and work in Halfhidden, and Kieran, my ex-fiancé, was determined to settle in Oxford near his ghastly parents.'

'Ghastly parents sound like a deal-breaker to me,' he agreed. 'Though they can't be as bad as Fliss. I think I only survived my childhood because my father paid for boarding school the second I was old enough.'

'How old?'

'Eight.'

'Poor little boy!' I said, my heart wrung at the thought of him setting off to live away from home at such a young age.

'Actually, I preferred it to being dumped by Fliss with whichever of her friends would have me, while she went off with the latest man, or into rehab or wherever. I spent very little time with her.'

'Are you fond of her?' I asked curiously.

He shrugged. 'A couple of times when I was home in the holidays and she'd just got out of rehab, she was entirely different and it would be fun . . . and then it would all spiral out of control and she'd lose interest in me again because of the drink and drugs.'

'Yes – and she drew my mother into that circle,' I said bitterly, even though that was hardly Rufus's fault. In fact, I thought he'd turned out surprisingly well, considering.

'Did you see much of your father – or the man you thought was your father?' I asked him.

'Very little. He married someone much younger a few years later and had a family. His wife was jealous of me and resented his having to support me. I haven't even met any of his other children.'

'Families can be so difficult,' I said sympathetically.

'So, to answer your original question – yes, I suppose I have some feelings for her but, as they say, it's complicated. And even more complicated since I learned that Baz was my father.'

He was looking withdrawn and brooding again, and it suddenly occurred to me that our early years had been equally traumatic, though in very different ways: he had never been allowed a proper childhood, while mine came to an abrupt end on the night of Harry's death. We were also linked through our mothers' friendship – if you could call something that proved so toxic by that name – as well as through Baz, which perhaps was why we seemed to understand each other surprisingly well.

I looked at Rufus, sitting there with his long legs stretched out, coffee cup in hand, and for the first time really clocked the whole stunning effect of those strangely merman sea-washed light green eyes, the silky dark chestnut hair falling over his forehead, the fine Roman nose and the cleft in his chin that suddenly made me want to reach out and run my finger over it . . .

He looked up and smiled as if he had caught my thought in mid-flight and I felt myself colour slightly.

'I'm sorry I was rude to you when we first met,' he said. 'I was still angry with everyone, but it was unreasonable to take it out on you, especially when I didn't know all the facts.'

'And I'm sorry if I was horrible to you about your mother. You can't help who she is, or what she's like,' I said.

'Friends?' he suggested tentatively.

'Friends,' I agreed. 'And I want you to meet Cameron and Lulu properly, too, because they're my oldest friends.'

'Well, I *was* thinking of going down to the pub tonight, to see Howling Hetty's famous skull, so Lulu might be around then.'

'We all will, because Cam's grandfather, Jonas, is going to tell the Haunted Weekenders all sorts of ghastly ghost stories this evening and we fancied listening in.'

'I'll probably see you down there, then.'

'Or we might meet up and walk down together,' I suggested as I fished my phone out of my pocket and checked to see if I'd missed any messages from Judy, asking me to bring anything back with me.

My phone had managed to switch itself to sulky silence, which it did sometimes, and I could see I'd missed loads of calls and messages. But I didn't even have a chance to check who they were from before it rang again.

'Izzy?' demanded a familiar voice, in a newly recognisable terse manner.

'Kieran?' I said, astonished. 'Have you been trying to get me?'

'Of course I have – haven't you noticed? I've even rung the Lodge, but there was no answer.'

'They were probably out with the dogs and I'm in Ormskirk, shopping.'

'Well, I drove all the way up here last night specially to see you – and I need to go back this afternoon.'

'You're *here*? Why on earth didn't you let me know you were coming?' I exclaimed, surprised. 'And where did you stay last night?'

'A hotel down the hill from the village, with some ridiculous name.'

'The Screaming Skull?'

'That's the one. How long will it take you to get here?'

'I – well, I suppose three-quarters of an hour or so . . .' I began, reluctantly. 'But—'

'Right. The restaurant looks decent, so I'll book lunch for twelve.'

'But why have you—' I began, only to find he'd cut the connection. It was a habit I was by now very tired of.

'That was my ex-fiancé,' I told Rufus. 'He's driven all the way up from Oxford to see me, without bothering to let me know, and he's going back this afternoon.'

'I gather he's at the pub.'

'Yes, and he's expecting me there for lunch at twelve.'

Rufus looked at his watch. 'Come on then, I can drop you off on the way back and I'll leave your filing cabinets at the Lodge afterwards.'

'That's kind of you,' I said. 'I don't know what he wants . . .'

'Presumably he wants you back.'

'He's going to be out of luck, then,' I said firmly. I suddenly realised how much I'd enjoyed the morning with Rufus and how little I wanted to see Kieran again, let alone have lunch with him.

When Rufus pulled up in the pub car park, we could see Kieran standing outside with his arms folded, as if I was a stay-out-all-night teenager. Then he looked at his watch and frowned.

Clearly he wasn't expecting me to arrive in a beaten-up old Transit van, because he didn't spot me until I got out.

I noticed he gave Rufus a hard stare as he drove off and his first words to me were not any kind of endearment but a snapped, 'Who *was* that man?'

'A neighbour,' I said, equally snappily, and he seemed to pull himself together and remember what he was there for. He kissed me – on my cheek, since I turned my head at the last moment – and said how nice I looked and how much he'd missed me.

'I wish you'd let me know you were coming, Kieran.'

'It was an impulse! I knew you didn't mean what you said and it would be easier to sort things out face to face.'

I was just about to enlighten him on the fact that I had meant every word, when he said we'd better go straight in to lunch.

On the way, we bumped into Lulu and I introduced him.

'Kieran? And I had no idea who you were!' she said, amazed, but he barely said hello before carrying on towards the restaurant. I made a face at her behind his back and she grinned.

The waitress and the only other female diner in the room clearly thought Kieran looked very toothsome – which I suppose he did, though I preferred him in dishevelled linen rather than his current smart-casual attire, new haircut and critical expression – yes, he was definitely turning into his father!

If I had any lingering fondness for him, it was the kind of feeling you get when looking at snaps of past happy times.

Over lunch, it transpired that he'd expected that at the sight of him I'd have fallen into his arms with expressions of rapture and abject apologies for the way I'd behaved. Also with promises to move right down to Oxford, although, he magnanimously conceded, I could have a quiet little wedding in my one-horse village first.

'If that's what you really want. I know your hippy-dippy upbringing means you have all kinds of strange ideas.'

'Too kind,' I said, tucking into my seafood ravioli. Lulu's brother, Bruce, really was an inspired chef!

I finished off every delicious morsel of that before breaking it to Kieran that, as I'd already told him, it really was all over. I wasn't going to go back to him.

'I really don't honestly think we would be happy, Kieran, but I do hope we can stay friends.'

This sop seemed to make him so angry that I predicted a serious case of indigestion before he was even halfway home.

'I see I've wasted my time – and I suspect I know why. It's that man who drove you here, isn't it?' he accused me.

I felt myself flush, and said angrily, 'Of course not, don't be silly! I've only been home for five minutes, so what sort of quick worker do you think I am?'

But I could see he'd already made his mind up, and by now I'd had enough both of the excellent lunch and the far-from-excellent conversation, so I grabbed my handbag and got up to go.

'Thank you for lunch, but I must get home now.'

'I'll drive you there.'

'No need – you get off on your journey.'

But he insisted on at least seeing me out and we were just walking across the car park towards the start of the path, where I hoped to shake him off, when there was a clip-clop of hoofs on the road and none other than Cara Ferris – now Lady Cripchet – came into view.

It was too good an opportunity to lose, so on impulse I called, 'Cara, wait!'

She turned her head and scowled blackly at me . . . and then her gaze slid past and fell on Kieran. She did a classic double-take, her eyes widening, then yanked on the reins. Her mount, a sturdy dapple grey, came to a halt, snorting.

'Cara, could I have a word . . .?' I began, but she ignored me, still staring at Kieran as if she couldn't believe her eyes.

He seemed equally stunned. 'Cara, is that you? Long time, no see!'

Cara slid off her mount and he kissed her with more enthusiasm than he'd shown to me.

'You know each other?' I said, stating the obvious.

'Yes, from Oxford,' Kieran said, and he didn't have to explain how well they'd once known each other because it was evident. 'We lost touch.'

'We did, but it's great to see you again,' Cara agreed. 'What on earth are you doing here?'

They seemed to have forgotten I was there again, but I reminded them. 'I've been trying to get in touch with you, Cara,' I said. 'Could we—'

'You know I don't want to talk to you,' she snapped. 'I don't even know what you're doing here, but I wish you'd go away!'

'We used to be engaged,' Kieran explained. 'Look, Izzy, I know you want to get off. Don't let me keep you.'

'No, and *I* certainly don't want to speak to you ever again,' Cara said emphatically, then added rudely, 'Clear off!'

There didn't seem any point in hanging about after that, so I left them to it, noting that Kieran was not now showing any sign of urgency to get back to Oxford.

I looked round before the turn of the path. The dapple grey was hitched to the pergola by the beer garden and Kieran and Cara were heading into the pub. She was almost as tall as he was, so their heads were very close together . . .

It looked as if I'd been dropped like a hot potato. So much for his protestations that he still loved me!

I turned and started to climb the steep path towards the Lady Spring, where I stopped to drink a cup of water: my soul was in urgent need of a slight purge.

Chapter 16: Howling Hetty

When I got home, Judy said that Rufus had not only dropped off my new filing cabinets, but insisted on carrying them through to my studio. Then he'd told Debo and Judy where I was, which was something *I'd* been too distracted to think of.

After that, they invited him to stay and eat my portion of vichyssoise soup and hasty pudding, which Judy had made for lunch.

'And never did I ever think I'd invite a child of Fliss Gambol's to share a meal under my roof,' Debo said. 'But actually, he was quite nice, so I kept forgetting.'

'So did I, while we were chatting over coffee in the Blue Dog. I think he's had a tough time the last few months and it's made him angry with everyone and everything, but underneath, he's OK.'

'And how was Kieran?' asked Judy.

'Awful! I don't understand how he could have so quickly turned into such a clone of his father, but I think I had a lucky escape.'

I told them how he'd obviously thought that the mere sight of him would send me contritely rushing into his arms and agreeing to anything he wanted. 'But then later he completely lost interest in me when he spotted Cara Ferris! It seems she was an old flame that never quite got extinguished and they were all over each other like treacle.'

'That was a bit sudden,' Judy commented.

'It was, but then so was the way I fell right out of love with him,' I said fairly – and then, right on cue, the man himself rang my mobile.

'Kieran?' I said, surprised.

'Yes, it's me,' he said tersely, 'and Cara's just told me what *really* happened on the night of that accident you were involved in as a teenager.'

Of course she'd told him that I'd *insisted* on driving, which made it all my fault that Harry was killed and her modelling career prospects ended.

'I'm sure that's not how it happened,' I protested, but my words fell on deaf ears, because he was already saying what a sweet, sensitive little soul she was and ordering me to stop harassing her.

'Oh, shove off, you credulous pillock!' I snapped, losing patience, and clicked off the connection.

'Hear, hear!' Debo said. 'I take it that was the final disengagement?'

'Permanently and irrevocably detached,' I confirmed.

'I'll break out a bottle of elderflower champagne then, shall I, and we'll drink to that?' Judy suggested.

Lulu rang later and apologised for not warning me that Kieran was there and not twigging who he was.

'Mum had taken the booking for the room, but then he didn't arrive, and they thought he was a no-show. But apparently he turned up after I'd gone back to the caravan, so late that Bruce was locking the place up for the night.'

'He should have warned me he was coming up – just as he should have let you know if he was going to arrive in the middle of the night. That was *so* inconsiderate.'

Mind you, in retrospect there had been so many occasions when he'd said he would meet me somewhere, or call me, and then hadn't. At the time, seen through the rose-tinted spectacles of love, this had seemed an endearing, if slightly irritating, foible.

'Two couples arrived earlier today for a Haunted Weekend, but the ones who came yesterday are Americans from Minnesota, and really fun,' Lulu said. 'They've gone off to see Rufford Hall and then Winter's End, because I told them it was haunted by a seventeenth-century ghost called Alys.'

'Good thinking. You might find a few more local ghostly goings-on for visitors' days out, too.'

'Yes, that's what I thought, so I'll have to do a bit of research. I put the American couple in the Blue Room and they said they'd hardly slept a wink last night, because of the manifestations, so they were delighted. They were convinced it was Howling Hetty.'

'But she doesn't appear anywhere in the building, does she?'

'No, not even in the public bar where her skull is.'

'Well, it's not my idea of fun, but I'm glad they're enjoying themselves.'

'I can understand why you fell for Kieran, now I've seen him,' Lulu said, reverting to the original topic. 'He's very attractive to look at, even if his manners aren't so pretty. He wasn't exactly friendly when you introduced us, was he?'

'No, in fact, he was quite abrupt and rude. You know, he seemed a totally different person until recently, so kind-hearted, generous and easy-going. Maybe he's a human chameleon?'

Lulu sang a snatch of 'Karma Chameleon' and then giggled. 'He was more like a human boa constrictor at breakfast! I think he ate enough to keep him going for at least three months. When he ordered extra sausages, he asked me if they were free range and I told him they were so free range they'd been running round the farm that very morning, humming the theme tune to "Born Free".'

'Did he give you his "you're barking mad" look?'

'Something like that,' she admitted.

'I'd talked about you often and said your family had the local pub, so he must have known who you were even before I introduced you . . . unless it didn't register. I've come to suspect he never listened to a single word I ever said.'

'I peeped in while you were having lunch and he didn't look very happy, though *you* seemed to be enjoying the food.'

'I certainly was. That brother of yours is such an inspired cook that even Kieran ranting at me couldn't spoil it! But Kieran was too miffed that I hadn't fallen straight into his arms to appreciate it and then I put the lid on things by telling him we were totally finished. But I could have saved my breath, because as soon as he clapped eyes on an old flame outside, he entirely forgot my existence. And you'll never guess who the she was!'

'I don't have to, because I saw him come back into the hotel with Cara Ferris, of all people. Then they sat in the bar for ages canoodling, until finally I had to ask him to go and remove his luggage from his room so it could be cleaned for the next guests.'

'I said he was inconsiderate.'

'*And* rude, because he just tried to wave me away as if I was an irritating insect and said he'd do it later.'

'I expect you sorted him out?'

'Oh, yes, I told him if his bags were still there in fifteen minutes, I'd have to charge him for another night's accommodation. And then someone shouted that there was a horse wandering round the beer garden, stealing sandwiches.'

'I expect *that* broke up the necking party?'

'It certainly did. Cara leaped up and dashed out, and he followed her. Then she must have ridden off, because he came back alone, paid his bill and left.'

'I expect that's the last we'll ever see of him,' I said, feeling quite happy about it. 'He had the gall to ring me up later and order me not to harass poor, sensitive little Cara about the accident.'

'Sensitive as old boots,' Lulu said, then added, curiously, 'How was your trip with Rufus?'

'Surprisingly fun. For a start, we've both had traumatic events in our pasts that are still impacting on our lives, so we have that in common. Fliss sounded like the mother from hell even before she went public about who fathered him.'

'Perhaps he'll turn out to be more reasonable about the kennels and everything than you thought, then.'

'Possibly, though he's no pushover. But you'll meet him properly tonight because I've invited him to Jonas's ghost story session. He wanted to see Howling Hetty's skull anyway. Is that OK?'

'Of course. Cam says he's recorded some sound effects and he's bringing Jonas down early so he can set things up.'

'Great. I think I'm walking down with Rufus – he said he'd give me a ring later.'

'Fast mover,' Lulu commented admiringly.

'Nothing like that,' I protested. 'I barely know the man. In fact, yesterday I was convinced I didn't like him in the least.'

'I know, I'm just teasing,' she said. 'Well, I'd better get back to it. See you later.'

After the ups and downs of the day, I found it hard to settle doing anything constructive, so I fetched Babybelle from her kennel and took her down to the lower pool, where she could bathe and I could sit on a mossy rock and contemplate life, the universe and everything.

It was peaceful, but today there were no guardian angel voices assuring me I was heading in the right direction. On the other hand, there was none telling me I was going wrong, either.

When I got home, Judy was spinning some of Belle's washed and carded dog hair. She said she would knit me a jerkin, but I wasn't entirely sure I wanted to look like Babybelle's skinny sister.

I met Rufus that evening just where the Sweetwell path joined with the narrower one leading down from the Lodge, and as we walked to the pub he asked me diffidently if my meeting with Kieran had been good.

I replied that it had been good in the sense that he'd accepted we were no longer an item. Then I told him about

Cara turning up and how they seemed more than pleased to see each other.

'Cara Ferris is the main witness to the accident, the girl in the back of the car, and I need to talk to her. But she hasn't answered my phone messages and today she told me to clear off.'

'Charming!' he said. 'I remember you telling me about her and that she's married to the owner of that big estate on the other side of the hill.'

'Grimside. Yes, she's Lady Cripchet now. He's a horrible little man more than twice her age and I've heard they don't get on. But she was certainly getting on with Kieran when I left. The minute she appeared, he dropped me like a hot potato.'

'Do you mind?'

'Not in the least. My pride might be slightly dented, but that's about it.'

It was still early when we got to the Screaming Skull, so thankfully there was no Dan infesting the public bar. For all I knew he could be shacked up in London for the weekend with the unsuspecting Rufus's mother.

Howling Hetty's skull, snugly tucked away in its backlit alcove, was today wearing a straw Easter bonnet decked with flowers, foliage, tiny painted eggs and fluffy yellow chicks. I detected Lulu's hand in the work.

Rufus silently contemplated the skull for some minutes. It was stained a dark reddish colour and was very shiny, probably from being first buried and then washed downstream.

'It's not a cheerful sight for a pub, apart from the Easter bonnet, is it?' he said eventually.

'Perhaps not, but it has to stay exactly where it is, because they tried moving it a couple of centuries ago and there were *horrible* consequences.'

'That's quite a heavy jawline,' he observed critically. 'She can't have been any beauty.'

'You know, I've often thought that myself! Come on – let's go through to the hotel bar. Cam's car was outside, so he and Jonas must already be here.'

I checked that Lulu didn't need us to help, but she and Cameron seemed to have everything well in hand. I introduced Rufus to Cam and Jonas, and then we had a drink in the bar until Lulu stuck her head through the doorway and announced, thrillingly, that anyone who would like to have their veins turned to ice and their marrow curdled should go through into the residents' lounge.

Clearly she'd missed her vocation and should have been writing horror novels, but I'd heard many of Jonas's stories before so I knew the evening was likely to be scary.

'That went well,' Lulu said happily, once the lights had been switched back on and the petrified punters had all exited back to the bar for stiff drinks. 'Jonas, you were brilliant and scared them rigid! If they don't see any real ghosts tonight, at least they'll all *think* they have.'

'I enjoyed it,' Jonas said. 'And I'll be happy to do it all over again whenever you like, on the same terms.'

When I'd introduced Rufus to Jonas and Cam, they'd both eyed him as if he might suddenly go all lord-of-the-manor on them. But they'd soon got over that and now he was helping Cam pack up the sound equipment he'd hidden in the lounge.

'Great sound effects,' Rufus said. 'I knew it must be your

doing, but the hair on the back of my neck stood up anyway, especially that bit where there was an icy wind blowing and a hand tapping at the window.'

'And mine,' I agreed.

'I've recorded the whole session tonight, too,' Cameron said, 'because I think Granddad ought to make a proper book out of his ghost stories. I know he's got lots more to tell.'

'I have that,' Jonas agreed. He'd accepted a whisky from Rufus, on top of all the Mossbrown Ale he'd already consumed, so he was now looking very merry.

I was sure he had lots more stories, too, though one of tonight's had borne a suspiciously strong resemblance to Cathy's haunting of Heathcliff in an old film of *Wuthering Heights* I'd seen.

'Come on, Granddad, finish your drink and I'll take you home,' Cam urged him. 'I promised Mum I'd have you back by half-past ten and she won't go to bed until you're in.'

'Lot of fuss,' Jonas said, but he must have been getting tired because he drained the last drops of whisky and left without further protest.

We helped Lulu finish tidying up the lounge and then, when she went off to lay the tables for breakfast, Rufus said he'd see me home.

We went out through the snug and the public bar, the quickest way to get to the path, though when I saw that Dan was now propping up the bar with his cronies, I wished we'd gone all the way round instead.

Catching sight of us, he said something in a low voice that made his friends snigger. I was positive I'd caught the name 'Fliss', though I hoped Rufus hadn't.

But whether he had or not, he stopped dead and gave them a look that wiped the smiles from their faces and had them turning away, pretending there was something rivetingly interesting behind the bar (other than Hetty's skull, which they were so well used to that I don't suppose it even registered any more).

Rufus turned and strode out, and I followed him into the fresh, cleansing night air. Under the lights strung along the path, he looked tight-lipped.

'Judy says Dan is all mouth and trousers,' I said, offering vague comfort for the curiously nasty little scene. 'He's certainly stupid if he thinks he can get away with making sneering remarks to his own employer.'

'We had a bit of a set-to earlier when I got back from Ormskirk and found him hanging round the courtyard – or trying to, because Foxy was sending him off with a flea in his ear.'

'I told you he's not liked locally, so she wouldn't want him nosing about,' I said.

'Well, seeing he was there, I took the opportunity to tell him in no uncertain terms that if he wanted to keep his job, then he needed to put his back into his work,' he said. 'He wasn't too happy about that. In fact, he insinuated that he'd got off with my mother when she came down and that meant he had a free pass to do what he liked.'

'Judy did say they seemed thick as thieves that time they came down to the Lodge together,' I said cautiously.

'He implied it was more than that and when he'd told her how I was treating him, she'd sort me out. I can't think why he would imagine telling me he'd got friendly with my mother would give him a get-out-of-jail-free card, but I only hope phone numbers are *all* they've exchanged,' he added darkly.

'I know Dan puts it about, but she wouldn't go for a man like him . . . would she? He's horrible.'

'She very well could,' he said, then caught sight of my face as we passed the last of the garden lights and stopped dead, staring down at me. 'You know something, don't you? Out with it!'

Seeing nothing else for it, I confessed. 'Lulu said one of the barmaids overheard Dan bragging that he'd been to stay for weekends with your mother in London. But it might not be true.'

'I suspected as much – and trust Fliss to muddy the waters! But I made it clear she had no influence over me, so he'd better buckle down and get the gardens and grounds back into some kind of order. I'm not standing for slacking – *or* impertinence.'

He both looked and sounded rather scary and I was glad it wasn't me his anger was directed at.

I followed Rufus through the beer garden towards the car park, where the path up to the Lady Spring started and, as always, it brought back painful memories.

'This is the way I came on the night of the accident,' I told him. 'I usually walked home with Cameron, but I'd left early because my dog was elderly and not very well.'

'Wasn't it too dark to walk up the path alone?' he asked.

'No, it was still just about light enough to see where I was going and it's a shortcut.'

'I'm still surprised you dared, now I know about Howling Hetty.'

'But she only haunts the drive – in that dip round the first bend, where the accident happened, actually.'

'Let's hope she stays there, then. After tonight, I think I need someone to hold my hand in the dark *anywhere* on the estate.'

'I feel a bit like that myself, because Jonas gave me goose-bumps,' I confessed.

'Come on then,' he said gravely, holding out his hand, and when I put mine into it he enfolded it in a warm, strong grip.

'There are no ghosts here, really, or only the ghosts of memories,' I said. 'Baz's old red Range Rover was parked right over there. He kept it mostly for Harry to drive, but he'd promised him if he wasn't caught for speeding or drink-driving again before his nineteenth birthday, he was going to get a sports car.'

'So, you were passing and they were already there?'

'Yes – and that scene's haunted my dreams ever since. Cara Ferris was sitting in the back – she's the daughter of the local husband-and-wife vet team, who have a clinic in the village, did I say? Simon Clew was sitting sideways in the driver's seat with his legs out of the car and his head down, as if he might be sick. Of course I didn't know then that Harry had spiked his drink.'

'Some people's bodies just can't cope with alcohol,' Rufus said. 'It's like poison to them.'

'Harry was standing by the car. When he spotted me, he seemed really pleased to see me, but he had an ulterior motive.'

'He wanted you to drive them back to Sweetwell.'

I nodded. 'Later, they said it was in case the police were waiting round the corner, which they used to do quite a bit then. But I've no idea how he persuaded me, because my memories, like the dreams, always end with him standing by the car, smiling and asking me to the party.' I shivered.

'Come on,' Rufus said, setting off up the path and pulling me with him. 'Let's go home.'

'Actually, I know Harry's perfectly happy now, because I saw him in Heaven while I was in the coma,' I found myself suddenly confiding in him.

'Really?' He seemed so genuinely interested that I told him about the near-death experience and being pulled down a tunnel towards a bright light.

'It was an Alice-falling-down-the-rabbit-hole feeling, because I was curious, but not afraid,' I said. 'Then all at once I was standing near a wonderful garden full of flowers in colours I couldn't even put a name to. The sky was brilliant azure blue and the air filled with soft, strange music . . . There were people in the garden and I really wanted to join them, but I couldn't,' I added regretfully.

'Why not?'

'As I moved towards the gate in the wall, my mother appeared in front of it and stopped me. Harry was standing right behind her, with my old dog, Patch, frolicking round his feet as if he was a puppy again – and that's when I realised I was in Heaven . . . or almost in Heaven. I didn't quite make it. My mother said it wasn't my time and I needed to go back, because I had important work to do.'

'And that's when you regained consciousness?' he asked.

'I was pulled back down the tunnel and into my body, even though I didn't want to go. The next thing I knew, Debo was shaking my shoulder and telling me to wake up.

Debo and Judy didn't really believe me when I said I'd been to Heaven. They thought it was the drugs and the blow to my head.'

'*I* believe you,' he said, to my surprise. 'One of my friends came off his motorbike and had a similar experience, only in his case his granny ordered him to go right back and sell his bike, then give the money to his auntie Dora, who needed it. So he did.'

'And did she need it?'

'Yes, her cat had been run over and had to have an expensive operation, so she'd got herself into debt with a loan company.'

'I was sent back to help other women improve their lives through my skills with textiles,' I said. 'I only went wrong when I met Kieran.'

'So far, my whole life seems to have been wrong,' Rufus said morosely.

'Perhaps, but now I'm sure it's turned right and you're *meant* to be here in Halfhidden, just as I am.'

Spring Cottage was dark and quiet, so Tom must have gone to bed. We passed Cam walking down the path after dropping his grandfather off at the shop and chatted for a moment. Although so dissimilar, Rufus and Cam had taken to each other and Cam invited him to go to look at his gallery next day. I said I might pop in to see the new folding doors, too.

It was only after we'd wished each other good night and parted company that I realised I was still holding hands with Rufus, and I wondered if Cam had drawn the wrong conclusion. But it seemed unfriendly to disengage my hand at that point, especially since Rufus insisted on taking me all the way to the Lodge, even though I told him I'd walked the path alone a million times.

'You'll have to brave Howling Hetty on the drive,' I pointed out and shivered again.

'Didn't you say she only haunted that hollow round the first bend, where the accident was?'

'Allegedly.'

'I'll go back down the path and cut round to the other side, if it will make you feel happier.'

'I wouldn't say happier, but certainly relieved.'

On impulse I invited him into the Lodge for coffee, warning him to be quiet since Debo and Judy would be fast asleep. I was surprised to find Babybelle in the kitchen, curled up with Vic and Ginger. There was a note on the table, explaining that some of the dogs had got out earlier, but Debo and Judy had heard them barking and quickly rounded them up. Only Babybelle had refused to go back, so they left her downstairs.

'The sooner you get some decent kennels and perimeter fencing, the better,' Rufus said, having read this missive over my shoulder.

'They don't all get out, and this is the first time any have escaped for ages,' I protested, though if you counted Babybelle, I suppose that wasn't strictly true.

Babybelle had marked our entrance into the kitchen by opening her eyes and thumping her tail on the hearth rug. But on hearing the sound of a biscuit tin being opened, she deigned to get up and lumbered over hopefully, followed by the other two dogs.

Rufus didn't stay long. I think he could see that I'd had such a drawn-out and emotionally draining day that I was exhausted.

As soon as he left, I went to bed, and although after Jonas's stories I was nervous about turning off the light, when I did, I remembered the comforting strength of Rufus's hand enclosing mine and instantly plummeted deep into sleep.

Chapter 17: Dog Daze

'Come on, Simon – you get in the back with Cara, so Izzy can get in the driver's seat,' Harry urged him.

'I don't want him in here with me, he might be sick again,' she protested.

But Harry was hauling Simon upright, even as I was echoing, blankly, 'The driver's seat?'

What seemed like seconds after my head hit the pillow, I shot bolt upright, wide awake again . . . but now the sun was shining through the rose-patterned curtains and it was morning.

I really would have to talk to Daisy again about my dreams – memories – whatever they were.

I went for an early dip, so it was at breakfast, while I was fending off a determined attempt by Babybelle to snatch the food from my fork mid-air, that I found out Judy and Debo had had an even more eventful time last night than I'd realised.

'The doorbell rang soon after you went to the pub, Izzy, but when I opened the door, there was no one there, except a big Alsatian that had been tied to the front porch,' Judy said. 'I could hear a car revving away towards the road, but it was out of sight.'

'It's a bitch,' Debo said.

'It certainly is,' I agreed heartily.

'No, I meant the Alsatian is a bitch. The poor thing's been used for puppy farming, from the look of her.'

'But she's not a *dangerous* dog, so she could be rehomed?' I asked hopefully.

'She doesn't seem dangerous, just very cowed,' Judy said. 'What do you think, Debo?'

'I think you're right, but we should get the vet to check her over before she moves on to Lucy's.'

'Fair enough, but will the Ferrises be working on a Sunday?' I asked doubtfully.

'I expect one of them will pop in for a look at her,' Debo said.

'And charge twice as much because it's also Easter, don't forget, and a bank holiday weekend,' I pointed out.

'It'll probably be Will, and I don't think he'll charge more than usual,' she said optimistically. 'Anyway, last night we'd just settled the Alsatian into a kennel and gone back to bed, when a couple of the other dogs escaped.'

'They must have been jumping at the gates and knocked the latches out, though they haven't done that for ages,' Judy said.

'It's odd how it's almost always weekends when they do,' Debo said. 'Don't tell Rufus they got out, will you?'

'Too late. I invited him in for coffee, so he read the note, too. But don't worry, he knows we're going to make things much more secure as soon as we can.'

'How lovely that you're getting friendly with him,' Debo

said brightly. 'I'm sure once he knows us all better, the nice Baz side of him will come out more and more.'

'I don't think he's like Baz in the least,' I said doubtfully. 'And he's certainly got his share of demons. But I'm sure he'll mellow, once the Halfhidden effect takes over. In fact, he already has, a bit.'

'It's the mineral water,' Judy suggested. 'We're all so chilled, we're cool as cucumbers.'

'I don't think he's had any of it yet,' I said doubtfully.

'Then he should,' she said, and actually, it was a good thought!

After breakfast I took a look at the new arrival. No one had mentioned that she was a *white* Alsatian – or she would have been, if her fur hadn't been so matted and dirty that it looked yellow. She was also little more than skin and bone.

My heart was wrung to think of all the puppies she must have had, which had probably been removed at barely six weeks. No wonder she had a cowed, beaten air.

But at least she didn't look remotely vicious and her tail thumped when I said softly, 'Poor old girl!'

'She's going to be all right,' Sandy assured me, on her way past with a wheelbarrow full of sacks of dog biscuit. 'Vet's just been. They must have dumped her because she'd had such a bad time with the last litter that she was no good for breeding any more. Will gave her a kennel cough vaccination and she's having a bath later, followed by worming, flea treatment and ear drops.'

'That sounds like a fun day for her! I hope she . . .' I began, and then, looking up, saw Rufus and lost the thread. The sun was glinting off his shiny, dark chestnut hair and, since a smile was softening the effect of that Roman nose and cleft chin, he looked less as if he was about to engage me in a gladiatorial contest that I was bound to lose.

'Hi, Izzy, I'm just on my way to Cameron's gallery. I wondered if you wanted to come and see these amazing folding room dividers.'

'I thought you'd be too busy to go. Aren't you opening your garden antiques centre tomorrow?'

'I am, but I've been up since the crack of dawn, so there isn't a lot left to do. Foxy's just arrived, too, although I wasn't expecting her on a Sunday *and* she says she's coming tomorrow as well, even though it's a bank holiday.'

'The Lane girls don't take a lot of notice of weekends. You'll have seen Sandy's here, too. Debo and Judy keep having to force her to take time off.'

'After tomorrow, Foxy will *have* to take Mondays off, at least, because that's my usual closing day. And on the others, I'm only open to the public from ten till four, or by appointment, so she doesn't need to work long hours.'

'I think you'll find that, like Sandy, she turns up whether she's paid for it or not.'

While we'd been talking, the so-far-nameless Alsatian had got up and slowly approached the front of the pen. Now Rufus spotted her and squatted down, eye to eye.

'Hello! Who's this?'

I told him the tale of her arrival, by which time he was stroking her head through the mesh and her tail was wagging eagerly.

'I've never had a dog . . . or any pet,' he said absently. 'I didn't have a settled home to keep one in, what with Fliss dumping me with her friends in the school holidays. Some of those had dogs or cats, though.'

Babybelle, who Sandy had lured back to her pen on the far side of the kennels, must have got the last morsel out of her treat ball, for she now gave a long, abandoned howl.

'Come on,' I said to Rufus, 'let's escape before she does!'

We found Lulu in the gallery, though she'd only popped in for a quick look at the new folding doors, since the pub was quite busy.

'That lovely American couple are leaving for fresh haunts today, but the others are staying till tomorrow morning,' she added, handing me a mug of coffee.

We watched as Cam demonstrated to Rufus the ingenious way the big glass and wooden room dividers smoothly and silently opened and closed, so that one minute we were in a huge gallery space, and the next in a studio.

'Boys and their toys,' Lulu said, and Cam grinned.

'I've found a few artist's donkeys and studio easels on eBay for when I start running painting classes here. Battered but fine,' Cam said.

'Donkeys?' questioned Rufus, puzzled.

'Like a bench that you sit astride, with an easel on the end,' Cameron explained. 'They're from a private art school that's closing down, only they're in Cornwall and it's a bit of a hike down there.'

'We could go together in one of my vans, if you like,' offered Rufus. 'If we started in the early hours and took it in turns to drive, we could do it in a day and I've got a contact down there who often has some unusual bits and pieces for me, too.'

'Great!' Cameron said. 'There's a "buy it now" option, so I will, and then we can work out when will suit you to go down with me and collect them.'

'I wish I could come; it sounds like fun,' Lulu said regretfully, then put her cup down and got up. 'I'd better get back.'

I went out with her, leaving Rufus helping Cam to hang paintings. It was good that he was getting on so well with one of my best friends, but really, I think he was just too afraid of Foxy to go back to Sweetwell!

Lulu drove off down the lane, and as I crossed the Green, the church bell (known locally as Little Knell, due to its being about the size of a budgie's toy) began clonking away in a slightly cracked, but not unpleasant, manner. Money had never run to getting it recast, because keeping the roof on the church had always seemed more of a priority.

Judy was among the locals heading up the gravelled path to the church, locks of her hennaed hair undulating in the breeze, like bright flames. I knew she'd been looking forward to the Easter service, which was always in addition to the normal monthly one, and she'd be helping the vicar's wife with the Easter egg hunt for the small children around the Hut later.

The faint strains of Jonas warming up the organ with a brisk rendition of 'I Do Like to Be Beside the Seaside' competed with the bell to lure the parishioners to worship, and I felt that God was in his heaven and all was right with the world.

All was evidently *not* well in Babybelle's world, for she was still emitting occasional howls, like a faulty burglar alarm. I thought I'd better take her for a run before I did anything else.

She determinedly headed down the path to the lower pool,

so I thought that she was probably feeling fitter already . . . or maybe it was just that she liked to get very, very wet.

On our return, she was pretty set on going back into the Lodge for lunch with me, too, where Debo told me that Rufus had stopped by on his way back from the gallery, to say hello to the new dog.

'Sandy said he'd already made a fuss of her earlier and she'd come right up to him.' Then she added, 'Sandy seems to be fine with Rufus now, by the way, so I think Foxy must have told her he was OK.'

'Good, because you don't want your staff frogmarching your landlord about,' I said drily.

'I'm sure she'll be fine, now he's shown he's a dog person,' Judy said.

'We've called the Alsatian Pearl,' Debo said. 'If Rufus could give her a home at Sweetwell, that would be perfect.'

'I wouldn't jump the gun, Debo,' I cautioned her. 'He told me he'd never been able to have a pet because either he was at boarding school or farmed out with some of Fliss's friends.'

'How cruel!' Judy said, her soft heart stirred. 'Some people just aren't fit to be mothers and Fliss is certainly one of them.'

'I think Rufus *might* be interested, though I told him that Tom was coming tomorrow to choose a new dog and perhaps *he'd* like Pearl,' Debo said.

'But Tom's already taken the greyhound,' I reminded her.

'Oh, yes, silly me,' she said innocently. 'How could I have forgotten?'

I finished designing the prototype of my sari/Grecian/ flamenco skirt, then rummaged about in the boxes, looking for a pretty fabric to make it up into. Time had flown by, so even though I knew Cam was coming to help me tweak the Izzy Dane Designs website into shape, I was still surprised to see him.

Completing the website was yet another important step, and once the first consignment of stock arrived and we'd done the photo shoot, I'd finally be ready to go live . . . so long as I'd finished sorting out PayPal and all the rest of it, of course.

'So much to think of, so little time!' I said to Cameron. 'I *thought* I had organised most things before I even got home, but now as fast as I tick one thing off my list, I have to add another.'

'Have you remembered that you'll have to register as self-employed for tax purposes? We both will.'

'Yes, and I've already started keeping an account of what I've spent on the business so far,' I said. 'Rufus must be an old hand at all that stuff, since he's been running his own business for years, so if we get stuck we can always ask him.'

'True. I like him now I've got to know him a bit, and it was kind of him to offer to go to Cornwall with me to pick up those easels and benches, wasn't it?'

I agreed. 'When we first met, we were at cross purposes, blaming each other for things that happened in the past. But now suddenly I feel I've known him for ages. It's very odd.'

'Perhaps that's why you were holding hands on the path last night when I passed you, then?' Cam teased.

I laughed. 'Oh, that was just a joke really, because Jonas had scared us silly with his stories.'

'And there was me, thinking you'd fallen instantly in love!'

'Rufus has, I think – but with a dog, not me!' I told him

about Pearl and then took him to see her. She'd been washed and treated by then and was looking much better. Sandy said she was eating like a horse.

Debo stopped scrubbing out a pen with the big stiff yard brush and came over. 'I'd like to keep her for a few days, until she puts on a bit of weight,' she said. 'And anyway, Izzy, you said Rufus was very taken with her, so we ought to wait and see.'

'Yes, I just told Cam about that, but Rufus may not want to take on a dog.'

'She'd make him such a wonderful companion,' she said. 'I'm sure he's a dog person, so he *needs* her.'

'Do you think she's even house-trained?' I asked doubtfully.

'Since it's likely she's been kept caged in a barn with a lot of other dogs, possibly not,' Debo admitted.

'That would certainly give Myra plenty to clean up, then – she'd go into bleach overload.'

Cameron said he'd better get back to Spring Cottage and I told him I'd see him in the pub that evening.

The years had concertinaed together so that I was slipping almost seamlessly back into the old ways: early morning dips in the pool, walks with the dogs and then, most evenings, meeting up with Cam and Lulu at the Screaming Skull.

'I told Rufus we'd be down there tonight and he'd be welcome to join us,' Cam added, as he turned to go.

So it seemed the old routines *were* changing, after all, just as my old dream had jumped from its usual track and was now running free.

When I set off for the pub, Babybelle was safely back in her kennel – and I hoped she'd stay there, though an occasional anguished howl followed me as I walked down the shadowy path to the Lady Spring.

Rufus and Cam were sitting on a block of lichened stone, waiting for me – I could hear them talking quietly, even before I saw them.

There was no sign of Dan in the public bar when we got there, which was a good thing – unless, of course, he was off in London again with Fliss. I expect Rufus was thinking the same thing.

The pub was busy, so Lulu could only get away to join us for half an hour, just in time to hear Cam and Rufus discussing when they would make the long trip down to Cornwall.

'When I bought the easels and donkeys, the seller said he had a lot of other odds and ends I might be interested in, if I'm starting up art classes,' Cam said. 'I'll see when we get down there.'

'If we're stopping at my contact's place too, we'd better take the bigger van,' Rufus said.

Lulu suggested that in that case it might be a good idea for Cam to try driving it a bit, before they set out.

Walking home, I thought suddenly how odd it was that in the space of only a couple of days, Rufus had gone from a total stranger to someone we were all comfortable with, as if he'd always been part of our group.

After we left Cam at Spring Cottage, it was good to have someone to walk with me the last bit of the path home – right to my door, in fact, though this time Rufus wouldn't come in.

'I have a few email queries to answer tonight. I'm hoping to shift that huge semicircular stone seat to an old customer

– and I'm officially opening the antiques centre tomorrow, don't forget.'

'True. You need your sleep; it's probably going to be a busy day.'

'I hope so . . . and why are we whispering?' he asked.

'So we don't wake Babybelle. She seems to have bat ears,' I explained. 'You're not going to walk up the drive, are you?' I added. 'Why don't you cut round the path again?'

'I'm really not worried that I'll come face to face with Howling Hetty, but I can see I'll have to exorcise her from my drive at some point, to make you happy,' he said in some amusement.

I thought that even if he did, I'd still be reluctant to walk past that spot at night, haunted for me as it was by more than just Hetty's ghost.

Chapter 18: Lucky Charm

'Me?' I gasped, astonished. 'You want me to drive you back to Sweetwell? But – I can't drive! I'm not even old enough to drive.'

'Of course you can drive! You were fine when I showed you how,' Harry said. 'Don't worry, I'll sit next to you and tell you what to do.'

He gave me that smile again, though this time fear lessened the impact.

It was a grey morning and I bottled the swim, deciding to go out for the early dog walk with Debo and Judy instead and visit the pool later.

First, though, I rang Daisy and told her how my dream seemed to be no longer recurring, but moving on.

'And I'm convinced they're really memories, because before, the scenes I dreamed about were like something seen underwater, but now they're floating up to the surface, so they're perfectly clear.'

'Very poetic,' she said. 'It's certainly possible that that should happen while you're relaxed in sleep. It will be interesting to see how far they progress.'

'However far it is, I still want to talk to the two main

218

witnesses to the accident, Simon and Cara. I've spoken to all the others now, though it didn't add much to what I already knew, except that Simon tried to see me when I was in hospital and they wouldn't let him in.'

'Have Debo and Judy told you I'm coming to lunch in a few days?' Daisy asked. 'I'm speaking at a conference in Liverpool and calling in on my way back.'

'No! They must have forgotten to mention it.'

'We'll talk then,' she promised.

Babybelle was delighted that I was taking her for her morning walk and, since she seemed to have struck up an unlikely alliance with Pearl, I had charge of both dogs.

I didn't put Belle on the lead and she stayed right behind me, nose to leg, as before. Then, as we came out by the house and were about to take the path that would lead us home by a different route, Rufus suddenly appeared round the side of the building, heading for the stable yard.

Ginger and Vic were romping freely all over his roughly hewn lawn, but Debo, unabashed, waved and called out gaily, 'Hi, Rufus!'

Babybelle and Pearl spotted him at the same moment and Belle instantly bounded off. I wasn't sure what she was going to do with him when she got there – bowl him over? Attack him? But I didn't have time to ponder further because, to my surprise, the lead in my hand gave a galvanic jerk as Pearl set off after her friend. She was a big dog, so I didn't have much option but to follow.

By the time we got there, Belle was greeting Rufus like a long-lost friend, but Pearl timidly abased herself at his feet, unsure of her welcome until he made a big fuss of her.

'You might as well admit defeat and rehome her,' I told him with a grin. 'It's obvious she adores you.'

'She's lovely, but I've never had a dog and—' he began.

'Oh, you'll be fine,' Judy assured him, as she and Debo, trailing dogs, caught up with us. 'She'll have to be spayed, because another litter could kill her, but as soon as she's over that, she can come to you.'

'But don't worry if you *really* don't want her, since I'm sure Tom will,' Debo put in.

'I'll have her,' he said suddenly, seeming to surprise himself.

'Great!' Debo enthused. 'And if there are any problems with her settling in, I'll give you the number of Chris, my dog whisperer, and he'll come and sort her out.'

'Right . . .' Rufus said, then added uneasily, 'What kind of problems?'

'Oh, I'm sure there's nothing major,' she assured him airily.

His brow wrinkled. 'You know, now I come to think of it, I'm sure I saw Tom out with a dog yesterday . . .'

'Come on, you two – time to get home for breakfast,' Judy said quickly.

'Good luck for today. I hope you get lots of customers,' I said to Rufus. 'I might pop in later and see.'

And then we beat a hasty retreat, though Pearl had to be dragged away from her idol and kept stopping to look wistfully back.

Lulu drove up later so we could go and see the garden antiques centre together, though she wouldn't be able to stay long.

'My Haunted Weekenders and some of the other visitors have left, but we're still quite full because of it being a bank holiday.'

'Soon you'll have Haunted visitors for whole weeks at a time, not just weekends,' I said.

'We often do have visitors for a week anyway. I expect the Haunted Holidaymakers will take themselves off every day to do the trail, or visit the other local attractions, so all I'll need to do is lay on the storytelling evenings and hand out the leaflets and maps.'

I hadn't intended taking Babybelle to the garden antiques centre, but since she'd flattened the netting of her pen and come in search of me, there was no choice. She refused to be diverted even by the rattle of her food ball, so we put her in the back of Lulu's small car. She entirely covered the rear seat and there would probably be a blanket of hair left when she got out, but Lulu said she didn't mind.

The centre seemed to have got off to a good start, for I'd noticed quite a lot of cars going up and down the drive already and there were several customers about when we got there.

Rufus was helping to load a lion-head wall fountain into the back of a big four-wheel-drive vehicle, while Foxy was cleaning the rust off an ancient wheelbarrow, while keeping one stern eye on the punters. She waved her wire brush at us.

I had Belle on her lead and resisted her attempts to drag me over to greet Rufus again. Luckily she didn't persist, but followed us as we had a good rummage about. Lulu bought a half-cask that had once held whisky but now had holes drilled in the bottom to turn it into a planter.

'Mum will love it and it'll look great by the kitchen door, full of flowers,' she said, and Rufus promised to drop it off later in the day.

'How's it going?' I asked him.

'Surprisingly busy. I thought it would take longer for word to spread that I was here.'

'Come down to the pub again tonight with me, Izzy and Cam, and we'll celebrate your opening,' Lulu suggested. 'It'll be quieter than yesterday so I'll be able to join you.'

'If you're sure you don't mind?' he said diffidently. 'I know the three of you are old friends and you probably still have a lot to catch up on.'

'Don't be daft!' she told him. 'Izzy said on the way here that she felt like she'd known you for ever.'

'Did you?' he asked me.

'We *all* do,' I said. 'Maybe it's the Salcombe in you.'

He bent to stroke Babybelle's head and she grinned and lolled her huge tongue amiably at him.

It seemed to remind him of our earlier meeting, for he said uneasily, 'That dog . . .'

'Pearl? Missing you already,' I said brightly.

'I mentioned her to Myra and she asked if she was house-trained.'

'Possibly not, but it will give Myra's cleaning a real challenge, won't it?'

'I think it's going to give *me* one, too,' he said gloomily, and then Foxy called him over to talk to a customer.

Lulu had to go then anyway, but since Rufus and Foxy were so busy, I offered to make them some coffee in the little office and, while I was about it, one for myself. There was a plastic box of fruit fairy cakes on the desk, which was probably Myra's contribution to the new enterprise.

When it was ready, I loaded the mugs and cake box onto a battered tin tray and left Belle snoozing under Rufus's desk while I took it out to where Foxy was working on the wheel-barrow.

I laid the tray down on a nearby stone bench and Rufus came and absently helped himself to a fairy cake, before wandering off, mug in hand, to talk to an elderly couple who seemed lost in reminiscence as they examined the antique watering can collection.

'Rufus knows his stuff, his interest's genuine and he's full of knowledge,' Foxy said, then added unexpectedly, as she stared after his broad-shouldered, slim-hipped rear view, 'He's a bit of all right, too – but I'm not his type.'

She took a slurp from her mug and demolished a fairy cake in two bites.

I wasn't sure exactly who would find Foxy their type, though I'm a great believer in there being someone for everyone, and I said so.

'One of the gardeners over at Grimside has his eye on me,' she admitted.

'Really? It's not Simon Clew, is it?'

'No! He's having it away with Cara Ferris-as-was. Everyone knows that!'

'*I* didn't!' I said, amazed.

'Well, you do now. And I reckon Rufus has his eye on *you*, because as soon as he could get away from his customers, he was across the yard to talk to you, faster than a fox after a chicken.'

I blushed. 'I'm sure you're wrong, Foxy. He thinks I look like some kind of pixie.'

'Well, so you do – and they're supposed to be lucky!' she said, and then guffawed, before going off to browbeat a browser into buying something he probably had had no intention of purchasing.

I felt a little shy after that, even though I was sure *I* wasn't Rufus's type, either. But I did think we might become good friends in time . . . so long as his mother wasn't around. I sneaked off home while he was still preoccupied.

Rufus was very quiet and abstracted on the walk down to the pub that evening.

The first thing he said to Lulu when we got to the Screaming Skull was, 'Dan wasn't here yesterday and I don't suppose there's been any sign of him today, either, has there?'

'No,' she agreed, 'not since Saturday night. But he hasn't been in as much as usual at weekends recently, anyway.'

'Then I think my suspicions are right,' he said sombrely. 'Izzy told me that he'd been boasting about spending weekends with my mother, and when Fliss rang me earlier, I heard a voice in the background and was sure it was him.'

'What did she want?' I asked.

'To warn me not to be taken in by your aunt Debo again,' she said. And she thinks I ought to give her notice to quit the Lodge.'

'But you can't do that,' Lulu said. 'It's Debo's for life, isn't it?'

'Yes, that's what I told her. Then she said she and Dan had got friendly – her words – and he'd told her I was coming down on him heavily, so I was to lay off.'

'She's put you in a difficult position, hasn't she?' Cam said sympathetically.

'She specialises in doing that. But I told her straight that if I was paying someone to work for me, I expected them to earn their wages, so whether he stayed or not was up to him. That's when I thought I heard his voice in the background.'

'Tricky,' I said.

'Oh, trust Fliss to add a complication to any situation,' he said. 'I told her I could hear him in the background and I knew he was there with her, and she said what he did in his free time was his own business, and then she put the phone down.'

'It is going to make things awkward, isn't it?' Lulu asked.

'Yes, but luckily none of her men friends lasts long, so I should think she'll get tired of him any minute now,' he said. The thought seemed to cheer him up a bit, so we went into the public bar and played darts.

Cam suggested, while we were playing, that Rufus should join the Halfhidden Regeneration Committee and come to the Hut meeting the following night, which would be a good way to get involved in village life, and he said he would.

When Rufus and I left, Cam said he'd stay for a bit so he and Lulu could have a look at what was to go on the hotel website about the Haunted Holidays.

'Are your friends . . . more than friends?' Rufus asked tentatively as we started up the path, the two pale moons of our torch beams overlapping ahead of us.

'I think it's heading that way,' I admitted, then explained about Cam rescuing Lulu from her horrible ex, and how it seemed to have brought them closer on the way back to the UK.

'Then I think Lulu got cold feet, imagining Cam was just being kind and comforting, and also that it would ruin our friendship. But actually, I really do think they've fallen in love and eventually they'll admit it to each other.'

Some startled creature went crashing away in the under-growth and I said suddenly, 'Sometimes lately I feel I'm being watched when I'm in the woods. I never used to have that feeling.'

'*Do* you think you're being watched?'

'Not really and there's never anyone there, so I'm sure I'm imagining it. But maybe Howling Hetty's expanding her territory, or . . . other ghosts.'

I shivered and he took my hand in his warm, strong grasp, just as he had the first time we'd walked up from the pub together.

Chapter 19: Ghosting

'Simon's incapable of driving – who'd have thought a drop of vodka would make him legless?' Harry said disgustedly. 'And if I get done for drink-driving again, I can kiss goodbye to that sports car Dad's buying me.'

'But if the police are waiting round the corner I'll be arrested, and Judy and Debo will be furious!' I said, my voice trembling.

'Of course you wouldn't be arrested. They'd just let you off with a caution,' he assured me.

I woke at dawn to a silent house. It was too early even for Debo and Judy to be up and about, but I was way too unsettled to sleep again.

I got up, collected my swimsuit and towel and then tiptoed downstairs. In the kitchen, Vic and Ginger opened their eyes and each gave me an incredulous look.

As I slipped out into the still, chilly morning air, I nearly changed my mind, but then crept on past the kennels. There was the sound of some stertorous doggy breathing, which I suspected came mostly from Babybelle. During that night she'd spent in the Lodge kitchen, the walls had practically vibrated with her snoring.

There was no sign of life yet in Spring Cottage and I started to get the feeling that all the rest of humankind might have vanished in the night. I think I've watched too many bad horror films.

But then, as I pushed through the old turnstile, I nearly had a heart attack – for a spectral white shape glimmered in the dark entrance to the cave above the pool, amid a few lingering swirls of early morning mist.

'Oh my God!' I gasped, stopping dead – almost literally.

The spectral shape waved. 'Hi, Izzy!' it called.

'Is that you, Lulu? You nearly gave me a heart attack!'

Once I was nearer, I could see she was attired in a white Victorian nightdress with long sleeves and a pie-crust frill around the neck, made out of about two acres of diaphanous cotton lawn. Her face was covered in stage make-up, whiter than any geisha's.

Cameron, who had been kneeling by the pool taking photos, got to his feet. There were dew-damp circles on the knees of his arty ochre-red canvas trousers and fine droplets sparkled in his flaxen hair.

'Hi, Izzy, we didn't think even you would be at the pool this early. It's freezing!'

'It certainly is, *and* clammy hanging round inside this cave,' Lulu said pointedly.

'You two carry on. I'm happy to wait till you finish before I have a dip because it doesn't seem such a good idea right now. Maybe the sun will have warmed things up a bit by then.'

'I think we're done, actually,' he said. 'Come on down, Lulu.'

'You didn't mention doing this last night, at the pub.'

'It was an impulse,' Cameron explained. 'I woke up really early and thought the touch of mist would make a great background, so I rang Lulu up and suggested it.'

'He woke me up to tell me,' she agreed.

'That nightdress . . .?' I said.

'I found it in one of the attics inside a huge leather trunk, along with loads of other Victorian clothes and a couple of hats.'

'We'll doctor the pictures of Lulu to make her look a bit more insubstantial.'

'She's pretty insubstantial already. I'm not surprised Bruce is trying to fatten her up.'

Lulu said, 'I'll be a genuine wraith if I don't put my clothes back on.'

'Couldn't you have worn them underneath?' I asked.

'No, because Cameron wanted to take some arty shots up above the spring where the Halfhidden Worm was supposed to live. I was standing on the rocks in Sacrificial Maiden pose as the sun came up, with it sort of shining through my nightgown.'

'So we're having postcards of sexy ghosts?' I asked, staring at Cam, who coloured slightly.

'It was just . . . easier to get the effect I wanted,' he said.

'Did the Worm come out to have his picture taken?'

'We're still working on that one,' he admitted. 'We need some otherworldly photos of the waterfall, too, and Lulu thought a ghostly Saxon warrior would be good, though I'm too skinny to fit the bill.'

'You might persuade Rufus,' I suggested.

'Good thinking. I'll give him a ring later. What did Saxons wear?'

'Tunics and leggings,' Lulu said.

'Sounds a bit eighties,' I commented dubiously.

'Not that kind of leggings,' she said. 'I don't think the Saxons invented Lycra, or even stretch cotton.'

'They didn't have cotton at all, did they?' Cameron asked.

'I don't think so,' I said, 'but I bet there's a costume that will do in the Hut storeroom, like one of the shepherd's outfits from the Nativity.'

'Oh, yes, those brown Hessian tunics,' Lulu agreed. 'Perfect!'

'I expect they're in the big wooden chest with the Father Christmas outfit,' I said. 'Nothing ever seems to get thrown away.'

'Hessian would be itchy,' Lulu pointed out.

'He'd be wearing it for only minutes, and he could leave his T-shirt on underneath,' said Cam.

While Lulu got dressed in one of the sentry huts, Cameron persuaded me to put the nightie on over my swimsuit and wade about the pool, trying to look like an ailing Victorian miss. Then I did a sort of drowning-Ophelia thing, clutching a handful of bluebells to my bosom, while he snapped away. I wasn't sure what he was going to do with *those* photos.

We all went into the cottage afterwards, where Tom, who was now up and about, made us hot coffee. The new greyhound, who had been renamed Queenie, seemed as much at home as if she'd always lived there.

'There was a white horse in the outbuilding when I went to let the hens out,' Tom said. 'But I'd seen you near the pool, so I thought it must be something to do with you.'

'It's my sister-in-law's horse,' explained Lulu. 'I rode it up here so Cam could take some pictures of it for the haunted

230

smithy – and I'd better get her back before Kate notices she's not in the paddock any more,' she added, getting up.

'I'm spending the day working on my business plans,' I said. 'I need to chase up the supplier about the clear plastic clothes bags I ordered, among other things.'

'Yes, and I've got lots to do at the gallery, too,' Cam agreed, so once Lulu had ridden off on the white mare, we walked together up the drive and I nobly forbore to question his story that he'd woken Lulu that morning by phone rather than, as I strongly suspected, in person . . . The nearest I got was remarking that Lulu was looking very cheerful that morning.

'Yes, she's soon going to be her old self again,' he agreed, not rising to the bait. 'See you at the Hut meeting later!'

I'd forgotten that last night Cam had asked Rufus to join the Halfhidden Regeneration Committee until he turned up at the Lodge, on his way there, unable to pass by without visiting his new love, Pearl.

If he had a Facebook account, his relationship status should read, 'in a relationship, but it's complicated'.

Lulu, Cam and Jonas were already at the Hut when we arrived, as were the dynamic duo of Freddie and Rita Tompion, who as usual had got everything ready: a table and chairs set out, the kettle on for coffee and a packet of gingernut biscuits arrayed on a paper plate, to which I added some flapjacks.

Rita suggested she take the minutes, and the meeting got underway to the accompaniment of Jonas sucking gingernuts that he'd dipped into his coffee.

Freddie said, 'First off, the Ramblers Association annual

clear-up day is Sunday the 22nd. That's when local volunteers join in with Association members to cut back the path all the way from Middlemoss to the Halfhidden Green,' he explained to Rufus. 'It's generally pretty clear up to the pub, it's just afterwards it gets overgrown.'

'We'll have to put a notice on the board outside our Lottie's shop, asking for people to help, but there's always a good turn-out,' said Jonas.

'I think I remember you mentioning this at the meeting,' Rufus said. 'Presumably it's to keep the path open for hikers?'

'Yes, and so the Middlemoss Morris Men can get up it easily,' Freddie said.

'Every May, they jog all the way up the path from Middlemoss to the village, stopping occasionally to dance,' I explained to him, since he was looking blank.

'I'm planning my first Haunted Holiday week to begin that weekend so the visitors can see some old traditions, as well as ghosts,' Lulu said.

'If the ghost trail is ready in time,' Freddie said.

'Oh, I'm sure it will be,' Lulu said. 'The path being cleared is a good start and Uncle Brandon asked me to put a sign up on the village noticeboard asking for volunteers to help clear the one up from the alpine nursery to the waterfall, too.'

'When does he want to do that?' asked Rita, taking notes.

'This Sunday. It's not far, so it shouldn't take so long,' she replied. 'Now, I sent you all the list of suggested signposts and information boards for your comments and Uncle Brandon is having them made at a cut price by a friend.'

'And we've nearly finished taking the pictures that are to be printed up as postcards,' Cameron said.

Then he showed everyone a rough draft of the haunted trail brochure. On one side was a map of the village, with the various attractions numbered to match information boxes around the edge.

'That looks good,' I said. 'What about the blank bit on the back, though? What's going there?'

'Advertisements,' Cam said. 'We thought some of the attractions further afield, like the Witchcraft Museum in Sticklepond, might pay for those.'

'So it would raise some money towards the printing?' Rufus said. 'Good idea. I know you said you'd make a small charge to everyone actually numbered on the map, which seems reasonable, too.'

'Hannah Blackwell's looking into reopening the tea garden at the Old Mill and her daughter Shirley would move back and run it with her, if she gets permission,' Lulu said.

'We're having a life-sized cut-out of the haunted grandfather clock made, to stand outside the shop, and Rita's ordered in some silver clock charms and extra watches,' Freddie said. 'There's not much room inside, so we thought visitors could have their photos taken next to the replica, instead.'

'I'll come and photograph the actual haunted clock, or Cam will, for a postcard,' promised Lulu. 'Cam's doing the haunted falls tomorrow morning.'

Rufus looked slightly sheepish, so I thought he must have agreed to pose for the Saxon warrior.

'So, signs, boards, maps and brochures, postcards, path clearing . . . all on their way,' Lulu said, with satisfaction.

'Tom has ordered more pamphlets to sell at the Spring,' Jonas said. 'And our Cameron says he's going to make all my stories into a book. What do you think of that?'

'I think it's a great idea,' I said. 'Is Tom stocking up on the souvenirs, too?'

'He said he had. The replicas of that clay Venus figure always seem to sell like hot cakes,' Cameron said. 'Mum's ordered resin skulls with "Howling Hetty" printed on them, though I told her they were a bit naff.'

'I should think they'd sell, though,' I said. 'Where does Tom get those reproductions of the ancient preggie lady sculptures from?'

'A potter over in Mossedge,' Cam said. 'His own work is good – really organic pots and ceramic sculptures – so I'll be displaying some of it in the gallery.'

'Terracotta skulls would be more tasteful,' I suggested, 'and pretty much the same colour as Hetty's.'

'But also more expensive,' Cam objected, 'not to mention a bit Damien Hirst.'

'I don't think he's got the copyright on skulls,' Rufus said.

We seemed to have wandered off the point a bit, but Lulu called us to order and we sorted out the last items on the agenda. Rita promised to type up all her notes and email them round.

Afterwards, Cam, Lulu, Rufus and I walked down the lane to the pub and had a drink in the snug. Dan, who was in his usual corner by the bar, had his back turned when we went through, but could be seen in the mirror over it, smirking horribly.

From the way his fists clenched, I'm sure Rufus must have noticed too and I thought that unless Dan *wanted* to lose his job, he must be the stupidest man in the entire world.

'So, all set for the Saxon warrior pictures in the morning?'

I said brightly to Rufus by way of distracting his mind, as we sat down in the snug with our drinks.

'I found a big tunic and sort of cross-gartered trouser things in the Hut,' Cameron said. 'They're roughly made, but should give the right effect from a distance.'

'The further the better,' Rufus said morosely.

Chapter 20: Not so Dusty

Harry took my hand and tried to draw me towards the car, but I resisted, my stomach full of the butterfly wings of fear.

'I thought you'd do it for me, Izzy,' he coaxed, his green eyes sparkling. Then, bending to whisper in my ear, he added, 'After all, you must know I want you to be my girl . . .'

I awoke with the words, 'If you believe that, you'll believe anything!' on my lips. Had that really been another memory? Surely even my sixteen-year-old self couldn't have been silly enough to think Harry would have ditched tall, stunning Cara, with her long, fair, silken hair, for a skinny elf with an urchin cut, who'd barely left the tomboy grazed knees and scabby elbows phase behind her.

I had no idea, but if it *was* a memory, then Harry was more devious than I'd thought him and *I'd* been infinitely more credulous.

Cara held all the answers, if only she would give them: but although I'd repeatedly rung her, there was never any reply and she didn't get back to me.

Simon was also proving elusive. He hadn't been seen much in the village since his return and, though I was told he was living in a cottage the other side of Grimside on the Middlemoss road, no one knew exactly which one, or even had his mobile number. It was all a bit frustrating . . . and the only way to move forward seemed to be to go up to Grimside in the hope of finding one or both of them there.

But not that morning, for exciting new ideas for clothes were bubbling up in my head and I was draping a length of star-patterned pink sari fabric round my dressmaker's dummy when Lulu burst into the studio unannounced, floundered over Babybelle, who barely seemed to notice, then waved a piece of paper at me.

'Thank goodness you're here! I've had the smarmiest letter from Guy, pleading with me to go back to him and saying the other woman was a mistake and he was sorry for everything. I was desperate to tell someone, and Cam's out.'

'Hasn't Guy learned to email yet?' I asked mildly, when I'd removed the dressmaker's pins from my mouth and stuck them in the howdah of my pewter elephant pincushion.

'Apparently not.' She dropped heavily down onto the old sofa, as if her legs would no longer hold her up, and the springs protested. 'Solange said he was paying a student to do the website bookings, but I suppose he can't very well ask him to write personal emails for him, too.'

'Oh, I don't know – I wouldn't put it past him,' I said, and then read the letter, which was alternately affectionate and threatening.

Darling Lulu,

I've made a terrible mistake because the moment you were gone I realised that I really do love you and I'm missing you so much. I couldn't bear the thought

237

of you with another man, though I'm sure you still love me, too, and haven't even thought of seeing anyone else . . .

There was a lot more of the same.

'Let's hope he doesn't find out about you and Cam,' I said.

'There's nothing to find out,' she protested, but then added, more honestly, 'or not much!'

I grinned. 'You just take things slowly and see what happens. And of *course* there's no way you're ever going to leave Halfhidden and go back to Guy.'

'Certainly not! Only he says if he doesn't hear from me, he'll come over.'

'For the wages he's offering, I expect he's having trouble finding someone to do even *half* the things you used to,' I suggested.

'Yes, that's pretty much what Solange said in her last email. Guy made a drunken pass at one of the women he'd hired to clean the *gîtes*, so now most of the local husbands won't let their wives go anywhere near him.'

'He's not the brightest bunny in the box, is he?'

'No, and now I can't imagine how I fell in love with him in the first place,' Lulu confessed. 'What can I say to put him off?'

'You'll have to make it absolutely plain that you're not only never going back to him, but you don't even want to hear from him again. Tell him you've made a new life here and moved on.'

'You're right and I'll also make it clear there's no point in him turning up anyway, because my parents won't have him on their property.'

'Let's hope he can take a hint, then,' I said. 'But on past form I suppose he might just ignore that and appear out of the blue anyway.'

'I'd feel a bit vulnerable in the caravan on my own at night, if I knew he was around.' She shivered.

'Why exactly *are* you living in the old caravan in the paddock? I've never asked.'

'Because Mum and Dad divided their apartment into two when Bruce and Kate married and moved in, and they kept the smaller one for themselves, so there's not really any room. And I was fine with that. I mean, when I went to live with Guy in France I told them I wouldn't be back and Bruce could take over the Screaming Skull when they retired. So when I had to come home, I felt a bit like an interloper.'

'I see what you mean, though I'm sure they don't think of it like that, they're just glad to have you back.'

'I told Bruce and Kate that I didn't expect a share in the business, just a job. That's why I need the Haunted Holidays to be such a success.'

'That still doesn't explain the caravan.'

'Oh, the staff accommodation was full, and anyway, I preferred being on my own in the caravan, though I'd like my own little house eventually, if I can ever afford it.'

I thought the way she and Cameron kept looking at each other, she could well end up making her home in Spring Cottage before long. But I didn't say so, because if she wanted a slow-burning romance after singeing her wings on Guy, so be it.

'I've felt perfectly safe in the caravan till now. And I know this would sound daft to anyone but you, but some evenings

I think I can hear old Conker munching the grass, or sighing, the way he used to.'

'But that might just be Kate's horse?'

'No, because it usually happens when she's put him in the top field.'

'Then I'm sure it *is* Conker. When I told the old Middlemoss vicar about going to Heaven and seeing Patch there with Harry, he said he was sure all creatures capable of love would find a place there.'

I'd been so grateful that the vicar had actually *believed* in my near-death experience and hadn't just been humouring me, like Judy and Debo, so that it felt as though I'd had the equivalent of a stamp for Heaven in my passport.

'Maybe Conker is a kind of equine guardian angel!' I suggested, and Lulu smiled.

'That's a nice thought.'

'As back-up, you could think about getting a guard dog,' I suggested sneakily. 'Debo's got a lovely brindle bull terrier who looks fierce, but is as soft as butter. That's probably why he got dumped: no good for fighting.'

She looked uncertain. 'I don't know . . . I mean, I couldn't leave him in the caravan all day, could I? And I'm not sure how he would get on with Mum's Yorkie.'

'He seems fine with other dogs and you could put a kennel in the shade of the trees by the caravan, for when he can't be with you.'

'I'll think about it,' she said.

'You do that – and you might as well come and meet him now, while you're here,' I said persuasively, for after all, I'd successfully matched Rufus and Pearl, so I thought perhaps the same technique might work with Lulu. Debo had driven off earlier to pick up a truly Desperate Dog, so really, we needed to make room for the new one.

Out in the kennels, Lulu regarded the scarred, brindle-coated dog and he lolled back and grinned, as only a bull terrier can.

'What's he called?'

'Debo said he looked just like Bruce Willis, so she wanted to call him Bruce, but Sandy ignored her and named him Dusty.'

'Just as well if I do have him, because he couldn't have the same name as my brother!'

'True, and if you called him Willis, it would end up as Willy, which is more than a bit embarrassing to be calling after your dog.'

'Dusty it is,' she agreed.

Hearing his new name, Dusty cocked one ear and then got up in a leisurely manner and came to the wire. I got him out so Lulu could meet him properly.

'Chris, Debo's dog expert, says he's scared of men and that's why he growls until he gets to know them, but he's not vicious, he just *looks* fierce. He'd make a perfect guard dog.'

Dusty rolled over with all four legs in the air, in mute invitation to Lulu to tickle his tummy and she obliged. 'Poor old thing,' she cooed. 'Look at those scars! Who could be so cruel?'

I knew it, it was a match made in heaven! She only promised to *think* about adopting him, but the clincher was the way Dusty's tail lost its jaunty angle and his ears drooped as he was returned to his kennel.

'He deserves a good home and some love,' I said.

'I'll have a word with Mum and Dad and see how they feel about it,' she conceded, looking back at him as we walked away.

Sandy, who'd been washing water bowls at the nearby tap, gave me a conspiratorial wink.

Lulu rang me later to say that her parents were keen on the idea of having a guard dog who would bark if there were any strangers about in the night.

'Well, there's no one quite as strange as Guy,' I commented.

'True, and now I come to think of it, he's not a dog-lover either,' she agreed. 'We'll have to get Dusty's kennel sorted before he moves in, but Mum and Dad said they'd pay for that and a fence round the caravan.'

'I could email you the link to the place I've ordered our new kennel block from,' I offered. 'They're very reasonable. Or the big pet store has a good range.'

'I'll have a look online later. I loved the fabric of that dress you were wearing this morning, did I say?' she added. 'Is it one of your own designs?'

'It is, and I really must get you or Cam to take some photos of the clothes samples for my online catalogue – when you've finished doctoring the haunted pics, that is.'

'That won't take long. Those Cam took yesterday look good and I already had loads of atmospheric photos of the falls, so we can just superimpose the ghostly image of Rufus on top.'

'Oh, yes, Cam was going to do the Saxon ones early this morning – I'd forgotten. I wonder how it went.'

'I don't know, because he had to go off and teach an art class afterwards, but I suppose we'll find out later, at the pub.'

*   *   *

Accompanied by my large and inconvenient shadow, Babybelle, I popped up to Stopped Clocks to get a new battery put in my watch and take a look at the haunted grandfather clock, which was tick-tocking away quietly in a dark corner.

When I got back, Judy said I'd missed a call from Rufus, who wanted me to go to Sweetwell after lunch.

'Did he say why?'

'No, but I made pecan puffs this morning, so you can take him some of those. We need to keep him sweet.'

'Maybe you should knit him a dog-hair scarf, too,' I said, and although I was joking, she took me seriously.

'Good idea! It won't take me long and I can finish off your jerkin afterwards.'

So after lunch I walked up to Sweetwell Hall, taking Babybelle and Pearl with me. They seemed to get on well together and Babybelle was clearly intending to go with me, whether I liked it or not. I thought it might be as well to remind Rufus how lovely Pearl was, in case he was getting cold feet.

We went along the drive, past the Fatal Spot in the hollow that was also Howling Hetty's favourite haunt. Darkened by the interlaced branches overhead it was an eerie place, even in full daylight and without an accident on your conscience.

We didn't linger, and a little way further came upon Dan, still engaged on the mammoth task of cutting back the encroaching trees and shrubs. He gave me an evil look as I walked past and made a threatening gesture with the roaring brush cutter.

Pearl immediately tried to hide behind me, but Babybelle, who had been plodding after me in her usual sedate fashion, turned and snarled at him, exposing a lot of sharp white teeth. I was really impressed and I think Dan was too because his evil grin vanished and he turned back to what he should be doing.

Sandy was in the yard, hosing down a random collection of ancient chimney pots, but she said I'd find Rufus in his office, where the man from BT had just finished installing the new landline.

When we went in, Pearl went straight to Rufus, looking up at him with soft, trusting eyes, but Babybelle slumped down just over the threshold with a weary sigh.

'Hi, Babybelle' he greeted her, amused. Then turning to me he said, 'You know I think she's looking a bit trimmer already, so it must be all the exercise.'

'And less food, though if she can steal anything remotely edible she does. Which reminds me – these are some home-baked biscuits from Judy.'

As I handed him the tin, Belle got up and moved to sit heavily on my feet.

'Picture of an adoring dog,' Rufus said, as she laid her head on my knee.

'I think that expression just means "you're a soft touch and I want something to eat",' I said. 'And don't even think about opening that tin of biscuits,' I added as he clicked on the kettle and reached for it. 'I'll be covered in drool from knees to ankles. Eat them when I've gone.'

'Oh, well,' he said resignedly.

'How did your stint as a Saxon ghost go this morning?'

'Hanging about a waterfall at the crack of dawn in a mini dress and leggings isn't my idea of a fun outing.'

'I wish I'd seen you!'

'You will – immortalised in guidebooks, leaflets and postcards,' he said gloomily. 'But Cam promised I'd just be a vague image of a superimposed ghostly presence, so no one would know it was me.'

'That's what he told me about the pictures he took of me in the pool and Lulu prancing about in a white nightie,' I said. 'They've probably all just gone viral on YouTube.'

He looked horrified and I giggled. 'No, not really! Anyway, Lulu will be helping with the photography – it's her hobby – so she wouldn't let him.'

'How are you getting on with Izzy Dane Designs?' he asked. 'Nearly ready to launch?'

'Cam helped me put the finishing touches to my website, so I just have photographs of the clothes to add and then, when my first stock arrives, I can go live.'

'Every time I see you, you seem to be wearing something unusual but pretty, so I predict it will be a huge success,' he said, which was a surprise, because Kieran always thought my taste in clothes was weird.

I found myself blushing. 'Why – thank you.' Then I changed the subject quickly. 'I passed Dan on the way here, cutting back the edge of the drive.'

I didn't mention the gesture with the brush cutter. Maybe I only imagined it was threatening.

'I hope he was working hard, because he's got a lot of idle years to make up for.'

'He did seem to be getting on with it, and it's clear all up one side from the entrance gates to the second bend now.'

'You were right about there having been a sit-on mower, by the way,' Rufus said, gently fondling Pearl's head so she sighed blissfully. 'I got round to asking Olly about it and he said he'd loved using it, but Baz had told Dan to sell it, so he'd had to use the old petrol mower again.'

'I don't see why Baz would tell Dan to sell it,' I said. 'He only bought it because Debo told him Olly was single-handedly trying to keep the garden in order in his spare time. That's when he told Dan to stop poncing about the grounds and get on with his job, which of course he didn't.'

'I asked Dan about the mower this morning and he looked really shifty,' Rufus said. 'He told me Baz had told him to sell it, but the man who'd collected it gave him a false address and the cheque bounced, so Baz had had to write it off.'

'Oh, yeah, pull the other one, it's got bells on,' I said sarcastically.

'That's more or less how I put it. I asked for the crime reference number from when he reported it to the police, only of course he hadn't done that.'

'Because he'd sold it and pocketed the cash?'

'I presume so, though I can't prove it. I've told him he's on a final warning and unless he shapes up, then he can start looking for a new job.'

His jaw was set, and if Dan didn't see that here was a man he shouldn't cross, then he was an even bigger fool than I thought he was.

'I've promised Olly I'll get him another sit-on mower and Myra says she knows the owner of a garage near Middlemoss, called Deals on Wheels, who can find me a decent used one.'

'Oh, yes, Judy got her last car from Dave Naylor, the owner, and it's a good runner. Cam hired a van from him the other day, too. He's cheap and cheerful, and he does tractors, too – anything with wheels.'

246

'How are you doing with your mission?' he asked. 'Have you got any further?'

'Only in my dreams,' I said wryly. 'And whether those are the right answers or not, only Cara can tell me. She and Simon are the last and most important witnesses I need to speak to.'

'Didn't you say Simon was working for Cara's husband at Grimside?'

'Yes, but I don't know his phone number, or even exactly where he lives. And Cara hasn't answered any of my messages, plus she was horrible when I met her the other day.'

'Unfriendly!'

'She always blamed me, especially for the scar she got in the accident – though actually now you wouldn't notice it if you didn't know it was there.' I sighed. 'I'm sure Dan will have warned Simon not to talk to me, but I thought since the herb garden at Grimside is open to the public, I'd go over there and hope to spot him.'

'If you don't see him, then you could ask one of the other gardeners to give Simon a letter, explaining what you want and asking him to ring you?' Rufus suggested. 'I don't see why he wouldn't want to talk to you, even if it does stir up bad memories.'

'Yes, good idea. He was always too scared of his father to do anything against his wishes, but now I should think he's his own man, wouldn't you?'

'It's been nineteen years since the accident, so if he's not, he never will be,' Rufus said drily.

'So, why did you want me to come up here today?'

'Do I need an excuse to want to see you?'

'Don't be daft,' I said.

247

'OK, I just wanted to warn you that Fliss might suddenly appear at some point soon. She rang me again and talked about coming down to stay.'

He rubbed his forehead, as if even the thought had given him a headache. 'I said if she behaved herself and didn't give Dan any more stupid ideas, she could.'

'What did she say?'

'Accused me of being feudal and then said I was letting Debo influence me against Dan, but I said I'd made my own mind up, based on the evidence. I only hope the damned man doesn't become my father-in-law,' he added darkly.

'*Has* she ever got married?'

'No, but she's definitely gone a bit odd since I moved here. Today she said if I'd only get rid of all of you at the Lodge, she could have it as her little place in the country, even though I know she hates the country. So unless it's to do with Dan, it's a bit baffling.'

'She's mad if she still thinks you can get rid of Debo and Judy, just because she wants the Lodge!'

'Well, I think we already knew that,' Rufus said.

'Let me know if she does appear so I can keep well clear and warn Debo,' I said. 'Are you coming to the pub tonight?'

'Oh, I don't know . . . I don't want to keep butting in.'

'You're not, and anyway, if Cam stays late I'll be glad of the company on the way home. I wouldn't want to walk through the woods at night on my own and it takes twice as long by way of the road.'

'I knew you had an ulterior motive,' he said, and smiled.

I'd updated Rufus on the Guy and Lulu situation and she must have got hold of Cam at some point that day and told him, too, because when we got to the pub he asked her if she'd replied to Guy's letter yet.

'Yes, and sent it off. I made it as terse as I could and said there was absolutely no point in his coming over here. I'm sure he doesn't really still love me, he only wants me back to do all the work, for nothing.'

'I hope he doesn't just turn up, because he's pig-headed and stupid enough to think he can talk you round,' Cam said. 'And what if he comes when you're alone in the caravan?'

'I was going to tell you, Cam, I'm getting a guard dog, one of Debo's Desperate Dogs,' she said, and explained about Dusty. Then Rufus said he was adopting one too and told Cam all about Pearl.

Cam said he was starting to feel left out, with no dog of his own, but Lulu said he could share Dusty and take him out for walks any time he felt like it.

'I've been out visiting local craftspeople who want to exhibit in the gallery,' Cam said. 'I've already got that ceramic artist who makes the Venus figurines for the Lady Spring, and a silversmith – oh, and a craftsman near Southport who makes bird sculptures out of driftwood – so that's a good start. I've rejected quite a few craftworkers, because I want really top-quality stuff.'

'Did you hear any more from the seller of those easels and benches on eBay?' I asked.

'Yes, and he's offering me a job lot of all the smaller items he's got left, like drawing boards and brushes, but I'll see what they're like when I get there.'

'We'll have to go next week,' Rufus said. 'I'm off to a country house sale up near Durham tomorrow and I won't get back till Friday. In fact, I think I'd better call it a night now and go home, since I have a very early start in the morning.'

Cam said he'd stay for a while, but I elected to go with Rufus and we walked back in the darkness under a velvety, star-studded sky, the conjoined warm glow of our torches showing the way.

Rufus escorted me to my door, as I knew he would, and it was as well he did because I could see the outer gate to the kennels was wide open and a familiar large, dark shape was bounding towards me.

'I suppose she's flattened her pen again,' I said resignedly, getting behind Rufus in case she tried to flatten *me*, too. 'But she was in one of the stronger ones, with Pearl – and anyway, the outer gate should have been bolted.'

But it was certainly ajar now, and when we investigated, we discovered poor Pearl curled up in a nervous ball at the back of the pen she'd shared with Belle, with the door swinging open.

'How odd. Debo or Judy usually check everything when they do the bedtime rounds.'

'Just as well we got back when we did,' Rufus said, bending to stroke Pearl and tell her she was a good dog for staying put. Babybelle had followed us in, but when we tried to leave, she immediately started to howl, so I had to let her out before she woke Debo and Judy up.

'I'll have to take her into the house with me,' I said resignedly.

'And I'll have to get off. I still have a couple of things to sort out for tomorrow. It's the first time I've left Foxy in charge, too.'

'She'll be fine and she can ring or message you if anything comes up, can't she?'

'Yes, I'll have my mobile on all the time. And Laurie, Myra's husband, is a nice chap and since he's off work this week he said he'd go down a few times to check she was all right,' he said. 'When he retires in the summer, he's going to do a bit of part-time office work for me. He says he'll need something to keep his mind active.'

'That sounds like a great idea,' I said. 'And I'll see you . . . well, Friday, perhaps, when you're back,' I added, and then he walked off into the night and I let Babybelle into the kitchen, where she settled down with Ginger and Vic as if that was her rightful place.

Chapter 21: Treasured

'N-no,' I stammered, dazed and blushing. 'But Cara . . .'

I half-thought he was only teasing, but he looked serious enough. He put his mouth to my ear again, which tickled, and whispered, 'Cara's old news – I'm finishing with her tonight. Off with the old, on with the new!'

'What's this about Cara?' a voice imperatively demanded from the back of the car. 'What are you telling her about me, Harry?'

I was dying to discuss my escalating dreams with Daisy Silver, so it was lucky that today was the day she was calling in for lunch, on her way back from some convention in Liverpool.

At breakfast I reminded Debo that she was officially opening Hidden Hoards on Saturday, at ten, and it was exactly as I thought: she'd entirely forgotten about it.

'But I'll make sure she scrubs up and gets there on time,' Judy assured me.

'Good, because Cameron's told the local paper you're opening it, Debo, and they're sending a reporter out. You'd better come into the studio and we'll decide which of my clothes you're wearing.'

'OK, but we'll have to be quick, because Chris is coming over this morning and he's bringing Snowy back. I want to discuss one of the other dogs with him, too, and then I'll take Snowy over to Jonas and see him settled into his new home.'

We picked out an outfit and then Judy suggested that it would look wonderful with a set of Indian gold wedding jewellery Debo had.

'I don't think I've ever seen you wearing any jewellery, Debo!' I exclaimed, surprised. 'Or only in magazine pictures.'

'Oh, it's not practical when I'm working, so I don't bother. I do have a few pieces given to me as gifts and they're in the little safe in the study. Baz insisted on installing it.'

'I had no idea you had a safe, either,' I confessed.

'I forgot all about it, to be honest, so I haven't opened it for years.'

The tiny safe was set into the wall behind a small medieval-style tapestry of my own making and the code was her birthday, the same numbers she always used for everything, which, as I kept telling her, was blindingly obvious to thieves.

Inside, it was totally crammed with leather jewellery boxes, including one containing the spectacular gold wedding set.

'You've got a treasure trove stashed away!' I exclaimed, stunned. 'Is it insured?'

'There seems a lot more of it than I remember,' Debo said, looking at it in a puzzled way as if it might have been multiplying behind her back. 'And I don't think I've insured anything individually.' She held up a finely wrought necklace so that her fingers seemed to be dripping rich, buttery gold. 'They were all gifts, so each one reminds me of the giver.'

'Various lovers,' Judy interpreted.

'Actually, I don't really *need* any of it, do I?' she said, opening her grey eyes wide. 'I expect it's worth quite a bit, so I could sell it and give you your money back, Izzy.'

'But surely it has sentimental value?'

'Yes, but I'll still have the happy memories and I don't wear it any more. Can you find out how we get the best price for it, Izzy?'

'If you're sure. But I don't want you to give *me* the money. Keep it for another crisis.'

'Better still, I'll use it to make sure you're all right, Judy, if anything happens to me and you lose the Lodge,' she said. 'An annuity, perhaps? I'll have to get some advice on the best sort.'

'I'm sure Rufus wouldn't make you leave anyway, Judy,' I said. 'Not now I know him better.'

Judy protested that she didn't need an annuity and they bickered off to the kennels together, though I removed the gold necklace from Debo's careless fingers and locked it back in the safe first. I'd have to do an inventory when I had time.

Daisy arrived early for lunch, since she couldn't stay the night and so needed to set off on the long drive back to London by early afternoon. It was lovely to see her again, and of course she, Judy and Debo had been friends since the sixties, so there was lots of talk and laughter.

I hadn't mentioned my changing dreams to Debo and Judy because I hadn't wanted to worry them, but I managed a brief chat with Daisy alone, when she asked me to show her my clothes samples in the studio while Judy was making the coffee.

I told her about the more recent dreams that were releasing a slow trickle of what might, or might not, have happened.

'But they're as sharp and clear as a memory, so I'm sure they must be.'

'Are they all like that?'

'No, occasionally they start out that way and then take a turn into one of those odd ones – you know, the kind where you're walking down the street without any clothes on. And I've got a new recurring dream, nothing to do with the accident, where I'm floating through opaque turquoise water with Rufus . . . but that's quite nice.'

'Rufus?'

'Rufus Carlyle, Baz's son by Fliss,' I said, feeling myself go slightly pink. I hadn't meant to mention the watery dreams! 'I thought he was going to be horrible, but he's turned out to be not as bad as we thought, considering who his mother is. In fact,' I admitted, 'he's quickly become a friend.'

I told her a bit about him and the way he'd been shunted around between school and various temporary carers as a child, and she said that he did indeed sound interesting, and a strong character to have built a business after a start like that.

'Though of course, he will have been damaged by that upbringing and the lack of parental affection, followed by rejection from the man he thought was his father.'

'Well, I'm damaged too – not by my childhood, which was wonderful, but by the accident that ended it. So, we sort of have something in common, don't we? Mind you, we also have a couple of major things that ought to drive us apart, like the way his mother's influence on mine led to her death and my having been the driver of the car that killed his brother.'

255

'Ah, yes,' Daisy said, 'how are you getting on with your investigation into the accident – your mission, as you called it?'

'I've talked to everyone who was involved except for the two most central witnesses, Simon and Cara. I don't know if Simon actually remembers anything, but Cara must know all the answers, if I could only get her to speak to me.'

'She's proving elusive?'

'Very – but I'm going to go all out to talk to both of them now, whether they want to or not. In fact,' I said, suddenly making my mind up, 'I'll go to Grimside tomorrow and look for them!'

'Be careful, Izzy,' she warned. 'When you open a can of worms, you can never get the lid back on.'

Then Judy called to say the coffee was ready and I told Daisy how Kieran had lost interest in me when he came up, once he caught sight of Cara, his old flame. She said it was a small world and coincidences like that no longer surprised her.

Just after Daisy left, my first consignment of stock arrived from India, which was very exciting, so I spent the rest of the day unpacking and sorting the airy cotton and silk dresses, tops, quilted jackets and floaty scarves. The main colour palette for my first collection was indigo, turquoise, terracotta and cream, with a sprinkling of garments in bold garnet red, emerald and gold. The tiny silver bells on the tie necks of the blouses tinkled and the boxes smelled of sandalwood, which evoked many happy memories . . .

I pressed everything, attached the tags and then put the clothes into clear plastic covers, on which I stuck computer-printed labels with the name of the design, size and colour.

Then, later, Judy ferried most of the stock over to Cam's in the car, where I hung everything in the stockroom and stacked the matching scarves in the shelf unit.

Cam was busily putting the finishing touches to the shop area, but the walls were now covered in pictures and the cube storage displayed pottery and strange wooden birds. The jewellery was in a glass case near the counter and he was just fixing up a light inside it.

'It's all looking good,' I told him.

'I'm nearly there – I even know how to use the till,' he said proudly. 'Though actually, Granddad's still better at it than me because he's looked after the shop quite a bit for Mum.'

'I've reminded Debo that she's opening the gallery on Saturday and we'll have her here in plenty of time.'

'Great! Lulu's got me some cut-price bubbly and Mum's doing cheese nibbles for the customers,' he said. 'Or at least, I hope some of the people who come to the opening will be customers, because I'm nearly broke now. The gallery will have to pay its way quickly.'

'I'm sure it will, and when you and Rufus have been to Cornwall next week to collect the easels and stuff, you can advertise the art classes, too, can't you?'

'True. I think that's going to be my bread-and-butter work. I had to give my notice in for the other art classes ages ago so they could find someone else to take them over, but all the travelling to get to them really ate into the payment I got anyway.'

Then he suggested we take the pictures of my clothes for the online catalogue early next week, when Lulu wasn't so busy and could model some of them too.

'And I want to rope Debo in a bit, because seeing her wearing my designs might go down well with older customers.'

'Great idea! If you have a famous model in the house, why not use her?'

'Lulu could take Debo's pictures on Saturday, since she'll be wearing one of my outfits then. I know there aren't any Haunted bookings this weekend, so she should be able to come. Unless they're short-staffed at the Screaming Skull, they don't really seem to need her, do they? But hopefully that'll all change after the Haunted Holidays go live on the website.'

Snowy briefly returned and then went off to his new life with Jonas, but I saw that two more dogs had been installed in his place, and one of them, a demented-looking Doberman, was flinging itself at its cage door in a way that made me feel glad it was to stay in the strongest kennel in the corner until Chris had dog-whispered it into a better frame of mind.

Poor Pearl was to be spayed next morning, paid for by Rufus, who would be up in Durham by now . . . and somehow, I didn't feel like walking down to the Screaming Skull on my own that night, though that was probably just tiredness. I texted Cam and Lulu not to expect me and told them I was going to go to Grimside tomorrow to try to find either Simon or Cara – or even both. Lulu kindly offered to pick me up and drive me there.

Right after we'd arranged that between us, Rufus rang me to ask how Pearl was.

'Perfectly happy,' I replied, amused. 'She doesn't realise she's having an operation tomorrow, you know.'

'No, but *I* do.'

'It'll be fine. How was the estate sale?'

'Not very good, but I'll tell you all about it tomorrow. I thought you might be at the pub, with Cam and Lulu.'

'No. My first consignment of clothes arrived earlier, so I've been really busy all day and I'm tired.' Then I told him I was going to Grimside in the morning, to try to buttonhole Simon, Cara, or both.

'Are you sure you don't want to wait for me to get back so I can go with you? This Cara sounds very unpleasant and you might need some back-up.'

'No, it's OK, and I think I've got more chance of them opening up if I'm alone,' I told him, and he said then he'd see me tomorrow.

Debo and Judy had already gone to bed, so he was the last person I spoke to that night (unless you counted Vic and Ginger). Perhaps that was why I instantly plunged deep into a strangely comforting dream of swimming with him, the second my head hit the pillow . . .

Chapter 22: Grimside

I woke the following morning feeling strangely blissed out, which I expect was the same effect people get from swimming with dolphins. I also felt resolute that I would make some progress with my mission that morning, or bust!

Lulu duly picked me up and drove me over to Grimside. Although the edge of the estate bordered the village, most of it, including Sir Lionel Cripchet's ugly redbrick Victorian mansion, was situated on the other side of the hill, a few miles by road from Halfhidden. Lulu had to get back after dropping me off, in order to welcome some last-minute Haunted Weekenders.

'Americans – parents and two teenagers. They'd heard about it from that nice couple from Minnesota and thought they could squeeze it into their own trip. I'll have to see if Jonas will come and do a repeat performance of the story-telling on Saturday, even if it is just a small audience.'

'I'm sure Jonas would do it *every* Saturday night, so long as you plied him with pints of ale, and Cam and I could come, and probably Rufus, too.'

'And a couple of the ordinary hotel guests might, so that would make a decent audience,' she agreed.

She pulled up near the front gates of Grimside, which looked forbiddingly like something you'd find at the entrance to a high-security prison, though a small board had been put out advertising that the herbivarium was open.

'You could give me a ring when you come out and I'll pick you up if I can,' Lulu offered, but I said no, it was OK, I'd walk home by the road because the exercise would do me good.

'If you're coming back past the pub, then you could pop in and tell me how it went.'

'I think you'll be too busy – didn't you say you had to go to the wholesaler's for more soft drinks later, too? But I'll email you if I manage to speak to Simon or Cara. If I don't, or they won't talk to me, I've written notes for both, explaining why I just want to ask a few questions.'

'Good luck!' Lulu said and I thought that *that* was something I could do with a good dose of.

I followed the sign to the herbivarium, which was in a walled garden not far from the entrance, and a gnarled and monosyllabic elderly man in a small booth took my two pounds and handed me a ticket and a leaflet.

I noted that the way out, as so often in homes and gardens open to the public, lay through the shop: no sales opportunity lost. It was the same up at the Lady Spring, where Tom liked to tempt the visitors with souvenirs and pamphlets on their way out through the rear section of his shed, having already sold them plastic bottles to collect up some of the precious water, along with their tickets, at the entrance hatch.

There were only a couple of other visitors wandering around the neat brick paths between the herb beds, and one solitary gardener who, to my disappointment, wasn't Simon.

But having paid my money, I spent some time looking round, and it was very pleasant within the sheltering walls, with the sun shining and bees busily humming around the rosemary.

When I thought I'd had my two pounds' worth, I asked the gardener whether he knew where Simon Clew was, but he was probably a close relative of the man who'd sold me my ticket, because he just said, surlily, 'I dunno,' before resuming his weeding.

I emerged from the shop without purchasing anything, to the disappointment of the woman behind the counter, and stood there irresolute, wondering whether to boldly head up the path beyond the 'PRIVATE. NO ENTRY' sign towards the distant house. Even if I didn't spot Simon, I could at least see if Cara was at home to unwelcome visitors. And if not, I'd be able to leave her note at the house and drop Simon's off with the elderly man at the ticket booth on my way out.

I'd just decided to pursue this course of action when Simon suddenly appeared from the large greenhouse next to the walled garden, pushing a wheelbarrow full of seedlings.

It took me a moment to recognise him because he was no longer wearing heavy glasses, but other than that he looked much as he'd always done: stocky, quiet, brown-haired and attractive in an unassuming kind of way.

'Simon!' I exclaimed. 'Just the man I wanted to see.'

He stopped dead, staring at me as if I was a ghost. Then he swallowed hard and said, '*Izzy*?'

'Yes, it's me. Long time no see, Simon. I almost didn't recognise you without the glasses.'

'Laser surgery, years ago,' he explained.

'How are you?'

'I'm . . . fine.' He swallowed again and looked around nervously, as if the Wicked Witch of the West – or possibly Cara – might be about to arrive in a puff of smoke and turn him into stone. 'I mean, Dad told me you were back and asking all kinds of questions about the accident, but I didn't think you'd turn up here.'

'I had to, because I didn't know how else to get in touch. And as I told Dan, I only want to ask you a few questions because I'm trying to get a clear picture in my head of what happened.'

'But you surely *know* what happened? I mean, you might have lost your memory, but they must have told you?'

'I'm aware of the facts, of course, but I've always found it hard to understand how I could have agreed to drive the car that night. So I wanted to talk to everyone involved and see the full picture at last – and then I'm sure I'll be able to put it behind me once and for all,' I explained.

'I do see what you mean, Izzy, but I was ill that night so *I* don't remember anything, either.'

'I know you had a bad reaction to the alcohol, but I thought perhaps you might recall a little bit. Debo and Judy said you wanted to talk to me at the hospital, too, and I wondered what about.'

He nodded. 'I did try to see you when it didn't look like you were going to die after all.'

'So, *do* you remember anything about that night?'

'Not much, as I said. The alcohol affected my system like poison and I've never touched a drop since. But then, I didn't know I was drinking vodka at the time. Trust Harry to do something so stupid,' he added, then sighed. 'Well, he paid for it, but somehow, I've always felt a bit guilty.'

263

There was a haunted look in his eyes and I felt some compunction about reminding him of the past, though at least he had some inkling about how I was feeling.

'Me, too,' I told him. 'And Harry really must have pulled out all the stops to persuade me to drive, because I would have been scared witless by the idea, whatever Cara said about my insisting on doing it.'

'No, I – well, that's what I thought afterwards, until Cara told me what really happened. She was angry with *you*, rather than Harry . . . and so was Dad.'

'I'd certainly like Cara to tell *me* what really happened,' I said drily. 'What *do* you actually remember, Simon?' I asked. 'Come on – there must be something!'

'Not a lot, apart from being in the beer garden earlier,' he confessed. 'After that, it's all hazy. I thought at first I'd been driving the car, but then, I *always* drove the car, so they said I was just remembering another occasion when I had . . .' he tailed off.

'That's interesting. I had a flashback and thought I'd been in the back of the car that night, but then I remembered I *had* been, only the week before the accident,' I said. 'I've often dreamed about that night, the same dream every time, but lately it's been changing . . .'

'You, too?' he asked, looking startled. 'Sometimes I—'

Just as I was feeling that we might have found common ground, he broke off abruptly and, following the line of his eyes, I saw Cara riding up the drive on a thin chestnut thoroughbred, whose clipped, velvet-smooth coat showed every bump and vein of the body beneath, like an equine anatomy lesson.

She was scowling as she slid off her mount in one elegant movement and strode over, her horse trailing behind her.

'What are *you* doing here?' she demanded. 'You're not wanted – can't you take a hint?'

'Look, Cara, I only need a brief chat about the night of Harry's accident – just once, and never again,' I said reasonably. 'I was explaining to Simon that—'

'*Go away*,' Cara interrupted rudely. 'Get off my property and stop bothering me.'

'I paid my two pounds to see the garden, like anyone else,' I pointed out mildly, 'and I don't want to upset either of you, only get a better understanding of how things happened.'

'It's all in the past,' she snapped. 'It's over.'

'It won't be over for me until I know everything there is to know.'

Simon and Cara exchanged glances. There was no mistaking the body language, or the look of slavish devotion in Simon's eyes. So Foxy had been right, but whatever was going on, Cara was in charge.

'Dad told me not to talk to her, raking up old stuff,' Simon said, looking troubled. 'When she didn't die like we thought she would, but started getting better, he didn't want me to talk to her then, either.'

'Of course he doesn't, Simon, when you nearly had a nervous breakdown over it at the time,' Cara said, taking a grip on his arm that was more custodial than possessive. 'Anyway, you remember nothing and I said everything I knew at the inquest.'

'But I'm not sure if I do recall little bits of what happened, or if I'm imagining it,' he said. 'I was just telling Izzy that—'

'Then don't. She's simply trying to offload the blame onto us.'

265

'That is *so* not true!' I said indignantly. 'I accept that I was driving, I'd just like to know why on earth I agreed to it and what caused the actual crash.'

'You insisted on driving back – you were a right little bossyboots – then you ran the car off the road, killed Harry and ruined my life, that's what happened!'

'That's a bit harsh, Cara,' Simon began.

'Shut up, Simon!' she said, turning a Medusa face on him.

'I can just about believe Harry persuaded me to drive,' I said, 'but there's no way I would have *insisted* on it, or that it could have been my suggestion, so I've always wondered why you said that?'

'Are you accusing me of lying?' she snarled, narrowing her eyes at me, then added in disgust, 'God, how could a man like Kieran ever fall for *you*?'

'Who's Kieran?' Simon asked, baffled.

'My ex-fiancé,' I told him. 'It turns out he used to know Cara in Oxford.'

'*And* he knows the truth about the accident, too, now,' she said spitefully.

'He certainly fell hook, line and sinker for your version,' I agreed.

Simon was looking puzzled. 'You didn't mention any Kieran to me,' he said to her.

'Cara, all I want is for you to tell me the truth,' I said. 'What you heard and saw, how Harry persuaded me to drive and how I came to run the car off the road where I did, rather than stop at the Lodge and let Harry take over. Then that's it – I'll drop the whole thing.'

'Then you're out of luck, because I've said all I'm going

to say. Now, I think you'd better go, before I have you thrown out!' She glared at me implacably.

'I can see I might as well,' I said, but as I turned to leave I saw Simon's troubled expression and wondered if he was having doubts about Cara's version of the story. Or maybe he was just worried by some other man's name coming up.

'We've nothing more to say to you, ever,' Cara said for both of them, and again she shot Simon a look that was both proprietary and illuminating. *Here's my creature, my plaything,* it said.

I wondered if the elderly and irascible Sir Lionel Cripchet, a small, red-faced baronet, prone to picking arguments with everyone he came into contact with, had any idea there was a whole Lady Chatterley thing going on practically under his nose.

Walking back, I pondered what had been said . . . and what hadn't, for of course I was sure they were keeping something back. I suspected Judy and Tom were, too, but at least I thought I knew what that was.

But Cara had definitely told one lie and it was interesting that Simon seemed as troubled by dreams and recollections of that night, which might or might not be true memories, as I was.

I was a mile down the road and the sky was clouding over in an apocalyptic kind of way, much like my thoughts, when a familiar large green van pulled up.

The window rolled down and Rufus said, 'Going my way?'

'Judy always told me not to accept lifts from strange men,' I said primly.

He cast a glance up at the ominous sky. 'The choice would appear to be to get in, or drown.'

I got in.

'Didn't you find anything at that country house sale?' I asked, as he pulled out into the road again.

'Not much, because they'd sneakily bought in a lot of modern rubbish and arranged it in the outbuildings with a few old pieces, to try and make it look as if it had been there for years. I wasn't fooled.'

'So, a wasted trip?'

'Not entirely, because I stopped at a contact's house on the way back, and he had some more old chimney pots for me. People love them as garden decorations and planters. I got a couple of stone horse troughs from him, too.'

'Judy has one of those by the kitchen door,' I said. 'She grows bay leaves for cooking in it, though I keep telling her some of the bigger dogs can pee that high.'

'I expect she gives them a good wash first before she uses them,' he suggested, and I hoped he was right.

'How's Foxy managing without you?'

'She sounds fine. I've checked a couple of times, but I don't think she's had any problems.'

'She's very capable and so is her sister, Sandy. Her end of the kennel paperwork was immaculate, with full records on all the dogs that had passed through.'

'So, did you have any luck at Grimside?' Rufus asked, and I told him what had happened.

'Cara's sticking to her story, even though I know it isn't completely true. I think Simon would open up if I got him alone, but I don't know that there's a lot of chance of that, or even that he remembers anything for sure.'

'Frustrating,' he said sympathetically.

'You know, I'm sure they've got a whole Lady Chatterley/ Mellors thing going on,' I told him. 'Though actually, with Cara, it was a bit more like Lady Macbeth; she was pretty snappy with him.'

'That might be more fascinating if I'd ever met either of these star-crossed lovers,' he said mildly. 'I don't suppose you've heard yet how Pearl's operation went?'

'No, but you can come in and we'll find out when we get to the Lodge,' I suggested.

Judy told Rufus that Pearl was fine and would be coming back next day. She'd be in the house while she recovered and then she could go up to Sweetwell after that.

He went off relieved.

We were all supposed to be going over later to the gallery to help Cam get ready for the next day's opening ceremony, but Lulu, when she rang to find out how the Grimside trip had gone, said she would be too busy to get away that evening.

So it was just me and Rufus helping Cam set out the borrowed champagne flutes and putting the final touches to everything, and when we'd finished, I showed Rufus the racks of swaying clothes in the storeroom. He seemed genuinely interested – so unlike Kieran had ever been.

And, speak of the devil, just before I went to bed that night, Lulu rang again to tell me Kieran had returned to the pub and was staying that night. I quickly checked my phone for missed messages, but he hadn't called me.

It was very odd, because he seemed to have totally lost interest in our getting back together the moment he set eyes on Cara. And anyway, surely this time he would have rung me first?

Perhaps he'd come back to *see* Cara? If so, then poor Simon might soon have his nose put out of joint!

Chapter 23: Hidden Hoards

'Just get in the driver's seat,' he coaxed. 'I'll be right next to you and you can pretend we're on the Sweetwell drive again.'

I woke up in the middle of the night calling out to my younger self, '*No, Izzy – don't do it!*' as if I was a time-travelling bystander who could change the future. It took me ages to get back to sleep after that.

I had to dash down to the Screaming Skull early next day to drop off one of my Izzy Dane Designs outfits for Lulu. I'd decided that if she and I and Debo were *all* wearing them to the gallery opening, then Cameron could get lots of good pictures for my online catalogue and there'd be fewer to take later.

She was busy with the hotel guests when I cautiously popped my head into the breakfast room, but there was no sign of Kieran. Lulu spotted me and, when she had a minute, told me he'd checked out right after breakfast and she'd seen him get into Cara's car, leaving his own in the car park.

So, my suspicions were right and it was definitely off with the old and on with the new – or maybe that should be back

271

with the even older? I could hardly feel hurt by this turn of events, considering I'd not only told Kieran I'd plummeted headlong out of love with him, but followed it up by saying we were finished.

However, Cara was not only married, but appeared to be carrying on an illicit affair with Simon, too, so the course of true love – or whatever it was – was unlikely to run smooth.

I can't say I gave it a lot of thought, because I had to dash back to change and make sure Debo did the same.

Of course, Debo made everything she wore look stunning. For the opening of Hidden Hoards she had on one of my Grecian-inspired sari dresses, a fusion of two cultures that must have worked, for it was much admired.

Cameron photographed her before everyone arrived. Then he took some pics of me in my pleated jade-green silk-mix top and simple draped skirt, and Lulu, who was wearing an amber dress that matched the citrine earrings I'd given her.

Rufus, who had also arrived early, said gravely that we all scrubbed up well and added that pixies should always wear that particular shade of green. But I knew by then when he was teasing me, and anyway, I'd realised that the words 'Saxon warrior' would forever have the power to silence him.

The throng at the gallery opening included not only locals, but some of the hotel guests. Debo, well primed, made a little speech about how this was another step towards the regeneration of Halfhidden, which would put it firmly back on the tourist map.

The local reporter took lots of details and ate his way through an entire plate of nibbles, without appearing to stop writing, though fortunately many of the guests who came into the gallery for a free glass of bubbly also bought things, or took one of the leaflets Cam had put out about the art classes he would soon be starting.

When the numbers finally began to thin, Lulu returned to the pub, and Judy and Debo, who were keen to change into workaday clothes and then fetch Pearl from the vet's, also left. Rufus, who had a delivery to make before heading back to the garden antiques centre, said he would call in later, on the way to the pub, to see how Pearl was.

He simply couldn't keep away – it *must* be love!

Pearl was still a bit out of it when Rufus arrived, not to mention miffed about having to wear a plastic cone on her head to stop her licking her wounds, but she was still pleased to see him.

When finally I managed to tear Rufus away from her and we got to the pub, Lulu gave us the next instalment in the Kieran/Cara saga.

'He came back with Cara, then she transferred some luggage from her car into his and they drove off in it,' she said. 'Presumably overnight – and Dad's mad, because she left her car here and he says they're using us as a public car park. It's not like either of them has even *asked* if it's OK.'

'So – you think they're starting an affair?' Rufus said.

'It certainly looks like it. Cara seems to have become a bit of a goer, doesn't she? Married, having an affair with the head gardener and now picking up with an old flame. I wonder where they've gone.' Then she got up. 'Oh, well, time to set up the storytelling session. Where did Jonas get to?'

'Playing dominoes in the public bar with an old crony,' Cam said. 'I'd better go and fetch him.'

Dan hadn't been there earlier when we walked through to the snug, and I'd wondered if he was back in London with Fliss. Rufus was probably thinking the same, though neither of us said anything.

In the end there was a good audience for the storytelling session, for several of the non-Haunted-Weekend hotel guests came. So, since we weren't needed to pad the numbers out, Rufus and I retired to the snug to relax and chat over a drink.

I don't know how it came about that we'd so quickly become comfortable together, but as soon as we'd stopped being prickly with one another, we'd seamlessly slipped into friendship. Perhaps it was that, despite being brought up elsewhere, he was very much a Salcombe, and so belonged here in Halfhidden.

Only his occasional mention of Fliss cast a slight blight on things for me, though he probably felt the same whenever I brought up the subject of Harry's accident. Now I'd had time to think about it, although Fliss *sounded* like a dreadful woman, I didn't suppose she'd set out to kill my mother on purpose, any more than I did Harry.

'Tomorrow I'm going to help clear the path up to the Fairy Falls, or Boggart Falls, or whatever they're going to call them, for an hour or two,' I said. 'Can you come, or will you be too busy flogging old rakes and wheelbarrows?'

'I might get away for a bit. Laurie's becoming interested in the business after helping Foxy and he said if he was home he'd always cover the office while she sees to the customers. It's going to be really handy when he's retired.'

'Yes, that's working out well,' I agreed. 'It'll be Cam's first proper day of opening at the gallery tomorrow, so I don't expect he'll be coming and I think Lulu will be too busy. Still, it's quite a short path and not very overgrown, so it shouldn't take long to clear.'

We got a lift back up to the Green in the car with Cameron and Jonas, since it had started to rain. Everything was quiet at the kennels, and when I let myself in after Rufus had walked off up the drive, the three dogs in the kitchen barely marked my presence with the opening of sleepy eyes.

My night was untroubled by dreams and I woke to a newly rinsed, brighter morning. I had a swim and then, after breakfast, Rufus called at the Lodge to see Pearl and to offer me a lift up to the Summit Alpine Nursery, where the path-clearing volunteers were to gather.

Babybelle, who had been lying in a comatose heap with Vic, Ginger and Pearl, insisted on coming with us and wouldn't be distracted, so in the end Rufus put her in the back of the old Land Rover.

'I didn't even know you *had* a Land Rover! How many vehicles have you actually got?' I asked, as we set off.

'Only the Transit van, the big van and this . . . oh, and a motorbike,' he added. 'They're all old. I don't even have to pay road tax on this one.'

'It's certainly a no-frills ride,' I said, for as we crossed the cattle grid at the entrance to the nursery, it felt as if my bottom had been passed over a cheese grater. 'If it ever had any suspension, I think you've lost it.'

Belle seemed to enjoy the ride and although I'd thought she might be a nuisance, she simply plodded after me to the bit of path I was assigned to clear, lay down in a patch of shade and promptly went to sleep.

275

There were plenty of volunteers, but I was the token one from the Lodge, since Judy was keeping an eye on Pearl, while baking, and Debo was awaiting the arrival of yet another Desperate Dog. I had high hopes that the canine numbers would still balance at the end of the day though, for someone who wanted a brindle Staffie was visiting, and we certainly had a good stock of those!

I'd been working for about an hour and was having a little rest in the shade with Babybelle when, to my surprise, Simon climbed up the path and lowered himself onto the grass next to me. His expression was troubled. I hadn't seen him earlier chopping back brambles, so I suspected he'd come specially to talk to me, rather than volunteer.

'I'm sorry Cara was so rude to you on Friday,' he began. 'But any mention of the accident still upsets her.'

'I expect it does, but I'm not going to stop asking questions until I know exactly what happened, so she might as well bite the bullet and get it over.'

'She doesn't even want *me* to talk to you,' he said, then paused, before adding, with more than a hint of question in his voice, 'She was out yesterday, then came back hours later with a strange bloke, put some luggage in her car and drove off with him again.'

'I think that was probably Kieran, my ex-fiancé. Remember, she mentioned him while I was at Grimside? Apparently, they're old friends.'

'Yes, I wondered if it might be him. I was there when they came out of the house, but she left without a word. I might as well have been invisible,' he added bitterly.

'Lulu told me Kieran stayed Friday night at the Screaming

Skull and then yesterday she saw Cara drive him back there, before transferring some luggage from her car into his and going off with him,' I said helpfully. 'Hers is still in the pub car park.'

'Right . . .' he said, his face like thunder.

'Isn't her husband ever home?' I asked curiously.

'No, and they lead very separate lives. He has a place in Scotland. He owns a small whisky distillery – that's how he gets his money – or he's off at his club in London.'

'I've heard rumours that you and she are . . . more than friends,' I said.

'You can't keep anything secret in a village. I hoped she'd agree to leave Cripchet, but she didn't much fancy slumming it on gardener's wages,' he said. 'But it seemed all wrong to me to be taking old Cripchet's money while having an affair with his wife, so I've already applied for a job back with the National Trust and hope she'll leave with me when I get one.'

'How did you come to be working for Cripchet in the first place?'

'I was staying with Dad for a couple of days' holiday and ran into Cara. She said the job was going and put a word in for me. It was better wages and a good cottage, though he expects a lot for his money and he's an unpleasant man to deal with.'

'Your dad has been unpleasant to *me* since I came home. He even threatened me and said I shouldn't have come back. Mind you, he seems to have it in for all of us at the Lodge.'

'He gets grudges. He was bitter about Debo ratting on him to Baz, just because he made a pass at her. And then she told him Dad was letting the grounds go . . . though, actually, even I could see that Olly was the only one doing any work.

Dad had it easy,' he admitted. 'Still, he's harmless really, you know that – all hot air. He never laid a finger on me when I was growing up and he's tried to do his best by me.'

'But Debo and Judy said it was common knowledge that when you were little he left you alone at night when he went out to the pub.'

Simon shrugged. 'He likes a drink – and he likes the ladies, too. We had neighbours on either side, so I never felt afraid.'

'Things are changing at Sweetwell now,' I warned. 'If he doesn't pull his socks up and do his job, Rufus won't be as easy-going about it as Baz was. I don't think Dan's attitude to him is helping, either.'

'Dad met this Carlyle bloke's mother when she was down and they've stayed in touch,' he said awkwardly. 'She's a pop star – or he said she was. *I'd* never heard of her.'

'Fliss Gambol. I think her heyday was the sixties and early seventies. And he's definitely stayed in touch; he's been boasting to his friends in the pub about going to London and spending weekends with her!'

This was obviously no surprise to Simon. 'Does Rufus Carlyle know?'

'He does. And your dad was sniggering to his friends in the pub the other night when Rufus was walking through and he heard Dan mention his mother's name, so to say he's not exactly happy with him at the moment would be the understatement of the year.'

I paused, for Rufus had come into view. He must have been working hard for he'd stripped off his shirt, revealing an impressively muscled torso and broad shoulders. He slashed back a clump of brambles and then, as if he felt me watching, turned briefly and gave me a smile.

'*That's* Rufus Carlyle.'

'I've seen him about, but I'd know him for a Salcombe anyway, with that colouring,' Simon said.

He got up to go. I rose slightly creakily to my feet, too, having stiffened up.

'If I give you my mobile number, can you ring me when Cara's back?'

'I don't know,' he said uncertainly. 'I reckon Dad's right and it's better not to stir it all up again.'

'Then the quickest way to stop me is for everyone to tell me exactly what happened,' I said, exasperated. 'I have a feeling you're keeping something back, too, Simon. Or is it just that you realise what Cara said about my insisting on driving you all up to Sweetwell that night couldn't be true?'

'No – no, I *don't* know any more,' he protested quickly, but he looked troubled. Then, turning on his heel, he plunged off down the steep path without another word.

I felt I'd had enough path clearing by then, and Rufus needed to go back to the Hall, so Belle and I hitched a ride with him. On the way, I told him what Simon had said, though I skimmed past the Fliss bits so as not to rub salt in the wound.

Judy had invited Rufus to dinner that evening and by then Pearl was much perkier than when he saw her in the morning.

'She's not house-trained, so there *have* been a few little accidents, but this afternoon she followed Vic and Ginger out for a pee, so she might just get the hang of it from watching the other two,' Judy observed.

'It would be a bonus if she was at least *partly* house-trained by the time I take her to Sweetwell,' Rufus said. 'Since Myra

279

heard she was coming, she's been stocking up with industrial amounts of disinfectant and Marigolds, and she says she's prepared for anything.'

Dinner was roast beef and Yorkshire pudding, followed by the last of the previous year's blackberries from the freezer, made into a crumble, served with thick cream.

Rufus and I felt a bit stuffed after that and took our coffee into the studio, accompanied by Pearl and Babybelle, while Judy and Debo went out to the kennels with Vic and Ginger.

'I've texted Lulu and Cam to say we won't be at the pub tonight, but I don't really think they'd have noticed we weren't there anyway,' I said, with a grin.

'Probably not. Things seem to be hotting up!'

'I suspect Cam spends some of his nights in the caravan, because he always looks self-conscious when he says he's going to stay on a bit and help Lulu set the tables for breakfast.'

'Why can't they just come out and admit they're an item?' he asked, puzzled.

'I'm sure Cam would, but Lulu needs some time to get over Guy. He was very controlling and dented her self-confidence. Now his mistress has left him, I only hope he *doesn't* come here, expecting her to be pleased to see him, because he's arrogant enough.'

'How do you feel about *your* ex and Cara now?'

'I don't feel anything at all, which is pretty shocking, really, considering how recently I was all set to marry him! I'm just a bit sorry for Simon . . . but maybe she's only having a fling with Kieran and will go back to him.'

'If he'll *have* her back. And there's the husband too, isn't there?' He grimaced. 'What messy lives some people lead . . . my mother among them.'

'You haven't got any ex-wives or fiancées lurking about, have you?' I asked him, impulsively.

'No,' he said shortly. 'Where women are concerned, I have trust issues.'

'Right . . .' I said, then changed the subject. 'Simon said he felt bad about working for Cripchet after he started having an affair with Cara, so he's already applied for jobs back with his old employer.'

'Do you think you can cross him off your mission list now?' Rufus asked.

'Probably. I don't really think he remembers anything clearly after they left the beer garden that night and though he's a bit reluctant to talk to me, I think it's mainly because, deep down, he doesn't believe what Cara said about my insisting on driving.'

I paused, then thought I'd better come clean and said, 'He knew all about his father visiting Fliss in London – in fact, he said he thought he was there again this weekend.'

'I'd guessed as much. I wish she hadn't got involved with Dan because it'll make problems if I fire him, which is more tempting by the day.'

'Yes, he could then say you'd fired him because of the affair.'

'I expect I could find lots of witnesses to say how little work he'd done for years, though.'

'Cam texted me earlier to say you're off to Cornwall at the crack of dawn tomorrow to collect all those easels and things he's bought,' I said.

'Yes, didn't I tell you? We fixed it up yesterday. Jonas

minded the gallery for an hour this afternoon so Cam could have a go at driving the big van up and down the drive, but it's not that huge so he'll be fine.'

'It'll be a long trip, even with the two of you taking turns.'

'But he'll be an expert van driver by the time we get down there. It was a good idea of his to keep his gallery opening times and closing day the same as mine, so we'll both always be off on a Monday.'

'My hours will be entirely flexible, which I suppose is one advantage of an online business.' I sort of hoped Rufus would suggest I go with them on the trip, but he didn't.

'How did the photographs from the gallery opening come out?' he asked.

'Brilliant! Cam and Lulu sent them across yesterday afternoon and we're going to take just a few more on Tuesday. And once the pictures are up – the business goes live!'

'That will be an exciting moment.'

'Yes . . . though I suppose it will take a while before anyone finds my site.' I sighed. 'I'd hoped to have talked to everyone about the accident before then, but I don't see it ever happening with Cara.'

'Are you still dreaming up new details?'

'Off and on. I'm sure most of them are real memories, though only Cara could confirm that. I do have some bizarre dreams, too, and another recurring dream about swimming up at the Lady Spring with—' I broke off, remembering exactly *who* was swimming about in that dream with me!

'Tom says you swim there early most mornings.'

'Yes, usually before breakfast. I got used to the heat in India, so it seems a bit chilly, but I'm getting toughened up again. You should come.'

'I thought you liked to be alone while you're swimming?'

'Sometimes, but now I know you better, I really don't mind,' I assured him, thinking that since he swam with me in my dreams anyway, he might as well do it in reality.

'How about if I send you a message whenever I'm setting out in the mornings and you can come if you feel like it?' I suggested. 'Sometimes I go later, or miss it altogether if something comes up.'

'OK – maybe *I* need toughening up, too,' he said.

'But you have to drink a whole cupful of the water from the cave first every time – it's a ritual and it's good for you.'

'If it's a purge of some kind, we ought to try pouring a bucketful into my impossible mother,' he said with a wry smile.

Chapter 24: Close Encounters

Dazed by what Harry had said, I was sitting in the car before I came back to reality. It was now starting to get dark and my hands, clenched on the steering wheel, felt sweaty with fear.

'Harry, there's no way I can do this!' I whispered, tears rolling down my face.

While I was swimming early next morning, I finally came to terms with the idea that I might now never manage to get any more information out of Cara, the last and most vital witness, and the only one who could tell me if my unfolding dreams were just that or actual memories. By now I was sure in my heart that they *were* true glimpses of the past . . . I wondered how far they might take me. Each time I woke up after one, I thought it might be the last, but if they ended then I would just have to accept that, too.

There was nothing like floating about in the Lady Pool to soothe, calm and give a sense of perspective.

I thought about Cam and Rufus, too, driving all the way down to Cornwall, and hoped they were having a good journey.

* * *

I worked all morning and then had lunch with Lulu in her caravan, a palatial trailer that used to be overflow staff accommodation before they renovated some of the attics in the Victorian part of the pub.

Workmen had just finished erecting a neat wooden fence around the caravan and there was a roomy kennel under the shade of the trees. I thought she'd managed to get everything ready extremely quickly, because although I'd ordered the new fence and a small, purpose-made kennel block for Desperate Dogs, they hadn't even been delivered yet.

After lunch we went out in Lulu's car to buy all the other things that Dusty would need, so that she was prepared for his arrival. I'd made a list and copied it for Rufus, too, for Pearl.

'Bed, bowls, collar, lead, food, brush – this dog's an expensive luxury,' Lulu complained as we wheeled an overflowing trolley towards the checkout.

'You didn't have to buy the most expensive collar on the rack,' I pointed out. 'And he could have managed to find his dinner even if he didn't have a white china pawprint-patterned bowl with "DOG" written on it.'

'He's had a hard time, I want to spoil him a bit,' she said.

'I might be doing this all over again with Rufus in a couple of days. Since he's never had a dog before, he's going to have no idea what to get, or how much it will all cost.'

When we'd loaded everything into the car, I said I'd like to buy a new dog-walking raincoat, since my ancient anorak had sprung leaks along the seams.

'I hadn't thought about all the walkies,' Lulu confessed. 'I suppose I'd better get something more waterproof, too.'

'We'll be able to meet up sometimes and walk the dogs together,' I suggested.

'That would be fun, and maybe we could take them to the beach one day, if the weather's nice,' she agreed.

We fell in love with the same raincoat, as we'd so often done with clothes in the past. They were made of water-proofed red cotton, with hoods and patterned linings – mine had sailboats and Lulu's, ducks.

'I've already got wellies and my old walking boots,' she said, 'so I think that's everything.'

Lulu came back to the Lodge to say hello to Dusty and have a cup of coffee. While we were snaffling freshly baked cheese scones from the rack, I had a text from Rufus, saying they were just starting back.

'So they'll be very late,' I said. 'I suppose they'll stop a couple of times on the way for something to eat and a rest.'

'At least he sent you a message, which is more than Cam sent to me!' Lulu said.

'I think it was from both of them, to both of us, really.'

'But you do seem to be getting on *very* well with Rufus,' she suggested meaningfully.

'Just like you are with Cam?' I raised one eyebrow.

She grinned. 'OK, no prying!'

'There's nothing to pry into. I really like Rufus as a friend, now I've got to know him, but there are a couple of major obstacles to anything deeper, like his mother's dis-astrous influence on mine and the fact that I was ultimately responsible for the death of his half-brother, whatever the circumstances.'

'Oh, I don't think he blames you for that. And it's not his

fault his mother is Fliss Gambol, is it? It sounds like he had a horrible childhood.'

'It does, and I'm sure he's never had much in the way of mothering because he loves it when Judy urges him to eat more, or get his hair cut. He might go right off her when she gives him a dog-hair scarf, though.'

'I always think the things she knits from dog hair are going to *smell* of dog, but actually they don't and they look really nice,' Lulu said.

'She has to put a lot of work into the hair before it's ready to knit – washing, carding and spinning.'

Lulu sipped her coffee and her face took on a pensive expression. 'Izzy, I'm afraid of falling in love with Cam,' she confessed, 'because if it all went pear-shaped, I'm sure it would destroy our friendship.'

'Don't you think it might be a bit late to worry about that?' I said drily. 'Anyway, it won't go wrong. You'll still be best friends – only with perks.'

'I don't understand how I can possibly have fallen in love with Cam after all these years. It was just that on the way back from the Dordogne, I suddenly saw him totally differently.'

'Yes, I gathered that! And luckily, it was mutual.'

'I was looking forward to the three of us being back together in Halfhidden, like we used to be, but if Cam and I get together, things *won't* be the same, will they?'

'Things are changing anyway, whether you want them to or not, but I'm sure the three of us will always be best friends.'

'Perhaps we should make that four, since Rufus seems to have quickly become one of us,' Lulu said. 'It's as if we've always known him.'

'I'm sure if Fliss had told Baz about him, he'd have brought him up here at Sweetwell with Harry, so we *would* always have known him! It's a very odd thought ... and things would have turned out very differently.'

'Well, unfortunately, you can't turn back time,' Lulu said, 'or I'd twist the dial to right before I met Guy and start again!'

I went into my studio when she'd gone. I could hear Chris and Debo out in the kennels, working with the aggressive Doberman, and the volleys of frantic barking suddenly ceased in the late afternoon, just as I was stepping back to examine my latest creation with narrowed eyes and a mouthful of bead-headed dressmaker's pins. I don't know if it was Chris's magic working, or simply that the dog's voice had run out, or a combination of the two. Whichever it was, the silence fell like a blessing on my successful afternoon's work.

I didn't text Rufus next morning to see if he wanted to join me at the pool, since I was sure after his long journey he wouldn't be awake yet, though I did have a message from Cam when I got back from my swim, saying he and Lulu were still up for taking the last of the catalogue photos this morning and Lulu was coming over right after breakfast.

They were both there when I arrived at the gallery. Cam looked tired, with blue shadows under his eyes, but said it had been a really successful trip.

'It was a small private art school selling up, so I bought a job lot of useful odds and ends. Rufus needs to unload the stuff he'd bought on the way back first and then he'll drop my things off later in the day.'

'What did Rufus get?' I asked.

'A small, battered blue dinghy, of all things. He said they make a really good alternative flowerbed, filled with soil and planted up.'

'I suppose that *would* look unusual and pretty,' Lulu said. 'I must tell Mum, because it might just be what we need to brighten up the front of the hotel by the sign.'

'It would certainly be eye-catching,' I agreed.

'He bought a load of big pieces of driftwood too, and three or four old stone mushrooms – I'm not sure what they were originally used for.'

'That's a mixed bag,' I said, and then, coffee finished, we did the photo shoot right there, because I'd decided to call my first offering The Gallery Collection.

When we'd finished, they both went back to the Lodge with me, so they could collect Dusty and take him to his new home. The gallery was open by then, but we left Jonas in charge of the till, the biscuit tin and a large mug of tea.

Dusty, despite being afraid of most men, seemed to like Cam. This was just as well, because I suspected Dusty wouldn't be spending a lot of time in his new kennel, but instead dog Lulu's footsteps, much as Cam did when he got the chance.

When they'd put Dusty in the car and gone, waved off by a farewell party of Debo, Judy and Sandy, I sent Rufus a brief message explaining I hadn't thought he'd fancy an early swim that morning, and he replied saying he'd been a bit late getting up anyway, and then he'd had an appointment with a solicitor about changing his name. Now he was in the middle of listing everything that would have to be altered, from the signs and vans, to the website and business cards.

Then he added that he'd call in later to see Pearl on his way to the Hut for the Regeneration Committee meeting and we could walk there together. It was just as well he did, since I'd quite forgotten it was Tuesday!

When Cam sent over the pictures he'd taken that morning, I put them straight up on my website, making sure I'd written the right prices and item codes by each one, a task more complicated than I'd anticipated.

Then, finally, I was almost ready to go live and feeling very nervous about it, but since I was sure my inner voice was urging me to do this, it just *had* to be a success.

The Regeneration Committee meeting went well: the leaflets, postcards and map had all gone to be printed and among the advertised businesses were Izzy Dane Designs, the Hidden Hoards Gallery, Stopped Clocks, Rufus Salcombe Garden Antiques, and the Old Mill Tearooms, even though they were still a future project, rather than a reality.

Lulu, inspired by that trunkful of Victorian clothes that she'd found in the attic, had decided to run a sideline taking photographs of visitors wearing them and intended setting up a little studio in the hotel.

Tom had already pinned to the village noticeboard outside the shop a reminder asking for volunteers to help clear back the Sweetwell public footpath on Sunday next and I said I'd go for a little while, even though my arms and back still ached from helping clear the path to the falls. I expect the exercise was good for me.

The four of us walked down to the pub after the meeting and I asked Lulu how Dusty was getting on.

'It's as if he'd always lived with us!' she said. 'I left him with Mum and Dad, being spoiled rotten, and even Bruce came out of the kitchen specially to toss him a chunk of chicken breast, still dressed in his full chef's whites.'

It was lovely to hear Dusty had settled down so well. When we arrived there was no sign of him and Lulu eventually discovered him curled up fast asleep in the hotel office with her mother's Yorkie, wearing the grin of a replete and happy hound.

After another dreamless night, Rufus joined me at the pool for an early swim. At first, it was very odd having him quietly swimming up and down with me in the flesh, rather than in my dreams, but I soon got used to it.

When we'd dried off and changed, we walked up to where the smaller path to Sweetwell branched off behind its wicket gate and as we paused, I said, 'Pub tonight?'

'Or – maybe you'd like to come to dinner?' he suggested, to my complete surprise.

'You mean, at the Hall?'

'Yes, and contrary to what Myra might tell you, I can cook. I do a mean kedgeree and my chicken curry brings tears to the eyes.'

'Are you inviting all of us?' I asked tentatively.

'No, I thought it would be nice if it was just you and me . . . if you like the idea, that is.' He released that rare and devastating smile at me and I blinked, my mind going temporarily a beautifully fuzzy blank.

Then I got a grip and said, making a joke of it, 'Oh, Mr Rochester, this is so sudden!'

'You have to come out of your quiet corner sometime, Miss Eyre,' he growled, twirling an invisible moustache in a villainous manner, then strode off up the path, the drying ends of his water-darkened hair glinting dark chestnut in the leaf-filtered sunlight.

When I got back and told Judy I'd be out to dinner because Rufus had invited me to Sweetwell, she and Debo exchanged meaningful glances.

'Don't get excited, because we're just friends. I mean, given what's happened in the past, it's not likely to come to anything else, is it?'

'He's so nice, I keep forgetting his mother's that ghastly woman,' Debo confessed.

After breakfast I retired to put the finishing tweaks to my website and then went back to working on the latest designs, though loud hammering and sawing outside made it a bit hard to concentrate.

Eventually I went to investigate and discovered Tom in the process of dismantling the last of the makeshift kennels. Although dog numbers were down, Sandy said it still made a tight squeeze fitting all the dogs left into the old kennels. But the new small block, which would back onto the garden wall where once an old greenhouse had stood, was due to be delivered any day. At least the fence panels had arrived and were stacked ready to go up. It was getting there.

Just as I was debating what to wear that night – something that wouldn't send out any wrong messages – Rufus rang, his voice back to sounding as strained and tight-lipped as when we'd first met as he told me that Fliss had turned up out of the blue.

'She's staying overnight and she was being her usual totally unreasonable self, so . . . well, we've had a bit of a row. She's gone out with Dan. I saw his car pick her up, but I think they'd arranged that already.'

'Is she going to be out all evening, do you think?' I asked tentatively, not liking the idea of coming face to face with her.

'Probably, but if you don't mind, I'll pick you up and we'll go out to eat.'

'Yes, fine,' I agreed, and so we ended up having dinner in the Green Man in Sticklepond, which had good food, even if it wasn't on the same level as Bruce Benbow's at the Screaming Skull.

I don't think Rufus had much appetite for it anyway. Over dinner he told me that Fliss had been at him again to throw Debo, Judy and me out of the Lodge, and she seemed unable to grasp that he couldn't even if he wanted to.

'And I certainly wouldn't want her living in the Lodge anyway!' he added.

'Surely she wouldn't want to? Didn't you say she hated the country?'

'Yes, and she'd soon tire of it and be off again. But I now know the reason *why* she's so keen, because she has to move out of her flat for six months, while the whole building is renovated. Her mother was from an old and wealthy Hungarian family who cut Fliss off long before I was born, but she does get an allowance and the London flat is in a property they own.'

'So she wants the Lodge until that's done?'

'So she says, and then keep it as her bolthole in the country, since when she does go back they'll have divided her flat up into two and it wasn't that big to start with.'

'People will rent something the size of a shoebox in London,' I said.

'They will, and of course she's never paid any rent, so she can't really complain.'

The grim expression, which I'd hardly seen for ages, crossed his face and his jaw set. 'I told her straight that she could forget about the Lodge and there was no way I'd have her under my own roof for more than a couple of nights, though I offered to store her furniture for her, if she liked.'

'Could she possibly have really fallen for Dan and thinks they'll live happily ever after in Halfhidden, and that's why she's so keen?' I asked.

'No, she's just having a bit of fun with him and when I told her she was making things difficult for me, because I was on the verge of sacking him if he put one more foot out of line, she said I was picking on him because of their affair.'

He brooded for a few minutes in silence.

'So, that's when she went off with Dan?' I said finally.

He gave a wry smile. 'I remembered that she has a really bad dog phobia so I told her I was getting a lovely big Alsatian tomorrow. Then I said I wouldn't have Dan under my roof, in case she was thinking of inviting him back there at any point, which was the last straw.'

'Seems reasonable to me,' I said. 'It's your house.'

He sighed. 'Trust Fliss to ruin what I'd hoped would be a nice evening.'

'Well, I'll allow you to cook me dinner another night, if it'll cheer you up,' I promised, and he smiled.

'I'll hold you to that,' he said, and then finally seemed to notice what he was eating. 'This is the most enormous plate of food I've ever faced. And what have they done to the vegetables?'

'Cooked each one in a different way,' I said, poking a whole small stem of charred tomatoes aside to reveal a pile of what looked like caramelised parsnips and a puddle of chopped leeks in a glutinous white sauce. 'It's all just a little too much.'

We talked more easily after that, and I gave him a copy of the extensive and expensive list of dog essentials that I'd written for Lulu, which at least diverted his mind from his mother's antics.

We decided to call at the Screaming Skull on the way home for a drink, though first checking that Dan's old Fiesta wasn't in the car park. There was no flashy sports car, like the one Lulu had said Cara drove, either, so it looked like she was back from wherever she'd been with Kieran.

We found Lulu and Cam in the snug, looking at a postcard of the haunted clock, which had the story printed on the back. The cards with the ghostly white horse had come out well, too.

Rufus and Lulu discussed dog essentials and he said he was going to be on the doorstep of the pet store at opening time next morning, clutching the list, so he could collect Pearl later.

He'd cheered up a bit by then. We were just thinking of going home when there was a sudden rumpus in the public bar and a husky female voice started singing something I couldn't quite make out.

Rufus blanched. 'That's Fliss!'

Lulu went to see what was happening, then reported that Fliss had just told the assembled customers her name and that she was a famous singer.

'Though most of them didn't look as if they'd ever heard of her,' she added. 'She and Dan are both a bit the worse for drink.'

'Oh God,' Rufus said.

'Don't worry, if they get too rowdy, Bruce and the barman will put them out,' she assured him.

'I think we'll go anyway,' he suggested, and I gathered up my bag and jacket. But before we could even get up, the door to the public bar was flung open and there, like a superannuated and unwanted genie, stood a tall, white-blonde woman with a haggard, wild face and a pair of red-painted lips that had been inflated to the size of a car tyre inner tube.

'There you are! Dan said you liked to hide out in here with your friends . . . and especially *one* little friend. So now I know why you don't want that lot at the Lodge to move out, don't I?' she husked, in a bathtub-gin-and-cigarette voice.

'You don't know anything, Fliss,' Rufus said. 'That's your whole problem.'

She eyed me curiously, from strangely dead eyes, while I stared at her, quite fascinated in a horrified kind of way and wondering if she used a small trowel to put her make-up on.

'So, you're Lisa's little mistake, then? You look just like your father, the way Rufus looks exactly like his – I'm only surprised Hugo Carlyle didn't twig before!' She giggled, swayed and put out a hand to the door frame to steady herself.

'But you're nothing much to look at, are you?' she said, considering me critically. 'Practically a hobbit, and you could do with a bit of slap and lippy on, darling, if you want to get a man's attention.'

'At least I haven't had my lips pumped up so much that my face looks like a baboon's bottom,' I said coldly, and Lulu choked on her glass of Baileys.

'Are you going to let her say things like that to me?' demanded Fliss of her son.

'Why not? You started it. And anyway, Izzy's quite right.' He looked at her, his expression angry and exasperated. 'You're drunk – better let me run you back to the house.'

'No way! I haven't had nearly enough to drink – not nearly enough of *anything*! Have fun, darlings!' she added and then wobbled off on her vertiginous heels. The silence that had fallen in the other room while everyone strained their ears to catch what was being said was replaced by a sudden babble that was only muffled when the door to the snug was shut.

That seemed to have put the clappers on our evening, so we left by the hotel entrance and Rufus dropped me at home. He wouldn't come in and said wryly that this wasn't quite how he'd imagined the evening ending and then, before I could digest the implications of that remark, apologised for Fliss.

'It's not your fault, and anyway, I feel I gave back as good as I got,' I assured him.

But coming face to face with the woman who, not long after I was born, had drawn my poor young mother back into her circle of drink and drugs had been difficult, to say the least. I'd have to keep reminding myself that Rufus was her son and nothing but friendship could be allowed to develop between us.

Rufus had only just gone when Lulu rang my mobile to ask if he was there with me.

297

'No, he's probably back at the house by now. Did you want him for something? I could give you his number.'

'I just wanted to warn him trouble might be headed his way. Fliss sang for ages after you left and then got really argumentative when Bruce came out and asked her to stop, so he told her and Dan to leave.'

'You think they're coming back to Sweetwell?'

'She told Dan they could carry on the party there. Then she invited all Dan's cronies, too.'

'I'd better ring Rufus right now,' I said, but even as did, I heard several cars going past.

'Your mother, Dan and his friends are on their way to Sweetwell,' I said urgently when he answered.

'I hear them,' he said grimly. 'But don't worry, they won't be here long.'

And he was right, because most of the cars returned down the drive only a few minutes later, followed, after an interval, by one final car that I recognised by the terminal rattle of the exhaust as Dan's.

Chapter 25: Bird of Passage

'If you don't, then Simon will have to and we'll probably end up in a ditch,' Harry said. 'Come on, Izzy – don't make such a fuss, you can do it!'

'Oh, for goodness' sake!' snapped Cara from the back seat. 'If you're going to drive, then get on with it before Simon's sick again!'

I'd had a brief text from Rufus later that night saying, *All sorted. Good night, sweet dreams*, but in the morning, when he didn't answer my message saying I was off for a swim, I was worried, until I remembered that he was going out to the pet store early to get all the things Pearl would need before he collected her.

It was a misty kind of day – that slightly damp, candyfloss type that seems to cling like a wet veil – so I decided to postpone my swim for a bit. The sun was attempting to get through, so I thought by the time I'd had breakfast it would probably be quite a nice morning.

While we were making inroads into the scrambled eggs, I gave Debo and Judy a brief sketch of what had happened last night.

Debo said indignantly that she would set the dogs onto 'That Woman' if she came anywhere near the Lodge, though if she meant Babybelle, Vic and Ginger, I imagined the first would sit on her and the other two lick her to death.

Later, at the Lady Spring, I spotted Tom doing something to his beehives and I waved. There was no one else about. The mist had vanished, so it was pleasantly warm as I swam lazily up and down.

No Roman soldiers or attractive, green-eyed antique dealers swam with me; it was all just birdsong and humming bees, and as soothing as ever.

All my jumbled thoughts slowly dissolved: the sudden and surprising surge of anger I felt at my mother for letting someone like Fliss draw her back into her toxic circle; at Harry for stupidly and thoughtlessly spiking Simon's drink on the night of the accident – and even towards my absent father, who'd played no part in my upbringing, financial or otherwise.

I had to let them all go . . .

As I came out of the enclosure, in a much better frame of mind than I'd gone in, Cam was just heading out from Spring Cottage to open the gallery.

'Cam, wait!' I called, and he stopped and turned till I caught up, so we could walk up to the drive together, though until the big clear-up next Sunday the path was so overgrown in parts that we had to walk in single file.

He already knew from Lulu what had happened at the pub last night, so I told him about the cars all leaving again, and Rufus texting that it was OK. Then we reached one of the narrower bits of path and I went ahead of Cameron, ducking to avoid some fiercely encroaching brambles.

Then all at once there was a sharp snapping noise and something zipping through my hair, followed by a sharp sting on the cheek.

'Cam, I think I'm being attacked by killer bees—' I began, half-turning, when suddenly he knocked me flat with a rugby tackle from behind.

'Really, Cam!' I gasped, winded. 'That's not funny.'

'Those weren't bees,' Cam said, looking round and then cautiously getting up. 'Look at the tree behind you.'

He hauled me to my feet, took out one of those nifty Swiss army knives from the pocket of his slightly sullied white linen trousers and dug something out of the bark.

'Air rifle pellet, I think,' he said.

'I've been *shot*?' I put a hand to my face and it came away with a trace of blood.

'No, you've been shot *at*, but it didn't hit you, thank goodness. A chip of bark must have caught you, but it's only a tiny scratch,' he assured me. 'And whoever did it is long gone – I heard them crashing about in the bushes.'

'Perhaps it was someone shooting rabbits,' I suggested, a bit shakily.

'It would have to be a very tall rabbit, wearing a red mac.'

'True, and come to think of it, all the locals know there's no shooting allowed in the grounds . . .'

I tailed off as an unwelcome thought struck me. '*Dan?* He wanted to stop me talking to Simon and he might not know I already have. *And* he'd love to see me, Debo and Judy off the place. I just didn't think he was *that* keen!'

'Oh, I don't think so, and I've never seen him out with anything other than a shotgun. It's more likely to be a careless teenage boy.'

'They'd be in school,' I objected.

'Skiving. I really don't think that Dan is mad enough to shoot at you, even with an air rifle.'

'You're right, I don't either now I've thought about it,' I agreed.

'Whoever it was has probably frightened themselves silly and gone to put the gun back where they got it,' Cam said. 'Come on.'

I felt a bit shaken, but we saw no one until we reached the drive, where Dan, wearing overalls and a face like thunder, was painting the rusty entrance gates. He was up a ladder and you could see the bit he'd already done, so it seemed even less likely that he'd just run down the path and taken a potshot at me.

Cam told him what had happened and asked if he'd seen or heard anything suspicious.

'It wasn't me, if that's what you're getting at,' he declared, looking both shifty and angry at the same time.

'I didn't think it was, Dan,' Cameron said mildly. '*Did* you see anyone?'

'No – and now I'd best get on with these gates, though what painting has to do with gardening, I don't know,' he said sullenly, and then turned back to his job.

I suspected he'd had a bruising encounter with a furious Rufus when he'd arrived at work that morning. He looked pretty jaded, too, so maybe everyone had gone back to his cottage and made a night of it.

My theory turned out to be quite right, because Myra came down later and described in graphic detail to Judy and me what had happened the previous night. She'd had a perfect view of the proceedings from her bedroom window.

'I was woken up by car horns honking outside and then I heard Rufus and his mother having a stand-up row on the front steps. There were three cars out front with Dan and his friends, and she wanted them all to come in. But Rufus said he wouldn't have any of them under his roof, other than his mother, and told them to clear off. But he put it a bit stronger than that.'

'I heard the cars going up and then going away again,' I said. 'Lulu had already rung me from the pub to say they were heading this way and I tried to warn Rufus.'

'That Fliss said she'd go with Dan, so he let her get her things, while Dan waited outside. I don't think he should have been driving, from the sound of him.'

'I'm sure he shouldn't.'

'And this morning, my friend who lives next door to Dan told me they all went back there. They made a shocking noise and she banged on the wall several times, because her husband had to get up for work early, and eventually it went quiet.'

'I wonder where Fliss is now,' I pondered. 'Dan obviously made it into work this morning, because he's painting the front gates.'

'That's because last night Rufus told him that if he wasn't at work by half-past eight on the dot, he was fired,' Myra said. 'What goings-on! And that Fliss is a strange woman. I was there when she turned up to stay yesterday afternoon, without a moment's warning, then ordered me to take her case up to her room!'

'What did you say?' asked Judy.

'I said, "Take it yourself, you lazy bugger."'

'Attagirl, Myra,' Judy said.

303

'Then Rufus came in and said he had no idea where she was sleeping anyway, and she'd have to make herself a bed up.'

'Poor Rufus, having a mother like that,' I said. 'She was drunk and made a scene in the pub last night, too, before they all headed up to the Hall. Still, perhaps she's gone home now.'

'Let's hope so,' Myra said. 'Rufus went out early and came back with stuff for that dog,' she added. 'Not that I agree with having dogs in the house, shedding hair and making mess.'

This severity was somewhat tempered by the fact that Pearl's head, minus the plastic cone, was now resting on Myra's knee. She gave her a bit of the ginger parkin she was eating and said, more mildly, 'I only hope she's house-trained.'

'*Nearly*,' Judy said encouragingly.

After Rufus closed at four, he came to collect Pearl and was back to being tight-lipped, terse and distant, even apologising again for what Fliss had said to me.

Luckily Judy absolutely insisted he have tea before he took Pearl home, and by the time he'd got himself around sandwiches, cheese scones and fruit cake, he'd thawed a bit.

Pearl lay quietly at his feet, but as usual Babybelle had to be fended off the cake stand. Debo came in after a while and helped herself to coffee and a sandwich.

'So, have you dished out all the dirty details?' she asked Rufus. 'We know what happened last night, so you might as well talk about it.'

'We were tactfully avoiding the subject,' Judy told her.

'Well, there's no point in tact when the whole village knows what happened,' Debo pointed out. 'You had a row, Fliss went off to Dan's cottage with him and his friends – if you can call that motley crew friends – and kept the neighbours awake half the night. But she's gone now.'

'Has she? How do you know?' he asked.

'Because she was on her way to the station after lunch when she spotted me coming out of the village shop and stopped her taxi. She told me to look for somewhere else to live, and said if I didn't get out of the Lodge voluntarily, I'd wish I had. So *I* said it was an empty threat . . . and then I asked her if she'd thought of suing her plastic surgeon, since the last facelift had clearly gone disastrously wrong,' she added brightly.

'What did she say to that?' asked Judy.

'Nothing, just told the driver to take her to the station and then she put the window back up.'

'I'm so sorry,' Rufus said.

Debo gave him the puckish grin. 'Oh, I knew it was all hot air, because you don't really want us to go, do you, darling?'

'No, though I *am* glad to see those rickety sheds and all the wire netting vanishing into a skip.'

'I saw Dan painting the gate earlier and he wasn't a happy bunny,' I told him.

'He was insolent when I got back from the pet store, smirking and saying I'd have to be nice to my future father-in-law, so goodness knows what line Fliss has been spinning him.'

'You don't think she really might marry him?' I asked.

'No, I'm only amazed it's lasted this long. Anyway, I put him on a final warning and then he said if I fired him just because he was seeing my mother, he could get me for wrongful dismissal.'

'That wouldn't wash, because everyone knows he's been slacking since Baz went to live abroad,' Judy said. 'We'd all say so.'

Rufus suddenly seemed to notice my grazed face for the first time and asked, 'What happened to your cheek?'

'She caught it on a branch on her way back from the Spring earlier,' Debo said, which was the story I'd spun them so they wouldn't worry, because I was sure it *was* an accident. 'Just as well it's being cleared back this weekend,' she added, then suggested Rufus and I take Pearl and Babybelle for a walk. 'A quiet one; don't let Pearl exert herself.'

Rufus had driven down in the Land Rover, so I said I'd show him Ashurst Beacon, a local beauty spot. The air always seems fresher up there and we sat on the edge of the stone monument, looking at the panoramic views, while the dogs wandered around the clumps of gorse and bracken. We didn't say a lot, but at least the silences were as companionable as they'd been before his mad mother popped her snake head up and hissed.

Rufus dropped me and Babybelle back at the Lodge and said he was going to have a quiet evening settling Pearl into her new home.

'I'm not sure I feel like facing everyone at the Screaming Skull anyway, after last night,' he added.

'No one will blame you for the way Fliss and Dan behaved,' I told him. 'And you'll have to brazen it out sometime.'

'Maybe tomorrow,' he suggested. 'And perhaps, eventually, we'll have that dinner together at Sweetwell,' he added, with a hint of his old smile, and I found myself hoping that we would.

*   *   *

Lulu and I arranged to meet up with the dogs at the Lady Spring after lunchtime on Friday, and walk together down to the lower pool. We were wearing our new, matching macs, since the day was cool and damp, and when we came across Rufus, who was taking a sedate ramble with Pearl, he said it was like running into two Little Red Riding Hoods at once.

He came on the walk with us, and Pearl would have liked to have got into the water with Babybelle and Dusty, but she'd have to wait a few days till the stitches were all healed and out.

We sat on the mossy rocks and chatted, and Lulu said that since there had been no further word from Guy, he must have got the message and the panic was over.

'Solange – my friend in the village – emailed me to say that Guy's horrible elder brother has moved in now, though I don't know what help he'll be, because he's a lecherous old soak.'

'Not your problem, thank goodness,' I told her.

'True. Well, I'd better get back,' she said, checking her watch. 'We have two lots of Haunted Weekenders arriving and the rest of the hotel is pretty full up tonight, too. Are you both coming down later?'

'Yes,' I said firmly. 'Rufus's feeling a bit shy, but he can't go into purdah just because his mother and Dan made a scene.'

'You're so bossy,' Rufus said.

'She's always been a bit like that,' Lulu assured him. 'Especially when she started working abroad for that charity.'

'Assertive,' I corrected her. 'That's different.'

'Bruce says Dan's barred for a fortnight. Rufus,' Lulu said. 'If he causes trouble again, it'll be for life.'

*   *   *

When we walked through the public bar later, Dan's cronies all looked very sheepish. Lulu said Bruce had told them to remind Dan that he was barred, and his girlfriend with him, in case he'd been too drunk to take it in.

'One of them told him Dan and Fliss had had a bit of a bust-up on the phone earlier, so they'd thought it was all over, but apparently they made it up again.'

'Pity,' Rufus said morosely, and since he seemed about to sink back into gloom, Cam chose to divert his thoughts by describing the shooting incident.

'Why didn't you tell me?' Rufus asked, staring at me with those unnerving, sea-washed light green eyes.

'Or me,' Lulu exclaimed. 'You could have been killed!'

'It was just an air rifle and it didn't come that close. Anyway, I didn't want to make a fuss because I'm sure it was just a teenager messing about. Whoever it was probably didn't even know we were there.'

'I don't want anyone shooting on my land,' declared Rufus.

'I don't suppose it could have been Dan?' suggested Lulu. 'Not shooting *at* you, just trying to frighten you a bit.'

'That did cross my mind at first,' I admitted, 'but he's all talk and no action, and anyway, he was up a ladder painting the Sweetwell gates five minutes later, so it can't have been him.'

Rufus suddenly looked as if an unpleasant idea had occurred to him, but if so he didn't share it, only saying, 'Well, I'd better get back. I've left Olly dog-sitting Pearl, so I don't want to be out for too long.'

'Olly loves animals and he's very kind,' Lulu said. 'She'll be fine with him.'

'I'll come with you,' I said. Cam, as he was doing with increasing frequency, said he'd stay and give Lulu a hand before he went home.

The air was cool and fresh outside, with a few faint stars like sharp pinpricks in the dark velvet sky, and all was quiet until we'd got well above the Lady Spring and the dogs began to bark.

'Something's set them off,' I said. 'Still, at least now they won't be able to get out, because they're all within the garden wall and there's a strong gate.'

'That's something,' Rufus said. 'It will look a lot better once it's all cleared.'

'The small new kennel block and runs *will* be just outside the garden, but by then the new fence will be up and—'

I stopped dead, because there in the torchlight was the huge dark shape of Babybelle, sitting by the side of the drive like a forlorn hitchhiker.

'How on earth did *you* get out?' I asked her incredulously. But as we neared home, with her plodding behind me, I could see the gate in the wall was swinging open.

'She might have managed to burst out of her pen by flinging herself at the door, but she couldn't undo the bolt on the garden gate,' I said. 'And I'm certain Debo and Judy are checking and rechecking to make sure everything is locked up properly before they go to bed. You don't think someone could be sneaking round in the evening and letting the dogs out, do you?'

'You're thinking of Dan?'

'I – no,' I decided. 'He's all hot air really, so I can't imagine him doing something like that. And didn't his friends say he'd just made up with Fliss? He's probably on his way to London.'

'Perhaps, but there's no saying when he set off – if he did. But you're right, it does seem a bit petty.'

'It was probably just accidentally left open, then – Debo thinking Judy had locked it and vice versa,' I said. Then added, 'Swim early tomorrow?'

'OK, swim,' he agreed.

Rufus was just slipping into the water when I got to the pool next morning and I had a total Elizabeth Bennet moment – the one where, having first been overwhelmed by the size of Mr Darcy's house, she spotted him in his wet shirt. And Rufus wasn't even wearing the shirt.

Golden sunlight was fingering the silky, dark chestnut of his hair, as if it couldn't quite believe that it was real, and suddenly I wanted to do the same . . .

And come to think of it, last night I'd fingered rather more than his hair, but then, I'm not responsible for what I get up to in my dreams!

Tom, helped by Brandon Benbow from the alpine nursery and one of his strapping teenage sons, spent half the day erecting the new notices and signposts for the ghost trail, all over the valley. Then Foxy and Sandy's father came down and gave the Green the first rough mow of the year, so things were starting to take shape.

That night Jonas had a couple of new *really* scary stories to tell in the pub and I was so petrified as we walked home that I grabbed Rufus's hand and held it tightly all the way again.

However, we saw nothing more frightening than the large, pale shape of a barn owl swooping silently past, and when

Rufus left me at the door, he said firmly that he wasn't detouring round the haunted bit of the drive any more to please me. If he did meet any ghosts, he said, they'd be a pleasant change from his mother!

Chapter 26: Skulduggery

'I'm scared – and if Judy ever finds out, she'll kill me!'

'All the more reason to get going now, then, so we don't meet her coming to look for you,' he said with a touch of impatience and, reaching over me, turned the key in the ignition.

It was a dry but overcast Sunday morning, which was actually better for the mammoth annual path clearing than hot sunshine. The volunteers, including myself and Rufus, who had again left Foxy in charge for a while, all met up in the pub car park and were assigned to groups working on different parts of the path, cutting back encroaching branches and brambles all the way up to the Spring where we were to convene for lunch.

We were all ready for it by then and most volunteers had brought their own sandwiches, if they were staying for the afternoon too. Tom provided cakes donated by Judy and Myra, cold drinks and tea made in a brown, mottled pot, big enough to accommodate an elephant.

Rufus had to go back to Sweetwell, but I thought I'd wait to see if Tom wanted a hand with the washing up before I gave up for the day. Call me a wimp, but I felt as if I needed a tepid bath and a lie-down in a darkened room. Muscles I didn't even know I'd got were aching.

I was just finishing off a piece of cake and thinking I'd start collecting the white china cups together, which Tom had evidently borrowed from the Hut, when to my surprise Simon appeared.

'Hi, Simon – I didn't know you were here,' I said. 'We'll have to stop meeting like this.'

He smiled weakly at the joke as he sat down beside me on the grass and said, 'I've only just got here.'

'Oh, well, I'm off in a minute and so are quite a few of the morning volunteers, so they'll be glad of some fresh helpers.'

'I came to talk to you, really,' he said. 'I – you know you said that it was your ex-fiancé that Cara went off with last weekend?'

'Yes, Kieran – they'd known each other before, in Oxford.'

'She didn't come back for a couple of days and when I asked her where she'd been and why she hadn't told me she'd be away, she said it was her own business if she wanted to spend a few days in Oxford with an old friend. And then . . . we argued,' he said miserably. 'She said perhaps we should cool things a bit, if I was going to get so jealous.'

'Well, I'm sorry, Simon, but I don't see what it's got to do with me. I'm not engaged to him any more, so he's a free agent.'

'She swore they were only friends, but he's back and he's been staying up at Grimside all weekend.'

'I assume Sir Lionel's still away?'

'He was back for a night midweek and then went to London. They lead very separate lives, but even so, he's going to be hopping mad when he finds out some man has been staying at the house with her.'

His jaw set grimly. 'When she went out to the stables earlier on her own, I asked her straight out what was happening. She told me we were finished and to stop pestering her.'

'I'm sorry it didn't work out, Simon.'

'I thought she loved me, but I can see now that she played me for a fool, till someone better came along,' he said bitterly. 'I'll be off to another job as soon as I can.'

'I'd still like to ask Cara those questions about the accident, but I don't suppose I'll ever get the chance now,' I said.

'She swore she'd told everything she knew to the inquest,' he said. 'But when you said at Grimside that you'd never have insisted on driving the car that night, I realised you were right, so she must have lied about that.'

'I expect it was just a bit of embroidery, to make herself look better,' I suggested. 'That's what Lulu and Cam think.'

'I wish I could remember more,' he said. 'Sometimes I think I can . . . but then, I'm not sure if I'm *really* remembering what happened, or it's just that I've been told about it.'

'I know what you mean, because I keep having the strangest dreams, more like memories. And there was one flashback when I was in the rear of the car with Cara – only of course, I *was* in the back of the car with her the week before the accident.'

'Dad says he saw me get out of the back of the car after the accident and you were in the front with Harry, and I believe him,' Simon said.

'Yes, I know, because Tom saw your dad lifting me out of

314

the front. I accept that I drove up from the pub, but what's puzzling me now is why Harry didn't take over the wheel once we were on the estate. He was safe enough then from the police.'

'I wondered about that, too,' he said. 'Well, I'd better get back to Grimside, because I've asked for Wednesday off. I'm going to talk to the National Trust about going back to work for them. There are two jobs going – under-gardener on a big property down south or head gardener at a smaller place up in the Lakes.'

'Good luck with that,' I said, as he got up and then helped me to my feet. 'Let me know how you get on. I gave you my mobile number, didn't I?'

He nodded.

'Do you think you could give me Cara's?'

'She made me promise not to,' he said. 'But then, she made *me* a lot of promises and look what they came to!' He got his phone out.

'Thanks, Simon,' I said as I put Cara's number into my own phone.

'She might not answer – she's not replied to any of my calls or messages,' he said and then, as he turned to go, paused and added, 'Dad had a bust-up with that Fliss woman on the phone the day she went back to London. I don't know what it was about, but she'd done something he didn't like when he'd left her alone in the house. He didn't realise I was in the kitchen till he put the phone down.'

'Oh? I'd heard they'd had an argument, because one of his friends was talking about it at the pub,' I said encouragingly.

'They must have made up again, because he went down

late Friday and he's still there. I didn't meet her when she was here, but everyone's talking about her, and not in a good way,' he said. 'I'm sorry my dad's been such a fool over her and messed things up with Rufus Carlyle. I warned him good jobs weren't that easy to get at his age and a woman like her wouldn't stick around for long.'

'I don't suppose he listened to you.'

'No, he said he'd heard Cara had got off with some other bloke, so I was a fine one to be handing out advice. And I suppose he's right, but I didn't *come* here to have an affair with another man's wife, I just fell in love with her.'

'I'm sure you'll find a nice girl wherever you go next, Simon,' I said, but he didn't look either consoled or convinced.

I was so stiff and creaky that evening that Rufus drove me down to the pub in the Land Rover, and on the way I told him most of what Simon had said.

'I think I'll have to accept that I've gone as far as I can with my mission, because Cara's not likely to say anything else now, even if I corner her. I sent her two messages to her phone once I got her number, but she ignored them. And I'm never going to be totally certain that my dreams really are memories, am I?'

'If they feel like memories, then they probably are.'

'Perhaps, but they're more sporadic now – and I'm just as likely to have the other kind of dream . . .' I tailed off, going pink.

He glanced at me sideways, pale green eyes glinting. '*I* dream sometimes that I'm swimming up and down the pool at the Spring with you and you're wearing that white bikini you had on the first time we met.'

'That would *only* be in your dreams!' I said, and he laughed and then told me how well Pearl was settling into Sweetwell.

'She has the occasional little accident, but she favours the tiled kitchen floor, so it's easy to clean up. Olly's besotted with her and keeps offering to take her for walks, which will be useful when she's totally recovered and more energetic. Myra complains about the mess, but is trying to spoil her to death with home-baked dog treats.'

'There, I told you it would all work out well,' I said. 'You were made for each other!'

We all decided that since Monday was Cam and Rufus's day off and the day Lulu was always less in demand at the pub, we'd take a trip to Blackpool next day. Rufus had never been there, so we thought it was time he visited this Mecca of the north.

'We can go up the Tower, buy sticky rock and ice creams . . . but not ride on the donkeys. If there are still donkeys,' Lulu said.

'It sounds wonderful . . . or it would if I was about eight,' he said ungratefully.

'You'll love it,' I assured him. 'In the autumn, we'll go again one evening when the illuminations are on all along the prom.'

'As soon as we get back, my Haunted Holidays website goes live,' Lulu said. 'And the Izzy Dane Designs launch is Tuesday, isn't it?'

I nodded. 'Everything's ready; it's just a bit like jumping off a cliff.'

'But you won't fall because you have little angels to hold you up,' she teased.

317

In the Land Rover on the way home, Rufus suddenly asked, right out of the blue, 'When Simon said he'd overheard his father arguing on the phone with Fliss, did he say what it was about?'

'No, not really.' I tried to think back to what Simon had said. 'It was something she'd done after he left her alone in the cottage that morning. I wondered if he'd heard she'd threatened Debo on her way to the train and thought that was going a bit far.'

'Maybe,' he agreed, but he sounded abstracted.

At the Lodge, he just dropped me off but wouldn't come in. But by then, I was so stiff anyway that I could barely move. I went straight to bed and went out like the proverbial light.

In Blackpool we did all the things I'd promised Rufus we would *and* more, including a tram ride along the prom, a visit to the funfair, a pink candyfloss-eating competition and fish and chips wrapped in greasy paper.

It was a good day, the sort that would linger as a happy memory for ever. Tired and happy, we dropped Lulu and Cam off at the pub, where they intended taking Dusty for a walk together before the launch of the Haunted Holidays on the Screaming Skull website.

At the Lodge, Tom had been really busy: the last pile of debris from the old kennels was in a skip that was in the process of being manoeuvred onto a lorry, and the land was cleared ready for the new fence – *and* the kennel block and pens had finally arrived and were stacked where they were to be built.

Luckily there was a good foundation at the back of the

wall, where the big Victorian greenhouse once stood, so Tom could build directly on that.

Rufus came into the Lodge with me, carrying the giant pink teddy bear he'd given me after he won it on the rifle range, and plates of rock made to look like bacon and eggs, for Judy and Debo.

'We could do with the sugar for energy,' Judy said, after thanking him. 'We've had an extremely eventful day!'

'You can say that again,' agreed Debo, slumped on the old sofa with her long, corduroy-clad legs stretched out before her. 'The new kennels arrived on a ridiculously huge lorry just after you'd gone, and then about every ten minutes after that, an official from the council, the RSPCA, or some other body turned up.'

'That's a slight exaggeration, but not much,' Judy said. 'There was one RSPCA inspector and three other assorted officials, but they were fairly well spaced out through the day. Most of them were here for ages, though.'

'What on earth did they all want?' I asked.

'They'd been anonymously tipped off that there was a problem of one kind or another with the kennels. The RSPCA man said overcrowding, unsanitary conditions and cruelty had been reported. Actually, we'd met before,' Debo said, not to anyone's great surprise, 'and when I showed him round and he saw the plans for the new block, he said everything looked fine to him.'

'I should think so too,' Judy said. 'Then after him, we had someone from the planning department, who'd been told we'd hugely extended the kennels without permission, but of course he could see straight away we hadn't . . . or at least, we had *temporarily*, but were restoring the land to what it was before.'

'So that was two,' I said. 'Who else?'

'That nice woman who'd been before to measure how loud the dogs barked, but now there are fewer dogs so the noise isn't that bad. I've forgotten what the other one wanted . . .'

'Something to do with checking we didn't have forbidden breeds, like American pit bulls,' Judy reminded her. 'But, of course, we haven't.'

'It's very odd they should all come on the same day. Who tipped them off?' I asked.

'They wouldn't say, but I expect it was Dan, because he's done that kind of thing before. Only not several at the same time,' Debo said.

'I hope you're wrong,' Rufus said grimly. 'I've already told him I won't have you harassed, but I suspect my mother's egging him on now. I think a few words with her on that subject are well overdue,' he added ominously, getting up to leave, so I expect the phone wires to London would be burning as soon as he got home.

I had a look at the Haunted Holidays on the Screaming Skull website and then sent Lulu a row of smiley emoticons, but that was the only excitement of the evening. I was so tired, what with the path cutting on Sunday and the day out at the seaside, that I went early to bed not long after Debo and Judy.

If I dreamed of anything during the night, I couldn't remember it next morning.

Rufus swam with me and then I took him back to the Lodge for breakfast, at Judy's invitation. She's convinced that he wouldn't get half as many gloomy moods if he was eating properly.

'I'm certainly eating a lot of *cake* these days,' he said ruefully, 'because Myra's always leaving them about in the kitchen under covers with notes saying "Eat Me" stuck to them.'

'How odd of her,' Debo said, puzzled. 'What does she *think* you're going to do with them?'

'It's just a little joke – something from *Alice in Wonderland*,' Judy explained.

'I'd better get back,' Rufus said. 'Though Foxy's always there to open up in good time. In fact, I'm starting to suspect she doubles back in the evenings and beds down in one of the wheelbarrows, instead of going home.'

'Well, it's good she enjoys her work, isn't it?'

'I suppose so. But I'll have to get back anyway, because today is not only your website launch, Izzy – which I hope goes well – but the day I officially change my name from Carlyle to Salcombe on everything. I've already done some of it, like ordering new business cards, but the ads on the side of the vans and the signs all need altering. It'll be odd not to be Rufus Carlyle any more,' he added, 'but also a relief, now I know I don't have any right to the name.'

'But you *do* have a perfect right to call yourself Salcombe, and you'll soon get used to it,' I assured him.

Once my website went online I worked on my new designs for most of the day, though I have to admit that I checked for Izzy Dane Designs orders about every five minutes. Lulu was doing the same with her Haunted Holidays and we kept texting each other to ask if anything had happened yet.

But in the afternoon I finally got a grip on myself and went over to the gallery, where I arranged all the packaging ready for when the first order *did* actually come in. Already it was becoming clear that it wasn't ideal having to go to and fro across the Green from my studio in the Lodge to the gallery, though I wouldn't be able to afford to rent separate premises till my business took off – if it ever did. Since I didn't drive, running the business from anywhere but Halfhidden would be a bit difficult, too. I hadn't thought of that before.

The Regeneration Committee meeting that evening was a short one because by now everything was pretty much in place. The postcards were printed and distributed, the new souvenirs – tasteful and otherwise – had arrived, and Hannah Blackwell had finally got permission to open her tea garden.

As we came out of the Hut, I asked Lulu if she had any Haunted Holiday bookings yet and she said no.

'I'd really like the first holiday to start the weekend of the May Morris dance, so I hope I get some by then.'

'I'm sure you will,' Rufus said, and then suggested we all go back to Sweetwell, because he'd found a Chinese takeaway in a nearby village that delivered. So we did that and watched a film in the small, cosy room at the back of the house that Baz had always called the library, even though the only books on the shelves in it were his own.

Keeping with tradition, the takeaway included a bag of fortune cookies. Mine said, 'Fortune favours the brave', while Rufus's suggested he laugh in the face of his enemies.

I think Lulu and Cam's must have come out of a different box, because theirs were on the theme of love. I told Rufus about the Chocolate Wishes shop in nearby Sticklepond, set up by an artisan chocolate maker and he said we should take a trip there soon so I could show him the Witchcraft Museum and the local big house and gardens, Winter's End, too.

'There seems to be a lot happening in Sticklepond these days,' Cam observed.

'Soon it will all be happening in Halfhidden, too,' Lulu said determinedly.

'I've been thinking, why is it that the dogs only ever seem to break out at night?' Judy said at breakfast next morning, buttering toast so leaden that the toaster had groaned under the strain of trying to pop it. 'And mostly Fridays, or at least weekends.'

'Babybelle can break out whenever she pleases,' I pointed out, but Debo was looking much struck, her own buttery knife suspended in mid-air.

'You know, that's very odd,' she said. 'Now I come to think of it, you're quite right. And what's more, even the nervous ones who you wouldn't expect to break out, sometimes do.'

'So, we're thinking sabotage?' Judy said. 'Dan, of course – who else would be that mean?'

'Or that stupid, because one of them could well have turned on him and given him a nasty bite. He's lucky they haven't.'

'He probably unlocked them and just crept off, hoping they'd push their way out,' Judy replied.

'You haven't got any proof yet that *anyone* did it,' I said. 'But funnily enough, Rufus and I discussed the possibility of it being Dan the other day when we found Belle outside and the garden gate wide open, but we didn't *really* think he'd do it. He's usually all empty threats and hot air.'

'Oh, but it's so obvious now,' Debo exclaimed. 'We should

put one of those CCTV cameras up, or a tripwire or something. And actually, I know someone who sells and installs all that kind of thing.'

'You would,' Judy replied.

'I'll give him a ring later and see what he suggests.'

'The mind boggles,' Judy said, and then they both giggled like teenagers.

'You could use Babybelle as a guard dog and leave her pen wide open at night,' I suggested. 'She can't get out of the garden gate unless it's deliberately unlocked and since she hates Dan, she'd probably pounce on him if he came in.'

'Good thinking,' Debo agreed.

Simon rang later to say that Cara had gone off with Kieran again on the Sunday night after he'd spoken to me and she hadn't returned. He'd also been offered, and accepted, the post of head gardener at the Lakes property, so had handed in his notice. Or at least, he'd handed it in to the estate manager, because Sir Lionel hadn't returned yet, either.

I wished him well, but I was pretty distracted because I'd just had my very first orders – three of them! I had to print out the invoices and packing slips and then go across to the gallery to parcel them up, ready for Judy to take down to the post office.

And as I said to Rufus on Thursday morning, as we floated side by side in the greeny-turquoise water of the pool, I'd soon be fit as a flea, constantly trotting to and fro across the Green.

He said, 'It would be much easier if you had everything under one roof.'

'I know, and maybe if the orders flood in I'll eventually be able to rent somewhere.'

'I could find you some space up at Sweetwell, when you're ready,' he offered unexpectedly. 'There's the upstairs of the office building in the courtyard, for a start, and it could be extended into the loft room over the stables next door.'

'That would be ideal – thank you!' I said gratefully, then I described how Debo's friendly security expert had already been round and installed a tripwire and a camera in the kennels, which would be switched on at night, and Rufus said he could do with something like that at the antiques centre.

'But it'll probably just show a fox jumping over the wall and driving all the dogs mad,' I said sceptically. 'I mean, only Babybelle has got out since they've been kept inside the garden perimeter wall, and that was only because the gate was open, which might have been accidental.'

'Well, you'll soon find out, won't you?' he said.

We arrived early at the Screaming Skull that evening and found Lulu standing in the public bar in earnest conversation with a small, bald-headed, side-whiskered man.

'Thank goodness you're here!' she exclaimed. 'Cam's taking an art class, so he'll be late. Mr Chumley here – Professor Chumley – is an expert on bones and he's been looking at Hetty.'

'I could tell you more if you'd let me pick the skull up,' said the man amiably.

'She can't do that, because moving her brings bad luck,' I told him, aghast.

'Professor Chumley says the skull can't really be Hetty's,' Lulu told us, having first looked round to see if any customers were within earshot. But luckily it was so early that only one elderly man was sitting at the other end of the room, reading a newspaper.

'I'm afraid it's more likely to be a male skull, though that's not certain,' the professor agreed. 'It's of great age and also it looks as if the individual was of African origin.'

We all stared blankly at him, except Rufus, who looked amused.

'There were Roman soldiers hereabouts, I believe,' he continued. 'Possibly he served in one of the African cohorts.'

'I'm sure you're quite wrong,' Lulu said firmly, now she was over the first shock. 'It's Howling Hetty.'

Professor Chumley said wistfully that he could tell us so much more if we would allow him to remove the skull for examination, but again this suggestion was met with so much horror that he quickly desisted.

More customers were arriving so we took him through into the snug, where Lulu plied him with free beer till Cam arrived and got him to swear he wouldn't tell a soul about his suspicions. He was interested to hear about the Roman remains by the Lady Spring and said he'd come back when he had more time to examine them.

'Well, if you do, don't mention the skull not being Hetty's, or you'll be run out of the village on a hurdle!' Lulu warned him, and he promised he wouldn't.

Chapter 27: Night Passage

As the engine roared into life, I felt as if I was trapped in a nightmare.

'Put your foot on the clutch and go into first,' Harry directed me calmly, releasing the handbrake and I blindly obeyed in a trance of fear.

The gears crunched and we moved forward jerkily.

I tried ringing Daisy when I woke next morning, but only got her answering service, so I'd left her a message. But I was so keen to tell someone about my latest dream revelation that I was sitting on a block of stone by the entrance to the Spring waiting for Rufus when he arrived.

I didn't waste any time describing it either. 'I mean, it finally confirmed what I'd known all along must be the truth: that I really did drive that car up to Sweetwell.'

Rufus said, 'I suppose it does, but your dreams are throwing a really bad light onto my half-brother. I mean, it was a stupid prank to spike Simon's drink in the first place, but to then coerce a sixteen-year-old into driving him home was selfish and cruel.'

'I think he *was* selfish, but then, perhaps we are all a bit self-centred when we're teenagers?' I suggested. 'Harry had a tendency to do reckless things, so I don't suppose he understood how afraid I felt. But what I really find hard to forgive him for is spinning me that line about ditching Cara so he could go out with me. That *was* cruel.'

And I said much the same to Daisy later, when she rang me back.

'I'm inclined to agree with your Rufus on this one, Izzy, because after all, Harry was nearly nineteen and so more than old enough to be responsible for his actions.'

'He's not *my* Rufus,' I said quickly and she laughed.

'I think you've mentioned him more than Harry since you got back to Halfhidden, but that's a healthy sign.'

'We're just friends,' I said with dignity, and then she had to go, though she asked me to update her if my dreams made any further progress.

'I will, if they continue,' I agreed, for I now half-expected each one to be the last.

Izzy Dane Designs was suddenly becoming more exciting now orders had started to come in and already I was getting some idea of what would be the most popular styles and sizes. My intention had been to create a core stock of designs, but annually change the colours, fabrics and embellishments. There would also be one-off special-occasion designs, too.

I knew I'd need to visit the two workshops making my clothes in India at least once a year, to choose materials and discuss designs, but I'd have to find someone who could run things here for a couple of weeks, before I could take any trips.

I was ready for a break by lunchtime, so Babybelle and I

met up with Rufus and Pearl and took a picnic up to the rocks reputably infested by the Halfhidden Worm. There was no sign of it, though you'd think it would have come out for some cheese and tomato sandwiches and ginger beer . . . unless, of course, it had heard about Judy's bread, because the sandwiches certainly had a lot of chew in them.

It was pleasant up there, relaxing on an old picnic rug on the short sheep-nibbled turf, but all too soon Rufus had to get back to relieve Foxy so she could have her lunch, and I needed to return to my designs.

I went into the courtyard to say hello to Foxy, and when I came out, Dan had begun sullenly mowing the triangle of grass where the drive branched into two.

As Belle and I drew level, he turned off the old petrol mower and said to me, 'I told you not to talk to my Simon about the accident and I hear you took no notice. You leave him alone, or else!'

'You're too late and you've got the wrong end of the stick anyway, because Simon wanted to talk to me,' I told him. 'Not that he can remember much about that night.'

At this moment, Babybelle decided to show Dan her impressive set of sharp teeth and made a low rumbling noise in her throat.

He eyed her warily, before saying, 'You'd do better to let it all drop – let the past lie.'

'I don't think I've got much choice, if Cara won't fill in the missing pieces,' I said, since I could imagine his reaction if I told him I already knew almost everything that had happened, because I'd dreamed about it! 'Was it you who tipped off all those council officials and the RSPCA about the kennels, Dan?'

He didn't reply, except to reiterate his stock response that we should all clear out, if we knew what was good for us, so I dragged Babybelle away.

I decided not to tell Rufus about this encounter, since he was already poised on a knife-edge to fire Dan and I didn't want to be the one to tip him over.

I wasn't seeing him that evening anyway, since he was going to be out late delivering something bulky to a customer. Cam was taking a night class as a favour for a friend and Lulu would be busy getting ready for her Haunted Weekenders' arrival, so I decided on a quiet night in.

Babybelle, naturally, wanted to spend the quiet night with me, but Debo and Judy eventually persuaded her out to the kennels, using the treat ball.

They came back saying they'd securely fastened up everything, set the new alarm and CCTV camera and left Babybelle's door closed but unlocked, though she wouldn't find that out until she leaned on it at some point – probably the minute she'd eaten all of the treats.

They retired to bed and I soon followed. But although I was tired, I was a bit afraid to go to sleep because of what my dreams might show me next . . . and if it was the actual moment of the collision, I'm wasn't sure I could bear it.

So I was still half-awake some time later when the alarm suddenly began to shrill, jolting me bolt upright in bed. Then the windows brightened as the security lights came on and there was a loud volley of barks, followed by shouting.

Debo, Judy and I all popped out of our rooms onto the landing at the very same moment, throwing on dressing gowns as we dashed out to the kennels, Vic and Ginger at our heels. There we discovered the main gate wide open and

Babybelle sitting on top of a black-clad man wearing a face-concealing balaclava and swearing blue murder.

'Get her off me!' he yelled, along with a peppering of four-letter expletives, but Babybelle just stared down at him, as though he was a not very appetising dinner.

'Good dog, Belle,' I said. 'Hi, Dan – fancy meeting you here!'

'Now, shall we ring for the police, or Rufus, I wonder?' Debo mused aloud.

'Or we could just leave him there till morning?' suggested Judy. 'Babybelle seems happy enough. Quite comfortable, in fact.'

Dan made a galvanic attempt to unseat Babybelle, but didn't shift her an inch, though the growling increased in intensity to a menacing deep roar.

'Gosh, she's a great guard dog!' I said, impressed.

'We know it's you, Dan, you mean-spirited little weasel,' Debo told him. 'You might as well admit it.'

'Why wouldn't I?' he said belligerently. 'I was just driving past when I thought I saw someone hanging round suspiciously and stopped for a look-see.'

'Past from where, at this time of night? You're barred from the Screaming Skull,' Judy said.

'I was over at the Falling Star in Sticklepond, wasn't I? And I was doing you a favour, stopping when I saw someone hanging around and then the gate open. But when I came in for a look, this stupid dog jumped on me.'

'And the mysterious intruder you saw had vanished? I'm not buying that, Dan, and I don't think Rufus will, either,' I said.

'The truth will be on our new CCTV camera anyway,' Debo pointed out, and Dan turned the air blue again.

'That will be quite enough of that,' Judy told him severely, fishing her phone out of her dressing gown pocket and scattering tissues and a packet of indigestion tablets in the process. 'I'll call Rufus – *his* gardener, *his* problem.'

'How do you have his number?' I asked curiously.

'I put it in my mobile when he came to tea,' she said. 'He's sort of our new landlord, after all.'

Rufus came down on the motorbike I hadn't seen up till then, wearing jeans and a sweatshirt over, at a guess, nothing. He looked tired, dishevelled and cross, which, perversely, made him look even more attractive than usual. I suspected that when Judy rang, he'd only just got home and gone to bed.

He assessed the situation grimly. He did grim very well.

'It's Dan,' Judy said helpfully. 'We seem to have solved the mystery of the dogs that escaped in the night.'

'Babybelle, get off!' he commanded, but she only obeyed when I called her, planting her great paws in delicate bits of Dan's anatomy in the process.

Dan picked himself up from the ground and pulled off the balaclava, stuffing it into his pocket, before repeating his story about the suspicious stranger.

'How inventive! Are you sure you didn't write the plots of Baz's thrillers for him?' said Debo with sarcasm.

'And do you often drive around at night wearing head-to-foot black and a balaclava?' Rufus asked, then stooped and picked up something from the grass. 'And this looks amazingly like a wrench to me.'

'I didn't spot that,' Debo said.

'It's not mine,' Dan said quickly.

'I think you should count yourself lucky we're not calling

the police – because if we did, I might ask them to investigate my missing mower, too,' Rufus said pleasantly.

'You just try proving anything on either count,' Dan said truculently.

'I think if we look at the CCTV footage we'll find your mysterious stranger is the Invisible Man, won't we?' Judy suggested.

'I was trying to do a good turn, I was,' he insisted. 'But if you don't believe me, please yourselves, because I'm going now.' He dusted himself off and turned to leave.

'You can go – with a month's notice,' Rufus told him.

Dan swung round and stared at him. 'You can't do that! I've been working here most of my life—'

'Or *not* working here most of your life,' Judy amended.

'You needn't work the notice, either, because I don't want you on my property ever again. And I'd like you out of the cottage by the beginning of June,' Rufus said implacably.

Dan began to bluster. 'You can't get rid of me that easily – I could take you to a tribunal and get you for unfair dismissal. I'm not leaving my cottage either and—'

'Judy, phone for the police,' Debo said. 'I've had enough of this. And by the way, Dan, I was talking to Freddie Tompion and it came out that he saw you selling the sit-on mower when he'd gone up to Sweetwell to play chess with Laurie. You shook hands with the man, took a wad of money and he loaded it up and went.'

'I never!' he said predictably. 'And I don't think you want the police involved,' he said to Rufus, 'not when it was your own mother's idea to let the dogs out and all the rest of it. She's a piece of work, she is! Even took my—'

But we were not destined to hear what it was that Fliss took, for at this point Rufus felled him with a single blow.

'You'll regret that,' Dan snarled, getting up again and tentatively fingering his jaw. 'I'll have the law on you for assault and—'

'Did any of you *see* me hit him?' Rufus appealed to us.

'No,' we chorused, as one.

'There you are, Dan – three witnesses say I didn't lay a finger on you. I expect you ran into something.'

Dan stared at him in impotent rage, and then all at once the fight seemed to drain out of him, though he gave us all a look of hate before trudging off down the drive.

'Good riddance,' Judy said. 'The sooner he's out of Halfhidden, the better.'

'So long as he's not stupid enough to dispute my firing him . . . or drag my stupid mother into it,' Rufus said.

'Oh, I don't suppose he will,' Judy told him. 'Do you really think she was egging him on to let the dogs out and send all those inspectors to the kennels?'

'Probably, because of her misguided idea that I'd let her live in the Lodge if you moved out – and Dan seems to think he's included in the plan. He'll soon find his mistake.'

'Yes, and now he won't even have the cottage,' Judy said. Then her face lit up. 'I've just had a *brilliant* idea!'

'Oh, not another,' groaned Rufus. 'I haven't recovered from having Foxy foisted onto me yet.'

'Don't be silly, you know she's just what you needed,' Debo said. 'Go on, Judy.'

'You could promote Olly to gardener in his stead,' Judy suggested, with the air of one pulling a white rabbit from a hat. 'Foxy could give him a hand with any major jobs – she's always up for a bit of overtime – and when his dad retires, he can keep an eye on things, too.'

'Would Olly want to give up his work at the alpine nursery to do the job full time?' asked Rufus.

'Yes, because when Dan leaves, he could have the cottage and get married!' Debo said brightly.

'Olly wants to get *married*?'

'He's been engaged for years to a lovely girl he met at the adult learning centre – she's a gardener, too. It's perfect! And the cottage is slap-bang in the middle of the village, so his family are all in easy reach.'

'Right,' Rufus said faintly. 'That's all organised, then!'

Chapter 28: Romantic Comedy

Tears blurred my vision. I blinked them back, then crept out onto the main road at a snail's pace and took the turn up to Halfhidden.

'There are more gears than one,' Harry pointed out, straightening the wheel before we veered off into the ditch.

'At this rate, it would be quicker to walk,' Cara said acidly from the back seat, where Simon had now burst into slurred and unrecognisable song.

I think Rufus must have slept in after a long drive to deliver the bulky garden antique, followed by the alarms and excursions in the kennels the previous night, because he didn't turn up at the pool next morning, and it was surprising how much I now missed his company, after years of preferring to swim alone . . .

Even my naked young Roman soldiers seemed to have ceased to haunt my imagination the moment Rufus came on the scene.

When he called at the Lodge later with Pearl, who'd just been to the vet's to have her stitches out, she was not only full of bounce but seemed a totally transformed dog, with white glossy fur and shiny eyes, usually fixed adoringly on Rufus.

He didn't stay long because he had to get back to the antiques centre and I was in the middle of printing out order slips to go into packages, but we'd be seeing each other at the pub as usual that evening anyway.

When the parcels were packed, Judy drove me over to the Middlemoss post office with them and then dropped me at the pub to see Lulu. It was fun the four of us meeting up most evenings, but I suddenly felt like a heart-to-heart, just the two of us, and she felt the same way.

It was still a bit early for the lunchtime customers, but we'd just settled down in the hotel bar with coffee when we heard the sound of people arriving and a familiar loud voice from the public bar. We looked at each other.

'Dan? I thought he'd been barred?'

'He has,' Lulu said, 'but the new barmaid probably doesn't know him.'

We peeped cautiously over the bar, where we could see through to where Dan was standing – or swaying, to be more accurate – attempting to chat up the barmaid, encouraged by a couple of his cronies.

'He must have got tanked up at the Falling Star first,' Lulu suggested, and I thought she was right, especially when he began shooting his mouth off about his recent grievances, slagging off Debo and Judy in very nasty terms and then saying how he'd get his own back on Rufus for firing him.

Lulu turned to me, raising her eyebrows.

'Rufus *did* fire him last night – I was just about to tell you.'

'Oh?'

'Fliss will see me right, when we get married, and Rufus can't very well throw his own mother out of his cottage, can he?' bellowed Dan, steadying himself with a hand on the brass rail of the bar. 'Let's have a drink!'

'He's deluded,' I said.

'He's certainly *drunk*,' Lulu said, catching the barmaid's eye and shaking her head. 'I'll go and get my dad and Bruce, so they can put him out before any customers arrive.'

He didn't go quietly, but eventually his friends persuaded him into the car and drove him away. Once he'd gone, Lulu fetched fresh coffee and I gave her a quick résumé of what had happened the previous night, resulting in Dan being given a month's notice.

'He's so stupid! If he'd just buckled down and worked really hard when Rufus took over, then I'm sure he could have kept his job . . . or he would if he hadn't also decided to have a fling with Fliss and then brag about it.'

'While he was ranting on in the bar, he sounded peeved that Fliss hadn't wanted to see him this weekend, didn't he?' she said.

'Perhaps she's getting tired of him at last. Rufus still thinks she isn't serious and that she's using him to try to get us out of the Lodge, so she can have it while her flat's being renovated.'

'But that was never going to happen, so she must be as thick as Dan!' Lulu said.

'Actually, sending all those people round from the council and the RSPCA might have caused us some real problems if we hadn't already cleared off the extra buildings and got the kennels back under control,' I confessed.

'It's just as well you came home when you did, then, and

once Dan's gone, things will be much more peaceful round here.'

'Last night Judy and Debo suggested to Rufus that he give Dan's job to Olly, because if he's earning more money and has the cottage, then he and his fiancée can finally get married.'

'Oh, wouldn't that be perfect – and a wedding we'd all want to go to!' she exclaimed. 'But could he manage the job on his own, do you think?'

'Oh, yes, he's very self-motivated and good at his work, but his dad can keep an eye on things. Laurie's retiring shortly and he's going to do a bit of part-time office keeping for Rufus, anyway. Foxy's an ace with machinery like brush cutters, too, so she can always put in a bit of overtime.'

Lulu sang a snatch of 'Things Can Only Get Better' and then told me she now had several Haunted Holiday bookings, so things were looking up all round.

I described Dan's drunken scene to Rufus while we were walking down that evening and added, 'I think Dan is going to be tricky until he leaves. But you're forever stuck with Debo and Judy in the Lodge – *and* me.'

That's OK, because I don't really want to get rid of any of you,' he said. 'As to Dan, while he may think he's the only lover in Fliss's life, she's never been a one-man kind of woman, so goodness knows what she's up to this weekend. Still, anyone except him!'

When we passed through the public bar, where Jonas was sitting with a friend, downing a pint of Mossbrown Ale, we were startled to see Howling Hetty was wearing a bright pink bobbed wig. I had no idea where Lulu got that one, but hoped it wasn't something she made a habit of wearing herself.

'She must be trying to make the skull look more feminine,' I suggested.

'I don't think it's really working for me,' Rufus said, following me into the empty snug just as Lulu and Cam entered it by the hotel door.

'The most awful thing!' Lulu exclaimed, looking absolutely distracted. 'Guy has read one of my old emails!'

She sank down onto the bench seat between me and Cam, and Rufus took a chair opposite. 'That doesn't sound very earth-shattering,' he said. 'I'm missing something?'

'It depends which email it was,' I told him. 'But he doesn't use the computer, so how did that happen, Lulu?'

'That student Guy's paying to look after the internet bookings sent her an email, too,' Cam explained. 'He said he'd got bored the other night so he'd hacked into her old emails. He was just reading one *you'd* sent to her, Izzy, when Guy looked over his shoulder.'

'Unfortunately, it was the reply to one of mine telling you that Guy's drinking was getting worse and how unhappy I was,' Lulu said, and Cameron put his arm around her shoulders and gave her a comforting squeeze.

'And then you asked me if I knew that Cam had broken up with his girlfriend in London and – well . . .' She stopped.

'Guy realised that actually Cameron *wasn't* gay and the brown stuff hit the fan?' I suggested. 'Right.'

'The student – Alain, he's called – warned me, because he felt guilty. He did manage to fool Guy into believing that that was the only email left and all the rest had been wiped, though, which is something.'

340

'Why would he think you were gay?' asked Rufus.

'Search me,' Cam said.

'It was only because you look quite arty – he has that kind of mind,' Lulu explained. 'And I admit I didn't tell him you weren't gay, because then he would have gone into jealousy-overdrive.'

'He seems to have done that now, but it might be a good thing, in a way,' Cam suggested. 'If he thinks we ran off to be together, then he isn't going to expect you to go back to him now, is he?'

'No . . . perhaps you're right,' she agreed, her forehead smoothing a little. 'I made it very clear I *wasn't* going back in the letter I sent him, too.'

Now she was calmer, I kindly informed her, as only a best friend can, that her hair looked like an electrified sheep and most of her Sultry Rose lipstick was on Cam, and she rushed off to tidy up.

Cam, unabashed, scrubbed the lipstick off with a tissue I gave him and then he and Rufus set up the sound-effects equipment for the storytelling session.

Rufus and I didn't stay for that one but went back to the snug for a while and then returned to the Lodge, where we found Babybelle smugly installed in the kitchen with the other two dogs. Debo and Judy must have given up the struggle to get her into her kennel tonight.

I made cocoa and found some almond biscuits, which we took into the studio, where we sat on the sofa together so I could show Rufus my photographs of the two women's work-shops in India I'd helped to set up, where my stock came from.

'I'll have to go out there later in the year and see them – in fact, I think I'll need to go out annually.'

'I've always wanted to visit India,' he told me wistfully. 'Perhaps I'll come with you.'

I wasn't sure if he was serious or not, but I said he could if he wanted to . . . and then, right at that moment, his mobile went off and I could hear Fliss's voice, loud and clear, even before he switched to speakerphone and mouthed her name at me.

'There you are at last, Rufus!'

'I tried to get hold of you earlier, Fliss,' he said. 'I've fired your lover and given him notice to quit the cottage by June.'

'Oh, never mind Dan now,' she said impatiently. 'I'm having such fun catching up with the old gang that I've invited them to stay at Sweetwell next weekend. There's plenty of room. We'll party and liven you and that old dump up!'

'Then you'd better *un*-invite them,' he said evenly, but with an undercurrent of anger. 'I'm not having any of that lot under my roof – in fact, if they so much as set foot on my land, I'll have them arrested for trespass. And after what we discussed last time we spoke, I don't even want *you* at Sweetwell – I told you.'

I wasn't sure what he meant by that last bit, unless he'd still been angry at her for inviting Dan and his friends up to the house last time – but she obviously hadn't learned her lesson.

'Oh, you know I didn't mean anything by it and you never used to be quite so stuffy,' she said disgustedly. 'It's that little girl from the Lodge, isn't it? She's turned you even prissier than you were before.'

'I'm actually at the Lodge with Izzy right now,' he told her levelly.

342

'Then I suppose it must be love's young dream and you're never going to throw them out: so that's it, then.' She changed tack abruptly. 'About Dan – he did leave messages on my phone, so let's discuss—'

'There's nothing *to* discuss,' Rufus interrupted. 'And he'd be crazy to take me to an employment tribunal because he wouldn't have a leg to stand on.'

'I don't care about him being fired,' she said callously. 'What I wanted to know was—'

But neither of us was destined to hear what she wanted to know, for Rufus cut the connection at this point and then turned his phone right off.

As always, after any contact with his mother, he went all inwards and gloomy and took himself off home, though he did suggest as he left that he could finally cook me that dinner at Sweetwell the next evening.

And although the grisly spectre of Fliss still hung over us, I said yes, anyway.

While we were swimming next morning, Rufus told me he was heading over to Yorkshire first thing on the following day, to pick up a wrought-iron antique garden love seat and, if the price was right, some old agricultural implements.

'People love them as garden features,' he said. 'There might be some other stuff, too.'

Then he added teasingly that he really *did* wish I'd wear the white bikini I'd had on when he'd tried to drown me, which seemed to have stuck in his memory for some reason, probably the wrong one.

'I know you're not serious,' I told him, because I knew now when he was winding me up. 'I don't think it did anything for me even when I was a skinny teenager and it certainly doesn't now.'

'I think you looked cute in it.'

'Like a drowned pixie?'

'I like pixies,' he said gravely, and then, on some sudden impulse, I scooped great handfuls of water in his face and he splashed me back. Then he picked me up and whirled me around, before dropping me into the water . . . and when I came back up, there was Tom, looking puzzled.

Then his face cleared and he grinned. 'I wondered what all the noise was, but I see you're just having a bit of fun – much like I did with my Pauline when she was a young lass.'

Smiling benignly, he pottered off back to his garden, followed closely by Queenie, but I went all self-conscious and told Rufus it was getting late, and we'd both better get back.

'OK, but I'll see you tonight,' he reminded me, and unleashed that rare and enticing killer smile.

Probably due to it being a sunny, warm day, there seemed to be loads of people out and about by mid-morning when I went over to Cam's gallery to pack an order. Many of them had the ghost trail map in their hands, which was a good sign.

The gallery was quite busy too and Jonas, his little dog, Snowy, at his feet, was sitting on a tall stool behind the till, his shock of white hair standing out like a halo, while Cameron was getting down a painting he'd sold to a customer – one of his own.

When Cam had a minute to talk, he told me he was going

with Rufus on the Yorkshire trip and I felt a momentary pang almost of jealousy because Rufus hadn't asked me, too. But of course, if he needed someone to help him haul large garden furniture into his van, Cam was a much better prospect!

By late afternoon I'd stopped working and was having a little crisis of the 'what am I going to wear tonight?' kind. I mean, I was having dinner alone with Rufus . . . but as a friend? Or was this a date? I didn't even know if he saw me in any other light but friendship, but even if he did fancy me, *could* anything warmer develop between us, given what had happened in the past?

I tried consulting my inner voice, but all it told me was to put on a pretty dress, get myself up there and see what happened – a message I suspected didn't come from my guardian angel.

So I strolled up with Babybelle as dusk was slowly settling, though I quickened my pace as I passed the fatal spot, for the birdsong always seemed to be hushed just there and the trees feel as if they're closing in, despite their having recently been cut back.

Babybelle hadn't been invited, but when we arrived, Rufus said he didn't mind an extra guest in the least and it had been a bit remiss of him not to include her in the first place. She and Pearl certainly seemed pleased to see each other and at least talking about the dogs broke the ice between us, for I'd been feeling strangely self-conscious when he opened the door.

'Come into the kitchen and talk to me while I finish cooking,' he suggested, leading the way through. 'In fact, I've laid the table in there, because it's cosier than sitting in the dining room. This isn't exactly a grand house, but it's definitely grander than any I've ever lived in before.'

'I like your little TV room,' I said, 'where we watched the film after the takeaway the other night.'

'Officially, that's the library, though the Salcombes don't appear to have been great readers. There are only Baz's thrillers and a few Victorian novels in there at the moment, but I'll unpack my books soon and fill those empty shelves up a bit.'

'Including the works of the Brontës?' I asked curiously. 'I'm surprised you know *Jane Eyre* so well.'

'I did my degree in English Literature . . . and I'm a romantic at heart,' he said gravely, so I wasn't sure if he was serious or not.

He took a bottle of champagne out of an ice bucket and poured us both a glass.

'We're celebrating something?' I asked.

'Lots of things, not least that I've rung Fliss and told her she's permanently banned from Sweetwell.'

'But she's still your mother; she might want to see you?'

'If she does, I'll meet her in London. But this is *my* place and my new life, and I don't want her in it, messing things up.'

I wouldn't put it past her to keep turning up anyway, but I didn't want to rain on his parade, so I smiled instead and raised my glass.

'Here's to success for Izzy Dane Designs and Rufus Salcombe Garden Antiques,' I said, and we clinked champagne flutes.

'And to the future,' he added, then as he turned away to stir something on the stove, he asked me whether I'd dredged up any fresh memories.

'One or two, where I'm definitely driving the Range Rover, and totally terrified about it,' I admitted. 'I don't know if the dreams will ever progress as far as the accident, but I suspect not. And anyway, even if they did, Cara's the only one who could confirm if they're right or wrong, and she isn't talking. She isn't even replying to my messages on her mobile.'

'So – the mission has ended, more or less?'

I nodded. 'It's probably going to stay mission unaccomplished because I'll never know why I didn't get out at the Lodge, or why I crashed.'

'You might eventually remember all the answers,' Rufus suggested.

'I don't know. I seem to have the other kind of dream more lately, the one where I'm swimming up and down the pool with you and—' I stopped dead, going pink.

Rufus was getting too easy to talk to!

'*And*?' he prompted, turning with a wooden spoon in one hand.

'Nothing, we're just swimming and it's . . . nice,' I said lamely.

He gave me one of his serious, searching looks and then went back to finishing off the paella, which smelled wonderful.

'No starter,' he said, 'but I told Myra you were coming to dinner, so she's left an apple pie and cream in the fridge for dessert.'

'Perfect, though I'll be fat as a pig after all that,' I said, as he piled paella onto dishes and sat down opposite me.

Babybelle subsided heavily and hopefully on my feet. I was so glad Rufus didn't have a glass dining table, because there's nothing more disconcerting than a dog sitting underneath one and longingly following each forkful of food from plate to lips.

347

After dinner we watched a film in the library and I picked out the solitary romantic comedy from the line-up of thrillers.

'I'd forgotten that was there,' he said. 'It was in a mixed box of stuff I bought at auction with some books I wanted.'

'What kind of books?' I asked curiously.

'Old gardening ones – I collect them. I've never had a lot of spare time to watch films, because I've been too busy building up my business. Clearly I need you to educate my tastes.'

'You should chill out more,' I told him, and he said he was working on it.

We sat cosily together on the sofa with Belle and Pearl curled up asleep on the rug, and finished the champagne. It might have gone to my head slightly, because when he walked me home later, accompanied by both dogs, he had to put his arm around me to keep me going in a straight line.

He was resolute about our not avoiding the hollow, too. 'This is my property and if Hetty wants to haunt it, she'd better get used to seeing me about,' he said. And maybe she heard him, because there was nothing even remotely spectral hanging about the hollow.

When we got to the Lodge, he had to find the key for me, and then, the moment the door was open, Belle almost knocked me off my feet while thundering past, eager to see if there was any forgotten food lying around the kitchen.

I staggered and Rufus caught me . . . and then pulled me close and kissed me. It was a long, slow-burning kiss and I'm sure my feet weren't touching the ground.

When our lips finally slowly parted and I opened my eyes,

I found myself staring into his pale green gaze from about two inches away.

'Good night,' he said softly, then set me down and strode off, whistling to Pearl to follow.

Or maybe he was whistling to me, because *I* nearly did, too.

Chapter 29: Floating

We floated together in the opaque turquoise water, holding hands . . . Then Rufus stood up, crystal-clear droplets sliding down over his muscled torso, and pulled me into a close and passionate embrace . . .

It wasn't surprising that I should have a steamy swimming-with-Rufus dream after that kiss, but I awoke next morning feeling that last night we might have stepped over an invisible boundary. (And after that, in the dream, I'd not so much stepped, as *hurdled* over several more.)

It was probably just as well that Rufus and Cam had left for Yorkshire early, so I hadn't actually had to face him at the pool with that dream still fresh – even hot – in my mind.

Last night's kiss was probably just the champagne talking, though, and even if it wasn't, his ghastly mother (who I thought unlikely to leave him in peace), and my involvement in the death of his half-brother, still appeared almost insuperable obstacles to any closer relationship.

Unfortunately, these sensible reflections didn't stop me from blushing when Debo and Judy asked me at breakfast if I'd had a nice time at Sweetwell.

'Yes, and Rufus is a great cook,' I said quickly.

'What exactly did he cook up for you, darling?' asked Debo interestedly. 'Something with a little passion fruit in it, I hope?'

'Don't tease, Debo,' Judy said, coming to my rescue.

I made my escape and went to check for orders, for it was strange how many nocturnal shoppers there were. I had two and, after printing out the packing slips, I walked across to the gallery to parcel them up. At this rate, I'd soon be wearing a groove into the Green.

I had to let myself in, because of course it was Monday and so closing day anyway, but I'd texted Lulu earlier to suggest that since Cam and Rufus had gone jaunting off to Yorkshire without even asking us (that rankled with her a bit, too), we should have a girls' day out in Southport.

She'd agreed and was to pick me up mid-morning, but instead tempestuously burst into the studio ages before I expected her while I was still finishing sketching an idea for a new dress. I had photos of hippies scattered all over the place and a Mamas and the Papas CD compilation playing, to get me in the right retro vibe.

'Izzy!' she exclaimed.

'What's up?' I asked, switching the music off, then swivelling round and staring at her. She gazed back at me, wild-eyed, waving a piece of paper.

Dusty swaggered insouciantly in after her, with one battered ear up and the other down. Babybelle, unimpressed, raised her eyebrows and sighed, heavily.

'Why have you brought Dusty? We're not taking the dogs to Southport shopping with us, are we?'

'No, I just forgot to leave him behind, because I've had

an actual *email* from Guy! He says now he knows all about Cameron, he's going to come and sort him out – *and* he's not going back without me.'

She brandished the print-out again.

'He *emailed*?'

'Not personally. He got that student, Alain, to do it for him.'

'How do you know?'

'Because Alain emailed after Guy had gone out, to say he'd had to do it, but he was sorry. He seems nice, apart from the hacking into my private emails thing. He's only working for Guy until he's saved up for a motorbike.'

'What does Guy mean, he knows about Cameron? That he isn't gay?' I asked, having read the bellicose and threatening email.

'Of course, if he wasn't so stupid he'd never have thought he was in the first place,' she said. 'Look at the way the women who came to Cam's painting week always drooled over him!'

'Well, I wasn't there for any of them, so I'll have to take your word for it, but I can imagine. That flaxen hair and those big blue eyes get them every time.'

'I think now Guy's finally twigged, he's jumped to the conclusion that we've been having an affair for years and *that's* why he's threatening to sort Cam out.'

'But it's probably just an empty threat?' I suggested. 'He can't very well make you go back with him if you don't want to, and anyway, he'd need someone to look after the place if he was away, even for a few days.'

'But his brother's moved in, remember, so he could leave him in charge. Solange says Guy's only renting out the four separate self-catering *gîtes* now, and not having any guests in the main house, so even *he* should be able to manage that.' She shivered. 'Guy could already be on his way over here!'

'I doubt it, he was probably just in a jealous strop when he dictated the email. Send him one back telling him that if he comes near you or Cameron you'll report him to the police for harassment and threatening behaviour.'

'Yes, I suppose I should . . . and I've just had four more bookings for the first Haunted Holiday, so I could really do without this hassle right now,' she said, exasperation beginning to take over from the initial panic. 'I've had to warn the family, just in case Guy does suddenly appear, and Mum and Dad wanted me to move into their flat, but I said I was safe enough in the trailer with Dusty to protect me.'

'And Cam,' I added innocently, and she blushed. Her parents were very strait-laced, so her living with Guy for years hadn't gone down too well. They certainly wouldn't let Cam stay over in the flat as, I suspected, he often did at the caravan.

'Izzy, you know when I said Cameron and I had decided just to be good friends for now and put anything else on the back-burner?'

'I do, but let me guess: you've discovered now that you've really fallen in love and want to be together all the time,' I suggested helpfully. 'It's been obvious for a while that someone had taken the brakes off the go-slow clause.'

She laughed. 'That was me! I suddenly saw that there was nothing to be afraid of: Cam wasn't Guy, he was the man I'd known my entire life as a close friend and he'd always be that. The love bit was just an added extra.'

'Of course it is, and it will work out wonderfully well, you'll see. I'm so happy for you both!' I gave her a hug.

'Cameron wants us to get engaged. He says my parents and his family aren't going to like it if we just live together, which I suppose is true, and anyway, he *wants* to get married.'

She looked at me slyly. 'So, if you and Rufus stopped staring longingly at one another when the other one isn't looking and got things going, maybe we could have a double wedding?'

'*Does* he look at me like that?' I asked involuntarily.

'All the time.'

I sighed. 'Well, whether he does or not, nothing can ever come of it except friendship, given all the ramifications with Fliss and Harry, can it?'

'You had dinner alone with him last night. I call that a date!'

'No it wasn't, it was just . . .' I broke off and got up. 'It's too complicated to even *think* about! Come on – Judy's in the kitchen and she can bribe Babybelle into staying with her. We'll drop Dusty at the pub, send a quick email to Guy, and then get off to Southport.'

So we did just that and also, at my suggestion, emailed Alain to say that if he let us know if Guy suddenly set out for the UK, we'd cross his palm with euros.

We returned home hours later, tired but happy, because there's nothing like a bit of retail therapy to calm the troubled soul.

Cam obviously felt the same way, because when he and Rufus called in at the pub on their way back from Yorkshire, he immediately got down on one knee, formally proposed to Lulu and then presented her with an antique diamond ring!

'After we'd collected my stuff, he had me all over York searching for the perfect ring,' Rufus said with a grin.

'I think he found it!' I said, admiringly, and then Lulu's parents, who had been let in on the secret so Cam knew the right size ring to get, brought out the ready-chilled bubbly and we toasted the happy couple.

Luckily all this excitement made me forget to be shy with Rufus about that kiss until *much* later, when he gave me a lift home in the van, leaving Cameron and Lulu still celebrating. He stopped by the Lodge to let me out, since he was keen to get back to Pearl, who was being dog-sat by Myra and Olly in relays so she didn't get lonely.

'I'm tired, too,' he admitted, 'though it was a successful trip all round. I got a very pretty old wrought-iron gazebo and a pair of gates, among other things. Foxy will help me unload them in the morning. Then you'll have to come up and see them.'

'I'd love to,' I replied and then, as I climbed down and was about to shut the door, he leaned over and handed me a small, tissue-wrapped package.

'Here's something I picked up for you today, because it had your name on it.'

'Oh . . . thank you, but you shouldn't have!' I stammered, flustered.

'It's a little thing of no great value, but fun,' he said. 'While you, on the other hand, are a small thing of *great* value and also fun.' Then he released that killer smile at me and drove off.

When I'd disentangled myself from Babybelle's enthusiastic

welcome, I unwrapped my gift, which was a quirky, dear little antique brooch in the form of a short-legged, square-eared dog, set with amber stones.

I slept with it under my pillow and dreamed, unsurprisingly, only of Rufus.

Chapter 30: Blighters

In the early morning, while we were swimming, I thanked Rufus again for the brooch and he said it was nothing, he'd just thought I'd like it.

'I do, it's lovely,' I enthused, though I was trying to maintain a sort of cheerful, brisk friendliness, so he'd know that I realised that the kiss the other night meant nothing serious. But I think he'd forgotten about it anyway, because he was his usual quiet self and went straight back to Sweetwell after our swim, intending to start unloading the van.

I had Lulu on the phone right after breakfast, full of the joys of spring and her engagement and saying what a surprise it had all been, as if I hadn't been there and witnessed it for myself.

'I didn't realise that Cam could be so secretive, but it was sweet of him, wasn't it? And Mum and Dad are delighted.'

I passed on Debo and Judy's warmest congratulations, but after that I only had to make the occasional noise of agreement, while she burbled happily on.

When she finally ran out of steam and rang off, and I was making a cup of coffee before going into the studio, Simon got me on my mobile: this was obviously not going to be a very productive morning.

'Sir Lionel's home, and he and Cara have had a blazing row right in the middle of the stable yard,' he announced. I was just wondering what that had to do with me, when he added, 'He told her that he'd had enough of her carryings-on and wanted a divorce and then *she* said she didn't care, because it had been a huge mistake marrying an old weasel like him and she wanted a divorce too, so she could marry this Kieran.'

'That was speedy!' I said. 'But really, Simon, if she's that fickle, you're well out of it.'

'You're right, and when she started taunting him in a really vicious way about how old he was, and so mean with his money, the scales really fell from my eyes.'

'Then that's a good thing, because you'll get over her all the quicker,' I said bracingly.

'I think I already have. And Sir Lionel managed to shut her up, by reminding her that she'd signed a pre-nuptial agreement.'

'That was super-cautious of him!'

'Cara's his third wife. The second one died, but he's still paying alimony to the first. Cara's much younger than he is and so beautiful that he must have known she was only marrying him for his money.'

'Oh, I don't know, Simon. Most rich older men with pretty young wives probably delude themselves that they've married them for love.'

'I was just a diversion; she was never serious about me,' he said, but in a resigned sort of way. 'I'll be off to my new job in a couple of weeks, though when Cripchet calmed down a bit and finished calling his solicitor, he came to find me and tried to get me to change my mind about handing in my notice.'

'I hope you didn't.'

'No way! I need to be off out of it. But when he said I was leaving him in the lurch, I had a brainwave and suggested he give my dad the job and the cottage that goes with it, because he fancied a change of scene from Sweetwell. And he has, too!'

'Let's hope he's not expecting a glowing reference from Rufus, then,' I commented drily. 'Still, Cripchet probably won't ever know that Dan was fired, because he's not plugged into the Halfhidden grapevine at all.'

'No, and he's hardly ever even at Grimside. But it's a relief to me that Dad will have a place to live and a job after I've moved away.'

'He'll probably find himself working more hours for his money.'

'Yes, Sir Lionel's a bit of a slave driver,' Simon admitted. 'I told Dad he'd be out on his ear if he didn't pull his weight.'

'Well, at least some good has come out of it all, though I'm sorry things didn't work out with you and Cara. I feel a bit guilty that Kieran only came up here in the first place because of me.'

'It doesn't matter. I can see she'd have dumped me as soon as something better came along, anyway.'

'And she's obviously never going to talk to me about the accident. She hasn't even answered my text messages.'

'You won't be able to try to see her again if she goes off with this Kieran bloke, will you? He lives down South, somewhere.'

'Yes, Oxford.'

Simon rang off, promising to update me on any new developments, though I don't know why. After all, it was really nothing to do with me any more.

The pared-down kennels looked so much neater that morning. While I'd been in Southport with Lulu, Tom had finally finished off the new block with a couple of coats of weatherproofing wood stain. Now Debo was painting the new fence white, while Judy had marked out where the rose bed was to be dug and begun to remove the turf.

I showed Rufus the fruit of their endeavours before we went to the last of the regular Regeneration Committee meetings. Everything was now either in place or, like the Victorian tea gardens, well on the way.

After the meeting, as Lulu, Cam, Rufus and I walked down to the pub, I told them about Cara and Sir Lionel divorcing – *and* that Dan had been offered Simon's job and the cottage that went with it.

Rufus, who'd seemed a bit abstracted till then, said, 'I already knew about Dan getting Simon's job. Fliss told me when she called to say she was having to move out of her flat.'

'What, straight away?'

'Yes. They gave her lots of notice but she refused to go until the noise and dust got unbearable and she had no choice.'

'But where will she go to, that's the million-dollar question?' I asked. 'You've already told her you won't have her at Sweetwell again.'

'No way!' he said firmly. 'She actually suggested that she

could have Dan's cottage, once he'd moved to the one that comes with his new job!'

'But – she can't,' Lulu objected blankly. 'Olly and his fiancée are going to live there. I mean, Olly's handed in his notice at the alpine nursery and set the date for a summer wedding.'

'I told her the cottage was going to the new gardener, but Fliss is coming down to stay with Dan anyway,' Rufus said. 'And when I said I thought things were cooling off between them, she said they were on her side, but she couldn't spend six months living with friends.'

'Until he moves to the new place, I don't suppose you can really stop him having visitors in the cottage,' Cam said.

'No, but I only hope she thinks better of it, because I might have a hell of a job getting her out when Dan moves,' Rufus said gloomily.

After that, he wasn't exactly a ray of sunshine for the rest of the evening. Luckily Cam and Lulu were too engrossed in each other to notice.

Judy drove Debo to the station next morning, because she was off on a modelling assignment. She left wearing jeans, an old sweatshirt and her ancient green waxed jacket, though once she got to Daisy's, she would as usual transform herself from everyday duck to elegant swan.

After she'd gone, persistent rain set in, making trotting to and fro from the Lodge to the gallery to process clothes orders more of a chore than a pleasure, though at least my new red mac didn't leak water through the seams and down the back of my neck, like my old one.

It was still raining when Lulu and I met to walk the dogs after lunch. Lulu was girding her loins for the very first

Haunted Holiday, which was to start next weekend, on the first Saturday in May, when, annually, the Morris men danced all the way up the paths from the village of Middlemoss to Halfhidden.

I was just thinking that, other than the threat of Fliss's unwelcome presence in the village, everything was going well, when late in the afternoon I had a text message from Lulu saying that Alain, the student helping Guy, had emailed warning her that Guy had gone off somewhere yesterday and hadn't come back.

'But Guy might just be off on a bender?' Cam suggested, when we were all down at the Screaming Skull later and discussing it. 'Despite his threats, he must know he's no chance of getting you back, so coming here would be pointless.'

'I don't know . . .' she said doubtfully. 'He's vain enough to think that one look at him and I'd fall into his arms again.'

'Kieran was harbouring that idea, too,' I said. 'Or at least, he did right up to the point when he set eyes on Cara.'

'If Guy does suddenly appear, perhaps we should introduce him to Cara?' Lulu suggested. 'She might like a *ménage à trois* of rejected lovers.'

'Dusty and I'll protect you, if he shows up,' Cameron promised.

'Or you could just bash him with that huge rock you're wearing on your left hand, Lulu,' I suggested, and she grinned.

'If he comes to the pub, Mum and Dad will get Bruce and the barman to throw him out,' she said. 'He isn't going to know I'm living in the trailer because he doesn't have any local contacts. I should be safe enough.'

*   *   *

362

'Do you still feel someone's watching you when you're alone in the woods?' asked Rufus, as we walked home. Cam had set out with us, then doubled back to the caravan, though I don't think he was fooling Lulu's parents. Still, I expect they felt better about it now Lulu and Cam were engaged.

'No, it seems to have stopped, and anyway, it was probably all in my imagination.'

'Or it was Dan, in which case it won't happen again now I've told him to stay off my property . . . though come to think of it, I don't suppose I can bar him from using a public footpath.'

'I suppose it could have been him lurking about, but he's never actually done me any harm. I'm certain he wasn't the one who shot at me, too.'

'*I'm* sure it wasn't, too,' he said rather grimly.

I stopped dead and stared at him – or what I could see of him, for even though we'd reached the moonlit clearing by the Lady Spring, it was still hard to make his face out clearly. 'You know who did it!'

'I do, and they won't do it again,' he said . . . and then suddenly, I knew, too.

'It was Fliss, wasn't it?' I demanded.

'I'm afraid so. She took an old air rifle and some pellets from Dan's unlocked gun cupboard on impulse, though she's an excellent shot and only meant to frighten you.'

'She did that, all right! And now I can see why you told her you never wanted her to come back to the village again.'

'I was furious with her – and I'm so sorry, Izzy.'

'Why? It's hardly your fault your mother's nutty as a fruitcake, is it? And I don't suppose she'll try anything like that again.'

'She'd better not,' he said grimly. 'Come on, let's get home.'

'I hope Guy *doesn't* show up,' I said, after we'd walked in silence for a few minutes and my mind had reverted to Lulu's problems. 'He's horrible. Also, he's bigger than Cam, though Cam did karate when we were teenagers, so maybe he could just chop him into little neat pieces.'

'I'm sure Cameron can take care of himself,' Rufus said. 'But there are lots of people around at the Screaming Skull, so they'd just throw Guy straight out again before it got to the rough stuff.'

'Yes, that's true,' I said, reassured. 'But Lulu really doesn't need the added hassle at the moment. She's got so many bookings for the first Haunted Holiday that the hotel will be bursting at the seams!'

'Jonas will enjoy having a big audience for his ghost stories on Saturday night, then,' Rufus said. 'I wonder if he's "remembered" any new ones.'

'Probably. He's obviously got a good memory for films he's seen and stories he's heard, as well as a very inventive imagination.'

And *my* imagination was also working overtime, but whatever scenario I'd thought might transpire when Rufus dropped me at the Lodge, there was no attempt to repeat that kiss. Clearly the unwelcome possibility of Fliss's advent had cast a blight over him, yet again.

Perhaps that was just as well, considering.

Chapter 31: The Stars in Our Eyes

I got through the Sweetwell gates with more luck than judgement and came to a halt just before the turn to the Lodge, praying that Judy wouldn't emerge before I'd got out.

'What are you stopping for?' asked Harry. 'Keep going!'

When Lulu met me in the woods late next morning, she said Florrie Snowball, landlady of the Falling Star in Sticklepond, had rung her parents up that morning.

'She wanted them to warn me that Guy was staying there.'

'But how did she know he was anything to do with you?'

'Because last night in the bar he got talking to Dan and was mouthing off loudly about how he was going to come over to the Screaming Skull to show me he wasn't the kind of man to be messed with! And Dan was winding him up by telling him he'd heard I was carrying on with Cameron Ross.'

'He would,' I said disgustedly. 'But I didn't *really* expect Guy to show up, did you?'

'No, and now I haven't a clue when he's going to suddenly appear. Florrie said he went out with Dan about ten and asked her for a key in case he was late, but she told him the place was locked up at half-past eleven and anyone coming back after that time would find themselves on the doorstep till morning.'

'Good for her! But I wonder where they went.'

'Well, we were woken up last night by Dusty barking, though we couldn't see anything. At the time, we assumed it was a fox, but it might have been Guy scouting out the lie of the land. By now, everyone locally must know I'm living in the trailer, so I suppose Dan will have told him, though he probably didn't realise I had a dog.'

'I expect you're right,' I said.

'Anyway, there's been no sign of him so far and Dusty needed a walk, so I thought I'd meet you anyway.'

'Have you told Cam?'

'Yes, and he got angry and wanted to go over to the Falling Star and have it out with Guy once and for all, but fortunately Jonas couldn't mind the gallery, so with a bit of luck Guy will have made his appearance at the Screaming Skull and been turfed out by Bruce and the barman by the time Cam shuts the gallery.'

'You'd better be really careful on the way back home,' I advised her, when we'd done a circular walk through the woods and come out again by the Lady Spring. Dusty and Babybelle were running ahead . . . or ambling, in Belle's case.

'I'll certainly be keeping a lookout for him, but it's a huge nuisance with the big weekend coming up.'

'It'll certainly cast a cloud over things if he hangs about for long – and let's hope this rainy weather clears for Saturday and the Morris dancing.'

'I would really like a nice day to greet the first Haunted Holidaymakers,' Lulu agreed.

I was worried Guy might be lurking in the woods near the pub, so although Lulu said she'd be safe enough with Dusty, I insisted that Babybelle and I escort her home. A bit of extra exercise wouldn't do either of us any harm.

We emerged from the safety of the trees cautiously and Lulu checked the car park for Guy's big blue Citroën.

'No sign of him,' she said, relieved. 'Come on, I'll give you a cup of coffee before you go back.'

The big door to the public bar was open and I followed Lulu and Dusty in . . . and then almost ran into the back of her, as she stopped dead on the threshold.

She had good reason. Her father and Bruce were having an altercation with a tanned, silver-haired man at the other end of the long room: Lulu's ex, Guy. His tall, muscular frame had run to seed a bit since I'd last seen him and his high complexion was turning to a mesh of broken veins, probably from all the boozing.

The room was heavily shadowed where we stood and at first none of them noticed us.

'My daughter wants nothing more to do with you, so you've wasted your journey,' Mr Benbow said. 'You might as well pack up and get back off to France.'

'It's none of your business! I'll soon sort this out and put a stop to her getting ideas about any other man. Now, where is she?' Guy demanded.

Lulu, still holding Dusty's lead, began to edge slowly backwards and we could probably have crept away had Belle not subsided heavily onto my feet, pinning me to the spot.

'Leave now before you're thrown out, and don't come back,' Bruce said evenly.

Guy's hands clenched into fists and his face reddened even

further with rage, so I'm not sure what would have happened next had Dusty not suddenly growled deep in his throat, attracting his attention.

His whole persona changed, chameleon-like, in an instant. 'Lu, darling, there you are!' he exclaimed. 'I was just telling your family that I was certain you'd want to see me and you were only pretending to have a fling with that friend of yours to make me jealous.'

'But I *don't* want to see you and I'm not pretending about anything. Cam and I are engaged,' Lulu said, standing her ground now she was discovered. 'I wrote to tell you I never even wanted to *hear* from you again!'

'I didn't take any notice of that. I knew you were still angry because you'd found out I'd been seeing someone else. But I admit I was a fool and I soon realised I wanted you back – and I'll make it up to you, Lulu, I promise,' he added persuasively. 'Now, go and get your things, and we'll head for home.'

I don't think he'd even registered my presence, a step or two behind her in the shadow of the door, or either of the dogs.

'It's too late, Guy. I mean what I say. I love Cam and we're going to get married,' she told him.

In an instant his expression changed to one of fury.

'Do you think I'd let you—' he began, then broke off as Bruce took one of his arms in a vice-like grip and said encouragingly, 'Time to go!'

'On your way, flower!' said Sam the barman, taking the other and urging Guy forward, with Mr Benbow bringing up the rear.

'Yes, do go away, Guy,' Lulu said, exasperated, and then

he totally lost his rag and shouted some foul things to her as he was dragged past us.

Dusty, who'd kept up his low menacing growl with his eyes fixed on the interloper, now helpfully tried to lunge forward and bite him, while Belle watched interestedly, clearly not feeling it was her fight.

'And out we go!' Bruce said, impelling Guy forward and down the steps. We could hear him alternately threatening and blustering his way back to his car, then slamming the door, revving the engine and driving off.

'There, that should be the end of him,' Mr Benbow said as the men returned. 'I don't expect he'll be back after that.'

'He must have changed his car. I hadn't thought of that, or I wouldn't have come walking right into the middle of things,' Lulu said.

'It's probably all for the good now that it's over with,' I suggested, having finally dislodged Babybelle and got the circulation back in my feet.

Some customers came in, looking curious, and Bruce said he'd better get back to the kitchen, and Sam behind the bar.

'We'll come through to the hotel with you, Dad: I was going to make some coffee for Izzy before she went home,' Lulu said, but since it was getting late I told her I'd better get back to the Lodge for lunch, before Judy sent out search parties.

'I'll see you tonight, though. And I hope that really *is* the last of Guy. Be careful until you're absolutely certain he's gone back to France, won't you?'

'I will, but don't tell Cam what happened if you see him,

or he'll lock the gallery up and go and duff Guy up at the Falling Star, or something daft.'

'Good thinking,' I agreed.

Lunch at the Lodge was Lancashire crumbly cheese, chewy dark bread and home-made fruit chutney, over which I entertained Judy with an account of the fracas at the pub.

Then afterwards, while Judy went to collect Debo from the station, I caught up with the kennel paperwork. A hint of carelessness had already crept into Debo's ways, with everything shoved into the roll-top desk, but I fished it out again and dealt with it.

Judy called me for tea and cake later, and Myra was there, too, having popped in for a cuppa and a catch-up on her way back from the shop – and to give us the unwelcome news that Fliss had arrived at Dan's cottage earlier.

'My friend, the one who lives next door to Dan Clew's cottage, saw her arrive this morning in a taxi, and she must have come to stay because she had six large pieces of luggage with her.'

'Oh, blast,' I said. 'That's going to upset Rufus.'

'Well, my friend wasn't too happy about it, either. She said she hoped they weren't going to be rowdy late at night, like the last time she stayed over,' Myra said. 'It beats me how a nice man like Rufus can have a mother like that!'

'I think we're all pretty baffled by that one,' agreed Debo.

As soon as I could, I sent Rufus a text warning him of Fliss's arrival and got a brief one back saying simply, '*I know*'.

It was no surprise that evening, then, that he was in one of his withdrawn, brooding moods when we forgathered at the pub.

'Fliss's furniture came in a small removal van this morning, and when I rang her to say she might have warned me, she told me I should be grateful *she* hadn't arrived with it but was staying with Dan instead!'

'Where did you put her stuff?' I asked curiously.

'In one of the unused stables in the courtyard. I've covered it up and locked the door, so it should be all right.'

Lulu attempted to divert his mind by describing Guy's earlier unwelcome appearance, but he only said morosely, 'Maybe I can hire Lulu's brother and the barman to throw Fliss out of the cottage if she tries to stay on after Dan moves out.'

'Oh, come on,' I said encouragingly, 'she's not going to be happy living in a small cottage with Dan for more than a couple of days, surely. After all, she told you she was tiring of him.'

'I expect she is, but she'll stay because she wants to take over the cottage when he goes, while that sucker Dan probably thinks she's going to move to his new place with him.'

'Well, look on the bright side, at least he's still banned from the Screaming Skull, so you won't have to see him and Fliss tonight,' Lulu consoled him. 'He's drinking at the Falling Star in Sticklepond instead and the landlady told us he and Guy chummed up in the bar there last night.'

'This Guy does sound like the sort of man Dan hangs out with,' Rufus said. 'They probably got on like a house on fire.'

'Lulu wouldn't let me go over there and have it out with him,' Cam said. He'd been brooding over his half of bitter since he'd found out what had happened earlier.

'He's probably packed up and gone, so there's no point,' Lulu told him. 'Come on, Cam, you might as well stop sulking and help me to lay the breakfast tables. We'll get it done early.'

They said good night and went out, and Rufus, still wrapped in his own thoughts, said darkly, 'I'd like to forget I have a mother, especially since every time you see her, Izzy, you must think of your own mother and that if it weren't for Fliss she might still be here.'

'I did when I first found out what happened, but now I've met Fliss . . . well, I'm sure she wouldn't have bothered to go out of her way to draw my mother into her circle again, would she?'

'No, she's way too lazy and self-centred. The most she might have done was rung round her friends and told them all to come to some party or nightclub. That would be about it.'

'And my mother didn't *have* to let herself be sucked back into that toxic circle, because by then she had me to think of. She made the choice.'

'Perhaps, but it would still be much better if Fliss wasn't around, reminding you.'

'But every time *you* see *me*, you must think about Harry and how you'd have known your only brother if only I hadn't been stupid enough to drive back from the pub that night.'

He stared at me, light green eyes wide with astonishment. 'Is that what you really think? But of *course* I don't blame you, especially now I know *how* he persuaded you. Harry brought the whole thing onto himself.'

'If my dreams *are* memories and it's all true.'

'We're way beyond doubting that now . . . and if neither of us is blaming the other for what happened in the past, maybe we can put it all behind us and move on . . . together?' he suggested, looking at me with just a hint of that smile.

He didn't define what he meant by 'together', but I agreed that yes, perhaps we could . . .

When we walked home, he took my hand in his as if he had a perfect right to hold it, and I swear that the air between us was so clear that I could see the million firefly stars of distant galaxies.

Chapter 32: Stopped

'I – I can't,' I said, unbuckling my seat belt with trembling hands. 'You can leave it here and walk up, can't you? Or drive it yourself, now you're on private land. I have to go – Judy will be setting out for the pub to collect me if I'm not home in a few minutes.'

'I did stop at the Lodge and I was trying to get out of the car!' I told Rufus, the second he slipped into the pool next to me in the morning.

I was shivering a bit, because there was a grey, watercolour sky and a brisk, chilly breeze, making a swim not such an inviting idea.

I think it had numbed Rufus's brain too, so, seeing his blank expression, I explained, 'You know I dreamed that I *did* stop at the Lodge?'

He nodded.

'There was a bit more last night where I was trying to get out and told Harry he could drive from there, but somehow he must have persuaded me to keep going. I suppose that accounts for why I wasn't wearing a seat belt when we crashed – I must have forgotten to put it back on again.'

'At this rate, you'll probably find out!'

'I don't know. Each time now I think I must have gone as far as my memory can take me,' I said doubtfully. 'But I suppose it doesn't matter really, because I already have all the answers to my questions.'

Except, of course, what made me swerve off the road, and I didn't really expect ever to be able to tie that end up into a neat bow.

When later Lulu walked up to the Lodge through the woods with Dusty, and I'd made tea and found some sultana and cinnamon swirls, she told me that Florrie Snowball had rung her mum again.

'Guy packed and left the Falling Star first thing this morning, which is a relief! She said he spent last night drinking in the bar with Dan Clew and a haggard blonde woman who kept trying to sing, so she was glad to see the back of him.'

'Fliss, of course.'

She nodded.

'When Mrs Snowball warned her that she'd be thrown out if she didn't stop her caterwauling, she announced that she was famous and people *paid* to hear her.'

'I bet Mrs Snowball wasn't impressed!' I said. 'I didn't really know who she was until I Googled her.'

'She told her she didn't care if she was the Queen of Sheba, she expected all her customers to behave themselves like decent people. Then she said at Fliss's age she shouldn't be wearing a skirt so short it was practically a belt, because people would start thinking the Falling Star was some kind of house of ill repute.'

I giggled. 'I wish I'd been a fly on the wall! But poor Rufus isn't happy Fliss's staying in Dan's cottage, though I'm sure she'll have got bored with living there before Dan even moves out.'

'I expect you're right,' Lulu agreed. 'Last night I was a bit too taken up with stopping Cam rushing down to the Falling Star for a confrontation with Guy to think of how Rufus was feeling, but it must be hideously embarrassing to have your mother shacking up in your cottage with the man you fired, especially now he knows she was behind the vendetta to get you all out of the Lodge.'

'And she was the one who shot at me in the woods,' I revealed.

'Really?' Lulu stared at me, wide-eyed.

'Rufus guessed right away, but I found out only the other night. She thought she'd just give me a scare. He says she's an excellent shot, so I wasn't in any danger, but it was the final straw that decided him he never wanted her to come back to the village again.'

'Well, I think he might be stuck with her, at least for a few days, from the sound of it.'

'Still, *Guy* has recognised defeat and gone home, so that's one problem permanently solved,' I said encouragingly.

'Yes, thank goodness, and now I'd better get back.' Lulu got up and Dusty, who'd been snuggled up to the inanimate fur rug that was Babybelle, followed suit, tail wagging.

'It's just as well Dusty's having a decent walk this morning, because I think I'm going to be too busy later to meet you and Belle. We're short-handed and I really want to finish setting up my Victorian photography studio today, too.'

'Where are you going to have it?'

'In that little room next to the reception, the one Mum and Dad always call the library, just because it's got two bookcases full of novels left behind by visitors.'

'I didn't even know it was there,' I confessed. 'I thought that it was a big cupboard.'

'It's barely big enough to swing a cat in, but I've rigged it up with a clothes rail and a curtained changing corner. There's that old chest from the attic, the one I found full of clothes, too. I've filled it with hats, mob caps, shawls and bonnets. Cam's ace at eBay now, so he got me a few more bits and pieces.'

'Was it still raining when you walked up?' I asked, as she pulled on her scarlet mac.

'Only a bit, and the forecast said it would clear late this afternoon and tomorrow should be cloudy, but dry.'

'That sounds perfect for the Morris dancing, not too hot.'

'*If* the weathermen got it right.'

'Fingers crossed.' I saw her out and said I might walk down later with Babybelle, in which case I'd have a quick look at her photography studio. But first I needed to stock-take and then put in an order for anything I thought I was likely to run low on.

'If not, I'll see you at the pub later anyway and you can have a quick look at my studio then.'

I shook my head. 'We're not going to be there tonight, or not unless we call in on the way back. Rufus is taking me out for dinner.'

'What, like a proper date sort of out?' Lulu demanded eagerly.

'I don't think so. He sent me a message earlier saying he felt like a change of scene, and did I fancy eating out somewhere.

And at least it'll give you and Cam a chance to get all smoochy without us cramping your style.'

'It still seems odd to me that I've fallen in love with Cam, after all these years as friends,' she said, her face taking on a now-familiar dreamy expression. 'I mean, we've known each other from infants' school.'

'I know, it seems odd to me, too, and it *has* changed things between the three of us a little – but in a good way.'

'I don't think all the change is *entirely* down to me and Cam,' she suggested, with a grin. 'Not now our trio has turned into a quartet!'

I did my stocktaking and ordering, and then felt like a bit of air, even though there was still no sign of the rain stopping.

Babybelle had deigned to go for a walk with Debo, Judy and some of the Desperate Dogs, so I set out alone. I quite like walking in the rain, when I'm not wearing a leaking mac.

As I passed the kennels, I could hear Sandy having a long conversation with Henry, a yellow-eyed lurcher who'd come in the day before. She seemed to have taken a particular fancy to him, even though he bared his teeth whenever anyone went near. Sandy reckoned he was smiling, but I'm not entirely convinced.

When I reached the pub, I found Lulu slightly shattered after a stint of emergency chambermaid duty, and ready for a break. She got us both coffees and we carried them into her new photography studio, which was indeed little bigger than a cupboard.

There she got me to put on a shawl and bonnet and sit

in the Victorian wing chair she'd arranged in front of a scrap-screen and a black wooden column with a potted fern on top, while she took some trial photos.

'These look good!' she said immodestly, flicking forward and back through the pictures and stopping to show me the best. 'I think this will turn out to be a nice little earner. And Cam's going to run his regular art class every Thursday afternoon, so that will bring him a bit of steady income too. Luckily, Jonas is usually happy to mind the gallery.'

Lulu still had lots to do and I wanted to go back and contemplate my wardrobe, in search of the perfect outfit for that evening . . . whatever it might bring. The jury was still out on that one, not to mention which way I actually *wanted* things to go . . .

There were now a few breaks in the clouds that revealed ragged patches of pale azure blue, so it seemed as if the weathermen might have got it right after all, even if I did still need my hood up under the heavily dripping trees.

I passed Spring Cottage, where, unsurprisingly, no one was to be seen, for it was now past four o'clock and the enclosure officially closed, and I'd just reached the spot where the narrow, steep path down to the lower pool divided off from the main one, when I suddenly had that horrible feeling that I was being watched again.

I stopped and looked round, but there was no one in sight, though I did hear a sudden sharp sound, like a branch snapping underfoot.

Slightly spooked, I set off again, but faster – and then, as I turned the bend, I came on the unwelcome sight of Dan, leaning against the wicket gate and smoking a roll-up.

'It's *you*,' he said, sounding surprised. 'I thought you were Lulu, with that red mac on and the hood up.'

'We've both got them – and what are you *doing* here?' I asked. 'Didn't Rufus tell you not to come onto his property?'

'Public footpath, isn't it?' he said insolently. 'I was showing a friend round and he's—'

He stopped dead and his eyes widened in alarm as he looked beyond me, back the way I had come.

'What's the matter?' I said, then felt, rather than heard, heavy footsteps coming up fast behind me.

'No!' Dan said urgently. 'No, Guy, it's not her, it's—'

I swung round, got a brief glimpse of a face engorged with rage, and a raised hand clutching a stick, then I ducked and ran for my life – only to stumble over a tree root, striking my forehead as I fell into deep, enfolding, familiar darkness.

Somewhere far above me a bright pinpoint appeared, drawing me upwards into light, heavenly colour and celestial music.

'Oh, not you again!' said an exasperated voice that I somehow recognised as my mother's. And all at once, I was hurtling back into the black depths.

Next time, I swam more slowly back up towards the light – not a heavenly one this time, just a mellow, greenish glow, filtered through freshly washed leaves.

I could hear Babybelle barking from what seemed like miles away, and something, or someone, was crashing away into the bushes.

'What the hell . . .?' exclaimed Rufus's voice. 'Dan, get away from her! And Izzy, don't move. You've had a bang on the head,' he added as I stirred, but since I seemed to have a tree root pressing painfully into my side, I rolled over anyway.

'Izzy, tell him it wasn't me that chased you, but Guy,' Dan's voice said urgently.

'He had a stick and he was going to hit me,' I whispered, clutching at Rufus's arm.

'Who, Dan?' he demanded.

'No, of course not! It was Guy.'

'See, it's like I said,' Dan said eagerly. 'Guy stayed with me and Fliss in the cottage last night and then he said he just wanted to *talk* to Lulu, so I told him she often came up here, and I was showing him the paths when Izzy came along. Only she had her hood up and he must have thought it was Lulu . . . I didn't know he'd do *that*, did I?'

'I'll be round to speak to the lot of you later – unless Izzy presses charges for assault, in which case it'll be the police,' Rufus snapped.

I sat up, slowly. 'I'm OK . . . though I think I've got a bump coming up on my forehead. I bet I have a black eye tomorrow.'

'Should you be moving when you've had a previous serious head trauma? I really think we should get you checked out,' he said worriedly.

'I'm not going to hospital,' I stated firmly, just as Pearl and Babybelle appeared, looking pleased with themselves. I suspected they'd just seen Guy off and I hoped they'd bitten him somewhere it hurt.

Babybelle turned her attention to Dan and began to advance in a menacing fashion, growling deeply. Looking terrified, he slowly backed away and then, when his nerve failed, turned and ran like a rabbit.

She didn't chase him, but swaggered over and tried to lick my face. I fended her off.

'What on earth are you doing here?' I asked her.

'She suddenly appeared at Sweetwell earlier, probably looking for you, so I thought I'd walk her and Pearl down to the Lodge. Then all at once they raced off down the side path and I followed and found you out cold, with Dan bending over you.'

'I get the scenario, but it wasn't really his fault. Help me up. I'm fine now.' I added, but instead he scooped me into his arms and carried me all the way to the Lodge – and then to my bedroom, with Debo showing him the way.

Judy insisted on calling a doctor out, even though I assured them I felt fine, except for a sore head and a slightly swimmy feeling.

Dr Jilly Patel, an old school friend of mine, agreed I'd probably be all right. There was no sign of concussion, she said, though if any symptoms developed I was to go to the accident and emergency department of the nearest hospital.

'But I think a good night's sleep and you'll be OK, apart from the black eye and a lovely bruise,' she assured me, handing me a couple of pills and a glass of water. I swallowed them obediently.

When she'd gone downstairs with Judy, I felt suddenly drowsy. 'I want Rufus to stay with me for a bit. He hasn't gone, has he?' I asked Debo, and she gave me her puckish grin.

'No, I'm sure he's still downstairs, pacing about like an expectant father. I'll send him up, darling.'

Rufus, reassured that I was going to be all right, was all set to go and do something of a violent nature to Guy.

'You can throw him out in the morning,' I said, 'when you've cooled down a bit. Stay and talk to me for a while, instead.'

I held out my hand and he took it and sat on the edge of my narrow bed, looking down at me with concerned eyes. 'I think it would be wiser if I left you to sleep.'

'I'd sleep better if you were here . . .' I said drowsily, then added, as the thought occurred to me, 'Where are the dogs?'

'Being fed with Vic and Ginger. And I've rung Myra to tell her where I am and that Pearl's here too, in case she wondered.'

'Good . . .' I murmured, and after that I must have dropped off, because I woke much later feeling better, apart from the tender spot on my head.

The room had gone dark. Rufus was now sitting on the window seat, looking out at the sky. The shape of his head and the set of his shoulders were all at once familiar and dear to me . . .

'Rufus?' I said softly, and when he turned his head, I knew he was smiling, even though I couldn't see his face clearly.

Rufus went downstairs to tell the others I was awake, fine, ravenous and wanted to get up, but instead Judy brought me dinner on a tray and made me take two more of the pills the doctor had left. I suspected they had sedative properties, since the last one had put me out like a light.

'You're much better off in bed till morning, darling,' she said. 'Rufus is staying for dinner, but he'll come back up to say good night before he goes home.'

When he came up, I said, 'This was not quite the evening I thought it was going to be.'

'Nor me. And I had all sorts of interesting plans,' he said, a hint of devilment sparkling in those sea-washed green eyes.

'I told Lulu that we might call into the pub on the way home, but I don't suppose she and Cam will have missed us.'

'It's OK, she rang earlier to say Kieran's staying at the pub again, booked in for two nights. I told her then.'

'Is he? I expect it's because Cara's husband's home, so he can't go up to Grimside,' I explained, suddenly starting to feel drowsy again.

'I'd better go now and let you get a good night's sleep,' Rufus said, sitting on the edge of the bed and looking down at me with that smile. 'You look lovely, even with a bruise the size of an egg on your forehead – and I suspect you'll even look pretty with a black eye tomorrow.'

Then he gave me what I think was meant to be the lightest of goodbye kisses . . . except that I wound my arms around his neck and pulled him in for a long, gentle smooch that went on and on until, at some point, held fast in his arms, I fell fast asleep.

Chapter 33: Dream On

Simon, who had suddenly stopped singing, managed to get out just before throwing up. Now he wrenched open the driver's door.

'I c'n drive, 'm all right now,' he slurred, and started to climb in.

'Wait a minute, Simon – let me get out, first,' I said, trying to push him back out again. 'And you should all walk from here, because it won't take a minute.'

'No way,' Harry said, and pulled me onto his lap. 'Get a move on, Simon.'

'No, let me out!' I protested, trying to release myself and panicking all over again.

'Yes, let Izzy go home, we don't want her now,' Cara agreed.

'Who says we don't?' Harry said with drunken stubbornness. 'Simon – put your foot down!'

'Oh, sweet!' said Debo's voice, then I heard the bedroom door quietly close and opened my eyes to find the morning sun lying across the patchwork coverlet – and, so too, was Rufus.

In fact, I was still wrapped in his arms as he lay, fast asleep, his face relaxed and peaceful. All at once, I wanted to run my fingers over that cleft in his chin and . . .

His green eyes suddenly snapped open and gazed into mine, then he smiled.

'Good morning! I can't believe I fell asleep and didn't wake up all night.' He disentangled himself, wincing, and then stood up to stretch.

'Me, too, but I feel fine . . . except that the bump on my forehead is sore.'

'And you really *are* going to have a black eye,' he told me.

'Oh, great,' I said. 'I think Debo just put her head in, by the way. That's what woke me up.'

'How inhibiting,' he said, stooping to kiss me, long and hard, so Debo's recent presence didn't seem to be holding him back *that* much . . . and then, as he released me, last night's dream came rushing back to me, memories sliding into place like beads along a waxed string.

'Rufus, I've remembered what happened after I stopped at the Lodge. I know *everything*! Well, practically everything,' I qualified, then described how I'd tried to get out of the Range Rover and Harry'd held me back. 'Simon drove off . . . and presumably *he* caused the accident!'

'So you've felt guilty all these years for something you didn't do?' he said, coming back to give me a comforting hug. 'And Cara let you carry on thinking that!'

'That does seem cruel,' I agreed. 'But oddly enough, although it should be a huge relief, I still feel guilty that I drove them up the hill that night and almost went off the road several times. So it *could* easily have been my fault.' I sighed. 'There are no happy-ever-afters, even with the truth.'

'Oh, I think we might pluck one of those out of the air,

eventually,' he promised mysteriously. 'But for now, I suppose I'd better go down and see what's happened to Pearl.'

'I'm sure Debo and Judy will have taken her and Babybelle out for a run with the other dogs, and I can smell bacon, so breakfast must be almost ready.'

'Then I'll collect her and get up to Sweetwell, because I need a shower and a shave before I finally see what the hell this Guy character thought he was up to yesterday.'

'I'm not certain he was going to hit me with that stick, you know,' I said. 'And in a way, he's done me a good turn, because I think the shock must have sparked off that last memory. And what's more,' I added, sitting up straighter, 'now I do remember what happened, I deserve a resolution.'

'What *kind* of resolution?' he asked, blankly.

'I want everyone who was closely involved in the accident to come together on the spot where it happened, and for there to be no more lies and secrets.'

'That's a big ask.'

'There's more: I want the Middlemoss vicar to be with us and say some prayers for Harry – and for Howling Hetty, too.'

'You want to exorcise my drive at the same time?'

'Not really, it's just I feel a blessing might lay *all* the old ghosts to rest.'

'I'll help you, if that's what you really want, but it won't be easy to arrange. I hope you're not expecting some kind of Hercule Poirot moment, when someone breaks down and sobs, "It was me what done it"?'

'No, because I already know what happened, I just want everyone there when I tell them I do, especially Cara, Dan and Simon.'

'When do you want to do it?' Rufus asked. 'I mean, it's the Morris dancing thing today, so I expect the whole of Halfhidden will be overrun with spectators and Haunted Holidaymakers.'

'Of course, I'd forgotten! Blow, it will have to be tomorrow, if the vicar can fit it in between services. But he's very nice, so I'm sure he will if he can.'

'But no Morris dancing for *you* today,' he insisted firmly.

'I don't usually dance, just walk up behind them from the pub and watch,' I protested.

'Not this time: take it easy, even if you do feel much better.'

'I'll only go out when they get to the Green, then,' I promised.

'OK, and now I really will have to go. I still want to speak to that lot at the cottage.'

'You won't do anything hasty, will you?'

'Probably not, but I'll have this Guy out of there, if I have to throw him out. I'll see you later – but not at the Green, because Foxy wanted to watch the Morris men in her lunch hour.'

'I'll ring you when I've spoken to the vicar, and then, once that's arranged, I'll contact everyone and persuade them to come – one way or another.'

'Well, I'll make sure *Dan* turns up, at any rate,' Rufus said grimly.

'And I'm pretty sure of Simon, Tom, Debo, Judy, Lulu and Cam. Cara's the difficult one, but I think I can see a way to make her come, if she hasn't already gone off with Kieran.'

'You take it easy, don't do too much,' he said, then left me to get up.

* * *

Judy would rather I'd stayed in bed, but I felt fine, full of energy and hungry as a wolf, and while I ate several rashers of bacon and two eggs, I told them my plans for a blessing on the drive.

At first they were inclined to think it was the bump on the head giving me odd ideas, but eventually I talked them round.

And the vicar, who was a fairly recent incumbent and hadn't even known about the accident, was very understanding when I rang and explained what I wanted. He thought blessing the spot and saying some prayers there was a perfectly reasonable plan.

The only problem was that, the next day being Sunday, it would have to be very early.

'Seven thirty?' he suggested.

'Perfect, because at least then it will be quiet. Later, there are bound to be lots of people doing the haunted trail, or driving up to the antiques centre. It won't take long. If you could pray for Harry and poor Hetty, our local ghost, then I'll say a few words about the original accident, and that will be it,' I said. 'I feel it will give closure to me and everybody else involved.'

'I'll be there,' he promised. 'I'll call at the Lodge and we can walk up together.'

When I told Rufus that the vicar was on board and Judy had offered to make sure Tom would be there, I added, 'And I rang Simon straight after the vicar and *he's* coming too. Apparently, there have been more ructions up at Grimside, with Cara insisting her two horses and her jewellery belonged to her, because they were gifts, and Sir Lionel forbidding her to take them. Though, actually, I think she might be right and she's entitled to keep gifts.'

'I would have thought so, and perhaps she's attached to her horses.'

'I suppose she must be, which makes her almost human! Simon said Sir Lionel's had to go off somewhere today, and as soon as he'd left, Kieran arrived and started loading Cara's stuff into her car and his, so I'd better try and get hold of her now.'

'I had an old customer to deal with earlier, so I couldn't get to Dan's cottage, but he's just turned up here,' Rufus said. 'I think he's looking for me – I'd better go.'

'Tell him he's got to be on the drive at seven thirty tomorrow, or I'll inform the police that it was he who tried to hit me.'

'You devious woman!' he replied, a smile in his voice. 'I'll ring you back when he's gone.'

When Rufus called me, he said Dan had come to explain what happened.

'According to him, he had no idea that Guy might be violent and he thought if he talked to Lulu, then he'd clear off back to France. Dan didn't like the way Fliss was making up to him.'

'Well, it's true Dan's never been violent, so that all sounds believable,' I said. 'Is Guy still at the cottage?'

'No. When Dan got back there yesterday, Guy and Fliss were loading their bags into his car – and they've gone off together.'

'You mean, she's gone to *France* with him?'

'That's what she told Dan she was going to do. But if Guy thinks he's found a replacement dogsbody for Lulu, then he's mistaken his woman. In fact, he'll find he's taken a tigress by the tail.'

'Serves him right, too, but it was a bit sudden, wasn't it?'

'Sudden is my mother's middle name,' Rufus said. 'I don't expect it will last too long, but at least it gets her out of my hair – and I don't somehow think she'll ever want to come back to Halfhidden again.'

'It will take her a very long time to drink her way through a whole vineyard, too,' I suggested.

'I hadn't thought of that,' he said, brightening.

'I'll tell Lulu in a minute,' I said. 'But first, I'm going to send Cara a message she *can't* ignore!'

'What?'

'*I know everything*. That should do it.'

It did, too, because she rang me within seconds of getting my message.

'What on earth do you want now? I'm busy.'

'I know, but I wanted to invite you to a blessing tomorrow.'

'A *blessing*?' she echoed blankly and then, when I enlarged on what was to happen, she said quickly, 'No way! I'm off at dawn, once the horsebox driver turns up. I'm getting divorced and marrying Kieran, but I'm taking my horses with me.'

'I'm sure you'll be very happy together, but you really ought to come tomorrow – because you see, Cara, I've got my memory back and now I know exactly what happened.'

There was a small pause.

'*Everything*?'

'Yes. So if you aren't there, then I'm going to make sure the whole story is splashed right across the daily papers. It's so sensational, I'm sure they'd adore it. Think of the lovely twists – minor gentry, divorces, deception, affairs, marrying the ex-fiancé of the woman you've implicated in an accident she didn't really cause . . .'

'I'll come,' she snapped, capitulating. 'But only for a few minutes.'

'A few minutes are all it needs,' I assured her. 'Then – it's over, forgotten, for ever.'

Chapter 34: Old Haunts

I woke up alone next morning, for although Rufus had come to dinner the previous evening, he hadn't stayed late.

'Have an early night and I'll be down in good time tomorrow for when the vicar arrives. How are you feeling about it now?' he'd said, as he was leaving.

'A bit nervous,' I confessed, 'but sure it's the right thing to do.'

'A little angel voice told you, right?' he said, half-teasing and I nodded.

'Something like that.'

'Well, I'm looking forward to getting it over, so we can put it behind us and move on with the rest of our lives,' he said, and though he didn't specify whether that was separately or together, the intensity of his goodbye kiss might have been a slight indication.

It was a dry morning and fingers of sunshine were filtering through the clouds as the circle of those closely involved with the accident slowly assembled in the shadowy, still hollow on the drive where, all those years ago, both a life and my childhood had come to an abrupt end.

Gareth, the vicar, who was a youngish man with bright copper hair, stood in the middle, waiting patiently until everyone had ceased to shuffle their feet.

I was hand in hand with Rufus, flanked by Lulu, Cameron, Judy, Debo and Tom, while Dan and Simon stood opposite, united in disillusion.

Cara, looking furious, arrived last, snapping, 'This had better not take long – we've got to get off to Oxford.'

She didn't add, 'before my husband gets back and finds what I've done,' but I guessed the subplot. Kieran hung about just behind her, looking daggers at me.

The vicar, seemingly unaware of any of these undercurrents, welcomed everyone and explained that we were gathered together to bless the tragic spot and to remember and pray for those whose lives had ended there, which neatly included Howling Hetty, should she be flitting about the woodland shadows.

Gareth had a light but clear voice, and I thought the very air seemed to quiver as he proceeded with the blessing and then led us into the Lord's Prayer.

After the last 'Amen' had been spoken, he smiled benignly round the circle and announced, 'Now Izzy would like to say a few words.'

I swallowed hard, let go of Rufus's hand and stepped forward, and an array of faces – sullen, angry, puzzled or loving – looked back at me.

'First, I'd like to thank you all for coming and say that I hope today will provide some kind of closure on the past for all of us.'

One or two people shuffled a bit, as if readying themselves to depart, so I carried on quickly, '*I* certainly need closure, because although I'd lost my memory of the accident, it's recently come back to me: *all* of it. I now know exactly what happened that night and I'm going to share that knowledge with you.'

'But you promised you wouldn't tell, if I came!' Cara cried angrily, and everyone looked at her.

'No, I only promised I wouldn't give the whole story to the *press*, that's all,' I told her. 'But what's said today I hope will stay a secret between us.'

'Go on then, darling,' urged Debo. 'We're all agog.'

So I described how Harry had persuaded me to drive the Range Rover up from the pub that night, even though I hadn't wanted to.

'And I stopped to get out, as soon as we got onto the Sweetwell estate.'

'But you *can't* have got out,' Simon said blankly.

'No, I didn't – but only because Harry pulled me onto his lap when I was going to and wouldn't let me go. And then – and I'm sorry to tell you this, Simon – you climbed into the driver's seat and drove on towards the house.'

He didn't look quite as shattered as I'd feared he might. 'I'd half-suspected that anyway,' he said. 'I sometimes thought I remembered being at the wheel, only Dad said—'

'I was just trying to protect you,' Dan interrupted, his face flushed with guilt, or anger, or a combination of the two. 'I never *said* Izzy was driving, I only said she was in the front, which she was.'

'I understand why you did it, Dan, and I can forgive you – though you lied when you said you'd seen Simon get out of the back,' I pointed out.

'So . . . you weren't driving after all, but Cara let you

395

take the blame all these years?' Judy said, staring angrily at her.

'We all thought she was going to die, so it wouldn't matter if we said it was her fault,' Cara protested, backing away slightly from all the accusing eyes. 'Then when she didn't die, it was too late to change the story.'

'I expect you and Dan were highly relieved when I couldn't remember anything about it,' I said. 'But now I do – or almost everything, because I can't recall what made Simon swerve off the drive.'

But just at the moment the words left my lips, I suddenly had one of those time-ripping-open moments and the very last bit of the jigsaw dropped into place with a heavenly hint of the 'Hallelujah' chorus.

Harry, laughing, kept a firm grip on me as Simon gunned the engine and roared off up the drive. He took the bend too quickly and was almost into the hollow before he saw, too late, the white-clad figure of a woman standing there.

'Howling Hetty!' Simon yelled, jamming on the brakes and jerking the wheel, sending the Range Rover careering into the ditch . . .

'It was Howling Hetty!' I exclaimed. 'She was standing there, right in the middle of the drive, where the vicar is.'

'Nay, lass,' Tom said heavily. 'That was no ghost, but my Pauline – and it's been on my conscience ever since. I thought I'd left her safely asleep at Spring Cottage, but I was later getting back than I intended . . .'

He exchanged a glance with Judy, and I thought I knew *why* he had been so late and felt so guilty.

'She got out again?' I asked, and he nodded.

'Wandered off in her white nightgown. I found her in the

woods later, when you'd gone to hospital, and I think she got the pneumonia that night that killed her.'

'But she'd often managed to get out and you couldn't be there all the time, Tom,' Judy said, gently touching his arm.

'No, what happened that night wasn't your fault, any more than it was Simon's,' I told him. 'Harry started the whole sorry chain of events himself, with a stupid prank.'

The vicar, who had been listening wide-eyed to these revelations, said he could see that today had brought not only closure, but forgiveness, and he was happy to have been a part of it. Then he bestowed another of his benign smiles on us and left, passing a small, red-faced elderly man on the way.

It was the cuckolded Sir Lionel Cripchet, and as soon as he spotted Cara, he yelled at her, 'What have you done with the bloody horses?'

'*My* horses? They're on their way to a livery stables near Oxford. You just try and get them back and I'll see you in court!' she told him viciously, and then snapped over her shoulder, 'Come on, Kieran, time to go!'

She brushed past her small, irate and gibbering husband with the stately elegance of a blonde giraffe and the moment of near-farce broke the tension that held the rest of us together. As slowly as they had arrived, everyone began to drift off again. Simon left with his father, and Judy and Debo took Tom with them back to the Lodge, followed by Cam and Lulu.

Finally, only Rufus and I were left in the hollow, which all at once seemed to have lost its still, dark, haunted air and was now full of fragmented, shifting sunlight and birdsong.

He put his arms around me and drew me close. 'I love

you – did I tell you that?' he said, dropping a kiss on the top of my head.

'No – but I don't think I mentioned that *I* love *you*, either, did I?'

'Not that I can remember and I don't think something like that would have slipped my memory. So – shall we get married and live happily ever after at Sweetwell?' he suggested.

'I thought you had trust issues?' I said, slipping my arms around his neck, so I could nestle closer.

'I do, but an angel voice just told me that my heart was safe with you,' he said gravely. Then, tipping my face up to his, he kissed me.

Chapter 35: Photo Finish

It was a warm day in June and the church bell, Little Knell, was joyfully clonking out to celebrate a double wedding as Rufus and I emerged from the church door hand in hand, closely followed by Cameron and Lulu.

The guests poured out after us and streamed towards the marquee on the Green, while the beribboned and excited dogs, released by Sandy, bounded around, barking.

We finally persuaded Dusty, Pearl and Babybelle to stand still long enough to be included in the family photographs, and then they were rounded up again by Sandy before they could find and demolish the refreshments.

'What a heavenly day!' I exclaimed blissfully, tossing my bouquet of white roses over my shoulder, where it was caught by Olly Graham's fiancée, Josie, which was quite appropriate, since they were next up to get married. Lulu's bouquet was snatched in mid-flight by Foxy Lane and I wondered if she had snared her gardener yet . . .

Rufus looked down at me and said, raising one dark eyebrow, 'Almost as good as the *real* heaven?'

'Just as good – but different. Heaven on earth,' I explained, sighing happily. 'And look how brilliantly everything's worked out. At Sweetwell I'll be close enough to keep an eye on the kennels, Lulu and Cam will be living in Spring Cottage with Tom, and Fliss is still in France, trying to drink a vineyard dry.'

'And tomorrow, we'll be in India,' he added, for Cam and Lulu had postponed their honeymoon till after the main tourist season, so had offered to look after Izzy Dane Designs, too, while we were away.

'This trip is going to be a mixture of business and pleasure,' I told Rufus sternly.

'I know which one should come first,' he said, his green eyes full of love and, laughing, I went willingly into his arms.

Recipes

Lemon Marmalade Cake

Ingredients
6oz/175g softened butter
6oz/175g castor sugar
14oz/400g mixed dried fruit
3 large eggs, or four medium, lightly beaten
1 heaped tablespoon lemon marmalade
9oz/250g self-raising flour

Method
Preheat the oven to 325°F/170°C/gas mark 3.

Grease, and then line with baking paper, a seven- or eight-inch round cake tin.

Sieve the sugar and flour into a large mixing bowl and then add all the other ingredients. Stir well.

Turn the mixture into the cake tin and smooth the top, then place on a baking tray in the centre of the oven.

After an hour and a half, check it. If the edges are starting to catch, loosely cover the tin with foil and bake for a further three-quarters of an hour, or until a skewer inserted into the middle comes out clean.

Leave for about fifteen minutes and then turn out onto a cooling rack. Remove the greaseproof paper.

The cake can be iced when it's totally cooled.

Quick and Easy Lemon Glaze Icing

Ingredients
4oz/110g icing sugar
2-4 tablespoons of lemon juice, fresh or concentrate
Finely grated lemon zest, if liked

Method
Sieve the icing sugar into a bowl and then *slowly* add the lemon juice until you have a spreadable, but not too runny, mixture.

Spoon onto the top and smooth out with the back of a spoon.

Missy's Dog Treats

This fishy flapjack-style recipe from Pat Elliott was a huge success with my dog!

Ingredients
5oz/150g drained tuna
5oz/150g rolled oats

2 tablespoons of cottage cheese
Half a red apple, grated
A medium carrot, grated
A pinch of ground ginger
1 teaspoon of herbs – I used thyme and oregano
Cold water to mix

Method
Preheat the oven to 375°F/190°C/gas mark 5.

Line a baking tray about 12 inches square, or a rectangular roasting tin, with greased tinfoil.

Put all the ingredients into a mixing bowl and *slowly* add the cold water, mixing well. You want to bind everything together, but not make it sloppy.

Spread the mixture evenly across the tin and smooth the top. This will make thin treats, rather than thick bars.

Bake in the top of the oven for twenty minutes, or until golden brown.

When cool, cut into training-treat size nibbles or one-inch squares. These are chewy, rather than hard, and should be stored in a plastic box in the fridge, though they can also be frozen.

Cinnamon and Sultana Swirls

Ingredients
1lb home-made puff pastry, or a 500g pack of frozen, defrosted at room temperature for about two hours

2oz/50g castor sugar (I like the brown type)
2oz/50g sultanas, roughly chopped
1 tablespoon cinnamon

Method
Preheat oven to 200°C/400°F/gas mark 6.

Line a baking tray with greaseproof paper.

Mix the sultanas, sugar and cinnamon together in a bowl.

Lightly flour a board and rolling pin, then roll out the pastry to about 12 inches by 8 inches, and a quarter of an inch thick.

Moisten the surface *very* slightly and then sprinkle the sultana mixture evenly across it.

Roll up as tightly as possible, like a Swiss Roll, and then slice into discs about half an inch wide.

Lay them flat on the baking tray, about two inches apart, and bake in the upper part of the oven for about ten minutes, when they will be puffy, golden brown at the edges, and delicious.

Leave to cool on a wire rack, store in a cake box or tin.